W9-AFV-334

ALSO BY LYNN RODOLICO

Small Change

Intimates

Heart and Soul

To darling Claire,
With our love, hoping you will
cherish this special book as do
we. Sent with SO much love ...
Mom and Dad

TWO SEAS

LYNN RODOLICO

Eccolo Editions

Copyright © Lynn Rodolico 2012

All rights reserved.

No part of this book may be used or reproduced in any manner whatsoever without written permission of the publisher except in the case of brief quotations embodied in critical articles and reviews.

This is a work of fiction. Names, characters, place of incident either are the produce of the author's imagination or are used factiously. Any resemblance to actual persons, living or dead is entirely coincidental.

Grateful acknowledgement is made for permission to reprint previously published material: excerpts from *"In Memoriam"* and *"Flower in the Crannied Wall"* by Alfred, Lord Tennyson; *"The Children's Hour"* by Henry Longworth Longfellow; *"Ithaca"* by C.P. Cavafy (translated by Edmund Keeley); *"Blackbird"* by Paul McCartney; Hannah Senesh's final poem; *"A Case of You"* by Joni Mitchell and *"anyone lived in a pretty how town"* by e.e. cummings.

Published by Eccolo Editions
www.eccoloeditions.com
ISBN: 978-88-906986-9-9
Epub ISBN: 978-88-906986-2-0

FOR ANTONINO

With whom everything is possible

and

LISA AND FRANCESCA

beyond our greatest expectations

The earth is all before me. With a heart
Joyous, nor scared at its own liberty,
I look about, and should the chosen guide
Be nothing better than a wandering cloud,
I cannot miss my way.

Prelude -- William Wordsworth

CHAPTER ONE

A year ago, after a long and often thwarted search, Kate and her husband, Niccolò, found a house to buy on the island of Sicily.

In a little FIAT 500 rental car, they followed a real estate agent down a long, isolated, winding road that was threatening to slide in more places than one. Eventually, they arrived at the ruins of a once-large manor house, now little more than a pile of rubble; at best a few walls have resisted the elements.

"Is there a well?" Niccolò asks the agent. He is scanning the horizon for power lines. "Electricity?"

"It has a well but no electricity," says the agent who has brought them here. He is a peculiarly built man who reminds Kate of Ichabod Crane: *tall, exceedingly lank, with narrow shoulders and long arms.*

"Footage?"

"There are 600 square meters."

Kate suspects the agent has a blood sugar problem because he is surreptitiously nibbling on something from his pocket, nuts or raisins. It is almost lunch time. He is making her hungry. Quickly, she calculates meters into feet: Just under 6,500 square feet, much more than they need for a holiday home. "600 square meters is too much," she remarks.

"All of which would have to be knocked down and rebuilt," Niccolò says. "There is nothing here to salvage."

The price is exorbitant, they soon are told, more than a million dollars, and for what? "The right to spend another half a million to rebuild," Niccolò says.

"If not more."

"The borders are bad," Niccolò points out, as if he needs further convincing. The Department of Forestry's barbed wire starts a couple of feet from the side of the road, land that has been confiscated from owners who haven't kept it up.

"But you have to admit, the view is pretty nice," says their nineteen-year-old-daughter, Electra.

Kate nods. "Actually, the view is spectacular, *exactly* what we are looking for."

Laid out in front of them is a vast stretch of the Mediterranean Sea. The contrast is striking between the white sand along the coast and the blue where the water deepens. In the midst of this splendor rises a mountain.

"If I turn my back on the building and forget the price, just focus on the view," Niccolò says, "you are right; this is exactly what we are looking for."

"That's Mount Cofano," the other realtor steps forward to tell them.

"Stunning."

This second realtor, acting on behalf of the owner of this ruin, has been listening carefully to Niccolò. When he is sure they aren't interested in buying this property, he says, "I know another house that might interest you. It is ready to move into."

"How is the view?"

"Practically, it has this same view, and it costs a lot less than this property."

"Then let's take a look."

The agent shakes their hands. "I am Rosario Manzo. Call me Rosario."

Niccolò, Kate and Electra say goodbye to Ichabod and follow the new agent away from the ruin.

Back on the main road, they drive up toward Erice, that mysterious, mythical town at the very top of the mountain that overlooks Trapani. It is rumored that *Psyche* first encountered *Amore* in Erice. As Niccolò concentrates on the curvy road, Kate glances back over her shoulder as the view of Mt. Cofano shifts in its poses. As they crest the mountain, the view to the east, of Mt. Cofano and San Vito Lo Capo, is replaced by a view of the city of Trapani spanning the valley to the west. The granite-gray buildings edge against a glistening slate-colored sea.

Beyond, beneath a dove-gray sky, three islands beckon like sirens. As the road switchbacks, the view alternates between Mt. Cofano and Trapani, equally spectacular but completely different: one made by man with a backdrop of nature; the other, nature un-tampered, pure.

The realtor makes a sharp, left-hand turn off the main road and onto a single lane. They follow. Directly in front of them is another ruin, the remnants of a castle that was invisible from the main road. Mt. Cofano stands stately in the background. This view is even more spectacular than the one they viewed below with the other agent.

The road is steep in its descent. They are forced into first gear.

"No," Niccolò implores, afraid they will lose the view. "No lower, please!" The umbrella tops of two towering Mediterranean pines present the crowns of their jade green heads as the car continues to descend. Finally, when they can't glimpse even a corner of Mt. Cofano or the sea, the agent stops at a curve in the road, space for two cars chiseled out of a mammoth, black granite bolder looming overhead. They cross the road into the shadow of the magnificent pines angled over a stately, wrought-iron gate, through which they can see a manicured garden leading up to and finishing in a small, neat, attractive stucco and tiled two-story house. They are at the gate of a Mediterranean Hallmark greeting card!

The walkway is smartly paved in large, flat cobblestones. A well-seasoned wooden railing, the kind used to corral horses, separates the garden proper from a meadow below. There are several acres of startling green winter-grasses, beyond which the view reappears. Mt. Cofano stands front and center: a mountain at the edge of the sea. If this were an opera, Cofano would be the uncontested prima donna.

"Praticamente, that band of bamboo is the border line."

"Are those two palms on the property?" Niccolò asks.

"No, they belong to your neighbor, Edoardo Olivero."

The agent's use of the pronoun, *your* instead of *their* or *the*, doesn't jar against their immediate sense of ownership. Kate is beginning to understand this man's expertise. For the first time she takes note of his features: an owl-shaped forehead, large front-facing eyes blinking behind the reflected light of his glasses, as if from too much daylight,

"Excuse me, *Signora*, but you aren't Italian." His hard features are softened by a slight rounding of his shoulders.

"I am American."

If it isn't her imperfect grammar or accent, her height gives her away. No matter how long she has lived in Italy—and she has been living in Florence for nearly a quarter of a century—she stands out in a crowd of Italians. Her daughters, too, because of their stature and high cheekbones, are considered foreigners, although they were born in Florence and their Italian is flawless.

"What brought you to Italy?" His thin lips are turned up in encouragement. "Where did you meet?"

This is an old, familiar question, and it elicits in Kate a fond, familiar memory.

"I don't understand why you need to go all the way to Italy," her mother says. *"You will just get married and have Italian babies—"*

"What's wrong with Italian babies?"

"Nothing, except that they will be too far away for me to visit them often."

"You said exactly the same thing when I moved from California to New York, and I didn't give you east coast grandchildren."

"How I wish you had! New York is much closer to California than Italy."

"You are getting ahead of yourself, Mother. First of all, I'm not going to marry an Italian, they all have mistresses. And second, didn't we have an agreement that you weren't going to pressure me about marriage?"

"I know. I did. And I have been very good, you must admit."

"You have been wonderful."

"But the agreement was I wouldn't mention marriage until you turned thirty."

"You have been very good, Mother. Thank you."

"But you are thirty-one! What do you have against marriage?"

"Nothing. Absolutely nothing. And I promise you, if and when I meet the right person, the man with whom I can envision

4

spending the rest of my life, I will marry him. But I am not going to marry just to marry. You must accept that."

"Tell me again why you are going to Italy when you have more lucrative work here?"

It was a fair question then as it is now. "I came to Italy to photograph Tuscany," Kate tells the agent, Rosario.

This is also the answer she gave to her mother and her friends. However, the real reason, the one she didn't talk about, not even to herself, was that she was looking for something that she hadn't found in either California or New York or anywhere in between. It was something she had glimpsed in every photograph she had ever taken, in every place she had ever lived, enough to know it was out there, but which she had never held for long; had never owned. Ultimately, moving to Italy for a year wasn't primarily about work; rather, it was her search for the meaning behind the image.

Kate's career in photography was an example of life taking over and pulling her along, taking her to places she would never have dreamed of venturing.

Sitting on the beach in Malibu, trying to figure out what to do with her life after quitting her teaching job at the University of Santa Cruz, thus removing her foot from the bottom rung of a ladder she had expected to spend her life climbing, the only thing that distracted Kate from despairing the bleak uncertainty of her future was a group of seagulls flirting with the edge of the surf. Her childhood friend, Carrie, had asked Kate to take care of her house, to feed the cat and water the plants, a month-long reprieve from reality before Kate had to arrive at a decision. Kate put down the book she wasn't reading and raised her camera to photograph the birds.

Two little girls clamored across the otherwise deserted beach, waving their chubby, cherub-like arms as they chased after the birds. At first Kate was annoyed at the noise, the intrusion of Carrie's neighbors. She wished the girls' mother, Megan, watching from the patio, would come out to claim them, restore Kate's solitude. But the girls' efforts to catch the seagulls were so futile and hilarious, that Kate couldn't resist photographing them. Their joy was contagious, despite Kate's best antibodies working against it.

Kate spent that night in the dark room she had improvised in Carrie's bathroom, developing the film, printing the best of the photographs. The next morning, she brought the prints over to show her neighbor. Megan was equally pleased. As they were on the beach looking at the photos, one of the little girls, Janie, climbed into her mother's arms, and laid her head of pale curls back against her mother's shoulder. With the Pacific uncharacteristically doing honor to its name, lying smooth and unperturbed, mirrored by an equally serene sky, its blue the color of a Madonna's robes, Kate brought out her camera and captured their intimate communion.

To make a long story short, the second little girl's mother was the lovely actress Natalie Wood, who commissioned Kate to do a proper photo shoot of her daughter after having seen the photographs of the seagull chase. When she saw the photographs of Megan embracing her daughter, she commissioned a mother-daughter portrait for herself. In less than a year, Kate's portfolio contained dozens of Hollywood's actresses and their children. In the third year, a pop star engaged Kate, then a Senator's wife, and it looked as if nothing could have stopped Kate's burgeoning career, until one night in her darkroom, as another famous mother and her adorable daughter emerged from her tray of chemicals, Kate realized she was bored by the repetition of her work.

What had first caught her eye, a purity in nature in harmony with its human element, was largely absent from her present work. As much as she tried to urge her subjects to be photographed outdoors, spontaneously, they all wanted to be posed in their beautiful homes, surrounded by their sumptuous belongings, as if their inherent beauty was not enough to sustain interest.

For a year more Kate continued assembling her favorite Divas and Daughters into the first of a series of coffee-table books. But her heart and her free time were increasingly spent outdoors, photographing nature, building a repertoire of seasons that eventually she persuaded her editor to look at. Unconvinced, Kate's editor, Nell, nonetheless arranged for twelve of the new nature photographs to be used in a calendar, on the condition that Kate would produce an additional three books of the Divas and their Daughters, a contract she completed in haste, before all the pages of the nature calendar had been turned. When the calendar proved a reasonable commercial success, Nell conceded that Kate could spend a year in Tuscany, photographing the seasons. This present project wouldn't earn her a large sum of money, but Kate hoped it would feed her in other, more important ways.

Moving to Italy was a risk, an unknown. She didn't know anyone, she didn't speak the language. It could have gone all wrong, in which case Kate would have had to move somewhere else in her search for that still, small voice.

How could she have expected her mother to understand something she barely understood herself, the flickering form of an intuition rather than a concrete plan. Her mother had served as an excellent role model, giving Kate the solid principles and values by which she proceeded through life, a gift Kate never underestimated. However, as good and constant as her mother was, Claire had little use for things of the imagination, for life's intangibles. Claire couldn't see or hear images in poetry, couldn't follow a metaphor in a novel or a photograph. She considered these things superfluous.

"I know it looks as though I'm quitting a successful career," Kate had told her mother, as she was leaving the country.

"For a second time! I still don't understand why you left teaching. It was much more secure—"

Kate didn't try to explain why she left teaching: it was a subject too sore to touch. "I can't sit at home in the garden because it is safe," she had told her mother, and hoped it would suffice in place of the explanation she couldn't otherwise offer.

Kate would never tell Rosario, but the irony doesn't pass unnoticed that on her first day in Florence, the man with whom she was intended to spend the rest of her life walked into her garden.

Perhaps because she couldn't understand the words around her—the gate keeper bringing her a set of keys, the 86-year-old housekeeper, Maria, explaining, Kate thinks, that she was leaving dinner prepared in the kitchen before she retired for the day—perhaps because Kate couldn't rely on language as she habitually did, her other senses had to step in to interpret the

7

scene around her. Whatever the reason, the effect was that her sight became crystal clear, as if she had been given glasses she hadn't known she needed.

Even though she hadn't been looking for him, she could see him.

Even though they didn't speak the same language, they were able to communicate. Did she mention that she was sitting in the garden? On her first day in Florence? And that while they didn't speak the same language, they understood each other completely?

The book of seasonal photographs that had brought her to Florence took Kate three years—twelve seasons—to complete, even though the images came easily, spontaneously, charged with new light. The completion of the book was interrupted first by her marriage to Niccolò a year after they met in the garden of the villa in Fiesole. It was slowed again by the birth of their two daughters, first Elizabeth, then Electra, twenty months later. Her mother was right: the only thing wrong with her daughter's happy marriage was that her grandchildren were too far away.

"Where did you say you met?" Rosario is waiting expectantly.

"In Florence. Twenty-four years ago." That is as much of their happily-ever-after story as Kate is willing to share at the moment.

The house they are approaching is enchanting. It has been recently reconstructed from a ruin, the agent explains, respecting the traditional style of Erice. Rocks have been stationed periodically on the roof to hold down the tiles. Massive, chiseled stonework frames the large windows and the front and terrace doors. They can see the stone-mason's technique in the circular swirls of the stucco. Built into the front wall of the house is an ancient stone ring.

Electra says, "The perfect place to tie up my horse!"

"If and when you have one!"

Rosario is struggling with the front lock, turning and pulling. "The key the owners gave me doesn't seem to work on the front door," he says, leading them around to the side of the house. They have arrived at a semi-enclosed patio with solid, stone pillars dividing the views: To the northwest is the castle ruin they saw from above, perched on an extremely sheer cliff. To the northeast are the meadow and the sentinel palms. As if in a carefully crafted painting, their attention is guided toward Mt. Cofano, and finally the sea, where their eyes linger, before returning to the palms and the meadow.

"Is there any danger that those rocks might tumble down?" Niccolò's attention has been arrested by the steep precipice and the ruins at its extremity.

"It hasn't happened in the last several hundred years."

"This isn't an earthquake zone?"

"No. Even if a goat were to wedge loose a rock or two, there is at least an acre between the crag and your house, grass and trees to slow any tumbling stones."

"Goats?"

"Gaetano's goats," he points back to the hill above where they left the cars. "Your other neighbor. That's his property. He isn't supposed to let his animals graze at the castle," shifting his pointed finger back to the rock face where eventually Kate squints into focus two, then three, then four black, gray and white goats camouflaged against the stratified rock. "That isn't Gaetano's property, but the goats escape. They like steep cliffs."

"Don't they ever become stuck?" The littlest one is descending toward a clump of yellow wildflowers at the very edge of the precipice.

"All the time. Gaetano has to rescue them."

Goat theatre. Kate could watch them all day, if she could hold her breath that long, wondering if one would fall.

"What is the altitude here?"

"Approximately 400 meters."

Another box is checked. They want a view of the sea, the fresh air from the sea, but not the heat or summer confusion of having a house on the shore. They are looking for a house that will stay fresh in the summer months. Goats are an unexpected bonus.

The patio on which they are standing is large enough for six at the table and a few potted plants; maybe a barbeque. Kate imagines breakfast, lunch and dinner out here, wrapped in a heavy sweater in the winter—it is much colder than they had expected Sicily to be—but always outdoors. Adjacent to the patio is an antique wash basin made of thick, uneven stone. It is large enough to wash the dog, rinse sand off an eventual grandchild.

A perfect place to work with seedlings. The faucets are brass griffins, their mouths the open spouts.

Niccolò and Kate are trying not to show how excited they are to have found this house.

There are screens on the doors and windows, unusual in an Italian home. "Are there mosquitoes?" This is a critical question as dining outdoors in Tuscany has been ruined by mosquitoes; where delicate, sweet night-blooming jasmine competes with the pungent odor of citronella candles.

"Never." He wrinkles his small, hooked nose. "Maybe a few down in Trapani, if there is a spell without wind, but never up here."

"Is there a lot of wind in Trapani?"

The agent looks at Kate as if she's asked what planet they are on, his hooded eyes flickering momentarily with hostility.

Niccolò saves him the embarrassment of an obvious answer. "Remember those windmills we saw this morning?"

"Ahhh, of course." Truthfully, Kate hadn't connected the reality of wind with the museum-preserved windmills dotting the Trapani coast. She has just asked a Dutchman if there is wind in Holland. No wonder he is blushing, embarrassed by her ignorance.

Rosario opens the side door, and they enter the house through the kitchen. It is a small, dark room dominated by a *cucina economica,* an enormous wood-burning stove designed both to cook and heat a room. The furnishings are odd bits with bricks propped under some of the legs; nonetheless, the countertops are of uneven heights. Every wall is hung with mismatched cupboards and over-loaded shelves. In short, a disaster.

It is not unusual to find inefficiency in the design of an Italian kitchen. Kate recalls entering her mother-in-law's kitchen for the first time and being confused by the lack of architectural design, to put it nicely, in an otherwise magnificently appointed house. In her mother-in-law's generation, anyone who could afford a cook and servants stayed out of the kitchen, and consequently the furnishings and design were haphazard; an accumulation of left-overs. Things have changed in Italy as servants have become less plentiful, as Italians have moved into a generation of people who enjoy cooking, who would rather have privacy instead of help. Modern Italian kitchens are often showplaces.

But this isn't one of them. However, underneath the might-come-in-handy-one-day-accumulation, the walls are tiled nicely, a simple, clean, white *craquè*.

The hallway from the kitchen to the living room is made narrow by a sideboard squeezed in. There are two doors on the right of the corridor. The first is a bathroom, full-to-overflowing with boxes of worn, laundered garden gloves. Stacks of newspapers and paper bags neatly folded and wrapped with string sit on top of a rusty washing machine. A virtual recycling center.

"This room would need to be re-done for sure. Probably the kitchen, too."

"At least there is a shower." Electra is following closely behind.

The living room is small but nice; which is fine with them because they aren't looking for a big house. Their house in Florence is a progression of large, incongruous spaces, very old, even by European standards. It is hard to clean, with lots of stairs. Their goal in Sicily is comfort and ease.

The living room, as with every other room, is crammed full of things. There is an attractive corner fireplace, but the mantel is covered with a vast assortment of religious and secular dust collectors. A painted wax gnome rubs shoulders with an anorexic Virgin Mary, and Christ on his cross leans against a donkey holding wooden matchsticks in his side baskets. The staircase is grand and spacious, a little too much for such a modest house. Marble has been used unsparingly: even the shelves in the closets are marble.

There is an odd dichotomy between the architectural design, the materials used, and the furnishings. It makes Kate curious about the owners.

Upstairs, there is one large bedroom with a window framing the splendid view of Mt. Cofano. At the far end of the corridor is a child's size bedroom, with double windows looking out on the Mediterranean pines at the front entrance.

In between these two rooms is a spacious bathroom.

"It's lovely," Kate says to Niccolò, her heart sinking, "but it's too small."

It could have worked when their daughters were young. The girls could have shared the small bedroom. Years ago, it might have been possible for them all to share the bathroom. But now their daughters are grown and need their privacy, as Niccolò and Kate have grown accustomed to theirs. Both Elizabeth and Electra are away at university, but they return home for holidays. To further complicate matters, Elizabeth, their elder daughter, in medical school in England, returns home with her English boyfriend, Stephen.

"There is no way we can fit into this house," Kate says sadly to Niccolò.

He is nodding, regretfully, taking one last look out the window in the hallway, running his hand appreciatively over the dark, polished hardwood that frames the view.

They descend the stairs reluctantly, heavy with disappointment. Everything else is just what they have been looking for. Maybe they could buy it only for themselves? But this is Italy. Kids grow up but they don't leave home. Even when they have their own lives, their own apartments, even after they marry and have children, they still come home for weekends and holidays. Niccolò and Kate's daughters are a bit more independent, having both Italian and American blood, which accounts for their decisions to study abroad, but their Italian blood runs thickly toward tradition and home they come at every excuse of a holiday.

"Maybe we could buy that little abandoned house up the hill, too. Then we would all fit."

"Did Rosario say it was for sale?"

"No."

Their disappointment increases as they pass through the living room again, admiring the rich, wooden arch that divides the living room from the entry hall. They appraise the handsome wood windows and their shutters, the hardware in black wrought-iron with brass knobs, picking up the detail from the stair railings. "It would have been perfect," Kate says again, just in case Niccolò didn't hear her the first time.

Rosario opens a door in the downstairs corridor. "Let's take a look at the basement. *Signora, stia attenta alla testa.* Watch your head." This is a remark Kate is used to, a comment that is directed always to her, even when Niccolò is standing right next to her, almost exactly matching her height.

The stairs to the basement are marble. The handrails are the same dark hardwood joined to wrought iron evident upstairs, smooth and sturdy under her hand. The ceilings are a little low, but they can stand up straight and there is a two palm span of space above their heads. Three sets of large casement windows give the rooms a light, airy feeling. It doesn't feel like they are in a basement, except that it is warmer here than upstairs, which means it will be cooler downstairs in the summer.

Naturally, the rooms are full to overflowing. It is even more crowded than upstairs, as if permission has been given to this room to cede to storage. Despite the overload of things, the space is discernibly the same as upstairs: one large room, the equivalent of the living room/dining room, and an alcove, the equivalent of the entry hall.

"The light is good," Niccolò says.

"It isn't humid."

"The ceilings are low but not impossible."

"I wouldn't mind having the downstairs to myself," says Electra.

The possibilities are opening up: Elizabeth and Stephen could use the small bedroom upstairs. There is room for a double bed. Electra could sleep downstairs in the basement alcove. Eventually, they could improvise a couple of sofa beds in the larger part of the room for their friends or cousins or as a naturally air-conditioned summer reading room.

Rosario unlocks another door and they are in an additional room full of tools and boots, a wheelbarrow, a child's crib filled with two foot lengths of firewood. *"Praticamente, questo è il ga-rà-ge.* This is the garage." An English word Italianized, pronounced with three syllables: *ga-rà-ge.*

Rosario strains as he pulls up the heavy, metal door and they are outdoors again, facing the cliff and the castle ruin, on a steep, tarmac driveway that curves back up behind the patio from where they entered the house.

Niccolò says, "You might be able to drive a car into this garage but you'd never be able to drive it out."

"No. No. They kept their car here," Rosario insists, pointing at an oil stain on the pavement.

"The driveway is much too steep. Twice in and the clutch would burn out."

Outdoors, they pause to orientate themselves. "Where is the property line on this side?" Kate asks.

Rosario indicates an overgrown hedge of laurel in the distance. There is an old stone wall which seems to have collapsed in some places, overgrown with giant prickly pear cactus. "And those rocks are the boundary to the north."

"Is there a well?"

"There are two wells, one in the meadow—" He gestures toward a large, round, stone-structure visible above the grass, "—and a smaller one, less profound, I believe, here close to the house." He points to a lichen-stained, hand-chiseled stone well, half-buried in tall grass, which must be several hundred years old.

"Do the wells run dry in the summer?"

"I wouldn't think so but you can ask the owner. In any event, the house is supplied by city water and that, I know, is abundant."

"I thought Sicily had a water shortage?"

"Trapani can run low in the summer. Rationing can start as early as mid-July. But Erice always has water."

"Why doesn't Erice give water to Trapani?" Electra asks. She has been busy taking photos but she has apparently been following the conversation.

"Ha!" he replies, as if she has hit a funny bone. "They would expect us to share, but practically they can de-salt the sea water." They can hear centuries of rivalry, another Florence – Pisa which works out its antagonisms in regional soccer matches. Niccolò wonders if Erice has a soccer team.

Niccolò and Rosario are talking hydraulics, well depths, and ring sizes. Kate photographs Mt. Cofano as its colors shift again, from bright and sunny to soft and alluring, seductively sensual rather than blatantly attractive. Electra points out three horses on the hill outside the front gate. As she points at them, one hee haws, proving itself a donkey, both shy and curious. Furtively, it edges forward on its hill above their cars, just outside the gate, trying to watch the unexpected activity while hiding itself behind the fronds of a dwarf palm.

"Mama! We would have horses for neighbors!"

"And a donkey."

Electra is as excited as Kate. "I think I'd better go back to talk to the agent," Kate tells her. "We don't know how much this jewel costs."

Niccolò is already asking the price.

Rosario takes out a notepad and a pen and jots down a figure, folds the note and hands it to Niccolò, who shows it to Kate.

We can do that, Kate thinks, even if it is quite a bit more than they had thought to spend. A house like this at the sea in Tuscany would cost twice as much, and it wouldn't have any acreage, nothing more than a small garden with neighbors on four sides. She tries to catch Niccolò's eye, but he won't look at her.

"Unfortunately," Rosario continues, "the owners have prematurely committed themselves to buy a house under construction down at San Vito. They need to sell this house quickly."

How can they sell it? Kate thinks. It is a dream. However, in the interest of bargaining, she keeps her enthusiasm to herself. Instead she asks, "Where will they live until the house is finished being constructed?"

"Oh, they never lived here, Signora. They have an apartment in Trapani. They just came up here in summer, and worked in the garden."

A place to store the junk they can't bear to part with, she thinks uncharitably, and then she remembers that to live in the country is not considered fashionable, especially if one has ancestors in the not-too-distant past who worked the land. In the 1960s, there was an exodus from rural living to factory work, and while some of these people maintained affection for the land and continued to cultivate a plot of ground, to live in the country without having a city residence was regarded as a kind of cultural illiteracy.

"How many acres are there?" Kate asks.

"Almost four."

Four is manageable. In Florence they have sixty-four acres of olive orchards, which is too much for the two of them. They are always running behind chores that should have been done the month before. They never manage to prune all the trees in a single year, and just when they finish, it is time to start pruning again. The Golden Gate Bridge syndrome: as soon as one end is finished being painted, it needs to be started again at the other end.

"The owner," Rosario says, "had a heart attack, and they find this acreage too demanding, too hard to keep up. So I suspect you could offer less and have it accepted."

Niccolò still refuses to look at Kate. He is looking down at a crack in the pavement. He toes it distractedly. "It's a nice property," he says finally, "but I'm worried about the foundation."

He lifts up a sheet of corrugated metal which has been placed over the window well of the basement, and discovers more cracks, some of them significant. Niccolò walks around the house, lifting slabs of marble which Kate had assumed were for decoration but which were clearly meant to hide flaws.

At the rear of the house, Niccolò points to a crack in the façade of the second story. "We should find out how serious that fissure is," he tells Rosario. "Is there a geologist we can consult?"

The breathtaking view has lost its predominance as the foundation of the house is brought into question.

"Are you interested in meeting the owners?" Rosario tries to recuperate, his lips pressed together, pale, bloodless.

Kate holds her breath while she waits for Niccolò to answer. She wants to buy this house. How can a few cracks matter with a view like this?

"Could we meet the owner tomorrow morning to ask a few questions? Could they bring the man who laid the foundation?"

"I'll make an appointment." Rosario is clearly relieved. He licks his lips, leaves them glistening. "Give me your cell number, and I'll call you if there are any problems. Otherwise, we will plan to meet here at eleven o'clock."

They shake hands, say goodbye. As they are turning the car to drive back up the hill, Kate asks, "Do you like it?"

"I love it. It is perfect." Niccolò says, "I'm going to offer quite a bit less than what they are asking, but I'll pay full price, if they won't take less."

CHAPTER
TWO

"**D**addy?" Electra speaks from the back seat. "Don't you think it is a mistake to buy the first house we see?"

"First house we see?" Niccolò and Kate laugh simultaneously. "We have looked at so many properties we are ready to give up."

"In this area?"

In this area alone, they have looked at more than thirty properties last May, each more hopeless than the last. Once beautiful homes, long abandoned, the gardens were all overgrown. Acreage had been sold off indiscriminately so that cement-block apartments pressed in on three sides. The agent was Signor Toma, and for some unknown reason, as they were leaving the office to begin their tour, the agent's father, Signor Toma Senior, positioned himself into the front seat of the FIAT Punto. The agent's sister, Signorina Toma, blonde and high heeled, offered to take the less comfortable seat in the back between Niccolò and Kate. Signor Toma Senior, a sprinkling of dandruff on the shoulders of his dark shirt, serenaded their tour by pointing out every house he had bought or sold over the last thirty years.

At the end of each futile viewing, the sister of the agent asked, *"Ti è piaciuta?* Did you like it?"

"It was nice," Kate answered politely, "but not what we are looking for."

"What is it exactly you are looking for?" she asked again each time.

"A spectacular view of the sea. A house that is very private and isolated from other houses."

"Then you will love the next one," she promised each time they piled back into the car.

Apparently everyone has a different idea of a spectacular view of the sea. One house would have had an impressive view if the owner hadn't planted a forest of cypress and pines between his house and the sea thirty years before, obstructing the view completely. "You could cut them down," agent Toma counseled.

"We could," Niccolò had responded, "but his neighbor liked the idea and planted a few hundred trees himself, which we would not be allowed to cut."

The last property they visited, in *Contrada Misericordia*, did have a spectacular, unobstructed view of the sea, with only one house nearby, to the rear.

"Why didn't you show us this one first?" Niccolò asked.

The agent smiled but didn't answer.

"Why has the house been left unfinished?"

"The owner ran out of money." Toma hitches up his trousers and then lets them settle again on his slender hips. "The building permit has another nine months before it expires. The blue prints are with an architect in Valderice, if you want to see them."

"Asking price?"

Toma mentions a sum.

"Flexible?"

"A little."

"We'll talk it over and call you tomorrow."

That same afternoon, Kate and Niccolò returned on their own to visit the structure. They climbed over an improvised fence, and sat on the exposed steel beams to talk.

"If the building permit expires in nine months, we would have to start work right away. That's going to put pressure on us."

"Emotionally and financially. How much do you think it will cost to finish construction?"

"A lot."

A car approached, and they scrambled to their feet.

"At least we can ask the neighbor how he feels about a house being built right in front of his view."

"We wouldn't want an enemy."

"*Scusi!*" Niccolò called out. "Excuse us! We are interested in the property next door. May we ask you a few questions?"

"Sure." The neighbor brought out a package of cigarettes, offered them the option before lighting his own. "To be honest, we'd much rather look out onto a finished house and garden than this eyesore."

"How long has it been like this?"

"Years. At least two." He inhaled contemplatively, his ears glowing pink, illuminated from behind by the last sun of the day. "Maybe longer."

"Do you know the owner?"

"Enough to say hello if we pass on the street." His accent was northern, phrases finishing with a Milanese lilt. "He's a high school math teacher."

"Do you know why he has decided to sell?"

"I heard rumor he had counted on an inheritance that didn't arrive."

"Hmmm. So he might accept—?" Niccolò mentions a sum.

He laughed. "I suspect he'd be thrilled. Last I heard he was asking forty thousand less than that."

This wasn't as amusing to Niccolò as it was to the neighbor. "It seems as though the real estate agent thought he found a sucker."

"I had the same problem when I was shopping for property," he confided. "They hear a northern accent and think they've found a gold mine."

"With us they hear northern Italian and American accents."

"Well, call their bluff."

The agent, Signor Toma, said he wouldn't even bother to inform the seller of Niccolò offer.

No Electra, we aren't buying the first house we've seen.

It took them awhile to recover from their disillusionment, but in the last four months they have accelerated their efforts and have come close, twice, to buying property on Sicily's north central coast, near *Gioiosa Marea*.

The first was a ruin with permission to build on six acres of coastal view, which the agent-architect apologetically announced had been sold to the owner's cousin when he picked them up at the airport to sign the purchase contract. The second near-purchase was found for them by the same agent-architect as compensation for the property sold before they landed. It was even more promising than the first but unfortunately, it, too, fell through, at the very last minute, after they had booked their flight and hotel.

"We might as well use our plane tickets to Trapani," Niccolò had said. "We'll see what else is for sale. Come on. Don't give up."

Kate *had* given up. She was completely dejected. She had lain in bed night after night, designing their future house so that the breakfast room window would receive the sunrise, the dining room the sunset, their bedroom above situated so that they enjoyed both. She couldn't believe that another dream had disintegrated into nothing. A habitual optimist, too many disappointments had finally worn her down.

Niccolò called his cousin in Palermo and explained their disappointment. Among his many other qualities, Niccolò's cousin, who is also called Niccolò, enjoys solving people's problems. If he can, he will. "You don't want to live on that part of the coast anyway," he said. "I'll call a few friends who live near Trapani and tell them what you are looking for."

Kate agreed to go to Sicily not because she believed they would find another property, but as Niccolò said, they had the plane tickets. The other reason for not staying home was that their elder daughter, Elizabeth, in Italy for only part of her winter holiday, was leaving on the 24th to spend Christmas with her boyfriend in England. They had been in Italy for Christmas last year. Stephen's family had the pleasure of their company this year. Ultimately, Kate agreed to go to Sicily because she didn't want the three of them sitting around missing Elizabeth.

Niccolò, Kate and Electra were tourists all day on the 26th of December. Electra wanted to visit the sea so they spent the morning at an old tuna factory in Bonagia where Kate photographed the fleet of antique wooden fishing boats and the gargantuan rusted anchors while Electra climbed over the rocks and dared to put her feet into the cold water. Before sunset they visited the salt beds and wind mills near the Isle of Mozia, and watched an enormous, almost-African sun disappear into the sea between the Egadi Islands. They enjoyed dinner in a tiny trattoria in which the chef/owner overindulged them with extraordinary fish, wine and other local specialties. And after dinner, thoroughly sated, with the wind picking up and the sky bright with stars, they walked to the *Torre di Ligny*, the farthest point west in Trapani. Following the narrow railed walkway to the sea-side of the Tower, where the Tyrrhenian slapped spray into the Strait of Sicily, Kate threw out a prayer into this darkly lit, mysterious place, and left it wavering between the two seas.

That night they slept like babies blessed, and in the morning they had an appointment to visit the property where they met the agent Rosario, who in turn introduced them to the house of their dreams.

One road leads to another, and despite a few detours, eventually they find themselves on the road to home.

They are early for their appointment the next day but the owners and Rosario Manzo are already there. An elderly couple, Concetta is the energetic one, Carmelo acquiescent. It's all too apparent in their handshakes: his limp, extending only to the tips of his fingers, while hers compresses the whole hand.

Their son is with them, as well. Marco looks Kate directly in the eye as he shakes her hand but holds her gaze and hand a few seconds too long. His eyes are the only steady item in a body full of nervous twitches. He might be considered handsome— tall, well-built—except that he has shaved his head, which is unfortunately shaped like a bullet, and his ears are disproportionately small. He takes Electra's hand with no intention of ever letting it go and pronounces "My God, you are beautiful!" Electra receives his compliment with the same indifference by which she receives all compliments. She is suspicious of superlatives. "Pretty enough" is how she would put it. Beautiful is for another category of woman, those who wear spiky heels and push-up bras. She retrieves her hand from Marco's insistent grasp with equanimity.

The owners are happy to see Niccolò and Kate, and invite them inside their house which is slightly warmer today than yesterday. The wood-burning stove in the kitchen is ablaze and has taken the edge off the chill in the room. The jackets they bought yesterday afternoon layer them against the humidity.

The fireplace in the living room is smoldering. One log has been consumed already, breaking down into cinders. A new piece of wood has been stationed on top, the bark ignited with fervent flames. Little clouds of smoke puff into the room as the wind outside increases. Concetta opens a window, which causes the smoke to dissipate along with the accumulated warmth.

Concetta gives Kate a tour of every room, moving so quickly that Kate has to hurry to keep up. The floor is paved with large squares of tiles in muted shades of cinnamon, sand, not-yet-ripe peach, dolphin blue-gray. Unique and beautiful. They are intentionally marred, freckled with brown tones. *Easy to clean*, Kate hears herself thinking.

With astonishing speed, Concetta finishes the tour of all three floors. Pride flows through her commentary—there is no apology for the clutter—but she leaves Kate no time for questions. They have arrived in the *ga rà ge*, when, abruptly, she grinds to a halt to give Kate a lengthy history of the crib in which the firewood is stored, which was, not surprisingly, Marco's. Before she can start on a history of Marco, as well, Kate asks her about a credenza in the basement. It is the one piece of furniture in the house that Kate likes, but it seems to have no relevance to Concetta except as a starting place for a historical tour of all the furniture in the house.

Concetta has two gears, spinning and stalled, the first for physical objects, the second for sentimental attachments.

"This table belonged to a neighbor who moved away from Sicily when his daughter married. He took most of his furniture with him when he went to live with her in Turin, but the daughter didn't have room in their apartment for this table, so we got it." The other histories are just as interesting. Kate is weary and hardly listening when they reach the kitchen. "This cabinet belonged to my uncle. It was too short for the kitchen, so Carmelo raised it up." Concetta opens the cupboard door and Kate sees what is admittedly an ingenious adaptation. However, the cabinet is Formica-covered pressed wood, and why anyone felt it was worth adapting, she can't understand.

On the patio Concetta says, "My father made this table." She lifts off a plastic table cloth for Kate to admire his handy work, but it, too, is constructed from low quality material. "If you want, I can leave it for you."

"Thank you, but we already have furniture for the terrace, for the entire house. Please take it with you. Take everything."

They are already speaking as if they had agreed on a price, as if a contract had been signed.

When Kate finally frees herself to find Niccolò, he, Rosario and Carmelo are talking with Mimmo Morano, the man who laid the foundation. With wild arm gestures and spittle spraying liberally through the gap between his two square front teeth, Mimmo Morano is justifying the faults in the foundation, dismissing them as insignificant. Kate feels an instant distrust—dislike—of this man, and can see that Niccolò, who is standing with his arms folded across his chest, doesn't like him either.

Concetta grabs Kate's arm, as if she had wandered into the men's room by mistake, and pulls her into the front garden. "This is *finocchio selvatico*"—wild fennel, she says, "excellent with *sarde*—sardines. And this is *gira*—wild Swiss chard, delicious with garlic!" Her fingers tighten on Kate's upper arm, as if suspecting resistance, but she is wrong. Kate wants to learn everything in the garden. "This flower looks like a dandelion weed, no?" She doesn't wait for an answer. "But look closely, its petals are as bright as if they have been painted with enamel. The dandelions we pull up and feed to our neighbor's chickens, but these little flowers we find in the hills of Erice and transplant them to our garden." She moves Kate along. "This is *Alloro*." Finally, something Kate recognizes: laurel. "This is *crescione dei prati*," which is good for thickening your hair. You don't need it but it works." Kate looks at Concetta's wispy hair and wonders if she has tried it. "This is *Boragia*, very good when it's young but don't think to eat it when it's mature, unless you want a mouth full of stickers! Ha!"

On the left side of Concetta's face, below her eye, is a dime-sized mole. She wears large, rose-tinted glasses, which partially hides it, but she lifts them repeatedly, each time she wants to identify a plant. *Bardana*, good for healing skin problems, *Luppolo*, good for everything, it seems, from stomachaches to headaches. Kate needs a notebook.

Concetta's list of edible plants lengthens into an undistinguishable jumble of look-a-like greens. The only relief is the occasional appearance of those tiny, lacquered-yellow non-

23

dandelions. When they have toured the entire lower garden, she pulls Kate along behind her on a path that leads to the upper garden. She is talking incessantly and her voice is very loud. It is starting to grate on Kate's nerves. She wants to be with Niccolò. She wants to hear the discussion with Carmelo and Rosario about the foundation.

Kate has to scurry to keep up with Concetta. Despite her wish to be elsewhere, she has to marvel at Concetta's energy, her agility. She must be close to eighty, then recalculates to seventy-five, if her son is what, thirty-five? However old she is, she is very fit. Not an extra pound on her, full of energy and determination. Downright bossy, if truth be told.

"What is this?" Concetta stops abruptly and demands an answer.

Kate tries to remember. "*Finocchio selvatico*? Wild fennel?"

"No, *Gira*." She pulls Kate farther along the path. "That is *Finocchio selvatico*. And what is this plant?"

This is like a bad dream, arriving at an exam unprepared. Kate doesn't even venture a guess.

But Concetta isn't waiting for an answer. She is moving along, throwing out questions, supplying answers. She is proud of her garden and once Kate understands that she probably won't fail, she begins to relax and enjoy what the owner is showing her.

Kate has also come to understand that Concetta is hard of hearing, which is why her voice is so loud, and probably why she doesn't wait for a response. It may also explain why she insists on grabbing Kate's arm and pulling her along.

At the top of the garden, Electra suddenly appears, and clutches her mother's arm, pulls her to one side. Kate is going to have bruises. "You have to save me. The Stalker is driving me crazy!"

"The Stalker? Marco?"

"Yea. I have another name for him but it isn't very nice."

"Just be kind," Kate reminds her.

"Mama, it's ridiculous. He's already suggested marriage, has told me how many children he would like to have! I know his whole life history! I can't move without him shadowing me."

"Be nice," Kate repeats.

"What can I do? He's making me nuts!"

"Smile and be polite. I promise I won't make you marry him."
Cofano catches her attention, takes away her breath. "Unless it
means a significant discount on the price of the house."

"Uffa!"

They are glad for their new jackets. As long as they are
moving around, they are warm and the mists don't penetrate
the waterproofing. However, when they return to the house, are
corralled into the living room to discuss business, the cold
pierces to the bone. It is colder indoors than out.

Concetta sees Kate shivering. "Come with me."

Kate jumps up before Concetta can grab her.

In the kitchen Concetta takes a small pot of water that is
boiling on the wood-burning stove. "Hold this," she says, giving
Kate an empty plastic water bottle. Without a funnel, she
attempts to pour the boiling water into the small opening of the
plastic bottle. How stupid! Much of it spills onto Kate's hands.
Her hands are so numb it is *almost* welcome. She is going to
have third degree burns *and* bruises.

Everyone has convened in the living room when they return
with Kate's improvised hot water bottle. Rosario has heaped
more logs onto the fire. There is less smoke now.

"Mama, Marco is going to take me up to see the horses."

Kate is glad that Electra is being a good sport, keeping Marco
occupied so that she and her Daddy can negotiate. "We'll finish
up here shortly," Kate says, as much for her sake as for Marco's.
Kate announces to Niccolò: "Marco is going to take Electra up to
see the horses."

"We will come up to join you in a few minutes."

"OK!" Electra says above a large, bright, fixed smile.

"OK," Rosario takes charge. "Let's talk price."

Concetta grabs Kate's arm. "Come with me, I forgot to show
you the artichoke patch." Kate swears she can feel her nails.

"Let's look later." Concetta assumes Kate won't be interested
in the business details but of course she is. "I'd like to be present
for this discussion."

Rosario continues. "Here is what *Dottore* Aragona is willing
to pay, after he has assurances from the geologist, of course." He

hands Carmelo a slip of folded paper, on which has been written a price. "Is that acceptable to you, Carmelo?"

There is a mute exchange between Concetta and Carmelo, short-hand gestures born from years of cohabitation. "I would be willing to come down another twenty-five thousand but no more," Carmelo says eventually, his mouth tightly puckered, as if he had forgotten his teeth.

Rosario sums it up, "We are twenty-five thousand euro from a deal. We can solve this quickly, right here and now, Carmelo, if you are willing to come down another fifteen-thousand. Can you live with that, *Dottore* Aragona?" He is on his feet, ready to offer congratulations.

Carmelo looks unhappy. "Why am I expected to be the one to yield on the price?" he whines.

"I have a thought."

Everyone looks at Kate. It is permissible that she is present, but she is expected to remain silent. Men deal with men in Sicily. Suspiciously, Rosario says, "You have an idea, *Signora?*"

Niccolò is always given the title of *Dottore* which is a sign of respect for those who have graduated from university, whereas Kate, with a degree more than her husband, is called *La Signora*. The Mrs. It is one of those things that would have driven her crazy in the States but here it doesn't evoke her ire. She has learned that *Signora* is also a title of respect. "If we spilt the twenty-five thousand equally, we are both yielding." Kate says, looking at Concetta and her husband. "Would that be fair?"

Rosario leaps to his feet. *"Affare fatto!* Done!" He shakes Niccolò's hand first, then Carmelo's. Carmelo looks stunned, his hand is limp.

Kate repeats, "Are you in agreement, Signor Beragno?"

"I guess so. All right." Slowly his face transforms from worried suspicion to joy. Eventually he smiles, showing a mouth full of tiny seed teeth. *"Venduta!* Sold!"

Concetta rummages through a cupboard and brings out a very dusty bottle. "This wine is thirty-nine years old. It is only for very special occasions, like marriage and birth and first communions. Today merits a glass."

"Oh, I love a good wine, especially a fine old wine," Kate admits, although Niccolò and she are not in the habit of drinking except at meals. Kate nods her acceptance before she registers that the bottle is less than half full and has a screw top. Too late! Concetta pours the wine into a water glass and gives it to Kate with obvious pride. It is easily the worst wine Kate has ever tasted, even worse than her mother's favorite sweet rosé. Its remarkably high alcoholic content must be what makes it valuable. Concetta starts to pour a glass for Niccolò.

"He can share mine," Kate offers.

"No," Concetta insists. "This occasion merits that everyone has their own glass. *Cin Cin!*"

They all agree to meet tomorrow morning, their last day in Sicily, to sign an agreement and leave a down payment. They have yet to set a date.

Carmelo suggests the first of June.

Niccolò likes the idea.

Kate doesn't.

They excuse themselves to the kitchen to discuss it privately.

"June will give me six months to accumulate money to pay for the house," Niccolò explains.

"You are right, but if we wait until June we will miss our first spring in Sicily. If we take possession on the first of March, we can spend Easter here. Wouldn't it be wonderful to have Elizabeth and Electra reunited in Sicily for Easter?"

"As usual, *La Signora* is right," Niccolò concedes as they return to the room. "Would it be possible for us to move in at the beginning of March?"

Concetta has heard the date perfectly, and is worried that there won't be enough time to move all their things.

"All of January, all of February," Rosario clarifies. "That is two full months."

In the end it is decided that they will try to be out by the first of March and if they need another few weeks, Kate and Niccolò will postpone their arrival. But Rosario is encouraging. "It won't take long. Assuming it doesn't rain, you should be able to pack it all up in a couple of weekends."

Kate has her doubts, although she would know a quick enough way to rid themselves of all this junk. She's just glad she won't have to deal with it.

Rosario comes with them as they drive up the hill to pick up Electra. He will introduce them to their neighbor, Gaetano, the owner of the horses and the donkey, and the goats. Concetta and Carmelo remain behind, to begin packing some things into their car.

"I saw he has a donkey."

"*Due asini*—two donkeys," Rosario informs them.

"Does he have a family?"

"L'asino?" Rosario's expression in the rear-view mirror does not reflect a high regard for Kate's intelligence.

"No, Gaetano."

"Ah, yes." He looks relieved. "A truly beautiful wife and a very nice daughter about three years old. They live in Erice, in the town center."

"They don't live here?"

"Oh no! Gaetano is a carpenter but his passion is for animals. Recently he had electricity brought to the stalls so he could have light for feeding his animals in the evening."

Gaetano's property is directly southeast of theirs, up the hill towards Erice. The road to his stables is long and winding, edged in high brush that scrapes their side-view mirrors as they pass. He has built a shelter for his horses and a pen for his pigs, too. Three little black ones squeal and scurry out to see who is approaching, then squeal and scurry back under the protection of their very large parents. There is a pen for goats but it is empty. There are no living quarters. Six or seven barnyard kittens crawl over a rusty tractor, sprawl seductively over the seat like lingerie models posing, but they can't stay still long enough for Kate to focus the lens of her camera.

Electra greets them with a tiny apricot colored kitten in one hand. "Doesn't he remind you of Figaro?"

He does. Thirteen years disappear as if they never existed and Kate is seeing their cat, Figaro, for the first time. They adopted him when Elizabeth and Electra were in elementary school, a kitten to cuddle and to teach them responsibility. Guess who is taking care of Figaro while their daughters are studying abroad?

"Come see the horses!"

Kate follows Electra and the kitten, which she knows better than to ask to adopt, Kate hopes, to where Marco is standing by three strikingly beautiful thoroughbreds.

There is a dog, too, big and dirty, with muddy paws.

Kate tries to avoid the Rottweiler as she has avoided Marco, but she is less successful. She tries to keep Electra between her and the dog as she has packed only one pair of trousers and needs them to stay clean. Finally, Marco comes close and whispers, "Signora, if you pet him once, he'll settle down and leave you alone."

So Kate rubs his ears and compliments his soulful brown eyes.

As they return to the barn Marco walks beside Kate, silent now, seemingly content. He has been so needy they have almost forgotten to notice how kind he is, how sweet, how his soul shines, like light reflected off a new sliver of moon, unprotected.

Muddy paws no longer pose a threat.

"Yeah, I get your point." Electra receives her mother's poetic version unenthusiastically. "You didn't have to babysit him all day and put up with no less than ten insinuations to the happily-ever-after." She shivers in revulsion. "The guy is so insistent, so clingy, I am like a magnet repulsed. How's them lines for poetry!"

With Electra still unwedded, they return to the house to say goodbye a final time to Concetta and Carmelo. As they are lingering at the front gate, disengaging their hands from one final handshake, they hear noises from up the road. Before they can fully register what is happening, a flock of sheep clamor down the hill, a chorale of shaggy, bleating beasts, a complaining counterpoint to the yapping sextet of dogs herding them home.

Rosario holds out his arm and says, "*Aspetti*—wait, it's best to let them pass. We don't want to get in the way of the herd."

Concetta and Carmelo are silent, also exchanging looks, as if worried that Kate and Niccolò might want to change their minds. Everyone is strangely silent until the sheep have passed; then Rosario walks out into the road and collides with a straggler. No one can determine who is more shocked, the last sheep or Rosario.

However, Niccolò and Kate are delighted! Their glee is probably ridiculous, too child-like, potentially embarrassing, but they are so happy to have sheep nearby. First goats. Now sheep. The sound of sheep bells jingling in the distance had been one of the prerequisites for their dream house in Sicily.

CHAPTER THREE

Perhaps it is the excess of things in the house in Florence or perhaps it is an emerging philosophy in their own lives; whatever the reason they decide they will have only what is necessary in their new house. Nothing more.

In Florence they look at what they already have to see what could be useful in Sicily, a strategy that allows them to eliminate some of their own, over-the-years accumulation. This is an ongoing tug-of-war in their home which started not long after they began living together. Niccolò had an entire room of *armadi*—closets—all full, and he was caught between wanting to clear space for Kate's clothes and not wanting to part with his own.

When Kate understood his conflict, she suggested, "Why don't we put the things you rarely use into garment bags and we can store them in a downstairs closet."

"*Va bene*—all right."

As they started sorting through Niccolò's clothes, Kate found that he had five tuxedos, a fact that amused but also confused her.

"Why would you need more than one?"

"One is for winter, one is for summer, and one is for the half-seasons, spring or autumn."

"And this one?"

"Ah, well, this isn't a tuxedo at all. It is a morning coat."

"When do you wear it?"

"In the morning."

They are on the verge of laughter. "Before or after breakfast?"

"For an occasion, an important marriage, for example, that takes place in the morning."

When Kate first met Niccolò, he didn't speak more than a smattering of English—most of which was computer English—and Kate spoke no Italian. Kate learned Italian more slowly than he did English, although now, many years later, her Italian is better than his English. Somehow, from the very start, despite this limitation, they have been able to understand each other, even without the common link of a mutual language.

"And this one?"

"This is a *frac*–tails."

"An important occasion after lunch?"

"Exactly. An afternoon wedding or an evening at an embassy."

"And a tuxedo?"

"Never during the day. Only at night."

"And you wear these often?"

"You'd be surprised how often the occasion arises. When I was a young man we wore tuxedos nearly every Friday and Saturday night. Debutante parties. Now I wear them more infrequently, probably not more than a couple times a year."

"Do you see a tuxedo wearing occasion in the near future?"

"At the end of the month my friend Giovanni is getting married."

"Morning, afternoon or evening?"

"Morning. Eleven o'clock." He points to the set of long, pin-striped tails. "The reception is a lunch."

"So you won't need these? Kate points to the three tuxedos.

"This one," he fingers the soft nap of light wool, "I'll wear to the party on the night before the wedding. I will call Giovanni to ask if I can bring you. I'm sure it will be all right."

The thought terrifies Kate. She has come to Italy for a year to collect enough seasonal photos for a book. She has brought a few pretty summer dresses with her, a few serious outfits for the autumn, but none of her clothes are appropriate for formal parties. She would have to shop, which throws her into further panic, as shopping for clothes qualifies as one of her least favorite pastimes. She would need to buy shoes, as well. No, she is not looking forward to this. What has been a blissfully simple cohabitation with Niccolò now seems fraught with perils.

Niccolò misinterprets her reticence as a result of not having made any progress emptying closet space. He opens the next cupboard. "Everything in here is a size too small for me now."

Kate is glad to change the subject. "Why do you keep them if they are too small?"

"Because they are all classic designs which I will pass on to my sons."

"What if you don't have sons?"

"Then I will save them for my grandsons."

It is moments like these that underline their cultural differences. Kate wonders if they will ever speak the same language, literally and figuratively.

"Niccolò, I see that clothes give you pleasure, but you should know that I am not particularly interested in fashion." Her only hope is to be honest with him. "The idea of shopping for expensive clothes, in a foreign city, is my notion of a nightmare."

"You have just won my heart." His expression of relief transcends all language barriers. "You are the first woman I have ever known who doesn't love to shop."

"I am glad you understand."

"I do. I sympathize. I feel exactly the same way." He leans close, touches the side of her face gently with the tips of his fingers.

Just that, an eclipse, a blink of a touch, and Kate is instantly reassured. To camouflage this unfamiliar sensation that has simultaneously wrapped her in a veil of tranquility and has left her feeling vulnerable, Kate teases: "You would never know it from all of the clothes in your closets."

He waves his hand dismissively. "It is my mother who likes to shop. I go along because it is a relatively uncomplicated activity we can enjoy together, an hour when we can pretend we have a normal mother-son relationship, that's all." He sighs deeply, then smiles. "But you will need to buy at least two dresses for Giovanni's wedding. One for the evening, one for the morning. Can you do that for me?"

"If I start buying Valentino dresses, Niccolò, I'll have to return home. I have enough money to last me a year, but not if I start shopping on *Viator Nabuoni*."

"*Via Tornabuoni*," he corrects automatically. "But don't worry. My mother will take you shopping. It's what she does best." He rubs her arms briskly, as if Kate were cold and needs to activate her circulation again. "She knows where to find every good deal in town."

If Kate had known then how difficult Niccolò's mother was, she would never have had the courage to go shopping with Fiammetta, but Kate didn't know, and they had a nice time together. Fiammetta liked Kate because she was tall and thin and looked a good deal like her second husband's sister-in-law, who was considered by many to be the most beautiful woman in Florence. Fiammetta liked that Kate looked good in the outfits she suggested. She liked that Kate was willing to follow her advice. Kate ended up buying dresses she never would have bought alone; in colors she never would have dared to try.

Honestly, Kate was grateful for the help. Fiammetta knew what kind of dresses would be required for the parties Niccolò frequented. She solved the problem of what to wear to Giovanni and Ginevra's wedding after only two shops, at a reasonable price on a street parallel to Florence's Fifth Avenue, *Via della Vigna Nuova*. Kate had liked an off-white light wool, but Fiammetta guided her towards red lace. "With your height, you shouldn't wear white. It will make you seem big. Tall is good. Big is not good. You dress too plainly. Red lace is dynamic. Feminine. Besides, only a bride should wear white to a wedding. Remember that."

In the end Kate bought the red lace dress. As it would turn out she would never feel entirely comfortable in it as it was too flamboyant for her taste. However, to be fair, Kate never received more compliments than when she wore that dress. Fiammetta knew what Italians would like.

Shopping with her future mother-in-law was less exhausting than Kate would have imagined, in part because they paused for refreshment between shops. Fiammetta let Kate pay for the cappuccino after their first purchases, but she insisted on offering the Campari Soda which concluded and celebrated their successful errand. Emboldened by the Campari and happy with her beautiful, not-impossibly-expensive new outfits, Kate said, "*Contessa*, if we were in the States, I would call you by your first name after a morning like this. May I?"

Fiammetta frowned; her carefully painted red lips the only stroke of color in an airbrushed, ageless, summer tanned complexion. Kate had obviously spoken out of line, and Fiammetta was trying to decide how to respond. But Kate was tall and thin and pretty, her son had been dating long enough, was edging toward forty, so Fiammetta indulged Kate. "I think you might. Yes, you may call me Fiammetta."

When Kate recounted this conversation to Niccolò later that evening, he said "Do you know that my sister's husband hasn't been granted that privilege yet, and they have been married for nearly three years."

"Why hasn't he asked?"

"He isn't allowed to ask. He must wait until he is invited to use the familiar form of address. My mother must make the gesture and she isn't inclined."

"Why?"

"It's a long story."

"But maybe now that I have broken the ice, maybe now she will make the gesture to your sister's husband."

"One of the things I love about you is your optimism."

Eventually, they settle on putting Niccolò's out-of-fashion clothes into a downstairs closet. The tight-fitting shirts that men wore in the sixties, the low-waist, bell-bottomed trousers were set aside, carefully preserved for sons or grandsons. One closet was enough for Kate's clothes. That would change over the years as frequent social occasions required her to accumulate more and more outfits. Kate is convinced that it is the need to wear something different for every occasion that keeps the fashion industry alive and thriving in Italy. Kate has even dedicated a shelf in her closet for clothes she no longer wears but which might please Elizabeth or Electra when they are older. She has a favorite black cashmere sweater with a white whiskered cat on its front, a gift from Fiammetta when Kate was pregnant with her grandchild, the cat gaining a third dimension as Elizabeth grew. Kate will enjoy bringing it back into circulation when her daughters are waiting for children of their own, pregnant with their own expanding traditions.

As their daughters have needed closet space of their own, poor Niccolò has had to yield space in his wardrobe to the three women in his life. The clothes from the sixties and seventies were given to charities after their girls were born. The winter tuxedo that was a little too tight in the waist was also given away. As their family grew, so did their family's possessions, and as they are contemplating what they can bring to Sicily, they find they have a lot.

There are two single beds in storage; two extra teak chairs and a patio table. There is a full set of glasses, water and wine, and dishes that Niccolò inherited from his father which have remained in their boxes in the basement. They are a beautiful, rich cream color, bordered with a wide gold band, but they were designed in an era when servants did the washing up, before dishwashers, and the gold isn't zecchino. No matter how pretty, neither Niccolò nor Kate is prepared to hand-wash dishes each night. Niccolò asked the girls if they would like the dishes for their future households, explaining that they will need to be hand-washed, and they declined. So they will enjoy them in Sicily as their everyday dishes —their only dishes—and if they lose their gold, they lose it.

In the same box labeled "Take to Sicily" is a set of white *demitasse* cups and saucers stenciled with blue sailboats that Niccolò bought long before he knew Kate. He bought them in anticipation of the day he would own a house at the sea. Kate happily wraps these better-late-than-never-dream-come-true *espresso* cups in an extra set of towels, which will also be useful.

How will they transport all these things to Sicily? They call rental vans, moving vans. They investigate on-line shipping by boat, by train. Nothing makes sense economically.

"What if we use Little Lord Junior?" Niccolò suggests, "As we did when we went to *Isola d'Elba*?"

When the kids were still in car seats, crowded into the back of their little Peugeot with their babysitter scrunched in between, Niccolò had attached their boat, Little Lord Junior, hardly longer than their car, and used it for transporting all the equipment a family needs for two weeks in a rental house at the sea. On Elba Island they used the boat for brief excursions away from the shore, but even then it was too small to accommodate a family.

As a couple, it had been fine for the two of them. They had enjoyed the boat on the Serchio River and Lake Puccini. It even worked when Lizzy was a baby. However, when Elizabeth was eleven-months-old, Kate lifted her out of the boat, placed her on the shore, told her to stay still, which she unquestioningly did, while Kate helped Niccolò pull the boat up on the shore and onto the trailer. Kate was young, strong and capable and didn't know she was pregnant. She borrowed a diaper from Elizabeth. Oddly enough, a few days later Kate experienced morning sickness. Her doctor said that a positive home test could result from leftover hormones, and gave her a more dependable test, which also proved positive. Kate had been carrying twins and one was lost on the banks of Lake Puccini.

O soave fanciulla

Their third daughter.
"How do you know it was a daughter and not a son?" Niccolò once asked.
"All babies start as female. This one never had a chance to be anything else."

Kate enjoys their possessions as much as the next person. She finds tangible pleasure in the way light reflects from the cobalt blue vases on their sideboard; in steadying an antique Caltagirone platter as she passes a dust cloth. But Kate feels as though their possessions have begun to own them, as if they are holding them hostage for a very high ransom. When she and Niccolò travel, he worries about thieves, and when they are home, they spend too much of their time cleaning and dusting. In Erice they will unburden themselves of the unnecessary. The windows will be their frames, the view the art itself. All the colors and textures they desire will be found in nature.

However, before they are free to commence on this new episode, they must tend to their farm responsibilities, finish their chores in Tuscany.

Grape growers insist that olive farming is easier, less time consuming than vineyards. That may be true—it undoubtedly is—but in order to maintain the olive orchards, Niccolò and Kate spend the majority of their days in the fields, year round, unless it is pouring rain or under zero degrees centigrade.

Before leaving for Sicily, the job they set for themselves is to control the borders and mow the fields. They must inhibit the forests from invading the groves and keep the grass low or they will return from Sicily to find their olive trees in a condition that makes the harvest difficult.

At the end of February, their agent calls to give them good news. The house is empty. They can move in on the 1st of March. Concetta will give them the keys at the end of the week, when they fly down to Trapani to finalize the contract.

It is an easy flight, one hour and ten minutes from Pisa, the same length of time it takes them to drive from *L'Antica*, their home in Florence, to Pisa. They arrive in Sicily the night before and are up early, but they are late for their appointment by several minutes as they've asked directions to Via Regina Margherita and have been directed to Via Regina Elena. In addition, as they are hurrying to correct their error—from one Queen's street to another—they are adopted by a dog that falls into step beside them. He matches their hurried pace. Kate swears he looks both ways before they cross the streets and when a band of abandoned dogs gather in front of them, threatening their progress, he chases them off, ushers them forward. By the time they reach the bank and have to leave this dog outside, they feel like they are abandoning him themselves.

When they enter the bank, they find an anxious, over-dressed Concetta and Carmelo. They have brought their son, Marco with them, as well as their sister-in-law, Anna. "*Poverina*—Poor thing." Concetta whispers in her loud voice. "She is widowed, sitting home alone, feeling so sad, so we invited her to come out with us today."

How a couple of bureaucratic hours with a notary will cheer her up, Kate can't imagine.

If Kate is puzzled, Niccolò is annoyed. "This is inappropriate behavior," he says to Kate, "Unacceptable." Unfortunately, he doesn't know what to do to correct the situation. The *Notaio*, the notary, who is a much more significant figure in Italy than in the USA, something akin to a state registrar, calls for additional chairs and the eight of them crowd into the small, airless office lent to them by the bank president. If the *Notaio* isn't protesting the additional presences, Niccolò will accept the crowd as well.

The Notary initiates the reading of the deed, his voice a rich, pleasing baritone. "29 February, at—"

"29 February!" Marco, who hasn't been given a seat for reasons of limited space, hovers behind their chairs, claps Kate on the shoulder with clammy over-familiarity. "A day like this occurs only once every four years!" Kate is reminded of Muddy Paws, and tries to be patient.

The *Notaio* holds up his hand, a judicial gesture demanding silence. Marco leans back against the door. He is wearing a dark violet shirt, and his striped tie, a monochromatic rainbow, incorporates every shade of purple from lavender to lilac.

There are twelve, single-spaced pages of border history, rites of passage and cubic meter limitations to endure before they are asked to sign the contract. Kate needs to pay close attention as this is not simple, conversational Italian. Marco ostentatiously stretches his arms over his head, tries to catch her attention; wiggles his fingers to elicit a smile. At a pause in the contract, Marco takes advantage of the Notary's need to catch his breath by declaring: "These are moments of strong emotion."

'*No Marco. It isn't,*' Kate can hear Niccolò's thoughts colliding with her own. '*Finding the house was emotional, deciding to buy it was gratifying, but clarifying boundaries and arranging for payment just needs to be endured.*'

The Notary clears his voice and speaks directly to Marco, his dark eyes serious enough to intimidate. "If you can be patient, we will be finished in a few minutes."

The Notary proceeds: "This agreement is directly between parties Concetta Vangelo, born in Trapani on 5 January—"

Concetta is 66 years old, only ten years older than Kate, only four years older than Niccolò?

"—and Carmelo Beragno, born in Trapani on 13 March—"

He, too, is only three years older than Niccolò. Kate looks at the two men seated next to each other. Carmelo looks a bit like a dried-apple doll. Instead, Niccolò's face is smooth, his skin taut; the only lines around his dark, almond-shaped eyes are from laughter. His hairline has receded in the last couple of years, but it is still plentiful; has turned a distinct dove-gray instead of black, but it is silky, asking to be caressed.

"—and Katelyn Griffitts-Aragona, born in Santa Monica, California on 1 April—"

He interrupts himself to add, "*Complimenti Signora*, I would have never guessed—"

This compliment is a matter of form, a kind of social decorum. One is a fool to believe this kind of flattery. It is used by every doctor, nurse, bank manager and, apparently, Notary.

"—directly between the parties, there is no agent present," he pauses, turning to their agent, "Is that correct, Rosario? You're not here?"

"That's correct."

Rosario not being present means that the agent's commission won't be recorded and therefore won't be taxed.

They finish the paper signing and now Niccolò and Kate need to do the paperwork for the mortgage. Carmelo, Concetta, the widowed sister-in-law, as well as the non-present Rosario file out of the office, but Marco takes advantage of the available seats and places himself to Niccolò's right. "Where is your lovely daughter, Electra? Why isn't she here? Please give her my warmest regards."

The Notary visibly counts to three, and then explains that Marco needs to wait outside with his parents while the bank papers are signed.

When Kate and Niccolò finish signing, they join the others at a nearby coffee bar. The Notaio is in a hurry, the cafe is crowded, there is no place to sit down, but somehow they find eight chairs and squeeze together around a table for two. It takes forever for the coffee to arrive. The Notaio checks his watch repeatedly. Kate is seated beside the widowed sister-in-law. Her husband had a stroke eighteen months ago and lay in bed unable to move or speak until two months ago. Relieved, yes. But it is still hard. She has two sons who live nearby; their wives come to visit every afternoon, bringing her grandchildren. She is not depressed, just adjusting. She hadn't wanted to intrude this morning but Concetta had insisted.

Having coffee together is one of those institutions that must be done, like kissing under mistletoe, even if everyone has already consumed two coffees, even if you are late for your next appointment. Equally obligatory is arguing over who will pay. The women do not enter into the discussion, nor does the

Notaio. In the end Rosario takes charge of the dispute between Carmelo and Niccolò and pays himself. As close to a tax as he will pay on this deal.

Concetta gives Niccolò two sets of keys but has forgotten the third set in her other purse. "You will have lunch with us, then we can all drive up to the house, and I will give you the last set of keys."

"Thank you. You are too kind. But we have already made plans to have lunch with Niccolò's cousin." Kate looks at her watch. "In fact, if we don't hurry we will be late."

"But when will I give you the other set of keys?"

"What if you bring them up to the house this afternoon?"

The lunch with Niccolò's cousin is a fabrication, a lie, but Kate and Niccolò want to see their house alone; hopefully empty. They are so excited they can't wait. Niccolò, who usually drives with a caution that belies all Italian hyperbole, now drives like Alonso, uncovering Ferrari-like performance in their rented FIAT 500.

Kate is barely breathing as she unlocks the front gate. She swings it open, fastens one side, then the other, aware that this is the first of many times she will open these gates, harbor them fast against the wind.

The first impression of their new house is how spacious it is, now that it is vacant. They walk from room to empty room, admiring the woodwork, the stone baseboards, the marble windowsills, the patterns on the floors, the sweeping circular strokes on the stucco walls. There is a lot less to do indoors than they had thought. The rooms are wonderfully well-proportioned. The downstairs bathroom, freed from its overload, is lovely, the tiles a pale, mermaid blue-green, a color that shifts slightly as the light changes.

Outdoors, Carmelo and Concetta have left many things, as if they ran out of space in the truck that hauled away their belongings. It's all right. They will have time to put it all in order.

Niccolò and Kate sit on the cold steps of the patio to eat their slightly soggy mozzarella and tomato sandwiches and drink bubbly, bottled-water-gone-flat, feeling as if a terrific wind has caught their dreams, lifted them into the choir stalls of heaven, leaving them to sing the refrain of this miracle. If they can know this degree of happiness once every four years, they are indeed fortunate.

Niccolò says, "The first thing I am going to do when we return next week is cut down those two trees. Why would anyone plant trees in front of the view? Even the view from the upstairs will be covered when the leaves open."

"The first thing *I'm* going to do is take away that lattice and transplant the climbing geranium," Kate says, indicating the dilapidated white plastic trellis hinged to the wall of the patio. "Why do you think they barricaded themselves against the view?"

Niccolò shrugs, then smiles shyly, almost bashfully, as if he has uncovered a secret. He wraps his arm around Kate's shoulder, brings her close, for warmth or from happiness, it isn't clear, it doesn't matter. They sit together quietly, listening to the anthem of their good fortune.

They are home.

If they can't be happy here, they can't be happy anywhere.

Kate doesn't understand until they arrive that she hasn't properly prepared for this encounter. Along with the third set of keys, Concetta brings an enormous tray of almond-paste sweets, a specialty from Erice, enough to saturate the blood sugar of a dozen guests, while Kate has forgotten to provide champagne or wine or even coffee. Kate doesn't have anything to offer. Even their almost-flat water is half-finished.

Concetta's irritation manifests itself as an avalanche of advice and instructions as she moves through the house:

"Don't remove these strings from the railings in front of the windows—" What Niccolò has been calling the Tibetan prayer flags. "—they keep the birds from building nests."

"Build a counter in the kitchen and eat in here, there is room if you tuck barstools under the counter. Don't expect always to be able to eat outdoors." She rubs at the broken skin on her hands, "from so much scrubbing," she explains.

There is the matter of the saints and the popular sayings inscribed on the tiles attached to the outside of the house, marring an otherwise clean line. On the terrace alone there are six. At the front door there are another eight. The best one is about motherhood, saccharine sweet but the image of the Madonna is pretty. For the worst there are several competitors.

"We know that you will want to take them all," Niccolò says, trying to be tactful, stressing personal taste and sentimental attachment. "We will want to put up our own tiles."

"We would like to come back to pick the *fragola di bosco*—the wild strawberries—and the last of the *fave*—the broad beans," Carmelo ventures.

"*Va bene. Va bene.*" Niccolò would prefer that they not return once he and Kate have moved in, for their sakes as well as theirs. It is heartbreaking to watch a house undergoing change and it takes a larger perspective than Concetta and Carmelo possess to see improvements as anything other than violation.

For Niccolò and Kate's sake, it is important that they are free to do what they want with this property; not have a set of eyes following their every move.

Niccolò resolves it easily. "Take anything and everything you want before we return next week."

"I could give you a good price on this satellite dish. You'd save on installation, too."

"No, thank you. We don't have a television."

"This table is good—" Concetta is referring to the stained plastic table with three legs between the two trees that block their view, "and steady," Concetta adds, "if you position it right."

"And this shade," she tugs on a torn curtain "will keep the sun out of your eyes in the afternoon. I know it's a little broken, but you'll be sorry if you take it down." She is talking about a wind-tattered bamboo shade that, when lowered, hides the view of the castle ruin from the terrace.

Kate can hear regret behind Concetta's seemingly angry words, as if she is afraid they will not take care of her house properly. Clearly they don't know the first thing about caring for a house if they don't know to provide a ceremonious drink for the previous owners. After nearly an hour, in which Kate accepts Concetta's criticism as her due for not providing a celebratory drink, they finally steer them down the stairs from the patio.

Concetta stops suddenly, holds her ground, and refuses to budge. Kate thinks she is savoring one last look at the view and sympathizes with her completely, when Concetta interrupts to

43

warn: "Whatever you do, don't cut down those trees, you will need them for shade in the summer."

"Shade?" Niccolò questions, after they have gone. "The sun rises in the east, passes to the right of the house and sets behind us. These trees have never borne shade. The most they can do is shade our eyes from the view."

CHAPTER
FOUR

Owning a house in Sicily changes the way they feel about their home in Florence.

They love their house in Florence but they do not own it. It belongs to Niccolò's mother. When they married, Fiammetta announced that she was going to give it to them, but that hasn't happened. Several years ago she suggested they might like to pay rent. It isn't a large amount; just enough to keep them from forgetting it isn't theirs. It is the change in her attitude, without apparent reason, that upsets them the most.

One day Niccolò and his sister will inherit this extraordinary property, which originally consisted of a tower and a fortress wall, dating back to the early 1400s. In the 1500s, the villa itself was constructed around the tower, and every subsequent century has enriched and enhanced the building.

Niccolò's mother inherited Villa L'Antica from her father, and she lives in it for two months a year, June and September. She passes July and August at the sea. For the rest of the year, when she is in her *palazzo* in Florence, a turn-of-the-century palace on the Arno River, Villa L'Antica is empty, except for the gatekeeper and his wife.

Niccolò's house is at the corner of the property. Originally part of the agricultural buildings, the high, vaulted ceilings on the ground floor retain traces of its origin. Their living room table is the massive stone wheel once used to press olives. The middle and upper levels of their house were originally used for storing grain and harvested grapes and olives, but aside from the traditional shaped windows, it is hard to recognize the building's origins. The view of Florence in the valley below is breathtaking, and the property is surrounded by sixty-four acres of olive trees, beyond which are more olive trees, belonging to neighboring properties. Niccolò and Kate live in full country, twenty minutes from the center of Florence.

For years Niccolò and Kate lived frugally so he could put aside money to restore L'Antica. But as the years pass and the villa falls further into disrepair, as the price of property in Tuscany escalates, as Niccolò and Kate move past the age of wanting to undertake enormous, expensive projects, they have arrived at the conclusion that maybe his money would be better invested elsewhere.

This has been a hard concept for Niccolò to accept. His maternal grandfather bought L'Antica as a summer estate, and Niccolò is very fond of it. When Kate looks at it she is saddened by the sense of neglect. She sees an enormous white elephant— forty rooms around a crumbling inner courtyard—a building that will deplete all their financial reserves as well as all their energy. But Niccolò sees it differently. He remembers the parties he hosted when he was a young man, the nights of dancing in the tower, the stolen kisses. He feels he is letting down his maternal grandfather if he doesn't rescue and restore the villa to its former glory. It goes against his nature to give up on it. It reflects, Kate fears, his hope that his relationship with his mother might be rescued and restored.

Niccolò has looked for solutions from every angle. With Kate he has spent endless hours discussing options, but no matter how hard they have tried, they cannot find the key. If Niccolò's mother were inclined to collaborate with her son, an answer might be possible. But it has become painfully clear over the years that Fiammetta doesn't really want a solution. She wants to lament the expenses of maintaining such a prominent property as a kind of testimony to her status, the way she and her friends complain about the quality of their servants and the decline in service in the five star hotels where they summer on the Italian Riviera.

From their corner of the garden, Niccolò and Kate see the villa falling into disrepair. The box hedge maze in the garden loses its distinct form. The ivy creeps up the walls and under the eaves, under the roof tiles so that when it is finally cut and then tugged free, the tiles will wedge loose and the roof will leak, giving Fiammetta further reason to complain. It's a vicious cycle.

Their house—which is not theirs—is lovely inside. Kate and Niccolò have made it warm and cozy; pretty in an unusual, eclectic way. The effect isn't Italian or American, traditional or contemporary but a coming together of their two selves. A designer would undoubtedly find objection to Niccolò's great grandmother's Murano chandelier hanging from the center of their living room—the cantina where olive oil used to be pressed—the highest expression of Venetian sophistication shimmering into rustic Tuscan simplicity—or the *Macchiaioli* portrait of Niccolò's great uncle's *amante*—mistress, an Italian Daisy Miller at the end of an evening out, seated on a throne-like chair, aching, it would seem, to remove her shoes to rub her tired feet. *Ennui* oozes out of the Impressionistic brush strokes into the bright open spaces of their country kitchen. Yet whatever the criticism, their house is a reflection of them, their personal choices. The imperfections are theirs, too—the spattering of coffee on the kitchen wall where Niccolò makes their cappuccino in the morning or the black resin stains on the pavement around their wood-burning stove, or the Christmas ornament that fell into a terra cotta vat—the likes of which Ali Baba might have hidden one of his forty thieves—which is too hard to reach, even with a long-handled broom, and is destined to remain at the bottom for perpetuity. They claim these imperfections as fondly as they own the rest.

However, the façade of their house is badly in need of repair, and Niccolò is not inclined to fix it, as it isn't his property. A catch-22 that binds their hands and hearts and makes them feels helpless, like children.

Ineffectual.

Until they bought their house in Sicily.

In Sicily the house is theirs, and they can do anything they want to it . . . once they are sure that Concetta and Carmelo won't return to reprimand them.

Their little boat becomes a vehicle of liberation. An ark. Or, as Niccolò says, as they are hoisting the second mattress on top of the first, between which are piled two spare lamps, their shades removed; several short stacks of books, extra bedding; blankets: a gypsy caravan. They are a good forty centimeters above the rim of the boat when they lay in the final blankets which will also serve to counter the bumps in the 1,300 kilometers of road between Florence and Erice. They cover their bulging boat—wasn't Kate just talking about unburdening themselves of possessions?—with a waterproof tarp and tie it down, criss-crossing it securely against the possibilities of rain or wind.

In the car itself they pack their suitcases, their computers; food for the cat and dog, plus the items Kate has open in the kitchen, a half bag of rice, a half kilo of spaghetti. It is pointless to leave it behind in Florence, it will just spoil. Undoubtedly it will come in useful in Erice.

Kate prepares a hefty picnic for themselves as they are not going to want to stop for meals if it means searching for a safe parking place for their full car and boat. They figure if they leave early in the morning, they should arrive before nightfall. 1,300 kilometers. Thirteen hours. Fourteen, at most.

Everything is ready for departure. Their alarm is set for five a.m. Everything, except their pets and their picnic, is in the car. By six they are driving down the hill with two drugged animals, the dog by Kate's feet, moving only to reposition himself in exactly the same tail-to-nose circle; and the cat, Figaro, on her lap, fast asleep except for the occasional, indignant demonic howl.

The sky shifts from magician's black to indigo blue long before the sun itself rises. Then clouds appear, a twinge of translucent pink against alabaster, the first sign the sun has risen, is being reflected, even if they can't yet see it. Kate has an uncomfortable feeling that they are being followed, and when she glances back over her shoulder she sees she is right. The boat is bumping along behind them, lurching side to side, as if it were full of Noah's animals.

All around them the hills turn from indistinct black to palpable green as trees emerge from night's shadow. In the early half-light, they are all the same, but as the sun rises, the differences appear, skeletons of *deciduous* among the evergreens, their ghostly winter arms raised, ready to receive the blessing of light, the promise of leaf.

Slowed as they are by the weight of their belongings, it takes them twice the time they had predicted to reach Rome, and twice again what they had thought to arrive at Naples, which brings them into rush-hour traffic in both cities. Their average speed is half what they anticipated. Kate has ample time to study the weekend passengers in parallel lanes, the husbands, the wives, the emphatic hand gestures which make every discussion appear as an argument. She studies the kids with their noses pressed to the windows, studying her studying them. Toddlers, precariously perched on unseat-belted mothers' laps, are far too close to the windshield for safety. *Everyone* is on their cellphone, and everyone is speeding along, in a hurry.

Except them.

At this rate it will be Easter before they arrive in Sicily.

There is nothing to do but prod along in the slow lane. Kate's legs have fallen asleep under the cat; he has seemingly increased in weight as they accumulate kilometers. Afternoon lapses into evening. The sky darkens, more subtly than it has risen, more a reversal than an evolution toward the next light.

Even though they have more than half of Italy to traverse, they decide to stop for the night. It's not easy to find a place that will accommodate a dog and a cat and a boat, but eventually they convince a hotel owner that their animals are well-behaved and they are given a room. Despite a fretful night interrupted by a fully awake cat's lament at finding himself in unfamiliar settings, they are up and out early, hoping to reach Erice well before dark, even if they are a day later than planned.

Traffic is lighter. It is Sunday morning and trucks are absent from the *autostrada*. Their speed is always less than they'd like as the boat keeps them cautious. Their picnic is diminished but they nibble on the remains, trying to ignore that the carrot sticks are wilted, the crackers soggy, the cookies crumbling, the apple slices brown. Dawn is a black-to-gray process, uninspired. Still, every kilometer behind them is one in the right direction. They sing along with the Beach Boys until finally their boyish antics become annoying, and inappropriate, as clouds gather and the temperature drops. Finally, they fall silent and just drive.

At the side of the road bare mountains rise to expose stratospheres of beige and gray rock. The presence of trees becomes secondary, a spattering of evergreens, the result of tenacious seeds gripping what seems like solid rock. Why does the rock dominate here, Kate starts to ask Niccolò, when all the other hills are covered in trees? But Niccolò is lost in his own thoughts. He looks tired, and Kate decides not to interrupt whatever internal dialogue he is pursuing.

Without realizing it, they have moved inland and climbed to 1,000 meters, away from the temperate coast. They are travelling at the same height as the clouds

Then the snow begins, first at a distance on the highest peaks. As they drive south they find it has already accumulated in drifts at the sides of the road. It is not snowing hard enough to create problems for the drivers. The asphalt glistens a reassuring, uninterrupted black as they ride along the curvy, scoliotic backbone of the mountains. Niccolò seems unconcerned.

The evergreens surrender first to the white, their boughs quickly burdened with the wet, heavy snow. Then the bare-limbed trees succumb, the snow imitating leaf mass. A tree in winter, without its leaves, is like a sculpture without its drape. Sometimes the figure is stronger nude; sometimes leafed.

Eventually, they descend from the heights of the Apennines. A river appears out of nowhere, flows stronger than ice. It is slowed at its frozen sides but not stopped. Sluggish, it rolls over its bed of water-worn rocks with a crystal clarity that makes Kate catch her breath, as if she herself had slipped into the icy water. At a curve, an island of ice dissects the river into two parts. A brace of ducks sits still as decoys. At the far bank an Egret stands, one leg tucked up into feather warmth.

As Kate is becoming acquainted with the white landscape, it abruptly vanishes, more quickly than it appeared. The sky is still dark with portentous clouds, but Niccolò shuts off the windshield wipers. Kate lowers the heat. She glances at the map, then confirms it with the car's navigator. They *are* making progress. They are nearing the toe of the boot.

At Reggio Calabria, where they embark for Sicily, there is a rising tide. They watch the cars in front of them straddle the dock and the ramp to the ferry boat, a decisive spray from the sea splashing their undersides. A man waves them forward, tells them not to worry, to just plunge! His word choice doesn't please Kate, but Niccolò guns the motor of their overburdened little car and they bump on board. Right behind them the ferry's tailgate rises, and off they go, across the Strait of Messina, seven kilometers of sea that separate the continent from the Isle of Sicilia. Here, too, two seas converge: the Ionian with the Tyrrhenian. The light sparkles like a million diamonds on the Tyrrhenian while the Ionian is a shade darker, more intense. It probably has something to do with the wind blowing from the north, causing the Ionian to catch the light, but the effect is that the two seas are distinct even as they merge.

In thirty minutes they are disembarking on Sicily. Their spirits are restored as if this brief crossing has brought them significantly closer to their goal. For the first time they feel near to home, certain that they will arrive. Niccolò stops for gas. They run to the bathroom. While Niccolò walks the dog, Kate buys a bottle of water and still warm *arancini*, two fist-sized balls of fried rice around a center of ragu and peas. Sicilian fast food.

The drive between Messina and Trapani is as relaxing as the rest of the trip has been stressful. Apart from a little traffic on the outskirts of the cities they pass, the *autostrada* is empty, literally, except for their car and their boat, giving the impression of being the only inhabitants on this island. The sun finally makes an appearance albeit intermittently. The sea, ever present on their right, shifts from Sunday afternoon's bright blue aria to the quieter, pensive serenade of evensong.

They do not stop. With the roads clear and newly paved, their appetites satisfied by the quickly consumed *arancini,* they press their luck and speed along, as fast as their over-loaded boat will permit.

It is dark by the time they reach Palermo, and they slow to a crawl through Sunday's late afternoon traffic. Whatever illusion of solitude they have enjoyed until now is destroyed. Everyone who was absent from the *autostrada* is present on the road through Palermo. Kate is wondering why the autostrada grinds to a halt for a series of interminable traffic lights when Niccolò says, "I don't understand why a city as important as Palermo doesn't have a freeway that bypasses the city traffic?"

"It's strange, isn't it? Especially if you consider that all the other cities in Italy, even the less important ones, have roads that circumvent the city."

They are decidedly tired when they reach the exit for Trapani. The Eucalyptus trees lining the end of the *autostrada* dance seductively in the yellow street lights, catching and holding the wind. Their silver, shimmering leaves transport Kate beyond her exhaustion, as if she were being lifted into their strong graceful arms, and shaken like a tambourine. Their arduous journey is at an end. Kate covers Niccolò's hand on the gear shift, and together they downshift into third. In twenty minutes they will be home.

The road that winds up to Erice, with its steep ascents, its series of switchbacks, is more of a trial with the boat. Aside from a few lights blinking down on the coast, the breath-taking views which might distract them are absent in the dark. The sea itself is shrouded, and Mt. Cofano is invisible. Niccolò takes it slow but steady, like a runner at the end of a marathon.

About halfway up the mountain they meet the first eddies of fog. It begins as a light swirl, just enough to whirl around the trees, then it thickens into a solid stream, pouring across the road, a lateral, time-lapsed waterfall, spilling over the edges as dramatically as dry-ice from the witches' cauldron in *Macbeth*.

Niccolò and Kate strain to see, but it is like peering into a tall glass of milk, looking for the bottom.

Kate feels her eyes begin to burn. Beside her, Niccolò is hunched over the steering wheel, as if a few inches closer to the windshield will improve visibility. His shoulders are tense, his arms rigid, his whole body focused.

They know they must take the first right turn, the road that leads to Trapani, but Kate can't see anything.

Few cars are on the road: those coming down hill are proceeding with extreme caution, minimal speed; their headlights illuminating rather than piercing the fog.

Then, like a shadow in a mirror or a glimpse into the beyond, the fork in the road appears, but it is too late to turn.

"*Porca Miseria!*"

"Damn!"

There is nothing to do but continue up the hill, the fog thickening as they rise. From memory they know that there are a few places along the way in which a car can make a U turn, but they don't dare, not with the boat, not in this fog when cars might be descending the hill blindly. Up the hill they creep.

Figaro meows, as if sensing their increasing anxiety.

Niccolò squints at what might be space at the side of the road and decides he's going to risk a turn. Expertly, blindly, he maneuvers the car forward, then back, then forward again, and they are moving downhill. They strain their eyes so they don't miss the turn again and eventually the road to Trapani presents itself, appearing as a chink in a white wall. As they drive downhill, the fog lifts a little, just enough to spot their own little road before they pass it.

Niccolò moves into the opposite lane to make a wide curve onto their narrow street, leaving a margin of several inches as he takes the turn. But the boat turns more tightly on its axis and from Kate's side window she sees the boat trailer's wheel lift off the ground several inches. The inside of the curve in the road drops at least two feet, not a problem for a car that has taken the curve widely, but a serious problem for a boat being towed.

Niccolò is negotiating the front of the car but isn't aware of the danger on her side. For an instant Kate envisions the trailer overturned, the boat pulled onto one side, possessions spilled. Kate breathes in deeply, as if this will remedy the situation, and holds her breath until the car completes the turn, the boat following on its trailer upright, intact.

As she lets out her breath Niccolò asks, "What's wrong?"

"Nothing." This has been the absolute worst moment of the entire trip.

"Hang on. We are almost home."

Home they are, so tired and stressed they almost forget to notice how pretty the garden looks as the car's headlights sweep over each bed of plants, before the fog moves in through the gate like a harbinger, to occupy their garden in ghostly swirls.

They would like nothing more than to climb into bed and sleep. They feel acutely the thirty-odd hours they have been travelling these last two days. But before they can sleep, they have to unpack because the boat holds their mattresses and sheets and blankets, not to mention their pajamas and toothbrushes.

The house is freezing. They work in silence, systemically, taking care of the animals first. The things that they will need tonight Kate places near the stairs, the things they don't need are stacked into a corner of the living room. With their jackets on they build up a sweat but never become warm.

"It is beautiful, isn't it?" Kate says when all their belongings are unloaded from the boat and car. "I can't believe it is ours."

A desire realized remains a longing until the mind shifts into possession.

"It is. It will be even more beautiful tomorrow, when we are rested."

The house is spacious in its emptiness, except for the mantelpiece which Concetta has left covered in dust-collectors: a painted, wooden Austrian girl feeding her goose, several ceramic ashtrays, the donkey; vases full of faded, plastic flower compositions. It isn't until they remove everything; put it all into a box to return to Concetta, that they see that the mantel is a stately piece of carved rosewood, beautiful in its simplicity.

"We must never let it accumulate clutter."

"Agreed."

Kate locates two packages of crackers and a tin of fish fillets; the last of their carrot sticks from the trip; two remaining apples and a bottle of water. She lays out their meager provisions on the altar above the unlit fireplace. Standing, Niccolò leaning against a wall, his forehead glistening as if he were too warm, they consume their celebratory dinner as wholeheartedly as if it were a proverbial feast.

By the time they fall into bed, on the two side-by-side single mattresses on the floor in their bedroom, in the position where their real bed will go, once they have one, they are sick with exhaustion. The wind has picked up and the glass windows rattle in their frames. They hadn't noticed the thin panes of glass, undoubtedly adequate for summer but not for cold or wind. They try not to be unsettled by the rattling.

"Remind me to buy silicone tomorrow," says Niccolò.

"You think you will need reminding, with this March wind howling?"

"At least we can silence the rattling, until we can install double glass."

They lie together, shivering. Even their pajamas have absorbed humidity from the cold, damp house. The mattresses feel like they are waterlogged, the goose-feather comforters on top of them are damp, too. They snuggle closer together for warmth, and degree by degree their muscles begin to relax.

The room is so dark Kate can't see Niccolò's face, even though she can feel his breath sweetly, softly on her face. Outside, there are no lights either. The closest light comes from the coast, little pinpricks of blue and yellow that become visible, then invisible, as the fog shifts uphill to consolidate in Erice's permanent halo. Kate's eyes start to close, she is beginning to warm up, she might be able to sleep after all, when Niccolò whispers, "I've gone into fibrillation. Can you find my emergency medicines?"

Medicines? Kate gropes along the wall for a light switch. Medicines? She knows she packed them. His regular heart medicine is in his briefcase, always close at hand, but where in the world did she pack his emergency medicine?

Eventually Kate finds them. She finds a bottle of water, finds a glass.

The rest of the night is spent sneaking pulse readings. His heart races like a jack-hammer, then stops for what seems like ages before it loops back into a slow, reggae beat, then speeds up frantically, as if there were a band inside his heart, banging to burst free.

The wind, too, races through the night. Every time Kate starts to sleep, the wind howls like some desperate animal, starts her own heart pumping loudly. Somewhere in the middle of the night it starts to rain; a heavy downpour that batters incessantly on the roof, gathers force like a raging river in the rain-gutter which must be directly on the wall outside their bed.

Kate is afraid.

She tells herself that her fear isn't rational, but the truth is, she is afraid. She puts her hands over her ears to shut out the noise but that only works until her hands start to relax, and then the wind dominates again. Finally, after what seems like hours of this fruitless exercise, Kate unravels Elizabeth's iPod from her purse beside her on the floor, and inserts the earplugs. Rachel Wood's rendition of *Blackbird* resonates through her fear:

Take these broken wings and learn to fly,
All your life
You were only waiting for this moment to arrive.

At sixteen this Beatles' song spoke to her need for freedom, but forty full years later Kate hears in it a prayer for healing.

She is no longer afraid. Everything is going to be fine. The house is sturdy—despite the cracks in the foundation. Nothing is going to happen. They will not wash away down the hill into a pile of rubble in Bonagia before they have finished unpacking. Niccolò will be well again, soon. He always pulls through. Throughout the night, long after she has disengaged the iPod, *Blackbird* keeps her company, the wind and rain relegated to a mere orchestral backup.

You were only waiting for this moment to arrive.

When morning light finally arrives, the wind and rain both have been replaced by another impenetrable fog, as if these harsher elements had only existed in a flight of her imagination, an interlude to this insistent fog. Perhaps Kate has imagined Niccolò's uneven heartbeat as well? In the eerie white light that filters through the window glass, Kate sees dark shadows under Niccolò's eyes, like day-old bruises. His breathing is raspy, his breath is stale. The wind and the rain were real last night: the fog is the present reality but not the only reality.

Kate leaves Niccolò sleeping and quietly goes downstairs, in search of a desperately needed coffee. Last night she left out a package of espresso, the coffee machine and a box of long conservation milk they brought from Florence, things Kate knew they would need for their first breakfast.

But the gas isn't on.

Of course it isn't on. Italians have the habit of shutting it down at its source whenever they close house, as the evening news regularly reports detonations and persons dead from gas explosions. However justified they are, Kate doesn't know how to deal with it. A part of her wants to crawl back into bed next to Niccolò and sleep until it is all resolved. Another part, the part that wants her coffee, is admonishing her to resolve it. And quickly! *You can figure it out. It can't be that hard!* Kate tells herself, while feeling like crumbling into total helplessness.

In the end the caffeine addiction pushes her forward. If Kate doesn't have a coffee, she will be useless. *'Think!'"*

Outdoors, Kate follows the gas line to the tiled utility shed behind the kitchen and tries the door. Naturally, it is locked. Why is she surprised? Back in the house she finds the basket of keys on the living room floor. There are dozens! Many are duplicates, but Kate tries a handful of keys before the door opens. Inside the shed there are two tall cylinders of gas. Kate twists the knob on the first one, but it refuses to budge. She tries the second with the same lack of success. She returns indoors again—always keeping an ear open to hear if Niccolò has awakened—and locates a wrench in the toolbox Niccolò brought in from the boat last night.

She feels like cursing her lack of strength. She feels like crying for not knowing how to do this simple task, for having relied on Niccolò for this kind of chore. Kate never meant to be this kind of woman, dependent, ignorant, unable to fend for herself. She wasn't helpless when she lived in America. What has happened to her?

Helplessness is replaced by a good dose of anger and finally Kate budges the rusty knob. The gas opens with an audible gasp, air de-compressing as it fills the empty tube.

Inside, she needs a lighter to ignite the stove. They don't smoke, and didn't think to pack one. Rummaging through the items Concetta left on the mantle, Kate locates matches in the side saddles of the donkey. God Bless Concetta!

With the gas on, Kate opens the coffee pot and fills it with water, packs down the *espresso* grounds. She heats milk in a pan, while scribbling 'microwave' and 'lighter' on a list that will grow to many pages before they are finished furnishing the house. When the coffee is ready, Kate tiptoes upstairs to check on Niccolò. He is sleeping soundly, snoring softly.

The cat is confused. The tranquilizer has worn off and he is befuddled. Figaro wants to go out but can't yet, not until he has made this house his home, and they can be sure he will return. Kate shows him his food; adds fresh kibble and water; lifts him into the cat box from which he jumps out as if his paws had been burned.

Instead, their dog has gobbled down his breakfast almost before Kate can finish pouring it into his bowl and is racing in circles. Kate lets Clover out—there is no danger he will run away; he is a Cocker Spaniel and never ventures farther than the sound of their voices. After two full days in the car, he wants to run. Kate knows he's been good, has been patient beyond all reasonable expectations, but she can't deal with him right now. His unleashed enthusiasm is a reproach to her low spirits. Somehow Kate has to keep him from barking so Niccolò can sleep. Could she justify giving him tranquilizer drops again? He wags his stump of a tail at her, cocks his head to one side as if to say, *anything is all right with me.* He is a magnificent dog, satisfied with however little or much they give him, always happy. The high point of his day is when Kate tosses him a bit of dry bread each morning, a moment he anticipates as excitedly as if Kate were offering him raw sirloin. Unfortunately, Kate can't even give him that today, poor fellow. She will take him into the front garden, throw a pine cone, stay close in case Niccolò calls her.

She should have been outside all along. She feels better immediately. The air is cold—although no colder than indoors—but fragrant, invigorating like the sea. Kate sips her coffee, inhales its aroma. The caffeine begins to work its magic, begins to restore her determination. A mist lingers close to the ground, conceals the front gate and most of the garden, all of the castle ruins on the cliff and the meadows, but below, in between a grove of cypress, Kate can see the port of Bonagia, the old tuna factory they visited in December, bathed in sunshine! They are shrouded in cloud but the rest of the world is sunny!

At the upstairs bedroom window Kate sees Niccolò's shadow flicker behind the glass. He knocks. She waves. With hand gestures Kate asks if he wants her to come upstairs. In his own version of this same silent language he says no. He steps away from the window, his form retreating into a silhouette, then an absence. The window is empty, a reflection of the branches that are still dormant: limbs without buds, without leaves.

Take these sunken eyes and learn to see
All your life,
You were only waiting for this moment to be free.

58

A classmate brought the Beatles' *White Album* into fifth period art class the day it had been issued: 22 November, 1968. The lyrics were about independence, about seeing the world uniquely. Kate was in high school and searching for answers. Poetry was a significant part of that quest. Some of their younger teachers were offering e.e. cummings and Allen Ginsberg, but her Civics' teacher was relentlessly traditional: he had them memorize Longfellow's "The Children's Hour" and Lord Tennyson's "Flower in the Crannied Wall", which the boys in her class insinuated had sexual overtones:

> *FLOWER in the crannied wall,*
> *I pluck you out of the crannies;—*
> *Hold you here, root and all, in my hand,*
> *Little flower—but if I could understand*
> *What you are, root and all, and all in all,*
> *I should know what God and man is.*

Kate memorized the little poem easily enough and earned her points, but its resounding existential question was lost on her. All the answers to all her questions were in that simple poem but Kate discarded it as old fashioned. How blind she was!

Take these sunken eyes and learn to see

"The Children's Hour" was longer but easy to learn as it had a story line. Although they complained about the dire *irrelevance* of these poems, Kate found comfort in and secretly yearned for the traditional rhythms of Longfellow's day.

> *Between the dark and the daylight,*
> *When the night is beginning to lower,*
> *Comes a pause in the day's occupations,*
> *That is known as the children's hour.*

Structures were breaking down in the Sixties but there wasn't yet anything to replace them. In private, Kate longed to be "descending the broad hall stairs", to spend an affectionate hour at the end of the day with her father and sisters: "Grave Alice and laughing Allegra, and Edith, with golden hair."

Unfortunately, their reality was starkly different. Her parents had divorced two years prior, and they were all, in their separate ways, floundering.

"Did you know Mommy and Daddy are getting a divorce?" Kate had whispered to her eldest sister, Annette, eighteen to her thirteen years."

"Of course, Stupid. *How could you* not have known?"

They were all miserable, separately.

Kate's mother had gone back to work; there were no cookies and milk on the table when Kate came home from school. The house was empty. *Too* quiet. Her friends were envious because Kate could invite boys over, but the one time Kate had invited a boy she had admired from her Spanish class, he took her oldest teddy bear, Timmy, and had pulled out one of its amber-beaded eyes with his teeth; then he laughed at her for crying 'over a dumb, stuffed bear'. But Kate cried as if she were Gloucester betrayed, her own eyes torn out.

No, Kate would have rather had her mother home, even if it meant doing more homework than she would have preferred.

Instead, when her mother did come home, she lay on her bed, still in her white hospital uniform. She had trained to be a hematologist before she married Kate's father, and, as university education in her generation served to provide insurance for women, her training came in handy after the divorce. She didn't ask Kate or her sisters to have cookies and milk on the table when she came home from work, and they hadn't been raised to consider that a parent would ever need a child's help.

Still, Kate must have sensed her mother's need. Kate remembers massaging Claire's tired legs in the evening, while being embarrassed by the stubble.

Living with her mother kept her qualities—and her short-comings—real to Kate, whereas by seeing her father only on weekends, Kate was able to maintain an illusion of him based on who she needed him to be. Even when they had lived together as a family he hadn't been actively present. He, too, lay on his bed when he returned from work, reading book after book, impressing her with his literary penchant. He did not help with homework, he did not discipline them, except at the dinner table where they all dreaded sitting next to him. He had an eight-foot mirror installed on the rear wall of their dining room, to make the room seem larger, he told his friends, but in truth so they could see themselves while they were eating. The mirror helped them learn to chew with their mouths closed; to not speak with their mouths full; to sit up straight and to bring food up to their mouths rather than lowering their heads to their forks. Elbows were never allowed on the table. Slouching earned a black-and-blue mark on the shoulder blade.

Weekends with the divorced version of her father never included table manners, as if he had divorced himself from any further parenting. Instead, their weekends were a study in minor-league jet-setting: flying to Catalina Island in a sea-plane or driving down to Mexico in his newest Mercedes Benz, or up the coast to Santa Barbara for brunch at the Biltmore. Clearly, he was trying to win their sympathies, to prove himself the superior parent. Kate didn't take sides but she *was* taken in by his charms.

At home, by comparison, Kate was all too aware of a sudden shortage of money. Her mother had opted for a larger percentage of their communal property in lieu of child support. She wanted to finish their relationship, not prolong their discussions about money.

Kate's mother was the eldest of seven children, born into responsibility and respectability in a small farm community in eastern Kansas. One's word was one's honor.

Kate's father was born in New York City, the youngest of three, the only boy; to parents who had emigrated from Russia as youngsters themselves. Improvisation replaced truth in much the same way that appearances substituted integrity.

They were an unlikely match.

Kate's mother must have been a pushover. Naïve, trusting, and ingenious in equal parts, Claire must have wanted to believe the casually privileged image he presented. How tempting it must have been to be flung beyond the mundane accountability by which she was raised, where the only expenses were necessary, into this world of extravagant abandon. Encouraged, she casually averted her eyes from what might have been warning signs.

Kate's father introduced Claire to Caesar Salad at Chasen's, *the* place to be for those pretending social status, and Mai tai cocktails at the Brown Derby, tipping the *maître d'* generously so they could sit in a booth near Glenn Ford and Rita Hayworth. After every date, he sent her flowers; not carnations, which she had received before, but rare cymbidium orchids. He drove a new car, which was exceptional enough in 1946 when the world was still reeling from the Second World War. He distinguished himself by driving a Hudson Commodore Brougham Convertible. Long after he had moved on to own other new cars, Kate remembered him telling the Hudson Commodore story to a roomful of friends, leaning back on the sofa, legs crossed in a debonair fashion; his cigarette held as a prop to punctuate his clever anecdote: after the King of Denmark saw him driving down the Sunset Strip in his Hudson Commodore, what could he do but go out and buy one for himself.

Kate's father was charming, and he convinced her mother that together they could conquer the world.

He was wrong.

After twenty-one years, they admitted their fundamental incompatibility. The marriage was dissolved easily enough, but the children remained unwilling testimony to their faulty judgment, caught up as they were in the undercurrent of inhospitable waters.

CHAPTER FIVE

Clover nudges Kate back into the present: he has dissected the pine cone she has been tossing for him; a scattering of kernels lie at her feet, either an offering or a reproach. Kate can't tell. She finds another pine cone lying at the edge of the flower bed, and throws it as hard as she can. It disappears into the mist, but Kate hears it clink against their front gate. An instant later Clover emerges, as if from a cloud, as happy as a puppy, his new toy fetched and transported to her with extreme delicacy. He settles himself at her feet, the pine cone held closely between his paws, and works to dissect it kernel by kernel.

The late sixties were not a happy time for Kate: too tall, too thin, with wavy hair that refused to be ironed straight. "Too sensitive!" her sisters told her, when their ridicule resulted in tears. Kate wanted a divorce, too!

From a payphone at Palisades High School Kate called her father, desperate. "You have to get me out of here!"

"What's wrong?"

"Everything! Will you send me away to boarding school? Please?"

"Wouldn't you rather have a car? That would give you freedom."

"No, Daddy. I need to get out of here, please!"

"Don't worry. I'll take care of everything."

Niccolò opens the front door of the house and calls to Kate. "Don't you want to come in? Aren't you cold?" He has put his coat over his pajamas, as though he has thought to join her outdoors, but has reconsidered.

"Are you feeling better?" Kate returns to the house, Clover at her heels.

He looks terrible, a pathetic imitation of his usually healthy, vibrant self.

"I thought I might feel better if I got up, but I think I will go back to bed." He looks at her. "You look as miserable as I feel."

"I am."

"I'm going to be OK."

"I know."

"Come upstairs with me."

"You don't feel like sleeping?"

"No. Keep me company. Talk to me."

Niccolò returns to bed and Kate straightens the covers over him; then she crawls under the covers on her side of the bed and pulls them up to her chin. They are both shivering. Niccolò reaches for her hand and tucks it under his arm for warmth.

"Talk to me."

"I was thinking about my father, when I moved away from home."

"Tell me."

"It is not a happy story."

"I'm listening."

She tells Niccolò about her father's promise to rescue her.

"Whenever someone says, '*Non si preoccupi*'—don't worry about anything, I automatically start to worry."

She laughs, "Even if it is your father?"

"You tell me."

Niccolò knows the consequences of this story, if not the details.

"The following weekend we drove up to Ojai Valley to look at a boarding school my father had heard of. The school was picturesque, quaint, bordered by corrals for horses. 'Each student is given a horse,' my father told me, 'to take care of during the year. It's supposed to teach you responsibility.'

'I think I could be happy here.'

'All right. It's settled. This will be your school next term.'"

"You didn't think it odd," Niccolò asks, "that you didn't enter the school to talk with the headmaster or the teachers?" He has turned on his side, has taken her warmed hand in his. His eyes are glassy but alert. "Or ask some students how they liked the school?"

"Obviously, my criteria weren't very demanding. The setting was pleasant, peaceful and far enough from home."

Who questions the waters when jumping ship?

"On Monday, I returned to Pali High, determined to make the best of my circumstances for the remainder of the academic year. I told all my friends I wouldn't be returning in the fall, and because I was leaving, the friendships which had proven less than satisfying suddenly deepened into something resembling the friendships I had been seeking. In June, as we said goodbye, we cried in each other's arms, promising to be the best of friends for the rest of our lives."

They sowed their isn't, they reaped their same

"Things were better at home, too, knowing I would be leaving soon. It was summer, my brother and I spent our days at the beach. I didn't see my sisters much, and my mother had been promoted to Chief Technologist of the Laboratory. She had a lot more responsibility, was in charge of some eighty-five employees, but she seemed less tired at the end of the day.

"In early July, two boys came to stay at my mother's house, Douglas Malstrom and his friend, Mike Thompson. Doug, as he told me I must call him, was the son of the minister of the Episcopalian Church in Los Angeles, which my family, all except my father, had attended when I was an infant. I remember it as *the church where I took my first steps*. When we moved to Pacific Palisades, my mother remained friends with the minister and his wife, and saw them once a year, though my father didn't like them. 'Saccharine Sweet,' he had called Mrs. Malstrom when he still lived with us. When Doug wanted to attend the John R. Wooden football camp held at Pacific Palisades High School that summer, my mother welcomed her friends' son and his friend."

"American hospitality," Niccolò comments.

"It was a great two weeks, almost like having brothers but without the incessant, salt-in-the-sugar-bowl teasing."

"And which one did you choose for your boyfriend?" Niccolò asks.

"No, it wasn't like that. Not at all."

"What happened?"

"When Mrs. Malstrom came to pick up Doug and Mike at the end of the two weeks, I told her I would be attending Ojai Valley School for my senior year."

'Why, that's a short distance from our little town,' she said. 'You could come up for a weekend.'

'You could come up for a few days before school starts,' Doug said.

"So I called my father to ask what date my new school began, and he said, 'I'll call the school, then call you back.'

"But when he called me back it was to tell me that the school was full, there was no room for me."

"No!" Niccolò says, his eyes dark with empathy.

"My father said, 'But don't worry, honey. I'll buy you a car instead.'"

Kate looks at Niccolò, as if Kate needs to explain. "I didn't want a car. I needed to go away."

"Did he even file an application for the school?" Niccolò asks.

"Did he call the school at all? Probably not. He most likely assumed I would stop thinking about it, like some toy I had asked for and then forgotten. Only talk.

"But at the time, I didn't ask that question. I wasn't yet ready to find fault with my father. I believed his story about the school being full."

Niccolò says, "A child needs a father to be a man of his word."

"Exactly! I had built a future based on an assumption that my father would take care of things, believing that a promise made was as good as a promise fulfilled."

Stupid! The old voice reverberates. *How could you not have known?*

Niccolò's calm, concerned voice cuts through the grating memory. "What did you do?"

"I couldn't stand the thought of returning to Pali High for my senior year. I had told everyone I was leaving. My pride was interwoven with maintaining my word. And I really needed to leave home.

"Then Doug's mother suggested that I come live with them. 'Santa Ynez has a lovely high school.'

"I remember Doug groaned and said: 'It's boring, nothing ever happens. You would hate it. Especially after LA.'

"I recall thinking that nobody born in Los Angeles calls it LA. I was so busy thinking about this reverse snobbism that it took me a minute to hear Mrs. Malstrom's invitation: 'Why don't you come up with us now, spend a few days and decide for yourself?'

"Everyone remembers where they were, what they were doing when Neil Armstrong took his first steps on the moon."

"I was in the mountains near Modena."

"I was in the Santa Ynez Valley, and I felt as though I had arrived in the promise land.

"Santa Ynez was a sleepy little town, exactly what I was looking for. The first day I was there Doug introduced me to Lori, a cheerful, pony-tailed blonde, a cheer-leader, for God's sake; a role I would have scorned in my pseudo-sophisticated Los Angeles days. But in Santa Ynez, a town where everyone— even adults whose kids weren't in high school—attended the Friday night football games, a cheerleader was respected, and Lori was about the nicest, friendliest, most welcoming person I had ever met.

"And I really liked Doug. He was sweet-natured, not like the boys I knew back home. He was only a year younger than I was, but he seemed much younger, perhaps because he had grown up in a small town, perhaps because he was the minister's son. Being in his company was a lot like being with my younger brother. I remember sitting with Doug on the window seat in his living room, looking through last year's Year Book, giggling but curious as he pointed out the people who would be in my class. I didn't think twice when he asked me to give him a back rub."

"So your story has a happy ending," Niccolò concludes.

"No," Kate breathes deeply. "At dinner that night, Doug's mother said, 'I'm afraid you're not going to be able to live with us, dear.'"

"Why?" Niccolò asks.

"Doug asked the same question, before I could ask it myself.

'Because you two—' she had said, looking first at me, then at Douglas '—are too close in age to be left alone together.'"

"She was worried about her son's virtue or yours?" Niccolò asks.

"I don't know. I was incredulous. I remember challenging her: "You are worried about Doug and me?"

'It wouldn't be right,' she had explained. 'I am not always home after school.'

"That's ridiculous," I had blurted out. "He's a baby. I have known him my whole life. We used to run through the sprinklers together, naked."

"Which lost you your ally, I suspect," Niccolò says.

"Exactly! I meant to defend my virtue, but instead I offended my friend. In the end it didn't matter. Mrs. Malstrom wasn't listening. 'I will find you another place to stay,' she said, getting up to clear the dishes from the table.

"Did she?" Niccolò asks.

"She did. She had already spoken with a woman who worked at the hospital in town, a Mrs. Graham, whose daughter was leaving for college. She had a room to rent."

"I bet you weren't happy to be pawned off on a stranger."

"No, but at least I wasn't going to have to return to Pali High in September."

Niccolò has shifted again from his side to his back, his head sinking into the pillows propped against the wall. "Were you happy at the Graham house?"

Kate checks his pulse. It is slow. Irregular. She wishes she could give him the happy ending he keeps asking for.

"At the end of the summer, I moved in with Mrs. Graham. She had just dropped off her daughter at Pomona College— which is in Los Angeles County—and offered me a ride back up to Santa Ynez. In fact, she asked me to drive. I was sixteen. I'd had my license for two full weeks. Mrs. Graham fell asleep as soon as we reached the Pacific Coast Highway, and woke up two hours later to tell me to take the San Marcos Pass from Santa Barbara to Santa Ynez.

"I remember that the heat increased as we left the coast, the roads diminished in width as they curved up over the steep, rugged Santa Ynez Mountain range. This was real driving! The chaparral was brown on the hills but I thought it was even prettier than when I came up in mid-July with Doug and his mother.

"Mrs. Graham's house was on a shady street in Solvang, the town west of Santa Ynez. The house itself was fussily furnished, with doilies on the back of the sofa, framed needlepoint, that kind of thing, which reinforced my sense that Mrs. Graham was very old, but which didn't explain her having a nine-year-old son, Glenn.

"In truth, I didn't give too much thought to Mrs. Graham or her son. I didn't even care about the gray, over-cooked spinach and the tough cut of meat, the unsalted, boiled potatoes. Eating was something that had to be done, it wasn't something to enjoy. Honestly, I was more concerned with having time to wash and straighten my hair, choose between the two new dresses my mother had bought me for going back to school, while imagining what my classes and classmates would be like."

"What were they like?"

"They didn't notice me. I saw Doug at the end of first period. He waved but didn't stop to talk. I saw Doug's friend from football camp, Mike, too, who hollered hello as he sauntered past with a group of guys, members of the football team, I gathered, judging by their identical jackets. Otherwise, no one seemed to notice me."

"How strange."

"I might as well have been invisible."

"Poor you!"

"But invisible, I began to relax. Suddenly I was free to be myself, instead of who I thought I was expected to be. It was strangely liberating.

"At nutrition break, as I was looking for a place to sit and eat the apple and cookies I had brought, I noticed a pretty, auburn-haired girl in the hall, greeting everyone; being greeted by everyone. She stopped when she reached me. 'Oh, you must be the new girl Lori told me about. My name is Carrie. How do you like it here so far?' As she was talking with me, people swarmed by, touching her arm, smiling at her, welcoming her back. She was obviously popular. In addition to her books, which she cradled in one arm, pressed to her chest, I remember she was carrying a rather large green plastic inner tube, the kind we used to float in before we knew how to swim. Everyone who passed had a comment to make.

'How's the doughnut, Williams?'

'Just fine. Thanks for asking.'

'The tail?'

'All gone, thanks.' Her smile was unselfconscious; contagious. "I had a little operation last month,' she confided. "I had an extra two vertebrae, kind of a tail, and it started growing, if you can believe that. So I had it removed. I have to sit on this silly thing for another couple of weeks. Come with me. I'll introduce you to some nice people.'

"Her friends were nice, although they were more reserved than Carrie. There was trust and affection moving between these people, but they all seemed so young! It wasn't how they were dressed, although I was the only one wearing a mini skirt. It was how they acted, the way my friends and I had acted in Los Angeles before we started acting cool, before we had to pretend to know what was going on, especially when we didn't. I actually saw a group of boys trying to look up a girl's dress!

"At the end of the first day, as I was settling down to do my homework in the hard, wooden chair in my bedroom, I thought about Carrie. Like Carrie, I had an extra vertebra, too. The difference was that she was telling everyone, calling it a kind of a tail, whereas I kept mine a shameful secret, as if I had failed to evolve. As I was reflecting on this difference, I noticed that things have been disturbed on my desk. I opened my bureau: someone had been rifling through my drawers. I couldn't tell if anything was missing but even so, I felt violated."

"No!" Niccolò says. "What did you do?"

"I took six one-dollar bills from my wallet and placed them under my gym socks in the top right-hand drawer.

"When I came home from school on the second day, three of the six dollars were missing. On my bed there was a note that said Blake had called, that he and Rachel were coming up to camp at Lake Cachuma the following weekend."

"What did you do about the missing money? And who was Blake?"

"The note helped take my mind off the money. Blake was my closest friend. He had graduated from Pali High the previous June, and was due to begin studying philosophy at UCLA. He lived in a mattress-on-the-floor apartment in Santa Monica with his nineteen-year-old girlfriend, Rachel."

"A bit like us now," Niccolò says, patting the floor beside him. "Did their parents approve?"

"I don't know if his parents approved, but they didn't prohibit it. Blake's father was an engineer for the Hughes Corporation, and his mother was a nuclear physicist at Rand. Blake and Rachel were into being poor, one of those no-place-to-go-but-down-options available to those of us born into the upper-middle-class comfort of suburbia."

"What did you do about the missing money?"

"That evening, as I was helping to put dinner onto the table, I lowered my voice to alert Mrs. Graham to the fact of the missing dollars.

She stopped dishing out the flaccid carrots. 'I am sure you are mistaken.'

'Actually,' I told her. 'I put six dollars in my top drawer, as a kind of test, after I had noticed that someone had been in my room yesterday.'

'Setting traps, huh?'

'I wanted to be sure before I spoke with you.'

'Three dollars isn't a large sum of money.'

"That's hardly the point," Niccolò interjects.

"That's what I told her. I told her I didn't appreciate having someone rummaging through my things."

"What did she say?"

Kate tries to imitate the moral indignation she heard in Mrs. Graham's voice. 'Are you accusing me of rummaging through your things?'

'Actually, I was thinking it might be your son.'

'My son is not a thief. I am sure you are mistaken.'

"In the face of utter denial," Kate tells Niccolò, "I had no choice but to yield. I said, 'I am sure you are right. I just hope it won't happen again.'"

"Dinner that night was uncomfortably silent. I swear I could hear Mrs. Graham masticating, elaborately, deliberately, twenty times for every bite. I could almost see her counting. When the last of the meat had been disposed of, when her lips had been patted dry, she turned to me and said, 'I am not going to be able to have you live here. I don't want a wild girl living in my house.'

'Am I wild?'

'You want to run off camping with a boyfriend at Lake Cachuma.'

'I don't want to run off.'"

"She was obviously referring to the note," Niccolò understands.

"Besides, he wasn't my boyfriend, I tried to explain. He was going camping with his girlfriend. I would visit them during the day."

"That sounds reasonable," Niccolò says, stifling a yawn.

"I thought so, too, but Mrs. Graham hadn't heard a word I'd said. 'My daughter never even thought of camping with boys. I can't deal with a wild person.'

"And I can't deal with an insane person," I thought but kept quiet.

"I went back to my room. I tried to study. I was supposed to read twenty pages for American History, but I couldn't concentrate on anything other than my imminent eviction. I knew I would have to call my mother, but I didn't want to. I knew she would tell me to come home.

"I kept thinking, 'What am I doing wrong? First Ojai Valley School fell through, then the Malstrom's, now this fiasco.' I didn't feel like a bad person. I didn't feel guilty of the crimes of which I was being accused. But obviously I was doing things wrong. When all the evidence was in, clearly I was to blame."

Kate waits for Niccolò to say something, but he is silent. She leans forward to look at him and finds he has fallen back to sleep, his head cradled by the pillows. Kate is glad he is sleeping, that will heal him faster than her story, but she is sorry she hasn't been able to give him the happy ending he was waiting for.

In those first days away from home, happiness wasn't a consideration.

Kate's future seemed balanced between the impossible and the improbable.

Nothing was clear. Even the history lessons which had been so obvious in class clouded in front of her, the words turned meaningless. Kate remembers she eventually gave up trying to study, put on her pajamas and got into bed without even brushing her teeth. Kate clutched her bear, bringing Timmy to the side of her face, feeling his worn but still scratchy wool against her cheek. He had been given to her by her Godmother, a woman Kate never met as she and her parents had stopped being friends shortly after Kate was born. Kate wondered if that had been her fault, too. Nonetheless, Kate had always cherished this bear as evidence that someone thought to celebrate her arrival, even though she was just another girl, a third daughter. The cloudy, yellow light from the street lamp outside her window reflected in the single tawny eye; the missing reflection was testimony to her many limitations. How could Kate hope to take care of herself, live away from home, if she couldn't even manage to keep her bear, Timmy, safe?

CHAPTER SIX

E*nough!* Reminiscing about high school and her poor one-eyed bear isn't going to make things better in Erice. Quietly, so as not to wake Niccolò, Kate crawls out from under the covers, shakes out a cramp in her leg, and pulls herself up to her full height. Nourishment: she needs to find food.

She can't take the car to shop for groceries because it is attached to the boat, and she isn't sure how to unhook it without risking damage.

Next time she will pay closer attention.

What Kate does recall is that curve in the road last night when she was sure the boat would overturn. She doesn't want to encounter that risk again. She also knows that the roads in Erice are so narrow that side mirrors need to be folded in to pass along the streets, even for small cars; roads unimaginable towing a boat. Kate doesn't mind appearing ridiculous if absolutely necessary but she'd rather not try to negotiate an empty boat through the narrow streets of a medieval town.

She paces the length of their garden, trying to find a solution.

Essere tra l' incudine ed il martello. Kate is caught between a rock and a hard spot. Or, as is written on a tile on the wall of their patio: *Stari tra l'incudini e u marteddu.*

Clover has run off with another pine cone, has taken it to the front porch to tear it apart. Lying on his back in a very un-dog-like position, the pinecone held firmly between his two front paws, never even noticing his lack of thumbs, he dissects it kernel by kernel with his teeth. Kate picks up another pine cone and inspects it closely. It is full of pine nuts!

The toes of her shoes are dark with damp as she leaves the paved garden path and starts walking to the upper garden where Carmelo planted his *fave*. Maybe there are some left. Neither Niccolò nor Kate is a fan of broad beans, but at this point they would welcome any source of protein.

Indeed, there are a few *fave* left, but they have grown past their prime, are tough and chalky. Better left to the birds.

Kate wishes she could remember which plants in the garden are edible, but they all look alike. As she is trying to distinguish one green clump from another, she spies a line of fine, green sprouts, like daffodil stems, poking out of the earth. When she digs down with her fingers she finds a scallion, then another, row after row of fresh, young, green onions. Kate hurries back into the house to collect a plastic handled steak knife Concetta has left in the kitchen, and returns up the hill with as much energy as if the sun had recharged her batteries, to dig scallions out of the dark, loamy soil.

Kate cradles the onions, imaging how they will enhance the rice she has brought from Florence, when she stumbles, literally, over a patch of broccoli: dark-green flowers on pale-green stalks in the middle of the lawn, hidden by the tall grass which Niccolò and Kate will need to cut, once he is well, once they have acquired a lawn mower. These young, handsome stalks and flowerets must have re-seeded themselves from last year's crop. Kate is careful to harvest above the future buds, already imaging future meals. These unexpected flowers are so tender Kate won't need to peel them, which is fortunate, as she doesn't have a peeler, and the only knife sharp enough is covered in mud.

Indoors, warmed by her digging, Kate unzips her coat while putting water to boil for the rice. It is only late-morning, not the right time for lunch, but they didn't eat anything much last night, and Kate imagines Niccolò will feel better if he eats something. While Kate sautés the onions, she takes off her coat. By the time she adds the broccoli, with a dash of soy sauce (soy sauce in the rice, as well, as they don't have salt), the aromas rise up the stairs to wake Niccolò. Kate is combining ingredients, throwing in the handful of pine nuts she has been able to crack open when Niccolò comes down, his face gray. They sit on the two wooden slatted patio chairs they brought from

Florence in the otherwise empty living room, their plates balanced on their knees. He looks old; his two day beard stubble doesn't help.

"I think I might live," he says, after the third bite of rice. "Where in the world did you find food?"

"In our garden."

They both smile for what seems like the first time in ages.

"Have I told you today that I love you?"

"Not in words, no."

"I do. And I am sorry I fell asleep while you were talking, I just couldn't stay awake."

"Sleep is good for you."

Niccolò stifles a yawn. Kate collects his plate and places it on top of hers, lays their forks next to each others'. "Why don't you sleep some more?"

"I think I will."

She carries their plates into the kitchen, rinses them quickly, and leaves them to dry. Kate decides it is time to resolve their grocery problem before they are hungry again.

Niccolò returns to bed, and Kate hikes up to Erice to buy bread and salt and milk, enough to feed them until they can shop properly.

She is out of breath long before she arrives. The road is steeply uphill all the way, made longer because of all the switchback turns. The breath-taking views are by turn shrouded in cloud, then revealed, the sea so blue it is almost black. Kate can understand why ancient populations worshipped the sun. At midday, the sun itself isn't spectacular but the objects it illuminates are: the white wall of a church sparkles as if studded by diamonds or centuries of faith. Even the simplest building radiates with substance.

Halfway up, the switchback rears away from the view of Mt. Cofano, and Trapani appears, gray and somber, spreading like a shadow toward the sea. Beyond are the islands, their names Kate can't remember, only Marettimo, the one farthest from shore, alluring, inviting her to pause and appraise their silhouetted, seductive forms. Ulysses' sirens have been said to have sung from the Trapani coast, and Kate can believe it, regardless of its historical truth. Even from this height she can hear them beckoning.

It is a good thing she didn't bring her camera. She hurries herself along although she would like to linger. Kate is not terribly worried about Niccolò. They have been through this many times and she knows fibrillation's route. Today he will be sluggish, by tonight his heart will be fairly regular. Tomorrow he will be well again, and Kate will need to remind him to take it easy. She has her cellphone with her, he has his. Still, Kate quickens her pace even as her eyes linger on the islands, appraising the light. There will be many occasions to photograph this gulf designed in the shape of a sickle which defines Trapani, the antique *Drepanum*.

At the lower gate of Erice the walk steepens yet again. Underfoot, the designed pavement has worn slick and smooth from hundreds of years of passage. The design is practical, to facilitate carts, foot traffic and floods of rain, but the effect is wholly aesthetic. The abandoned streets and the fog reinforce the timeless illusion. Kate could be in any century. The shops are closed and shuttered and will remain closed until Easter brings the first tourists. She must photograph this town before it is lost to the crowds. In the main square, Kate asks directions from the only open cafe.

"Everything is closed on Monday mornings, but you can try the supermarket."

A supermarket sounds promising! Kate is directed forward another fifty meters to a tiny shop stocked to the ceiling with anything and everything Erice's three-hundred year-round residents might need. It is a long way from resembling the supermarkets in California or their more recent, lesser brothers in Florence, but Kate is as happy to find this shop as if it were Gelson's on Sunset Boulevard!

"Do you have any bread?" Kate asks, winded.

"Oh *Signora, mi dispiace.* I am so sorry. Not on Monday morning." The shop owner must see the pained expression on her face for she quickly adds, "Wait, I'll call a restaurant to see if they have bread they can spare."

She is quick and efficient, but the phone rings unanswered.

"Do you have any crackers or —?"

"Wait, I'll call my mother. She was driving to Valderice this morning. I will see if she bought an extra loaf of bread." She dials a number on her phone and speaks quickly in a dialect

Kate can't understand. "She does!" The shop owner is as pleased as Kate. She nods to a young man—her brother, her assistant, or perhaps a fiancé—and says, "Giovanni will fetch the bread." Kate has to insist he take her coin. Three minutes later he is back, bread still warm, turning away from her gratitude as if it were inappropriate. *"Si figuri!"*

To show her appreciation, Kate buys as much as she can carry home: local fish, San Pietro, caught and frozen last week by the shopkeeper's brother-in-law, excellent quality, Kate is assured. Fresh mozzarella, braided or in balls? Cow's milk or Buffalo? Kate asks for tomatoes. No *Signora, ancora no*. Not yet. Not until May, at the very earliest. But Asparagus yes, and three lettuces: *lattuga* from *Chiesa Nuova*, *Romana* from *Valderice, and Arugula* from *Purgatorio*.

Purgatory? Kate thinks but does not ask. There is much to learn here. Kate buys *Tropea* spring onions, their cerise and purple stalks so striking that she buys a bunch even though she has scallions in her garden. Finally, unable to resist, she buys five kilos of blood-red oranges.

Her arms are aching, threatening to pull out of their sockets by the time Kate reaches home. Her knees feel like buckling from the steep descent, but her spirits lift when she reaches their gate, and sees their little house.

Ultimately, it was Carrie who threw Kate a life-saver in Santa Ynez. She found her between classes the next day; her habitual cheerfulness turned serious when she heard of Kate's problems with the Grahams. "Poor you! I wondered how you would do living with them. But don't worry. You can come live with me."

"Really?"

"Of course! I'll talk to my folks right after school. Here's my number. Have your parents call my parents this evening. Gotta run. Can't be late for Biology!" And off she went, carrying her books and the ever-present cushion.

It was much easier telling her mother that Kate was going to have to leave the Graham's house with an alternative in the offering. Still, Claire thought it was best if Kate came home. Kate could go to another school, if she wanted, Santa Monica

High. She could ride with Claire in the mornings. Claire would drop her off on the way to work.

Kate let her mother talk, then gave her Carrie's phone number, and made her promise to call back the minute she finished speaking with them.

When Claire called back half an hour later, she was in a better mood. "I had to explain from scratch," she said, "as your friend Carrie had forgotten to tell her parents that she had invited you to move in."

"Oops."

"I spoke with Mrs. Williams. She is very friendly. She said their house is small, that you will have to share a room with Carrie, but that you are more than welcome."

"Carrie is incredibly friendly."

"Then I spoke with Mr. Williams. He is less friendly. He is a retired sheriff. He also said you were welcome, but he added that one false move and you would be—*out on your butt*— to use his exact words. Do you think you will be able to follow his rules? You've never lived with an authoritarian father."

"I do. I will. I will make this work."

"Good. If not, you will come home."

She met Carrie's mother the following day after school at the Graham's house when she came to pick up Kate. Anne Williams' bright green leprechaun eyes twinkled mischievously as she helped lift Kate's two suitcases into the trunk of the car. Although Mrs. Williams must have been at least in her forties, Anne—as she insisted Kate call her—seemed young and girlish. She was friendly and respectful with Mrs. Graham as they said goodbye, then rolled her eyes as they were driving off. "Bet you are glad to be away from that soggy old Graham cracker."

"I am." The second three dollars had disappeared from her drawer, as well. "Thank you for letting me live with you."

"We will have fun."

Jack Williams was a big bear of a man, as tall as Kate but massive. His tenor voice was powerful, intimidating. He repeated verbatim what he had told Kate's mother: "One false move and you are out on your butt!"

"Oh, Daddy," Carrie said, wrapping her arms around her father, nuzzling his neck with the tip of her nose. "You're going to frighten her to death."

"Honestly, Jack!" Anne joined Carrie, wrapped her thin, freckled arms around her husband's ample girth. "Stop before she thinks you mean it."

"I do mean it!" His stern complexion was softened by deep brown, long-lashed eyes.

"Have you ever seen more beautiful bedroom eyes?" Anne teased him, giggling.

Kate had never seen her parents kiss or hug or even hold hands. The last time Kate had snuggled with her father was when she was five, when they were waiting for her mother and newborn brother to come home from the hospital.

Suddenly, Kate found herself living with people who liked each other—loved each other—and weren't embarrassed by it!

She developed a figure in the year Kate lived with the Williams family. She would never be voluptuous, like her elder sisters, but her newly acquired curves allowed her to feel less self-conscious about her body.

The room Carrie and Kate shared was tiny. Their entire house would have fit into Kate's parents' master bedroom in Los Angeles, but the atmosphere at the Williams' house was grand. Carrie studied on her side of the room, Kate on the other, in a healthy, collaborative competition. Kate started bringing home A's. Anne cooked during the week, savory stews and huge slabs of tender beef. Carrie and Kate harmonized as they did the dishes: *He Ain't Heavy, He's your Brother.* Jack cooked on the weekends: five egg omelettes overflowing with sautéed green peppers, tomatoes, cheese oozing onto the plates, or mountains of pancakes with blue berries or strawberries, whatever they wanted, as if feeding them was a pleasure, not a chore. Jack made sure Kate was dressed appropriately before she went out on a date and sent her back into her room to button up if he thought her outfit was provocative. Everyone yelled if Kate stayed too long in the bathroom. Carrie and Kate sang their hearts out as they drove to school, Simon and Garfunkel's *Bridge over Troubled Waters*; the Jackson 5; The Carpenters, The Hollies. Kate had discovered what a family could be. Finally, Kate had *descended the broad hall stairs*, had become someone's *laughing Allegra*.

When Kate peeks in on Niccolò, he is sleeping. He looks pathetic lying on a mattress on the floor, his inherent elegance compromised. The covers are more on the floor than on the bed. Their clothes from last night are in untidy piles, the suitcase open and spilling its contents. Such disorder! Not what they imagined when they departed from Florence. Kate forces herself to resist the temptation to tidy up. It is more important that Niccolò sleep.

Concetta has left the house clean and provisioned with anything they might need until they settle in: Band-Aids in case they cut themselves while still unfamiliar with the house; candles, matches, paper and pine cones to light the fire place, two place settings of dishes: their every comfort anticipated. In the kitchen Kate unloads the groceries but can't put them away until she empties the shelves of all that Concetta has left for them. Kate takes a second cup of *espresso* and milk and sits on the steps of their little patio. She stares through the trees at the sea. There was wind again as Kate descended from Erice, it has lifted the clouds but hasn't brought sun; it has left white caps on the sea.

It is cold, very cold, and as Kate stares at her blue-tinted hands, she wonders what are they doing here? Have they made a mistake? It is stunning here, but they have travelled to many beautiful places and haven't bought a house. Maybe they should have rented first? Maybe this is why the price was so reasonable. The December cold remains December cold even in spring. Hadn't Carmelo said one needed a blanket even in the summer? And they were worried about the Sicilian heat! God, what have they done?

The two tall palms whirl like helicopter blades in the wind, and Kate can feel her thoughts reeling at the same high speed, as if hypnotized by their movement. Between their neighbor's cypresses, Kate can see the port of Bonagia where it is sunny again, while here it is almost dark. They are living in a cloud but Kate is not feeling god-like. On the contrary, if this is Mt. Olympus, the message they are being sent is not a sunny one.

In the distance Kate hears the clanging of sheep bells; their bleating sounds forlorn. She strains to see them pass in front of their gate, their whorls of white wool a blur in the dark fog. Like

82

spi.its in the night, she hears their passage more acutely than she sees them.

A box of books has been dropped in the entrance and Kate rummages through until she finds something to read. She's already read everything in this box at least once, but every title is worth reading again. After all, it's not about plot; it's about language, of being in the company of carefully chosen words. Karen Blixen's *Out of Africa* catches her attention. So does Rilke.

There is a calendar in the box, too, the February photograph one she took years ago, a winter river frozen beneath an ancient Roman arch. She studies it critically. She would do it differently now. It takes her a second to remember what month they are in, then another moment to calculate what day of the week it is. March 3rd. Monday. Elizabeth and Electra will be flying down on the 17th. That gives them exactly two weeks to ready the house for company. Two weeks! At this moment it feels impossible. There is so much to do, and she feels as frozen as the river in her photograph.

It is completely dark now, inside and out. The only light comes from two ceramic sconces on the stairs which they must return to Concetta when they have found light fixtures of their own. If Kate were home, she'd make herself a cup of tea at this hour, but Kate forgot to buy tea bags in Erice. Cold and uncomfortable, she sits on the stairs and starts to read Rilke's *Duino Elegies*:

Who, if I cried out, would hear me among the angels?

Clover comes to sit at her feet, his muzzle resting on the damp toes of her shoes. Figaro comes out of hiding from a half unpacked box, and settles himself down in her lap, curling in for a long stay. Rilke writes as if reading her thoughts, raising his voice in a northern Italian wind, walking into the *Bora* gale, as Kate submits to the Sicilian *Scirocco*.

Strange, to see things, that seemed to belong together, floating in every direction.

What's this sadness about, Kate asks herself. Niccolò's not going to die. He's not going to abandon her. A lack of sun isn't a

83

problem, either, not for one who has lived through winters in New England and New York, summers in San Francisco and England. Whatever this problem, it is momentary. Kate can deal with a little wind and cold. Eventually she will learn to decipher this weather, learn to deduce from where the wind blows.

She stays in this position long after it is comfortable—her feet blocked, her legs heavy from the weight of the cat, her mind too distracted to continue reading—simply because she can't make herself move.

CHAPTER
SEVEN

The next day is better. When Kate awakens it is to find Niccolò smiling, his Nutella brown eyes sparkling with renewed health, as if sprinkled with sugar. The wind has quieted, the fog has dispersed. It is still very cold, but at least the window panes aren't rattling. While Kate makes coffee, Niccolò showers, then shaves, without a mirror—there are no mirrors in the house! Another thing to put on their list!

Shaving consumes all of Niccolò's energy but at least he is out of bed. He sits in one of their two chairs, wrapped in his all-weather coat, and talks with Kate as she starts to organize their suitcases and boxes.

"I was wondering, do you have any happy memories of your father?"

She pauses to consider. "Yes." More than unpacking, Kate is designating boxes to their appropriate rooms to be unpacked later as they have no place to put their belongings yet. Until they have dressers, their clothes will remain in their suitcases. Until they have a cabinet in the bathroom, toiletries will stay in a box on the floor. Kate is doing what she can: hanging towels on the racks, putting soap and shampoo and cream rinse into the shower. However, to answer Niccolò's question, she settles herself on the bottom step of the stairs, in what is quickly becoming her favorite place to sit. "I have two cherished memories," she tells him. "Both of them are from about the same age, six or seven. The first is one time when my mother called the family to dinner and both my father and I arrived at the bathroom at the same time to wash our hands. Instead of making me wait, my father took my hands and washed them together with his. I had never noticed that my hands were small until I saw them enfolded into his large, adult hands. I remember how happy I was, as if it were yesterday. It was lovely.

Niccolò doesn't seem overly impressed. "And the other happy memory?"

"My father sometimes went out for a walk after dinner, and sometimes, if I promised to be quiet, he let me join him. I remember walking around our neighborhood, the other families still at dinner or mothers in the kitchen tidying up, feeling so honored to be out walking with my father, holding his hand."

"But you had to be quiet."

"Well, I seem to remember that I often had to promise to be quiet if I wanted to be near him, but I would have given up speech entirely if he had required it of me, anything to have had his company to myself." Kate laughs, "I used to watch bowling with him on Saturday afternoons even though it was the most boring program on television. But he let me sit beside him on the sofa."

"As long as you were quiet."

"Don't diminish the few happy memories I have!"

Kate gets up and kisses Niccolò's baby-soft cheek, puts her arms around this man who has more than compensated for her father's failings. Kate no longer blames herself for her being unlovable. She realizes now that she was just a casualty of a man racing and swerving to find his direction, that little kid in the back seat, buckled in for the ride, unaware that the man at the wheel didn't know where he was going or how to drive. Despite all the beautiful new cars, her father never discovered his destination. He was always striving for something new, something better, something of value, and made the mistake of looking for it outside of himself. Kate believes his marriage failed largely because the woman he chose was better suited to an image of who he thought he might like to be, rather than finding a wife who could appreciate and nourish his real qualities. Unable to sustain his image, he became less at peace with himself and more at odds with his role in the world. Unwittingly, he married disapproval. The image he tried to create for himself—transforming himself from the son of accented emigrants into a Brooks Brothers husband of one of America's original WASPs—was more to disguise himself from himself than a means by which to fulfill his potential. What sorrow remains for Kate from those early, unfortunate years has shifted from herself—that lonely, unloved child—to him, a man who never came close to knowing himself or the people who might have loved him, given half a chance.

It's not what we are born with that counts, it is what we do with it that matters.

Wraiths of mist whirl down from the castle ruins, engulfing their valley in near darkness, even though it is noon and the sun is high in the sky somewhere else. With this weather they are unlikely to eat outdoors before Easter. Niccolò gives Kate a hand and they carry their patio table into the dining room. Upstairs, Kate straightens the covers on their bed; puts their room in order so it looks less struck by a hurricane. After lunch they both nap, huddled together on their mattresses. The house is still insufferably cold, but they are warm under their mountain of blankets.

In the early afternoon, their agent, Rosario, drops by with a tray of marzipan pastries from Erice.

"Why didn't you call me?" He is appalled that they have not asked for help. "I would have been happy to drive you into town for groceries. I am certain I have an extra electric blanket you can borrow."

Kate doesn't know what strange pride has kept her from calling him. To be honest, it never even occurred to her that she could have asked for help.

"Would you be able to help me unlatch the boat from the car?" Kate asks Rosario.

In a second it is done. It was so easy to ask!

They stand in the garden, watching Mt. Cofano perform her tricks, the light shifting from dark to light on the water and the mountain. The two date palms engage the slight breeze, their fronds moving in the same direction as the swaying bamboo but at a different pace, catching a swifter breeze. These palms are part of the landscape of Kate's youth, the invincible guardians of her first memories. They stood sentinel along the palisades in Santa Monica, catching the winds from the Pacific. When Kate became old enough to worry about tidal waves, they belied the dangers, reassured her of her safety: in their hundred years of life they bent to the power of the Pacific but never broke. Where there are palms, Kate is allowed to feel safe.

Eventually, Niccolò joins Kate and Rosario. He is looking much better.

"I see Concetta left us all the tiles," he says to Rosario. "I wonder why?"

"They were reluctant to remove them from the walls, afraid if the plaster broke it would be a big job to patch the walls."

"Ok. We'll do it. We'll try not to damage the tiles or the house."

"If they break, they break."

"Exactly. We'll put the ones intact into a box for them. They left other things behind—gnomes and trolls between the plants in the garden—which we will box up, as we find them."

A car approaches and stops outside their gate.

"*Permesso?*" An elderly gentleman is asking permission to enter the garden. He is well-dressed in an outdated style, an elegant figure despite a noticeably rounded back. Several dogs of various sizes and breeds trail behind him.

Rosario greets him with enthusiasm and familiarity. "Edoardo! Come meet your new neighbors."

Rosario makes the introductions. "This is your neighbor, Edoardo Oliviero. Edoardo, please meet Dottore Niccolò Aragona and his wife, Kat-tie."

"Katelyn," Kate introduces herself. Rosario can't pronounce her name and has given up trying, as Kate has given up trying to correct him. She never uses her full name, not even on the works she exhibits or publishes, but single syllable names are not easy for Italians, and she would rather be called by her full name than Kat-tie.

Edoardo is eyeing them suspiciously. "I saw your names on the mailbox. What kind of name is Griffitts?"

"I'm American." Kate doesn't feel inclined to explain to a total stranger why she has adopted her mother's maiden name.

"American is good. And you?" he indicates Niccolò.

"Sicilian."

"Sicilian is less good. From where?"

"Trapani. Martogna. My grandfather was Niccolò Aragona."

"The historian or the revolutionary?"

"The historian. My *great* grandfather was the first to plant the new unified tricolor flag in Trapani before Garibaldi landed in Sicilia."

Their neighbor nods. "My brother," he crosses himself, "lived on Via Aragona. I am pleased to meet you." He shakes Niccolò's hand, then takes Kate's hand and bows over it. "I like Americans. Welcome to Sicilia.

"*Aspetti.*" Their new neighbor returns to his car, trailed by the dogs, and comes back carrying a bottle wrapped in brown paper. "This wine is older than you are, Madam, and as strong as your husband. So be warned."

She is amused that he has waited to meet them before offering the wine. They have obviously passed some kind of test. "Do you have time for a glass now?"

"There is always time to raise a glass to new friends."

"Would you like to see the house? We don't have furniture yet but if you'd like to see it?"

"I'll wait until you have had time to settle in."

"I would invite you to come in from the cold, but I am afraid it is colder inside than out."

"I prefer the out-of-doors anyway, thank you." Their neighbor and Niccolò sit on the low stone wall in the garden. Several of the dogs settle at their feet but one dog jumps up onto the wall to sit at their neighbor's side—a comic gesture because of its disproportionately short legs—and lays its ridiculously long eared head on their neighbor's thigh. Rosario follows Kate to search for glasses.

Indoors, Rosario pauses. Kate thinks he is noticing the changes from the last time he was here, when the house was crowded. Instead, he is looking at a large, flat screen in the corner of the living room. "I thought you didn't have a TV?"

"Why did you think that?"

"Carmelo told me you weren't interested in buying his satellite dish."

"We don't use it as a television, only as a monitor screen to view my photographs or to watch films when Elizabeth and Electra are home."

"What about sports? The evening news?"

She shakes her head. Niccolò reads the news on-line. Kate hears what is happening in the world because he repeats out loud the important events. What they miss on the evening news is the scandal: details that aren't constructive or informative, merely sensational; stories that don't enrich their lives but fill them with clutter. Worse, the voices of the broadcasters are loud and false; glib; insincere. Give her a newscaster who reports deaths from an earthquake with tears in her eyes and she'll reconsider inviting these people into her home. In the meantime, their absence is like a beautiful view uncluttered by billboards.

She has the glasses. Rosario holds the door open to let her pass.

Niccolò looks up from his conversation with their neighbor and smiles. "Who is that?"

"Where?"

"There. On the hill."

Rosario and Edoardo look to where Niccolò is pointing. "Ah, that is Gaetano."

"The carpenter?"

"Yes. Come to rescue his goats."

"Gaetano is Erice's most celebrated carpenter," their neighbor Edoardo reports, "not only for the quality of his work or his high prices, but for the length of time required to complete a job."

"We'll keep that in mind. I was thinking to ask him to replace the glass in the windows. But if he prefers to spend time with his animals instead of at work, perhaps we should reconsider."

"You've been here for what—two days? And already you've figured out Gaetano! Let's drink to our new neighbor's judgment of character!"

The bottle is full but there is the tell-tale screw-top so Kate pours as little for Niccolò and herself as is socially polite— Niccolò shouldn't be drinking, anyway—and larger amounts for Rosario and Edoardo. *"Alla vostra salute!"* To your health.

"Alla nostra salute," Niccolò responds. "To our health." He takes a small sip; then cradles the glass in his hand so its contents can't be seen. Kate does the same.

Rosario leans forward and pours himself another glass while Edoardo tries to find out Niccolò's political views. "If I remember correctly, your grandfather was a dedicated Monarchist. Are you?"

"We live in a realm without a sovereign. A benevolent ruler would be much better than the politicians who are wasting our taxes."

Edoardo raises his glass.

Rosario gives them the name of a furniture shop in Trapani which they visit that same afternoon, after he and Edoardo have left.

Niccolò turns up the car heater full blast and speeds down the hill, no longer concerned about bumps that might over-turn their trailer. They are warm and unencumbered, and they find the furniture shop with only one wrong turn.

It is such a relief to have Niccolò well again. Kate says, "*Menomale c'è tu*—Thank God you are here."

Niccolò smiles, an enigmatic smile that manages to convey pleasure and amusement, plus something else. He pauses to absorb the sentiment she has expressed; then corrects her Italian. "*Meno male che ci sei tu.*"

Hearing it from Niccolò's mouth, it sounds as if he were expressing his own thoughts, not merely correcting hers. She repeats the phrase, and hopes the words will sink in. She would like to perfect her Italian, but she fears she has reached a plateau. In any event, she justifies, the purpose of language is to communicate, isn't it, and if an idea, a sentiment, is clearly communicated, so what if the words are imprecise? At this point in her life, Kate admires the *effort*, the *intention* to communicate, more than perfect elocution itself. Taking pleasure in hearing her sentiment expressed correctly, she repeats, "*Meno male ci sei tu.*"

In the furniture store, the first three rooms are devoted to Baroque styles, white lacquered furniture with gold curlicues, flowers and angels. In the rear room they find a nice, dark wood bedstead, a simple yet substantial headboard with matching bedside tables.

"It isn't bad."

"Not exactly what we had in mind but possible."

They don't have any experience buying furniture. Almost everything in their house in Florence comes from Niccolò's family. Their things don't match exactly, they weren't designed to go together, their bedside stands and dressers, their tables and chairs are of the same era, they are complementary and pleasing in an eclectic way, if not of a set. And because everything they have is very old, everything has something wrong with it, a wobbly leg, a missing pommel knob. These are not pieces restored to new, bought in an antique shop, but pieces inherited, passed down from generation to generation.

"*That* bed frame could work," Kate suggests. A saleswoman has been following them. Kate asks her how much it costs.

"This is solid wood," she answers, although Kate would have thought all beds were made from solid wood. She tells them how much it costs, then adds an additional five-thousand euro to the initial price for the entire set, which includes the bed frame, the two bedside cabinets, the set of drawers and the armadio. "The mattress is separate."

It seems like a lot to her and Kate can tell by the way that Niccolò turns away it seems high to him, too. Everything else is expensive, as well. Or ugly. Or ugly and expensive.

They don't want expensive furniture in their house in Sicily. They want to be able to lock the door and walk away without worrying about the contents attracting thieves. What they want is sturdy and simple, reasonably priced. Kate checked on-line before they left Florence to see if there was an IKEA, and found there was an up-and-coming IKEA listed to open—four years ago! Apparently IKEA and the people who control Palermo couldn't come to an agreement.

Speaking of which, whenever Kate mentions to any of their friends their plans to live in Sicily, their first question is "What about the Mafia?"

Her answer is that they aren't important enough to be bothered by the Mafia. If they were opening a business, perhaps they'd be concerned, but not as homeowners.

Kate doesn't really know what she is talking about, but it sounds logical.

Since they have purchased their house, Kate has asked her own questions: "Is the Mafia present in Trapani?" Everyone replies with an embarrassed expression that reminds her of when she asked Rosario if there was wind in Trapani.

More recently they received a more elaborate answer from a man they met at a dinner party, a lawyer with political connections. "The Mafia doesn't exist anymore, not in any real sense." The dinner conversation had turned political, as it inevitably does between the first and second courses. "They made a grave error by attacking a public figure, by dynamiting Falcone's car in 1992," explained the lawyer.

"I remember when Falcone was killed."

"When that happened, the Mafia was hunted down, snuffed out. The big guys are gone. What remains is a mafia-mentality, a lot of *picciotti*—little guys—acting tough, like Al Pacino."

"But aren't there drugs—?"

"Yes, of course there are drugs and guns but only in the way that those things exist in any city."

Whether or not this man's appraisal is correct, the truth of their situation is that they have never come into contact with the Mafia. If it is here, it is invisible.

Kate is naïve but not stupid. She suspects the Mafia exists in ways they can't begin to imagine, not only in Sicily but all over the world, with its different names and functions. Kate started to say to their dinner companions "I wasn't born yesterday," or "I'm not a virgin", but instead Kate said, "Non sono mica nata vergine." "I wasn't born a virgin."

Eventually, these new friends stopped laughing, and the lawyer continued.

"The Mafia that does still exist is the Mafia in the original sense of the word; that is, if the state won't take care of things, they will themselves. Sicilians are people of honor."

They leave the furniture shop Rosario has recommended without buying anything and continue to look for furniture in the way they do everything, exploring, getting lost, turning down this street and that, along the way picking up other things they need: an electric heater, a microwave, a small mirror. They find more expensive Baroque bedroom and dining sets; elaborate ceiling lamps that would brighten any sheik's home. As they are looking they are also stopping into small grocery stores, buying a few things, comparing prices. Little by little they are getting to know Trapani. Slowly but surely they aren't getting lost at every turn.

But still they haven't found furniture.

After several days without success, they decide to explore IKEA-less Palermo, and on the main thoroughfare, that stretch of road that interrupts the *autostrada*, they find a large store selling sofas. They buy two for the living room, a supple white leather, as soft as kid gloves, the same color as the hand-hammered marble stairs, clean and fresh, easy to care for, assures the saleswoman. In the same shop they also find a sofa bed which they will put upstairs in the little bedroom for Elizabeth and Stephen when they come at Easter. In ten days.

In a second stroke of luck, they find another large warehouse that has everything they need: a handsome, brass bed-frame, good, solid wood bedside tables and dressers, brass reading lamps for the bedroom, mattresses, everything.

But they can't convince a salesperson to help them.

One salesman is deeply involved in conversation with an attractive, provocatively-dressed young woman. Begrudgingly, he disengages himself from his potential date. Impatiently, he listens to what they would like to buy, punches out a few numbers on his calculator and says it will cost more to transport it to Trapani (an hour away) than the full price of the purchase. When he sees that they are not thoroughly discouraged, he adds, "And delivery will take at least thirty days."

Niccolò and Kate try to shop where the people are nice, give their business to those who really want it. They leave all their items un-purchased to let the salesman return to his courtship.

But they still need beds. And dressers. A dining table. Chairs. Desks. The clock they haven't yet found to buy is nonetheless ticking.

"I have to tell you something," Niccolò confides, taking Kate's hand in the large parking lot as they search for their car. He sounds inexplicably serious.

"What?"

"I can't stand sleeping on a mattress on the floor any more. I thought I was flexible, that it wouldn't be a big deal, but I'm getting depressed. It makes me unhappy to sleep on the floor."

"I'm relieved. I had thought you were about to confess an affair." He raises his eyebrows, tempted to make a joke. "Don't

94

worry," Kate assures him. "We'll make a bed our first priority. We will find a frame we like."

"Let's just buy a good mattress with a base and legs. The frame can wait until later."

Back in Trapani, in the block between the cemetery and a pornographic cinema on a street called *Via della Madonna di Fatima*, they notice mattresses stacked on the sidewalk, leaning against a wall. The owner is standing in the doorway of a shop that gives new meaning to the expression *hole in the wall*, but as they have looked everywhere else, they might as well look here. They tell the owner what they are looking for, starting with the mattress. He leads them through a narrow passage to a second room where under the stairs he has a dozen mattresses.

"What do you want? Best? Medium? Or send-guests-away-after-three-days-quality?"

"We want a best quality queen-size mattress, a metal frame with the tallest legs you have."

He doesn't waver. He wrestles out a blue and white ticked mattress wrapped in thick plastic, then an uncomplicated, sturdy metal frame. From a box with two diverse lengths of legs he selects the longer ones. "Next?" He isn't interested to know that they want the tall legs so they can see the view of Mt. Cofano while lying in bed.

They tell him the items on their list, and one by one he shows them what he has. He, too, has lots of baroque furniture, lots of curlicues, but he also has plain, solid, nicely appointed, reasonably priced dressers; a dining room table that seats six comfortably but extends to accommodate twelve, and handsome chairs, high-backed and dignified; a desk for Kate, lovely with an inlaid panel of dark green leather. They like it so much they buy another one, slightly smaller, for Niccolò.

"When do you want all this delivered?" The owner of this shop hasn't introduced himself, hasn't offered to shake their hands; hasn't even bothered to smile.

"As soon as possible."

"This afternoon OK?"

"This afternoon would be perfect."

"Gabriele!" he hollers out onto the street. "Get your useless self in here."

Gabriele is the shopkeeper's son, a massive, church-pillar kind of guy, probably thirty years old. He sheepishly ducks his head of black curls as if he expects his father to hit him. "Gabriele will drive up this afternoon. Give him directions. Give him your phone number, too. He always gets lost."

After lunch, Gabriele and his brother, Pietro, carry the furniture from their truck into the house and position each piece in the right room. Pietro is wearing a bright yellow tee-shirt, several sizes too large, and Gabriele is wearing the same size tee-shirt, which on him is several sizes too small, bright red. Ketchup and Mustard: Someone's mother has been shopping the sales.

They are nice, happy-go-lucky guys out from under their father's callous rule. Pietro is thin and blonde with slightly startled turquoise eyes, so different in looks and nature from his dark, bushy-browed brother, and his father, that Niccolò is reminded how often Sicily has been conquered; dominated in ancient times by both blue-eyed, blonde Saxons and dark-eyed, dark-skinned Arabs.

When they have finished twisting in the last brass bureau handle, Gabriele says shyly, "We have a chest of drawers that would fit nicely into your bathroom, if you would like."

They take measurements for the upstairs and downstairs bathrooms. When they have finished, Kate tells him that they want to replace the square plastic wash basin in the downstairs bathroom with a real sink, and ask where they might find one. "If you follow me down the hill, Signora, I'll take you there now. I'll introduce you to the owner, my cousin."

"If you don't mind? Thank you. Let me find my coat."

"When you finish, we can pass by the shop to see if you like the bathroom cupboards."

Niccolò is looking tired. "If you don't mind, I'll stay here—"

"Good idea. Try to rest."

"I will, now that we have a real bed."

Gabriele becomes Kate's guardian angel. He waits patiently while she looks at several models of sinks. The shop owner quotes a price, and then lowers it—gives them the plumber's discount—when Gabriele steps forward. Gabriele carries it to the car, always shy, always ready to duck away if Kate decides to cuff him on the ear.

She returns home with a bathroom sink replacement, and the promise of bathroom cabinets delivered before dinner.

Niccolò greets her with a grin. "See anything different?"

She touches his cheek. "You shaved?"

"And showered, but that's not what I want you to notice. Look around."

She sees it immediately: the absence a presence: He has cut down the two trees that have been blocking their view!

"You aren't afraid Concetta and her husband will come back to haunt you?"

"Well, actually, I gave both trees a serious pruning first to see if they could be saved, but finally I overcame my reluctance and down they went."

"It's amazing. You have opened the whole front view."

"Wait until you see the view from inside the house. Go look out the entry hall window."

Suddenly, from inside the house, at every window—the entry hall, the kitchen, their bedroom, the guest bedroom—Cofano is so close it can almost be touched. It is as if they hold a shell to their eyes and see the waves whispering, releasing themselves with a murmur against the shore.

That same evening, when Gabriele and Pietro deliver the additional furnishings, Kate asks Gabriele if he knows where they can buy counters for their kitchen. He takes the measurement of what Kate would like, and says he'll stop on the way home at a shop that cuts counters to measure.

"I suppose you want me to install it, too?" There is no accusation in his voice, only courtesy.

"Could you?"

"It's not part of my job, but I'll do it."

Two days later, Gabriele and Pietro drive up with the faux marble counters. The cabinet that Carmelo adapted to a greater height becomes the base for the counter they are installing. Having anticipated the problem, Gabriele brings along another piece of basic kitchen furniture, a set of four drawers on which to balance the other end of the counter.

"How did you know what to bring?"

"My Mamma says you can't have too many drawers in the kitchen."

They don't have *any* drawers so this is the perfect solution.

Gabriele has also procured a roll of finishing material for the edges of the counter. As they are completing the job, he asks to use their *ferro da stiro*.

"I don't have an iron."

He thinks Kate hasn't understood. "*Un ferro da stiro*—an iron," he repeats, gripping an imaginary one and pantomiming the ironing process. "I'll be careful. I won't damage it."

"I'm sorry, but I don't have one."

Pietro takes over the questioning, his bright, blue eyes incredulous. "Signora, you don't have an iron?" The brothers stare at her as if she's confessed that there is a body buried in the basement. "But how do you iron your clothes?"

"I don't. I hang them up carefully when they are damp from the washer and our clothes dry without wrinkles."

The brothers are alike in their disbelief, twins in their sympathy for her poor husband. The dangers of marrying a foreigner have materialized in front of their eyes. Their mother's warnings have just been validated beyond a doubt. *Moglie e buoi dei paesi tuoi.* Choose your wife and oxen from your own village.

Gabriele snaps out of his stunned expression first and concludes, "We will bring one up tomorrow when we deliver the patio chairs you ordered."

As they are leaving, Edoardo arrives, this time with his wife, Angelica. She is slight and delicate, and on her face is a habitual expression of concern. Her short, thin hair is mostly gray, but her manner and movements are girlish. Bashfully, she presents Kate with a basket of eggs. "The basket is for you, too."

Kate likes this woman instantly. She feels her enter her heart, as naturally, as unobtrusively, as a sea breeze ruffling her hair. "Has Niccolò told you that I love baskets?" Angelica looks pleased with herself. "Thank you." Kate has the sense of being in the presence of an angel.

Edoardo takes charge. "Half the eggs in the basket are from ducks. Half are from chickens. They are miserly now, producing barely three eggs a day. But once the sun starts to shine, there will be more than enough for everyone."

The basket is full of eggs, all different shell colors and sizes; an authentic Easter offering.

In addition, Edoardo has given them the promise of sun.

CHAPTER
EIGHT

When Elizabeth and Electra arrive on the 17th of March, the house has been furnished. Not having been here to see the transformation from empty to functional, they take it for granted. Nor can they appreciate how warm the house is. They don't complain about the cold, but they keep their sweatshirts on, collars up, zipped to their chins. Electra, who was with them when they found the house, is stunned by the changes, and Elizabeth, who is seeing it for the first time, is surprised by how big the little house is. Mostly, she is impressed with the view. "The palm trees make it look like a postcard!"

"Come on, Lizzy," Electra says, picking up her bag and her sister's. "I'll show you your room."

"Don't I get to choose?"

"No. I was here first, I chose. But don't worry; I gave you the better room."

Sisters reunited.

There are things to do, of course: they have no bookshelves, the books they brought from Florence are stacked in crates. Electra doesn't have a bedside table. She has to lay her book on the floor and leave her bed to turn off the overhead light. But Niccolò and Kate are proud of their progress. They have put silicone around all the windows and while the glass still shakes in its frame, it is the muted tingling of a baby's toy rather than a death rattle.

Electra has taken over the downstairs. They have put the two single beds from Florence onto stands they bought in town, one on each side of the downstairs alcove, with a long, low dresser between them under the high set of windows. The bedspreads retrieved from storage in Florence are Laura Ashley, with small pink and white flowers. A gift from Kate's mother, they have been set aside since adolescence. Kate has covered the beds in Electra's alcove with the reverse side up so that they are all white, with only a border of pink, and Kate is surprised, and touched, when she finds that Electra has turned them back to their childhood sides.

Her willingness to embrace her childhood, despite her twenty years, shows itself in her demand for a birthday cake, even though she celebrated her birthday in Holland one week prior. She chooses a chocolate cake, which in Florence would have been one of the easier cakes Kate makes. But in Erice it means starting from scratch.

Not scratch, as in making do without a cake mix: all cakes in Italy are made fresh. By scratch, Kate mean shopping for cake pans, baking paper, a timer, an oven thermometer; vanilla, baking powder, baking soda, chocolate, cocoa, the whole long list. To be honest, the only thing Kate does have is eggs!

The cake is more a success as a sign of her affection than as a culinary treat. To cover the imperfections, Kate melts bittersweet chocolate together with a little butter and powdered sugar, which creates a glaze to disguise the defects, and buys lovely Sicilian ice cream—a variety of flavors, to further distract. They light the twenty pink candles and sing the song, a verse in Italian, a verse in English. Niccolò films the first slice ceremony as he has done for every birthday of their lives, but this year no one hurries him along. They don't need to worry about the ice cream melting on the first birthday celebrated in their cold, new home.

"Presents?" Electra asks, noticing the absence of wrapped packages on the table.

Kate hands her an envelope. "This is from your Daddy and me."

Inside the envelope is a card on which are ten, badly-drawn horses, cut out and linked together like paper dolls. Electra says, "You have signed us up for art classes? Mother-Daughter bonding time?"

"Hardly!"

"We have found a stable in Trapani," Niccolò explains. "Your present is ten riding lessons!"

Electra jumps up to give her daddy a kiss; then she kisses Kate. "You couldn't have given me a more perfect gift!" Electra started riding a few years ago and her only criterion, it seems, for happiness in whatever city she is living, is the presence of a good stable. "I can't wait to see the horses, meet the instructor."

"And my present to you—" Elizabeth begins.

"Not a recycled iPod, I hope!"

"Hey! That was a great gift," Elizabeth says. She turns to her parents for confirmation. "Wasn't it?"

"It was."

Once they got used to the idea.

Last year at Christmas, Niccolò unwrapped a very familiar iPod from Elizabeth. Electra teased 'so we are now recycling gifts for Christmas?' The remark brought a laugh but didn't explain why the iPod they had given to Elizabeth four years before when she graduated from high school was being returned to them now as their Christmas present. She explained, 'Stephen gave me a new model for my birthday.' They have seen it; it is as slim as a credit card. 'And I wanted you guys to have as much pleasure as it has given me.' They smiled and thanked her, but Kate had her doubts. She couldn't see either Niccolò or herself walking down the road or travelling by train wearing earphones. Some of their friends swear by their iPods but Kate has never been tempted.

The gift started to make sense a few days after Christmas when Elizabeth took all the family's CDs, and put them onto Niccolò's computer to be downloaded onto their "new" iPod. It took several days and in doing so, it gave them a glimpse of how Elizabeth must look when she is studying: head down, highly focused, not distracted by conversations flitting through the room. The result is an album of their family's musical history: the usual Italian favorites, Lucio Battisti, Vasco Rossi, Eros Ramazzotti; a tuxedo-attired version of Rod Stewart acquired after the kids left home and Niccolò and Kate could slow dance to the sweet sentimentalism, un-criticized while preparing dinner; Joni Mitchell's "A Case of You" which stops Kate in her tracks no matter what she happens to be doing. It doesn't speak to her present situation, thankfully, but it reminds her of the desert she traversed to arrive here; songs from turn-of-the-century Naples, emigrants belting out homesickness for Santa Lucia, their sun, their motherland, voices that communicate the sorrow with which they live far away from their native home.

Thanks to Elizabeth, their family's music is easily accessible, and plays as randomly as if they were all home together, making their individual selections.

"My present to you, Electra, is an all-expense weekend with me in London, whenever you want in your twentieth year."

"That will be so great!" She hugs her sister.

"And Stephen's present," Elizabeth adds, "is to stay at home so you and I can have the weekend alone together."

"Cool!"

"Just kidding. Stephen will give you his present when he gets here."

"Best birthday ever!" Electra says, convincingly, dipping her finger into the chocolate frosting pooled at the base of her cake.

They quickly discover that having Elizabeth upstairs in the little bedroom is not going to work once Stephen joins her. Niccolò and Kate's bedroom shares one inner wall with the stairwell, but the other bedroom shares *its* inner wall with the bathroom; more exactly, with the toilet. Every tinkling of water is heard as if no doors were closed. Niccolò and Kate like Stephen immensely. They are glad he will be their guest, but none of them will enjoy this kind of intimacy.

Electra is a good sport and moves upstairs several days before Stephen arrives. Elizabeth and Niccolò move the two single beds together downstairs and place a patio chair at each side for improvised bedside tables. They will have to use the bathroom beside the kitchen but at least they all will have privacy.

"And if we were to transform the garage into a guest room?" Kate suggests one morning at breakfast on the terrace.

"Put French doors inside the garage door," Niccolò picks up, as if he, too, has been contemplating the same idea. "We can pull down the garage door when we go away but leave it up for light and air when we have company."

"It wouldn't need much."

They have simultaneously risen from the breakfast table, Elizabeth and Electra behind them, and have walked down the steep driveway leading to the garage. Niccolò pulls up the metal door. He glances around to see who might look in. "There's enough privacy."

"Except for the goats," Electra adds.

"We'd just have to make sure that no one circles around this side of the house when this room is being used," Elizabeth cautions, tucking her ash-auburn fringe behind an ear.

The first impression Elizabeth gives is pretty and friendly. She has learned to push past a childhood shyness that was sometimes mistaken for aloofness; nowadays, people are warmed by her sunny character. She is pleasant and accommodating; even her posture bends down so as not to tower over the people with whom she is speaking. But take Elizabeth out of the lime-light, put her in front of her books or computer or seat her at a lecture, switch off her socially accommodating light and her prettiness is transformed into real beauty.

Kate has been accused by her daughters of being partial, of losing her photographer's objectivity when appraising them, but even though Kate loves them, she is not blind. True, if they are judging by the standards of Hollywood, their lack of makeup alone disqualifies them as instantly as does their straight-forwardness, their lack of coy. But look at Elizabeth's profile when she is focused elsewhere and you will see indisputable classic beauty: a Greek statue, one of the major goddesses, come to life; the marble illuminated from inside, glowing. The straight, dignified line of her nose joins a forehead smooth with wisdom. Set her into motion, watch her walk, and you will swear her feet aren't quite touching the ground, her movement is so light, so graceful; other-worldly. Look into the dark liquid of her eyes and you will find yourself staring into the depths of infinity. But don't let her catch you staring or she will turn self-conscious. A smile will appear and she is transformed into mere prettiness again.

"We'll need to buy a double bed, two more bedside tables, and another dresser," Kate calculates.

"The floors would need to be polished, the walls plastered," Niccolò says.

"It would give us another real room."

"And you could have your room back, Electra."

"But I'll be able to hear you from my bedroom," Electra protests. She is the only one of them who isn't convinced.

"What if we put in a second door?" Kate suggests. "There would be almost three feet of space between the two doors. We could even put a clothes hook between them, kind of a closet that will muffle noise. Would that be OK?"

"It will be great," Elizabeth assures her. "You'll see, Electra. Can we finish it before Stephen arrives?"

"We can try," Niccolò says. "The French doors will have to wait, as well as the plastered walls, but an improvised room is possible."

"Will it be Elizabeth's room?" Electra wants to know.

"Let's call it the guest room. Elizabeth will use it when she is here with Stephen. We'll make our friends comfortable in it when they come to visit. And you will use it when you have a committed relationship."

"*If*," Electra pouts.

"*When*," Kate says, bringing her younger daughter close for a hug.

With the restoration of the garage, Niccolò and Kate have their privacy restored. The little upstairs bedroom becomes Niccolò's study. All their guests are delegated downstairs.

The entry hall is designated for Kate's study. Her days in the darkroom have been replaced largely by the technology of digital imaging. She needs an orderly space if she is to concentrate, and she won't leave stacks of papers or equipment on her desk as Niccolò will. He needs to see the work that is waiting to be done. If it goes into a drawer, it is lost. Kate keeps her middle drawer available for projects in progress and remembers to look through the papers periodically. The only things Kate keeps on her desk are her computer, her Hasselblad, and a calendar onto which she scribbles their appointments.

Her desk is the first thing you see when you enter their house, and being so close to the front door means that every time Kate need to stretch her legs or relax her mind, she is close to the garden. Her days are spent moving between her camera, her computer, the plants in the garden and the view of the sea, in the company of the three people she loves most in the world. So what if it's a little cold.

It always takes a moment to become used to having their daughters home again. It has little to do with them, really, and more to do with the dynamic that changes when four people instead of two occupy one space. Kate must adapt to the change of being herself, the person Kate feels herself to be when she is alone, or with Niccolo, which is the same, only chattier, to the role of mother.

The role of mother has changed over the years. It started out of nothing, gained experience and confidence as Kate found what worked and what didn't work, as their daughters grew and expressed their needs.

Of course the mother Kate was when their girls were young is not the mother Kate is expected to be when her mostly grown daughters return home. Her new role of mother doesn't leave much room for advice. Kate has to remind herself that when they are away they are in charge of their own lives, can take care of themselves. She and Niccolò are available to help them, of course, and advice is given if asked for—and sometimes even if it isn't. But when they were little, Kate advised them daily, helped them through every little encounter. None of them wants that any more, yet the old habits are hard to break. It takes her a minute to remember that Elizabeth and Electra already know everything Kate can teach them.

Then why are they always asking her for recipes?

Stephen's presence, three days before Easter, further enhances but complicates their reunions. Neither Kate nor Niccolò feel comfortable appearing for breakfast in pajamas. It takes a minute to become used to having a fifth person present. The sixth will be easier, Kate suspects.

Or not? Stephen has already said that he doesn't look forward to sharing Niccolò's attention with Electra's future boyfriend.

"*If*," Electra reminds them.

Any day now.

Their real estate agent, Rosario, stops by just before dinner on Good Friday as they are returning from *I Misteri* in Trapani. Even though his role as agent has been fulfilled, he continues to check on them; to make sure everything is all right.

Often Kate is grateful for Rosario's continued interest. Sometimes, like now, she wishes he would call first.

"Did you enjoy the procession?" Rosario asks.

"Perhaps *enjoy* is the wrong word, but I found it deeply moving." They are exhausted, physically and emotionally. Kate still has to think about what to cook for dinner, and because Stephen and the girls are here, she will have to prepare more than pasta.

Or does she? This is Good Friday. They are meant to eat simply.

Rosario consults his watch. "You are home early."

"We watched the procession for—" Niccolò checks his watch, too. It is almost eight o'clock. "—five hours."

"It was intense. Very tiring." Kate hopes he will take the hint.

"Not if you think that *I massari*—the pageant-bearers—continue to carry those heavy, life-size statues for twenty-four hours, all night and all tomorrow morning, throughout the entire city. It's quite an experience! The crowds on the sidelines become more and more passionate as they move through the eighteen Stations of the Cross. Everyone will have tears in their eyes tomorrow afternoon as the *Madonna* makes her way back into *La Chiesa del Purgatorio*."

Kate can believe it. She feels like crying, and they only stayed for a fifth of the procession. The music alone, a dark, menacing, repetitious tome has lodged itself in the bones of her memory, welded itself to the inebriated sway of the funeral garbed, beret-wearing pall-bearers. She is going to wait a day or two before reviewing the photographs she took today, but she is sure she has captured the importance of the procession. This is the first time in years that Kate has photographed people. Her camera's memory is loaded with close-ups: humanity's sorrow, joy, happiness and hopelessness, that range of emotions never permissible in the soft-focused romanticism of her famous photographs, even if the theme—Mother and Child—is the same.

"Do they do this every year?" Stephen asks, his dark brown eyes further darkened with questions too complex to express. Of all of them, Stephen has been the most startled by the procession, perhaps because his upbringing has been the most Anglo-Saxon, the least Catholic.

Elizabeth has translated and Rosario responds. "They do, *praticamente*, as you saw it today, for almost four hundred years."

"Exactly the same?" Electra challenges. "The statues looked Eighteenth and Nineteenth Century."

"Aside from the flower compositions at the base of the statues, and a few minor details, it is exactly the same as it has always been."

"Rosario, I'm about to start dinner. Would you like to stay?"

"No, no, Franca is expecting me home practically any minute. I just stopped by to bring you an Erice Easter specialty." He presents the wrapped and ribboned package he's been holding. Inside is a marzipan lamb, so large and authentic looking, with its whorls of white frosting, it might be confused with a real lamb, the runt of a litter.

They are all offering their thanks, expressing their gratitude, when Kate notices Stephen lean close to Elizabeth, their foreheads nearly touching, his enviable olive complexion and dark hair a paradoxical contrast to Elizabeth's creamy skin and light hair, as if he were the Italian and she the Brit. He whispers, "What exactly is one meant to do with it?"

"I think we're supposed to eat it," she whispers back, laying a hand on his forearm.

Sure enough, Easter morning, they prepare for the sacrifice.

But where do they start? It seems heartless to cut off its tail; worse to sever its head. Knife poised above the innocent beast, Electra suggests, "Slice it in the middle. We can each have a piece, and then you can join the two ends together again."

The lamb is so sweet they all have difficulty finishing the slivers of marzipan on their plates. At this rate they will be consuming the lamb until next Easter.

Kate is going to have to eat something real for breakfast or she'll collapse before lunch. Stephen is obviously having the same thought, "Would you mind if I sliced some bread?"

And so they find a solution to eating the lamb, a little piece of marzipan spread onto bread, as if it were marmalade. Every time Kate passes through the kitchen, she catches one of the family pilfering a piece of the lamb's middle.

There is a lot more noise when their daughters are home, a lot more dishes. Kate spends much more time in the kitchen; the meals are more elaborate, and the time they spend at the table is a larger percentage of their day. They have been known to clear off their breakfast dishes in time to set the table for lunch, or clear lunch dishes in time for the evening meal. It would seem that all they do is eat.

But food is just the backdrop, an excuse to pause in their daily activities to reunite, to sit across from each other to appreciate the transformation which has occurred in the time they've been apart.

They can see the old family dynamic reassert itself when Elizabeth and Electra fall to teasing. Their barbs are familiar and funny, the tips less poisonous for being dipped deeply in affection. Their accusations of Niccolò and Kate as parents are fond and familiar, too: "I still can't believe you forgot to pick me up from school! You just forgot. Admit it." Electra's indignation is as fresh as it was when it happened, more than ten years ago. "How could you have forgotten your daughter?"

"Second daughter," Elizabeth reminds her. "They remembered me. I'm the one who counted. Don't ever forget that, second daughter."

An unhappy memory is hooked and reeled to the surface; the time Kate's father didn't pick her up for their two-week summer's vacation. Leslie and Stuart, her elder sister and younger brother were already with him. Annette, the eldest, felt she was too old to spend summer holidays with their father. Kate didn't mind going last or alone, as she had been told she could bring a friend.

But as their agreed-upon appointment passed, her friend Carrie started calling, wanting to know when they were leaving. "Do I have time to wash my hair?" she asked.

Four decades before the invention of the cellphone, Kate had no way to contact her father. She was deeply embarrassed by her lack of information. "Go ahead, wash your hair," she told Carrie. "I'll call you when he gets here."

Three days later—seventy-two hours of waiting and at least a dozen puzzled calls from Carrie—her father phoned. "Sorry, Honey, but I won't be able to take you on vacation this year."

"Oh, it's OK," she lied, straining to sound blasé; hanging up before her voice betrayed her.

No explanation asked for or offered.

Kate looks at her daughters, hears the laughter in their voices, and feels the hook release its grip. With time, Kate has forgiven her father all his short-comings. He wasn't a bad man, he wasn't mean, he didn't abuse them or let them go hungry, but he was unprepared to be a father, and Kate suffered profoundly from his lack of expertise. If Kate were to meet him today, she would recognize a man not at peace with himself. Kate feels sorry for him; almost as sorry as she was for the little girl who felt everything he did wrong was her fault. True, Kate forgot to pick up Electra one time from school, one of her many mistakes in assisting her daughter to adulthood, but Kate is certain she didn't make Electra feel it was her fault.

Kate looks at Niccolò who is reveling in their daughters' silly conversation, as proud of them as if they were resolving the world's health issues, and thanks God that her children have a father they can count on. They will have issues to solve in their lives as everyone does, but he has given them a base of love and affection that will let them proceed securely. By being a good father, and a constant, loving husband, by constructing a life for them based on trust and honesty, he has helped her heal old sorrows. The dead, heavy weight of past heartache has almost completely ceased to pull her down.

To sit at the table together is to celebrate, if you will, the life they have crafted together, to reap the rewards of all the years when parenting was a full time job, requiring patience and constancy interlaced with comprehension and flexibility. Sitting with Elizabeth and Electra at the table, Kate couldn't wish them to be any different than the people they are becoming, although Kate does wish they would remember to ask for the water pitcher instead of reaching.

On *Pasquetta*—the Monday after Easter, Edoardo stops by in the afternoon and introduces Niccolò and Kate to his son. Matteo is twenty-five years old, an agile, attractive young man, with enough similarity to Edoardo to be able to see that Edoardo was a good-looking young man, before he had the accident which curled his spine, as Rosario has explained.

"I know you!" Kate says.

Matteo is shocked. "You do? Are you sure?"

"I saw you on Good Friday, in the *Misteri* procession. You were among the *massari* carrying the Madonna."

"With all the thousands of people you saw in Trapani, you remember me?"

"I do."

"My wife has a 500 GB hard disc memory. She doesn't miss or forget anything."

"I forget things all the time," Kate says, "he just doesn't remember."

Edoardo laughs. He likes it when Kate teases her husband.

"I noticed you because you looked as sad as the Madonna you were carrying." She must have taken a dozen close-up photographs of him. "I was wondering if you were truly sad or acting the part?"

"He was probably tired!" Edoardo answers for his son.

Matteo looks at her to see if Kate is satisfied with his father's answer, or if Kate wants something more. Kate nods. "Under the weight of those heavy statues, moving together with the other *massari,* in unison, almost as *un corpo*—one body, it is impossible to remain detached from Christ's ordeal. I felt as though I was actually carrying Jesus' mother through the streets of Jerusalem."

Niccolò and Kate glance at each other. They have followed the Stations of the Cross in Jerusalem, but for them it was a disappointment, an empty experience, as if Christ's suffering had all been sold off by the street vendors. They found more chaos than cosmos: the message of rebirth evaporated into the dogmatic heat of an over-crowded, inharmonious city.

"The true meaning of Good Friday can't help but sink in," Matteo pauses. "The Madonna must be the saddest of all those mourning. Christ rises, he is triumphant, there is the miracle of life after death, but that doesn't change the fact that Maria has lost her son. She is the true object of our sorrow."

He blushes. He has said more than he has meant to.

"It is an exhausting event," Niccolò adds. "I found the music haunting."

"The music certainly sets a somber, mournful mood."

"I am glad he made a respectful impression," Edoardo injects. "He's been sleeping for the last twenty-four hours. We had to resurrect him finally today at noon, with a double espresso."

"As you say, *Signore*, it is an exhausting event."

"Please, call me Niccolò."

"Niccolò." Matteo nods at their lamb dissected on the dining room table, an absurd creature now, mostly head and rump and tail.

"That's a good approach."

"Do you know this Easter specialty?"

Edoardo laughs. "It's one of those gifts you fear receiving more than one a year."

"A little like *panettone*," a dry, muffin-like cake, traditionally served as dessert at Christmas. Professionals receive dozens of them from their clients and patients, and in turn pass them on to their relatives and friends.

"Exactly."

Matteo studies the lamb. "In our family, we scoop the marzipan out from the back."

"Leaving a shell?"

"Yes."

"Next year we'll try the hollowing technique."

"It works pretty well, until the end, when it falls apart."

"I am sorry you missed Elizabeth and Electra. Stephen drove them to the sea."

"In this weather? Is he German?"

"No. English." Then Kate understands his joke. Germans are the only tourists who swim in Italy in all seasons. "They thought they glimpsed sun at Bonagia."

"Maybe." Edoardo doesn't sound hopeful.

"If they aren't too tired—" Matteo starts.

"Or too frozen—" Edoardo interrupts, and tells them a long, complex tale of two tourists who were shipwrecked on Favignana at the start of the 19th Century.

Matteo sits back, lets his father finish recounting a tale he has clearly heard before, then resumes. "If they aren't too tired, my brother and I could take them out for a drink after dinner tonight, show them around Trapani."

Again Edoardo interrupts his son with a half-related tale. Kate begins to suspect Edoardo is interrupting his son intentionally to see what Matteo will do. Consistently, Matteo retreats. He can't like it, but he doesn't protest. He is honoring his father. His self-esteem isn't damaged. Edoardo, on the other hand, is clearly taking pride in displaying his son's respect of authority. Kate suspects it is a duet they have been singing, with varying degrees of harmony, their whole lives.

"Thank you for the invitation, Matteo. I'll have Elizabeth or Electra call you as soon as they come back from the sea."

"**D**id you have fun last night with Matteo?"

"Yes!" Elizabeth is pouring cereal into a bowl. She has an intolerance to milk so she eats it dry, which always reminds Kate of a hamster. "He is so sweet. And really funny."

"His brother, Sergio, is nice, too." Electra is spreading the lamb marzipan on toast, making sure all the corners are covered. "And what was the name of that shy guy who studies in Bologna?"

"I can't remember, but he was cute, too."

"No one can understand why Electra is going back to Holland, if she is studying Business and Economics in Rome."

"Did you try to explain?" Kate asks Electra.

Elizabeth answers, in between bites of dry cereal. "I told them that Electra's university program is as hard to understand as she is herself."

"Hey, that's not fair. It's easy. I am studying Economics and Business at Luiss in Rome, with a year in Holland, at Utrecht University. How hard is that?"

"Almost everyone was able to follow that much," Elizabeth concedes. "But when I started to explain that it's not the usual classic *Economia* program but a pilot program in English, for only a handful of students—"

"Thirty."

"Whatever."

"We'd all had a few drinks by then," Stephen adds, spreading an almost transparent layer of marzipan lamb onto sliced bread.

"And that she wasn't in Holland as an Erasmus student, well, I lost everyone."

"It's not so complicated if one is used to variation, but for Italians it has too many variables to be comprehensible."

"Anyway, we had an excellent time. Matteo's girlfriend is gorgeous! Doesn't she remind you of Angelina Jolie?"

Elizabeth nods, her mouth full of cereal.

"Matteo has a girlfriend?" Kate asks.

"He does."

"And she is extremely sexy!"

"Who is sexy?" Niccolò has just walked into the room. He is carrying cappuccinos for Electra and Stephen, walking slowly so they won't spill.

"Matteo's girlfriend."

"Did *you* have a good time, Stephen?"

Stephen accepts his coffee gratefully. He is always quiet but quieter in the morning. "Yes, we had a lovely time."

"Lovely!" Electra imitates.

Stephen grumbles something into his coffee. He doesn't like being made fun of by his girlfriend's little sister.

Elizabeth doesn't give it too much weight. "Yes, it was absolutely lovely," she confirms. She smiles at Stephen and he brightens; the moment passes.

Electra says to Stephen, "I've been trying to get Figaro's attention, but he has been sitting at your feet since you came in for breakfast. Are you slipping him fish and chips?"

Stephen laughs.

Elizabeth laughs, too. "Do you remember the oil you gave us last night to put on Stephen's foot?" He had blistered his feet wearing new shoes and Kate didn't have any vitamin E oil so she offered him one of Niccolò's Omega-3 capsules, which he slathered on his blistered toe. Elizabeth continues, "I woke up in the night to hear Stephen laughing."

"Figaro was on the end of the bed, busily licking my toes."

"Omega-3. Fish oil."

"I think you have a friend for life."

"A shame I'm so ticklish."

"Oh, I forgot to tell you. Matteo and Sergio are taking us out again tonight," Electra adds. "Sergio is leaving this weekend for Lebanon—he's in the military. Matteo is giving him a going-away party. They are picking us up as soon as I come home from riding."

"I can't believe we already have a group of friends in Sicily, and we've only been here for what? A week?"

"Eight days."

"I can't believe we have to go back to uni the day after tomorrow," Elizabeth says. Stephen groans. Electra joins him. "The sun is finally out. It's warm! Can't we just stay here? Will you support three university drop-outs?"

"Of course, as long as you are prepared to haul manure for the garden, drive the tractor during the harvest, bottle and label and pack our orders, cook and clean and do all sorts of other dreary chores."

"Speaking personally," Stephen adds. "I think I'd prefer to complete medical school."

"I should think so! You are so close. You'll be graduating next time this year."

"Next year and a few months. It's been a long haul."

Elizabeth started medical school at eighteen, as European students begin their specialized studies straight out of high school, but Stephen completed an earlier degree in Biochemistry before deciding he wanted to study medicine. He is only one year ahead of Elizabeth in their five-year medical course, but he is five years older in age.

"Next August he'll be working in hospital," Elizabeth says proudly.

"Remind me," Electra interrupts, "not to holiday in England next summer."

It always takes a while to become used to having their daughters *leave* home again. The house is quiet. Figaro walks from room to room looking for a trace of the affection he fled from while Electra and Elizabeth were home. Clover brings them not one ball but two. From her computer in the entry hall, Kate sends a message to Niccolò upstairs at his desk: "Thank you for helping me in the garden this morning. I know it is not your passion, but I do appreciate your strong arms and good will, and I hope you will enjoy the final product."

When Kate returns to her desk after having made herself a cup of tea, she finds the following message: *"Grazie a te che mi hai fatto vedere il sole in una giornata di pioggia...* "Thank you for having made me see the sun in a day of rain."

Doing laundry fills the empty space left by their children's absence and by the time the sheets and towels are folded and put away, ready for the next visit, Niccolò and Kate have reclaimed their solitary equilibrium. They stop sending each other messages.

With the house furnished and most of the details resolved, they begin to understand the essence of what this house means to them. It is not about furniture or food; it isn't even about the plants in the garden. It is something fundamental, like being able to hear themselves think again. It has something to do with being who they find themselves being rather than who they have been pushed and pulled to be in the past. It has something to do with receiving and reciprocating the generous spirit of Sicily. There are lessons to be learned here, and they are patient students.

"But what do you do with your days?" a friend asks.

It is a question that never needs to be asked. Their days are full from morning to night and there are always things they want to do that remain undone.

"But what do you do?"

It's not so much what they do, Kate finds herself thinking, as the spirit with which they do it. They try not to plan their days but let them unfold. They delight in the taste of their coffee each morning, but also its texture, its color: the dark, mysterious

115

design where the coffee has penetrated the thick head of foamed milk, calling to be interpreted like ink blots, tea leaves or cloud formations. They marvel at the flavor of the blood orange marmalade they made in February, and remind themselves to make more next year as they will surely run out before the oranges ripen again, at the rate it is being consumed. As they clear the breakfast table, they listen to an owl's last call of the day, his night their day, hearing that he has moved his home from the rocks beneath the castle, and is now residing in or near a cave at the east end of their meadow. When they drive into town for errands, they talk about the books they've read, about the nature of tragedy, the nature of forgiveness, abstract ideas transformed by personal experience. When they carry groceries from the car to the kitchen, they notice how a sparrow's flight is different from a crow's, how a male and female hawk hover above the cliffs all but motionless, before abruptly diving into the crannies for their family's breakfast. They look up from their daily activities to catch a swallow at play or to watch their cat stretch himself indulgently in the sun; a study in perfect contentment.

The meadow itself is nature's theatre. In Tuscany, where every field is planted with olive trees, open space is a rarity. To have a large open meadow right in front of their house is a luxury, and they give it their full attention instead of rushing toward unimportant, insignificant distractions.

"So you don't do anything all day," their friend concludes. "You must be bored to tears."

On the contrary, they are cohorts with Darwin and Shelley, Thoreau and Keats. They also need to wash their car a lot; another gift from nature.

CHAPTER NINE

Pasquale and his wife, Lucia, have brought Kate a beautiful bouquet of *Calle*, two dozen, long-stemmed Easter Calla Lilies, stunning in their austere simplicity.

"Thank you. You are so thoughtful." It is Sunday afternoon, two weeks after Easter. Niccolò and Kate have been in their house for over a month, and Niccolò has invited Pasquale and his wife to visit. "I even have a tall vase."

Several months ago, someone called Tommaso Aragona asked permission to befriend Electra on Facebook. Given that they had the same last name, a surname that is not common even in Italy, she accepted his invitation. As it turned out, Tommaso, who was working in Switzerland, was born in Trapani. Of course they were related!

Electra knows her Daddy's passion for history and ancestry so she put them in contact. Tommaso himself didn't know much about his family's history, but the little he did know came from the uncle of a friend of his. Tommaso put Niccolò in touch with Pasquale, who in turn collaborated with Niccolò to reconstruct four hundred years of Aragona history in Trapani. On line he was interesting and helpful, and Niccolò enjoyed their exchanges enormously.

However, when Niccolò and Kate came down from Florence to sign the contract to buy their house at the end of February, as Niccolò had mentioned in an e-mail to Pasquale, they found him waiting for them at the airport.

"Sicilian hospitality," Pasquale announced. He is a short man, and wiry; his plain, non-descript features are completely obscured by a pair of quirky, Elton John-style glasses.

"But we have rented a car," Niccolò protested, embarrassed by Pasquale's unexpected presence.

"You shouldn't have. I am at your disposition, always. We have prepared our guest bedroom for you."

"You shouldn't have. We have a reservation in a hotel in town."

"Tell me which one, and I will lead you to it."

Much later, when Kate and Niccolò had time to speak between themselves, when they were able finally to liberate themselves from his company, they heard the threat in Pasquale's words of hospitality. He had, as he promised, driven them to the hotel, had stayed to talk with its owner, had made the owner promise to treat them like royalty, had insisted on taking them out for a coffee and pastry—on the far side of Trapani even though there was a coffee bar in front of the hotel, even though they had told him they didn't drink coffee except first thing in the morning and had things to do before their appointment with the Notaio the following day. Before he freed them, he made them promise to stop by for drinks at his home so they could meet his wife, after which they would go out to dinner at a little place he knew. To make a very long day tolerably shorter, by the time they said goodbye after dinner that night, a meal in which they were coerced into eating far more than they wanted, Niccolò and Kate had decided that they would try to limit Pasquale's presence in their lives.

But that doesn't preclude a Sunday afternoon visit.

Lucia is looking around the garden. "I told you they'd have flowers," she says abruptly to her husband. "They live in the country."

"But I don't have lilies, and I love them," Kate interjects. "Thank you."

"You should have listened to me!" She isn't listening to Kate. "I told you they'd have a garden."

Kate is embarrassed by their sudden onset of bickering. As naturally as a reflex, Niccolò tries to curtail the argument. "Did you notice the view? Isn't she pretty?" He gestures out to Mt.

Cofano who is, in fact, unusually gorgeous on this Sunday afternoon, as if she's dressed up for the occasion.

"You are new to this area—" Pasquale explains, taking off his large, outlandish glasses and polishing them on the corner of his sweater. "—but we are used to all this." He gestures imprecisely; then turns his back on the view. "You, too, will grow weary of looking at the same ol' rock day after day."

Kate can hear what Niccolò is thinking: *same ol' rock?* It is like calling Michelangelo's *David* a hunk of marble or the *Matterhorn* a sledding hill.

Nature is anything but consistent in Sicily. The northern coast is agreeable to the eye with its gentle curves and pretty coves, its stretches of white, sandy beaches interrupted dramatically by black, rocky lava *scogli*. In the midst of this predictable and pleasing view rises the dramatic Mt. Cofano, as if it had been picked up from the Alps, like Dorothy's house in Kansas, and plopped down in Oz, changing a simple view into Technicolor. Sicily's Sugarloaf.

In the instant since Pasquale has gestured dismissively, Mt. Cofano has shifted again from bright, straight-forward realism to a slightly out-of-focus impressionism, a Monet emerging momentarily before it diffuses yet again into a multitude of Seurat pin-points.

"Would you like to see the house?" Kate ventures.

"No, not particularly," says Pasquale, stepping indoors, unseeingly. "I'm not concerned with the haves or have nots of others." He seats himself in the middle of the sofa, making it impossible for anyone else to sit beside him, and folds his hands to initiate an aggressive left-against-right thumb-war.

"Lucia? Would you like to see the house?"

"I'd love to."

The tour is quick, the house is small, but Kate is happy with the results of their efforts as she shows Lucia upstairs and down. She is pleased to witness through another person's eyes how each room is attractive in its simple, uncluttered way, revealing Niccolò's personality and hers, reflecting the integration of their diverse but compatible selves.

"Very nice," Lucia pronounces as they return to the living room. "Of course I understand that it isn't finished, you will need paintings and carpets. Things."

"Actually, we have pretty much finished furnishing it."

"But you don't have any closets."

"We aren't going to have closets."

Lucia looks puzzled. She has chosen a hard chair instead of the sofa, as her back is bothering her.

Kate continues, "We are hoping that our clothes won't exceed the two dressers we have in our bedroom. If we have closets we will have to buy clothes for each occasion, and that will end the simple life we hope to live here."

Now Lucia is squirming. She has dressed up for the Sunday afternoon visit, not too much—this isn't evening or even a party—but she has chosen an attractive skirt and silk blouse, several strands of pearls, rings, stockings, shoes that match her outfit and a purse that matches the shoes. She looks at her hostess's outfit as if registering it for the first time.

Kate is wearing a nicely tailored pair of navy trousers, the ones she always wears when she changes out of her work or stay-at-home clothes, and a white cotton V-necked sweater, which, truth be told, she confiscated from Electra's charity pile. Some of her favorite clothes come from the things Electra and Elizabeth clear out of their closets. Kate is wearing a strand of pearls—a gift from Fiammetta for the birth of her granddaughter, Elizabeth—and matching earrings, the same earrings she wears every day, which Niccolò bought for her during the first year of their marriage. She is also wearing two rings, the same rings she wears whenever she is not washing dishes or rolling dough or gardening. They don't lose their value or their beauty by being worn daily.

Lucia fingers her pearls, nervously, touches each one individually, dutifully, as if reciting a prayer, as if praying for something to say to this unfamiliar woman.

Pasquale is recounting to Niccolò their Easter fiasco. "Our Sunday lunch was minutes from being on the table when our lights went out! Poof! We couldn't even finish cooking the pasta that I had spent all morning rolling out for Lucia."

"How frustrating."

"I worked for *ENEL*"—Italy's electric company—"for forty years. You would think someone would remember me, have pity on me, and come out to give us a hand, even if it was a holiday."

"What did you do?"

"I had to call an electrician. It cost me nearly a hundred euro to have the problem fixed. And he took his time in showing up, let me tell you. We didn't sit down to lunch until four o'clock!"

"What was the problem?"

"It was no big deal," he says, waving his hand in dismissal. "Something to do with a fuse."

Lucia sighs deeply, absorbed in her own memories of their Easter debacle.

"Can I offer you another glass of wine?" Kate asks. "Another piece of cake?" Kate has learned what is expected of her on these occasions. Concetta would be proud.

"No," Lucia shifts uncomfortably, straightens the pleats in her skirt. "I shouldn't indulge. These extra pounds aren't helping my back pain."

"What are you doing for it?"

"What is there to do?"

"Have you tried swimming?" Kate's mother's companion, Ron, has back problems and finds relief by swimming.

"I should be swimming, the doctor says that would help, but it's impossible."

"Why?"

"Because I teach each day until four," she says angrily, "and I have homework to correct in the evening."

"You do have a busy schedule, but couldn't you find an hour or two a week?"

"You don't know the half of it. You think I come home to find the house in order? Even though he sits around all day complaining he has nothing to do, now that he is retired. He could pick up a few groceries, couldn't he? No. I have to do it on the way home from work. Bags of groceries, piles of essays to correct. They don't help my back."

"They certainly don't."

"No, there's nothing to do but suffer." She continues to finger her pearls.

Kate has to be careful not to be pulled into Lucia's lament. If she could be useful, if she could help Lucia to solve her problem, Kate would be happy to participate, but Lucia doesn't want help. She wants to replay her record of unhappiness. Kate would rather not join her. She sets a look of sympathy onto her face as Lucia's harangue against life's injustices spews forth. She thinks of Ron, how Kate has never heard him complain about his back problem. To be honest, she's never heard him complain about anything, not even the tremor in his hand and jaw which Kate knows concerns him, his doctor, and Kate's mother, Claire.

Kate touches the smooth perfection of her own strand of pearls, one by one, beginning to understand the attractiveness of the rosary: by not having to keep track of the words themselves, Kate's mind is able to meditate on the mysteries within the prayers.

A few summers ago, Kate took Electra to visit her mother in Colorado, where she moved from California at eighty-some years of age to be closer to Kate's brother. Stuart fled Santa Monica after the 1994 earthquake and has been living happily ever since in the foothills of the Rocky Mountains. In addition to spending time with her grandmother—and her uncle and his family—which is the major reason for their visit, Electra had asked to shop at a large, outlet warehouse. Ron, bless his heart, had offered to accompany them.

"I am afraid you will be bored waiting for us."

"No, I'll bring a book," he says.

Electra was looking for polo shirts. The insignia over the heart didn't have to be an alligator or a polo pony, but the shirts needed to fit perfectly, which meant taking the time to try them on. In an hour they had found six shirts, and had spent less than half of what they would have paid in Florence.

Ron was patience personified. When Electra had finished, he joined them in line with four books and two wine glasses.

"Let me pay for those, Ron. It is the least I can do. You have been so tolerant."

"Thank you the same, but I prefer to pay for them myself, no offense intended." Ron is a trim, good-looking man five years younger than Kate's mother, with a headful of thick, white hair and sweet, baby-blue-eyes. He grew up in Missouri, and has not lost any of his Midwestern twang, despite forty-five years living in California before Colorado.

The cashier had rung up his books. "These glasses are on special, four-for-the-price-of-two." She had showed him the sticker. "Get yourself another two."

"That's all right," Ron had drawled. "I only need two."

"You are paying for four; you might as well take them."

"That's all right," Ron had repeated. "I only need two."

Back at the house, Kate had repeated this episode to her mother. Claire had explained that Ron had knocked over and chipped two of their wine glasses, and had been looking to replace them. They have a carefully measured three inches of wine at five, a ritual that marks the end of their day. They used to have peanuts, as well, but their doctors have said no. If they slip over their designated weights, if their belt buckles start to require another notch, they skip the wine on Tuesdays and Thursdays. They are both trim and healthy and well into their eighties. Discipline about weight is one of the things Kate admires about them, but it pales in the face of the lesson Ron has given her about bringing into the home just what one needs, even if the extra is offered at no extra cost.

Kate experiences a time warp, or Lucia has circled back on herself. The story is exactly where it was when Kate stopped listening. "There is nothing to do but suffer." Lucia hasn't noticed Kate's absence.

Niccolò is having more success with Pasquale. They are discussing ancestors; the one subject they have in common. Kate tries to think what she might say Lucia, a conversation that might prove useful to both of them, but all the subjects Kate presents—cooking, travel, the sea, their children, even singing—all the topics Kate throws out produce further examples of her guest's unhappiness. Kate decides to try again to divert Lucia from her groove of agony and introduces the most mundane subject she can think of, the weather.

"Is it always cold at Easter?"

"It is. People will tell you differently but I know the truth. I have relatives who live in Tuscany, and when I was a child, our families would visit each other during the Easter holidays and again for *Tutti i Santi*—All Saints Day—in November. November in Tuscany is always cold and miserable but we could sometimes still swim in Sicily. Easter is always cold here—there is no chance of sitting on the beach in March or April—whereas it is likely to be sunny in Tuscany. Spring in Sicily is beautiful but always cold.

She is absolutely right! Kate has been looking at this all wrong, figuring spring would be warmer in Sicily than in Tuscany because it is a thousand kilometers farther south.

Spring in Erice is as cold as autumn in Tuscany whereas Kate has photographical evidence of her children in the garden in shorts in April. It isn't the end of their cold, it almost always rains in May, but March and April are usually warm and sunny.

At the end of their visit, Lucia and Pasquale rise to say goodbye. Pasquale compliments them on their beautiful home as Lucia squeezes her hand, emphatically. "Thank you for a wonderful time. I haven't enjoyed myself so much in years."

Kate wonders if she has misjudged their entire visit until she sees that they are arguing again, before they have reached their car parked at the front gate.

"After forty years working for an electric company," Niccolò says, "he doesn't know how to flick a fuse switch." Kate is putting pasta water on the stove for dinner. Niccolò is rinsing their glasses and plates to put into the dishwasher. "Never again." He shakes his head. "Even the flowers were full of ants."

"It wasn't so bad," Kate says, bringing down a skillet to heat the tomato sauce.

"Are you kidding? All she did was complain."

"Yes, she grumbled a lot. And she's clearly depressed." In the midst of all her misery, Lucia has nonetheless bestowed on Kate a jewel of knowledge. "She told me how to organize our spring and autumn calendar so that we will enjoy Sicily and Tuscany more. That unexpected gem made all the rest of their visit worthwhile."

Spring is better in Tuscany. Autumn is better in Sicily. And Niccolò is right: they will never invite them again. As their cupboards need to be kept clear of clutter so does their social life. There is plenty of space for friendships, a certain amount for social obligations, but no room left for whiners and complainers, even if they bring stunning bouquets of essential, ant-ridden lessons.

CHAPTER
TEN

They are walking through the narrow, cobbled streets of Erice. Kate is photographing the extraordinary architectural details as the mist swirls and lifts to reveal a roguish gargoyle, an elaborate, medieval arch, a richly decorated courtyard. Cloaked in a fog that has inhabited these streets since the beginning of time, it is not difficult for them to imagine that they alone inhabit this austere, mystical town; that the occasional person who brushes past in the fog is but a phantom from a previous era. Despite a jarring cacophony of unsynchronized church bells announcing the noon hour, there is a stillness to this place that can't be disturbed, an atmosphere more holy than what Kate often encounters in churches.

"Nicco! Niccolò!" They hear Niccolò's name being called, but his is not an uncommon name in Italy, where boys are named for their grandfathers, limiting the number of names in circulation. Nonetheless, Niccolò glances around and sees a tall, thin man desperately waving a Curious George straw hat at them in front of the Church of San Giuliano.

"Do you know who he is?" Kate asks her husband dubiously, as they walk forward, smiles plastered onto their faces.

"I have no idea. I don't know anyone here, except Edoardo and Rosario."

The man who has been waving at them clearly knows Niccolò. "You don't remember me!" he says coyly. "I'm Eugenio. Eugenio Nasi. I would have recognized you anywhere!"

Niccolò isn't good at recognizing faces, even one as animated and particular as this man's, but names have a way of staying in his memory. "Eugenio!" They are embracing, old friends reunited, but Kate can see that Niccolò hasn't yet remembered from where he knows this man. "This is my wife, Kate."

"Enchanté" He removes his hat to reveal an abundance of too-brightly-dyed crayon-yellow hair, and bends dramatically low over Kate's hand.

What might Kate say that will help Niccolò locate this man in his past?

Eugenio supplies the key. "Have you kept in touch with the Martelli's? I haven't seen them for years."

Now Niccolò remembers. "I believe they moved to Australia several years ago." He says to Kate, "Eugenio was one of my friends from the infamous Martelli parties, when we were boys."

"The tuxedo parties?"

"Exactly."

"Were you in school together?" Kate asks this animated man whose eyes finish with a cross-hatching of wrinkles.

"Thank you for the compliment, dear," Eugenio says. "But I am ages older than your darling husband." He fingers the border of the large, floppy hat in his hands, turning it distractedly. "Didn't the Martelli family give the most extraordinary parties?"

"They did," Niccolò agrees. "Usually finishing with *cappuccino*, *brioche*, and a sunrise."

"No one gives parties like that anymore. We have been reduced to buffets! Finger foods, for the sake of goodness." His voice has risen an indignant octave. "Paper napkins!"

"Where have you disappeared to all these years?" Niccolò asks, seemingly unperturbed. "It's been ages. Do you have time for a coffee?"

"I don't. It's a long story but my father died last year—"

"I am sorry."

"Condolences."

"—and I am restoring his house here in Erice. I am expecting the carpenter in a few minutes. I just popped out to buy bread. I arrived last night and don't have any food in the house yet. But come over for dinner tonight. It will be wonderful to catch up."

"Tonight isn't possible—" They don't have plans but how can they accept when he's just said he's doesn't have food in the house. "—but come to us for lunch tomorrow."

"I'd love to. But Friday night, you come to me, no excuses. A group of friends are coming to dinner. Buffet style," he giggles, covering a mouth of crooked teeth. "Paper napkins."

Eugenio's friends, almost exclusively Sicilians, are all gathered for cocktails when Niccolò accompanies Kate into the inner courtyard. Torches flicker along the walls, lighting the faces of two dozen unfamiliar figures. Whatever wind there is tonight blows high above the courtyard walls, but Kate is glad she brought a shawl.

An elegant, Cole Porter look-alike approaches Niccolò and says, "As a young man I had the privilege of meeting your grandfather." He bows over Kate's hand and introduces himself as "Renato Ravidà." It is a peculiar name but it registers easily as there is a street in Trapani by the same name. He touches the coat sleeve of another man, and brings him into their little circle. "And this is Ettore Bassi." They shake hands with a bright-eyed, bearded man who arrived at the party at the same time they did. "This is his wife, Graziella," he presents a tall, elegant, beautifully dressed woman who has joined them. "My family," continues Renato, "hosted the reception after the ceremony in which your grandfather was awarded honorary citizenship to Trapani."

"I thought your grandfather was born in Trapani?" Kate says to Niccolò.

"He was. But by the time he became famous, he was a resident in Florence."

"Trapani honored him with the keys to the city."

"May I present my wife, Diana." A pocket-Venus in stature, Renato's wife carries herself proudly, with a gracefulness that makes her seem tall. "She knew your grandfather, too."

"Not personally," Diana takes Kate's hand, then Niccolò's. "I never had the honor, but Niccolò Aragona holds a very dear place in our family history." Her eyes moisten.

"How is that?"

"When my great-aunt, Zia Antonietta, was a student at *Collegio della Santissima Annunziata*, she fell in love with your grandfather."

Santissima Annunziata is a school in Florence, renowned through the centuries for boarding girls from Italy's aristocratic families.

Niccolò is enthralled. "You are illuminating a mystery I had never hoped to solve."

"You knew of my great-aunt, Antonietta?"

"Not by name, no. But when I was a young man, a few years after my grandfather had died, I was visiting his second wife, and she let a detail slip." Renato and Ettore lean forward to follow his story more closely. Diana is mesmerized. The offered tray of miniature sausage is ignored. "I had been in love with a girl," Niccolò proceeds, a little tentatively, "but her parents forced her to break off our engagement. I was broken hearted—"

"Understandably," says Diana.

"My entire life I had visited Grandfather on Sunday afternoons, and when he died I continued the habit. One time, at the height of my desperation, I confided my heart-break to his second wife, and she said, "Don't make the same mistake as your grandfather, marrying hastily to compensate for a disappointment in love."

"Zia Antonietta."

"Zia Antonietta."

Diana wipes tears from her eyes. "Of course her parents expected her to marry well. Your grandfather was at the start of his career, he wasn't yet famous."

"What happened to your great-aunt?"

"Of course she married," Diana has regained her composure. "But not the marriage of her dreams, I'm afraid. She had three daughters before she died in her late-thirties. I know she followed your grandfather's rise to success! I found news clippings of Niccolò Aragona's many accomplishments in her dressing table, which I inherited from her eldest daughter when she died. The irony, of course, is that after your grandfather became famous, Zia Antonietta's father recognized his value as a historian. They corresponded for many years." She pauses. "I hope your grandfather was happier in his marriage."

"After his disappointment, he married hastily, as my grandfather's second wife insinuated. An arranged marriage to a wealthy woman, noble, but almost past the age of marriage. She, too, had three children, sons—my father was the youngest—and she, too, died young, when my father was in his twenties and engaged to marry my mother."

"What a sad story." The man with the beard, Ettore, has tears in his eyes, as well. "I hope his second marriage was happier."

"Grandfather married again a year after my grandmother's death, to a woman who had been his student. That marriage, I believe, was a happier one for him, but it wasn't well received by my father or his brother, who were understandably still grieving the death of their mother. Unfortunately, it's a wound that still festers in our family."

"Zia Antonietta and your grandfather would have been happy together, I am certain." Diana smiles bravely.

"And you two would have been related," Renato says.

They wouldn't have existed, Kate thinks but has the good sense to not speak.

"Come," Ettore says. "I'll introduce you to one of Zia Antonietta's grandsons, my cousin Agostino, one good thing to come out of this sad tale about your grandfather."

"Ettore! If you will present me, I would like to speak with this woman about Shakespeare." A distinguished looking, white-haired gentlemen crosses the room, and bows over Kate's hand; then shakes Niccolò's. "Lorenzo Donnacelata," he introduces himself. "I hear your wife is a Shakespearean scholar."

"She is."

"Hardly," Kate says, registering another unusual name easily because it, too, is a street name in Trapani. "I specialized in the English Renaissance in graduate school—Shakespeare was my passion—but that was a million years ago, a previous life."

"I understand you taught Shakespeare at the University of California, Santa Cruz."

Eugenio has been talking. This is all information he pried out of her at lunch the other day. Eugenio is a question asker, an information gatherer. The Town Crier, Kate now understands. She wonders what else Eugenio has been telling his friends?

"Mostly I taught a lot of Freshman English."

"Do you miss teaching?" He pulls out a chair for her, and Lorenzo and Kate, Niccolò and Ettore all settle themselves in the wobbly, rattan furniture.

"Not at all."

"Why did you stop, if you don't mind my asking?"

This is a subject Kate doesn't speak about easily, a topic too painful to address directly, despite the passing of nearly thirty years; almost like lifting up her dress to reveal her extra vertebrae. But for some inexplicable reason, Kate finds herself trusting this gentle-man, willing to confide at first sight.

"I left teaching for two reasons. As I started to establish my career, my mentor became my tormentor and felt obliged to destroy everything he had encouraged me to construct."

"This is not the first time I have heard of that happening, in academia and elsewhere."

"It was devastating at the time, but in the long run I can't help but be grateful. He would turn in his grave if he heard me saying he had done me a favor, but I am happier now than if I had stayed in academia. It can be a very small world."

"What was the other reason?"

"I suspect that part of the reason I went into teaching in the first place was to boost my self-esteem—you know, everyone hanging onto my every word, scribbling notes as fast as I could speak. But once I was in front of the lecture hall, I discovered I didn't like being the center of attention. I found it made me extremely uncomfortable. I am much more at ease behind a camera, focusing on others."

"Is that what you do now? You are a photographer?"

Kate and Niccolò answer at the same time.

"Yes, she is a photographer."

"I am more of a farmer."

Niccolò and Kate laugh in unison.

"Farmer-photographer," Kate says.

"Photographer-farmer," says Niccolò, at the same time.

"In Tuscany," Kate tries to clarify, "we farm Niccolò's family's olive orchards."

"Always with a camera hanging around her neck."

Kate tries to turn the conversation away from herself. "Are you an academic?"

"No—no," Lorenzo laughs. "English literature is just a little hobby of mine. By training, I am an engineer, although my professional life has been spent as a manager for a consulting firm until I retired a few years ago." He leans back in his chair, stretches his legs, crosses his ankles. "But I love the English

Renaissance—Shakespeare, in particular. I saw an extraordinary production of *Hamlet* last month, at Wyndham's Theatre in London's West End. Jude Law played Hamlet. I had my doubts, a famous film star, but he was quite surprising. They compared him to Ben Kingsley's performance, directed by Buzz Goodbody—"

"—at Stratford's Other Place! I saw Kingsley's performance! It was one of the most amazing theatre experiences of my life."

"I can imagine."

"It was the first time I had seen Hamlet portrayed as mad, which makes sense if you think about it; after all, that's what all the characters have been saying about him."

"Jude Law's Hamlet was certainly off-balance, and angry; probably the angriest Hamlet I've ever seen. You really believed him capable when he said: "*Now could I drink hot blood.*""

"I think you've lost your wife," Ettore says to Niccolò.

"You may be right."

Ettore and Niccolò stand simultaneously. "If you will excuse us," Niccolò says, "We'll leave you two enthusiasts to discuss Shakespeare."

Ettore says, "I'll introduce you now to my cousin, Agostino. He's a wonderful man. It's his wine we are drinking tonight."

"It is a Grillo? It has a nice finish."

"It is," Ettore continues, moving Niccolò across the room. "If you and your wife would like to visit the vineyard, I am sure Agostino would be more than happy to give you a tour."

"The one aspect of Law's performance that I didn't much like," Lorenzo continues, recapturing her attention. "He had no sense of humor."

"That's a pity. Hamlet is perhaps Shakespeare's wittiest tragic hero."

"*For yourself, sir, shall grow old as I am, if like a crab you could go backward.*"

"With its implicit stage direction! Hilarious!"

"Unfortunately, Jude Law speaks terribly fast."

"It is part of his style."

"I'm sure it wasn't a problem for native speakers, but I was glad I knew the play well, or I would have lost a good many of his lines."

"Your English is excellent."

"You, my dear, are very kind."

As Lorenzo's conversation continues, Kate recalls why she loved Shakespeare: for every human predicament, there is a character to embody the emotion; from jealousy and the need for revenge, to love, requited and otherwise. It is all there. Just as Kate is beginning to flex a muscle she hasn't exercised for nearly thirty years, Lorenzo's wife, Caterina, comes to join them, together with Ettore's wife, Graziella. "You can't keep her to yourself all evening, Lorenzo. We want to talk with her, too."

"Are you Shakespearean enthusiasts as well?" Kate asks, moving over to make room for these attractive women.

"Hardly!" The idea amuses both women. "Eugenio was telling us that you live in Tuscany, in the hills overlooking Florence. That must be beautiful."

"Florence is my favorite city in Italy! Graziella says.

"The most gorgeous city in the world!"

"Eugenio told us you've bought a house in Erice. Do you like living in Sicilia?"

"We love it," Kate says. "It's magical. The people are so kind, so generous."

"I remember when Lorenzo brought me to Trapani to meet his family," Caterina recounts, "there were so many parties!"

"I had five aunts," Lorenzo adds, "and each one hosted a dinner party."

"He's forgetting to mention the lunches and afternoon teas! At the end of each day my mother and I would try to reconstruct who was related to whom. And how many cousins did you say you have?" Caterina teases, flirting with her husband.

"I've never tried to count them all," he laughs, "but plenty!"

"All of whom had to inspect me," Caterina recalls.

"I'm sure you passed with flying colors," Kate says.

"She did. Everyone loved her."

"So you aren't Sicilian?"

"No. I'm from Livorno. I met Lorenzo when he was studying at the Naval Academy. He was so handsome," she sighs.

He still is, but Kate can imagine how striking he must have been in his formal, naval dress. Caterina is very pretty, too, although she looks disturbingly like Niccolò's mother, albeit a younger, fresher version.

"I left Sicilia when I was seventeen," Lorenzo explains. "To study at the Academy."

"We spent our early years of marriage in Milano—"

"—then moved to Genova for twenty years before Lorenzo retired."

"So you've never actually lived in Sicily."

"No. We come every summer, with our children—"

"—and our grandchildren now—"

"—and sometimes at Easter, if the weather seems promising."

"A few days in November, for the feasts."

They finish each other's sentences without interrupting or talking at the same time, an intricate two-step they've perfected with time: no one's feet are stepped on.

"Sicilia is an ideal place to holiday—"

"—but we wouldn't want to live here all year long."

"It can become a very small town."

Graziella, who has been quiet until now, adds, "yes, very."

Sicily may be a small town but it is a welcome relief after living in Tuscany. Kate believes in form: it is like the blank spaces in art. Without it, the colors, the figures, all risk running together; but Kate resents it when form becomes an excuse for exclusion. She agrees with Niccolò's grandfather's comment about the noble class: all the zeros in the world add up to nothing without a number in front to give it significance.

Last year, at a dinner party in Florence, Kate found herself seated near a woman whom she has greeted at parties over the past twenty years but had never engaged in dialogue. Making conversation, Kate asked if she had children.

"Six," she reported.

"How old are they?"

She started the list, which ranged from thirty to nine. When she spoke about her twenty-year-old daughter who was passionate about horses, Kate mentioned that *her* twenty-year-old daughter also loved to ride. "We should introduce them, when Electra is in Florence at Christmas."

Kate could see this woman physically recoiling from her. However, as they were seated across from each other and would be until dinner was over, this woman found what she considered a polite response. "Of course." Her long, pointed nose held high. "If the occasion presents itself."

Apparently, Kate will never learn. She saw this same woman at another party, right before she and Niccolò came to Sicily. Kate greeted her by name. 'Oh, good!' their host said, taking their coats. 'You are friends.'

'Acquaintances,' this woman clarified.

In Kate's opinion, this woman missed an occasion to stay silent.

Refreshingly, at Eugenio's party, there is sincerity shining in the eyes of the people with whom she speaks. Niccolò comes and goes, sometimes bringing with him a new acquaintance; sometimes to join her in a conversation. He has discovered another old friend, Silvia, who also divides her time between Florence and Sicilia. Kate finds herself relaxing, which is not always the case in a room full of unfamiliar people, but here she can't help but let down her guard, surrounded as she is by an atmosphere of genuine affection. Renato and Ettore have told her about their olive farms, have offered to sell her oil, *at a good price*; then laugh when Kate tells them about their three thousand trees in Florence, and offers to sell them oil *at a better price*. Renato lays his hand on Ettore's shoulder, a gesture that is both brotherly and respectful. Kate asks them if they have known each other a long time.

"All our lives!"

"We played together as children."

"We also have in common that we both left Sicilia at eighteen."

"Our parents sent us to university in the north."

"That doesn't sound typically Sicilian," Kate says. "I would have thought you would be urged to stay home, to take over the family business."

"In my case," Ettore says, "I know it was hard on my parents, especially my mother as I was an only child. But I would have thought Renato's parents were glad to have him out of the house."

These two men are older than Kate, older than Niccolò, perhaps by as much as ten years, but it is hard not to see beyond the years to the two boys who continue to tease each other. Brothers in the best sense.

"And when did you return to Sicily?"

"I retired ten years ago," Renato says. "My wife inherited a property and wanted to return to Sicilia."

"And you?" Kate asks Ettore.

"We live in Milano, but we come back for the summer. My wife still works. She has a rather large clientele to follow in the north."

It takes her a minute but Kate is beginning to connect husbands with wives. Graziella, Ettore's wife, was a model in her younger days, and one can see by the way she carries herself that she was at home on the runway. She is obviously as smart as she is pretty, for she moved from modeling to fashion design as the first flush of her youth passed. Her eyes are magnetic: clear, bright emerald green, fringed by long, thick lashes that will never need mascara. Diana is married to Renato: they are the group's unofficial leaders, Kate suspects. Every gesture, every comment, is courteous and courtly. Lorenzo and Caterina combine sophistication with self-effacement, and are endearing for their total lack of pretension. Silvia isn't married but seems related to everyone present. She is an academic, a history professor at the University of Florence, and she is full of enthusiasm for Sicily's history. Renato's cousin, Aurora, on the other hand, who has lived on the island all her life, strikes Kate as sweet but potentially tedious. Kate hears the whisper of gossip as she passes by with a plate of food—"*Poverino*, it doesn't look good. He's going to have to have his hip replaced and even so—" Kate is not tempted to linger. Otherwise, everyone at Eugenio's party is interesting, friendly and welcoming. Kate senses the possibility of real friendship. These people have been friends for generations, and oddly enough, everyone here seems to have a street named after him in Trapani.

In all of Italy, streets are named after the country's prominent citizens: poets, writers, scientists, historians, political leaders; or saints. The street names keep Italy's renowned citizens from slipping into obscurity. They offer a pedestrian level of culture to everyone who knows how to read a street sign. It makes sense, really, that all of the people at

Eugenio's party would have streets named after them. They are all from old Trapanese families. Their ancestors were the heroes in the unification of Italia or important literary figures, architects or founders of museums. Niccolò's family has contributed to Italy's glory, as well, and now Kate understands why they have been included.

"We hope you will come to our house on Sunday," Ettore says, at the end of the evening. "It's more or less the same group of friends, but my son will be there, too, and a few others."

"We'd love to come," Niccolò says.

"May I bring something?" Kate asks.

"Just yourselves. Eight-thirty. We live in *Piazza Umberto Primo*. There's a brass hand as a knocker."

"I know the house!" Kate says. "I've photographed it."

"She's photographed every detail in Erice," Niccolò says. "It makes for slow walking."

"It's a beautiful little town. It merits attention."

"Until the summer crowds appear," Caterina says. "Then we can't open our front door without a stream of tourists trying to flood in."

"They live in the ex-Sacristy," Ettore explains, "of the *Santa Maria della Grazia* church."

"That must be beautiful."

"As long as you don't hope to sleep late on Sunday mornings," Lorenzo says.

"We are having a little gathering, as well," Caterina confides. "A week from Tuesday. Very simple. I am not an accomplished cook like Graziella—"

"I'm not a great cook—" Graziella protests. "Don't raise their expectations."

"I hear *you* are a wonderful cook!" Renato's cousin points at Kate.

The comment surprises Kate, catches her off guard. "Actually, any success I have in the kitchen is because I have good ingredients to work with. Only that."

"You are being too modest," cousin Aurora insists. "Eugenio told me you are a marvelous cook. I bet you have all kinds of secrets. What kind of pans do you use?"

If Aurora had asked Kate what kind of camera she used, what lenses she favored, she might receive an informed, enthusiastic response, but *pans*? The only thing Kate knows about pans is that food needs sufficient space to cook evenly, especially in a skillet. "Big ones?" she offers skeptically.

"Ha!" This isn't the answer she was waiting to hear. Kate hears disappointment in the emptiness of Aurora's laugh. She has disillusioned her by not offering a brand name. Kate knows that good pans make cooking more pleasurable, but she has never made the investment; for Christmas or a birthday she inevitably ask for bulbs, not kitchenware. As a result Kate can give this woman a bouquet of tulips but not an educated answer about pans.

"If you don't have other *pans*—" Caterina continues, "I mean *plans*, we hope you will come to our little party."

"And if you have time before then—" Lorenzo hands her an embossed card "—I would enjoy continuing our interrupted conversation about Shakespeare. However, be warned, I won't be able to offer you anything to eat. I'm the worse cook present."

"He can't boil an egg!" Caterina laughs.

"—but I can pour a drink!"

"If he doesn't cut himself opening the bottle," says Ettore.

When they finally say goodbye to their new friends, when they finally have thanked Eugenio for his hospitality, have promised to call him the following day, Niccolò and Kate walk silently back to the car, hand in hand. Tonight's conversations replay in the quiet, evening air.

Apparently, Niccolò is also recalling conversations. "I never thought I'd know the name of Grandfather Niccolò lost love." He shakes his head.

"It is amazing. Did you see, Diana had tears in her eyes?"

"I had tears of my own."

The heels of their shoes click in synchronization against the smooth, worn, marble cobblestone; overhead, a window is fastened, a shutter pulled closed. A mist swirls around the lamp posts. It must be after midnight.

"I am never going to be able to keep all those names straight," Kate says.

"It doesn't really matter."

"I guess not. It's just a dance, a waltz, a ballroom full of swirling, colorful personalities."

"Do you feel like walking a bit?" Niccolò says, moving her to his right side. "I wouldn't mind a little exercise after all that food."

"And all that wine!" Kate adds, taking his arm. "We're not far from Torre Pepoli."

"Zia Antonietta was a Pepoli," Niccolò says, as they climb the steps to the garden.

"How do you know?"

"Diana told me, while you were talking with Lorenzo."

At the entrance to the park there is a bench, a long semi-circle carved out of stone. "Take a seat here," Niccolò instructs, placing her at one end of the bench. "Slump down a little, keep your ear close to this column." He walks away, settles himself at the other end of the bench and leans into the column.

Intimately close, Kate hears Niccolò's voice, as if he were cupping his hand and whispering directly into her ear.

"Finchè è bello, la mattina, risvegliarsi vicino a te."

She is shocked by these mysterious acoustics. Kate looks at Niccolò, at least fifteen feet away. He is smiling.

Kate bends down and whispers, in the softest voice she can manage, "Morning, afternoon, evening, it is all fine when you are near."

"I hope you didn't mind me speaking of Bianca tonight."

It's as though he is right next to her. She can almost feel his breath on her ear.

How can she object to a love that preceded her by twenty years?

She can hear a need for reassurance in his voice, this man who has never given her a moment to doubt his fidelity.

"You don't mind not being the first in my life?"

She laughs, an inappropriate, single note that causes Niccolò to pull away at his end of the bench. Niccolò has had many girlfriends before her, if only one serious love.

"Amore." Kate watches him draw in close again. "As long as I am your last love, none of the rest matters."

CHAPTER ELEVEN

Edoardo has the habit of stopping by mid-morning to say hello to Kate and Niccolò, en route from his home in Trapani to his property in the country which he visits every day but only lives in during the summer months. They are neighbors in the best sense of the word: borrowed sugar affection generously lent over their non-existent back fence.

"When will you move up for the summer?"

"When it is too hot to sleep in town."

Often he brings them a gift: a jar of Angelica's preserves, *Amarene*, sour cherry, or a bag of lemons from their garden in Trapani. They sit outside on the low stone wall under the giant pines, in the company of all his dogs—dogs that have been abandoned and have found their way, half-starving, to his plot of land, sensing they won't be turned away. They exchange tidbits of news. The weather is always discussed. It continues to be dramatic, even though it is warmer now. They discuss plants: what is in bloom, what needs transplanting. Edoardo has a penchant for trees that were abundant in his childhood, which are slipping into extinction. Kate agrees with his logic, even if the trees themselves aren't always attractive.

One dog, Orecchiella, begins each visit at Edoardo's feet, but without any of them realizing it, he ends up next to Edoardo, his head resting on his master's knee.

Orecchiella is a very peculiar looking dog, longer than he is tall, with large, erect ears pitched in alert above a perpetually worried, too-human expression. Kate reaches forward to scratch him between his ears, to ease the crease between his brows, but he buries his head under Edoardo's arm: a one-lap dog.

At the end of the day, after Edoardo has changed back into his city clothes, he will stop by again, giving the unstructured day a frame. He brings eggs or a bouquet of flowers, "for you, *Nica*, not for him," he announces, establishing a flirtation which shifts day-by-day, sometimes sincere in his admiration of a flower she has cultivated against odds, sometimes as a teasing reprimand. "Niccolò has good taste but you don't, Lady Kate! Otherwise, you wouldn't have married him!" The humor isn't elevated, but the sentiment it expresses is genuine. For all his familiar teasing, Edoardo never oversteps the boundary of good taste.

"You know the eggs you gave us yesterday?" Kate says. "When I cracked open the first one, I was impressed by the brightness of the yoke. The next yoke was a different color from the first, the size slightly smaller, paler. The next was different, too. Six eggs, not one equal to the others."

"Of course not," Edoardo replies. "They are from six different birds."

At first Edoardo's gifts embarrassed them. If they bought something to give them in return—ice cream or chocolates—he and Angelica were *mortificati*—mortified, and the next day he would appear with more gifts than usual.

In April, shortly after Elizabeth and Electra returned to university, Niccolò and Kate learned to make cheese. It was something that Kate had wanted to learn ever since she read *Animal, Vegetable, Miracle*. They never had success with Kingsolver's mozzarella recipe, but with practice they have become proficient with *pecorino* and *ricotta* and *ravaggiolo*.

Kate knows Angelica likes her *ricotta* still warm, with lots of whey. Edoardo has a passion for the soft cheese, what they call *ravaggiolo* in Tuscany and *cagliata* in Sicily. Their son, Matteo, likes the *pecorino*; the more aged, the better.

They buy thirty liters of still-warm ewe's milk twice a month and spend a day making cheese. Their goal is to put aside several rounds of *pecorino* to age so they will have presents for Christmas. But their popularity with the *pecorino* is greater than their production and they have had to increase it, if they hope to have anything set aside for the holidays.

Finally, they have something of interest to offer Angelica and Edoardo. Their cheese is the first thing for which Edoardo has actually asked.

Well, hinted at.

"Angelica finished the *ricotta*. She heated up the whey and ate the *ricotta* warm. Again, you have made her happy," he tells Kate the morning after another gift of cheese.

"We're so pleased."

"Matteo and I consumed the *pecorino*." He sweeps his hand in the air, an abbreviated, upward whirlwind gesture, a sign of approval. "It was finished in a minute."

"Wait. I'll give you another one."

"Only if you have one to spare. I won't lie, it was delicious."

"You are doing us a favor," Niccolò says, having learnt a way to make it easier for them to accept. "We have made too many."

When Edoardo first started dropping by for a visit at the end of the day, Kate was unprepared. She didn't know what to offer. A glass of wine? A cup of tea? Cookies? Kate was not raised to insist and after the third offering she let it drop.

Now Kate knows that Edoardo will inevitably stop by for a few minutes before heading home, so she prepares a pot of verbena tea ahead of time, or offers him some of the cold espresso she has learned to keep in a jar in the kitchen. If he arrives hot and tired, she will offer him a glass of wine, but if she has tea already made, they have an alternative to wine and coffee.

Apart from the house-warming gift, the wine that Edoardo brings is light and easy to drink, made from his *Insolia* grapes. It isn't sophisticated, it isn't a blend of flavors, it isn't aged in barrels, but it isn't overloaded with sulfates and it doesn't give them a headache. It is, Kate imagines, what wine used to taste like before the oenologists stepped in: the grapes from which it was made.

"A glass of wine will stop perspiration," Edoardo tells them.

"That sounds like an old wives' tale," Kate says.

"I thought so too, the first time someone told me. I thought it was just an excuse to drink a glass of wine. But it works."

"It makes sense, chemically, if you think about it," Niccolò reasons. "The alcohol enlarges the blood vessels; the body doesn't have to work as hard to cool itself."

Edoardo rolls his eyes. "Just pour yourself a glass and sit."

With perfect timing—not a minute too long to risk boring or imposing on his hosts, nor a moment too brief, which might suggest he hasn't enjoyed their company, has just stopped by for a glass of wine—Edoardo rises. He bows in Kate's direction, ever-so-slightly, an authentic, gracious, courtly gesture; but when he repeats it to Niccolò, it is almost imperceptibly transformed, conveying a hint of irony, of self-mockery.

Kate excuses herself, returning with a week-old pecorino wrapped in waxed paper. Edoardo says, "A million thanks. But you shouldn't give it away, you should let it age, it is even more delicious when it is seasoned."

She returns to the pantry where their cheeses are stacked and dated, and wraps another, older cheese in waxed paper. When Kate gives Edoardo the seasoned pecorino, he takes her hand and bows deeply. There is no mockery in his expression of affection and appreciation.

"We'll see you tomorrow, Edoardo."

"Inshallah."

God willing.

CHAPTER TWELVE

This morning's sunrise was spectacular. As Kate photographed, she felt she was witnessing the creation of the world itself, not just the beginning on another day. She woke Niccolò, urged him to come downstairs so they could watch it together on the terrace. As they had their coffee, an enormous mass of clouds poured down from Erice and joined the sunrise. At first it looked as if the colors would dominate, the first waves of gray flickered pink and rose tones, but the gray descending from Erice covered all the colors, even the sun itself, and for several moments the sun and its reflected colors were obscured. Eventually, the sun rose above the masses and the clouds moved on to blanket the sea, altering the pale blue to slate. There was a movement on the water, not waves, not whitecaps but a kind of surging, as if the color-change had permeated the sea and changed its course.

Kate has been waiting to receive the inspiration for her next book of photographs, and suddenly she understands what it will be: Clouds. Clouds above the Sea. She can hardly wait for tomorrow's sunrise; can hardly wait to look through her files to see which photographs she can use.

"Your editor is going to love this project," Niccolò says ironically. "You couldn't have chosen a less commercial subject."

Elizabeth calls them as they are clearing the breakfast dishes. Normally she isn't up this early, but Stephen is in America, completing his fourth-year medical school elective at Stony Brook Hospital on Long Island. Elizabeth has just finished her third-year exams and is packing to join him. They will spend their summer touring the States, from coast to coast.

"So how has it been without Stephen these past six weeks?"

"Except for the first couple of days, which were pretty dismal, I haven't really missed him."

"Is that good or bad?" Kate asks.

"It's good. You know how you always told me a healthy relationship was an **H**, not an **A**."

Of course Kate remembers: two free-standing individuals well-connected but not leaning on each other and therefore destined to collapse if the connection dissolves.

Kate is impressed that Elizabeth listened; that she remembers.

"Well, I had an epiphany," Elizabeth continues. "I realized that Stephen and I are together because we enjoy being together, not because we are afraid to be alone."

"That's very good to know."

"But I am going to miss *you* this summer!" she insists, dropping her grown-up wisdom, indulging a regressive moment.

"It's a hard choice, my dear, diamonds or rubies."

"Hmmmm."

"Fortunately, you don't have to choose. Come down to visit us when you return from the States. Don't you have a week before university starts?"

"We do. But we can't come straight away. We've promised Stephen's parents we would visit them. He hasn't seen his folks since before Easter."

"All right." It is one of the few disadvantages of a boyfriend who has a good relationship with his family.

"But we will come down right after classes start, for a long weekend."

"I'll count that as a promise!"

"Mama, we love Sicily. We would come down every weekend, if you and Daddy bought our tickets."

This is not true, their lives are busy with studies and friends, but it is a nice thought.

Elizabeth shifts from sentimental to practical as effortlessly as she skipped from wisdom to immaturity, without skipping a beat. "The only thing that is missing from our house in Sicily is a pool."

"You are right, but we've had so many expenses recently, and your Daddy doesn't like to spend money he doesn't have. But one day we will put one in."

"Yea. Yea." She has heard this before. At L'Antica they have been talking with Niccolò's mother about installing a pool since the summer Elizabeth learned to swim.

But no matter how often they discussed a pool with Fiammetta, no matter that they found and agreed upon the ideal location; no matter that their offer to pay for half the pool was increased to pay for all of it, from the excavating equipment to the pool construction itself, to the finishing touches, border tiles and lawn furniture; no matter what, somehow that pool was never allowed into existence.

A pool isn't a necessity in life, it isn't like indoor plumbing or a roof over their heads, but it would have made the difference between a summer endured—Florence can be unbearably hot and humid—to one enjoyed, a place where the heat was a welcome excuse to spend the day relaxing in cool water.

"It could be a dramatic backdrop for your June cocktail parties," Kate tried to persuade her mother-in-law years ago.

Fiammetta liked the Hollywood image, Kate could tell.

"It could be a place for Elizabeth and Electra's friends to gather in the summer months."

Kate should have stopped while she was ahead.

"But they will make noise! They will leave their towels on the chaise lounges. They will move the lawn furniture, leave it in disorder."

She was probably right. Kids do make noise, especially when they are having fun.

Finally, it wasn't up to them. Eventually, they stopped proposing sites, stopped calling pool companies for quotes. In the end, Fiammetta spent her summers at the sea anyway. What did she need a pool for?

Just another reminder that their hands are tied in Tuscany.

"Don't worry, Lizzy. When we can afford a pool, we will install one."

"In the meantime, why not put in a little pool? Like a Jacuzzi."

Why not? Elizabeth is right: if they wait until they are ready to install a real pool, years might pass. If they lay the blame of being pool-less in Tuscany on Fiammetta's doorstep, what's stopping them now in Sicily? A little pool might be the perfect solution.

"When does Electra arrive for the summer?"

"She flies into Palermo in ten days."

"Give her a big hug for me."

"I will."

"And if she borrows my clothes, tell her to put things back before she leaves. She still has my Champion sweatshirt that she borrowed last Christmas."

"Actually, I have it. Electra left it in the laundry basket. I wear it in the evenings. It warms me like a hug."

"Oh, in that case, enjoy it."

For several days Niccolò and Kate wander the property looking for the right place to install a pool.

"What if we made it look like a pond?" Kate asks, pausing at a spot that has granite outcropping, which might, somehow, be incorporated into a pool design.

"What about a fountain?" Niccolò suggests, after they visit their friend Renato's estate in Trapani.

They cross off a Jacuzzi from the list as they aren't really interested in jet streams, just pure, clear water.

Sunday afternoon, when Kate is on the phone with Carrie, her best friend from high school, Niccolò tip-toes into the living room and whispers, "When you finish, I've found the place for the pool."

Kate covers the mouthpiece. "Give me five minutes."

A few minutes later, Kate joins him on the patio. "Where?"

"There!"

Bordering their patio is a large flowerbed, about eight feet by five. It is filled with earth from which grows a bush of rosemary, another of sage and a scattering of low-lying strawberry plants. It is where Figaro goes when he wants to soak up sun without having to worry about Edoardo's dogs' impromptu visits. The massive outer wall of this flowerbed sustains the patio, and is built of the same square stones that have been used to construct the pillars of the patio itself.

"*Bravo!*" If Kate squints past the plants, she can see that he has found the perfect place for their pool. In fact, it looks like it was destined to be a pool, but someone mistakenly filled it with plants.

It is just large enough for two people.

And it has been right in front of them all this time.

"All we have to do is empty it of earth."

"We'll be enjoying our pool this time next week!"

Naturally, it takes much longer to realize the pool than they think it will, but that afternoon they start digging. First they have to find a place to transplant the rosemary, sage and strawberries. Then they have to build a pulley device to lift out the buckets full of dirt that Niccolò is digging, which Kate overturns into the wheelbarrow and distributes along their driveway.

Three back-breaking days later, they are still digging.

"How deep did you say you wanted to make it?" Kate asks, tired and ready to quit.

"Deep enough to have water up to here—" He indicates his chest, "when I stand up."

They have three-quarters more to excavate.

Every morning they dig and haul away earth, another six to eight inches. Every afternoon Edoardo stops by to measure their progress, to mock them for how slowly they are progressing. He makes fun of them for wanting a pool at all. Kate assumes he is teasing them because the sea is so close at hand, but Edoardo, like many islanders, has a negative disposition towards the sea. He is right: in every family, in the not-too-distant past, there is a drowned mariner. However, if one is inclined to enjoy the water, his reasoning continues, the sea is conspicuously close. To him it makes no sense that they are building a pool.

Their logic differs: there are some days when they don't feel like driving to the sea. All they want is a half-hour of refreshment: a dip into cool water between one chore and the next. And in August, when every good Sicilian from all over the world returns home to visit his relatives, the normally empty beaches become crowded. A pool will let them retreat from the August crowds and still let them have the pleasure of water.

They can see by the way Edoardo lifts his chin that he is not convinced.

Edoardo's afternoon visits give them an excuse to stop and rest. Kate's back is aching, and Niccolò is tired, too. Kate brings out wine and tea, then cheese and bread sticks to absorb the alcohol. The dogs that trail Edoardo position themselves at the bottom of the steps. "Is that a new one?" Kate asks, noticing a small, skinny, black-and-white pup, his head cocked to one side like the RCA megaphone dog of her childhood.

"I found him in the garden this morning, waiting his turn for whatever food was leftover. I started to throw a stick at him. I have enough dogs to think about without adding another, but he moved toward me, so trusting. How could I send him away? *Vieni qui*—Come here, Nica!"

"*Nica!* You can't call him *Nica!*" Kate protests. "That's my nickname."

"All right, then. *Mica. Vieni qui!*"

Up the patio stairs Mica stumbles, tripping over himself, happy to be received by his Savior, regardless of his name. The other dogs follow—six or seven, too many to count—to settle under the table at Edoardo's feet.

As Edoardo bends down to touch their heads, Kate spies a package of cigarettes poking out of his pocket. "Edoardo! I thought you had stopped."

"I have. Well, almost. I can't drop to less than three a day." He breaks off a bit of breadstick and feds it to Orecchiella, who has, against the odds of short-legged anatomy, jumped onto his lap. With feigned subterfuge, Edoardo tosses the remaining pieces of breadstick down the stairs, after which the other dogs, which Edoardo knows aren't really welcome on the terrace, obediently return to their station. *Mica* stays by Edoardo's feet, unsure into which class he falls, the one allowed onto Edoardo's lap or the ones who must stay off the terrace. "Worse," Edoardo continues, "I think about cigarettes all day, the way I used to think about women."

With notable difficulty, Edoardo has reduced his forty cigarettes a day to thirty, twenty, ten and finally three, struggling to overcome a fifty year addiction because he understands that their concern is an expression of affection for him, for his family; for his eventual grandchildren.

"How many today?" Kate asks, both morning and evening.

Her strategies and maneuvers to help him quit smoking have earned her the nick-name Patton, which he qualifies quickly, never wanting to offend, by admitting his utmost respect for that American General. Kate prefers his other nick-names for her, *Lady Kate* or *Nica Nica*, which means "little one". Given Kate's height, it takes an impressive figure of a man to call her little, without appearing ridiculous.

"But once you stop altogether, a week without any cigarettes, the nicotine will leave your body, and you will be free. The desire will pass."

Again he raises his chin, not convinced. "Besides, what's the point?" He removes a handkerchief from an inside pocket, presses it against his forehead. "It's an awful lot of work for nothing."

"But you can recuperate many years of life. You are still young!"

He waves his hand in the air, dismissing her compliment. "How old do you think I am?" He squints at Kate, offering a challenge.

From the age of his sons—twenty-five and twenty-six—and from Angelica's age, Kate will guess sixty-five, although based solely on appearances and mannerisms, Kate would have thought him much older.

"Sixty-five? Sixty-six?"

"Sixty-six exactly! Someone has been talking!"

"Sixty-six is young," says Niccolò.

"It is. And I have had a good life. But I don't want to give up those last three cigarettes."

"Don't you want to enjoy your grandchildren in good health?" He nods, thoughtfully, as if considering her point. "They need to know their Nonno Edoardo full of energy and strength." He nods again, envisioning his grandchildren perhaps, the tricks he will play on them, the manners he will be sure they learn. "You can live to be eighty-five, Edoardo!"

He laughs, breaking his contemplation. "*Nica*, if I live to eighty-five, I will give you a diamond!"

"If you live to eighty-five, Edoardo, that will be my diamond!"

"Anyway, these aren't cigarettes. He pulls out a *Nazionali Esportazione* cigarette pack from his shirt pocket and taps out a folded square of newspaper. "They are seeds. *Agastache. Labiatae.*"

"Is it what you have growing behind your fish pond?" Long spikes with abundant swirls of white flowers and liquorice-scented leaves; they attract the most amazing assortment of butterflies, varieties Kate hasn't seen since she was a child in California.

"The same plant, but those by the pond are Liquorice Whites. These are Liquorice Blues. I have them on the far side of the lemon grove."

The lemon trees on Kate and Niccolò's property are dwarfed; they have produced little despite being well fertilized and pruned. Edoardo's lemon trees are magnificent, tall and broad-limbed, the leaves shiny and healthy, not shriveled by frost; their boughs so heavy with lemons it hurts Kate's back to look at them. Edoardo's secret is that many years ago when he inherited the property, he planted cypress all around it. His lemon trees are protected from the salty mist rising up from the sea as well as the bitter cold wafting down from Erice. In short, he has sacrificed his view for his lemons.

"Wait. I want to write down the name of the seeds. Spell it for me?"

He hands her a pen, a scrap of paper he has in his pocket. Slowly, he proceeds. "F-l-o-w-e-r."

"F-u-n-n-y."

There is writing on the side of the pen: *Scaduto Agenzia Funeraria.* Kate laughs. She passes the pen to Niccolò. He laughs, too. Roughly translated, *Scaduto* means Expired. It is the family name of a Funeral Agency.

"Does the name come from the profession or the profession from their name?"

"Good question. They've been undertakers for a long time. They buried my grandfather. And my father. I always ask for a pen when I see them. It's the only way I can be sure I'll have it back when someone borrows one from me."

Kate hands him back the pen.

"She and I," Edoardo says to Niccolò, "work wonders in our gardens. At this altitude, with the severe weather changes, every blossom we realize is a miracle."

150

He rises to leave, drying his forehead with his handkerchief before putting it back into his coat pocket.

"You need another glass of wine. You are perspiring."

He wags a finger in refusal. "Not even wine will help today, it is so hot. I told Angelica to ready our bedroom. I'm sleeping here tonight. If she wants to return to the city, she can, alone." He tucks his pen back into this pocket. "I will send up Matteo this afternoon to give you a hand with the digging."

"Thanks. We'll see you later."

"Inshallah." Edoardo rises, and as if at court, his choral of attendant dogs rise simultaneously.

After Edoardo leaves, Kate says to Niccolò, "We should go down to visit Edoardo's garden this afternoon, give him the satisfaction of viewing his flowers."

"Right after lunch."

Matteo stops by to dig for awhile, but after he fills one wheelbarrow, they insist he stop. He is younger and more muscular than they are, he has a strong sense of duty, but they have to be careful or he will wear himself out helping them.

"Guess what I found this morning tucked under the rosemary hedge in front of our house?" he says. "Four puppies! I was watering the garden when a little ball of dark fur started growling at me."

"Sandy's puppies?" Sandy is an abandoned beagle-mix who has been pregnant repeatedly since Edoardo took her in.

"No, not Sandy's." Again they are settled on the terrace, this time with water and cookies still warm from the oven. "One of the shepherd's dogs."

"More dogs," Niccolò says, looking out at the audience of mournful brown eyes which have followed Matteo up from his house, alert for a thrown crumb, a moment of attention. "Just what this valley needs."

"*Davvero*—how true." Matteo registers the tarnish on the other side of the coin, but like his father he can't deny the needs of these dogs. He can't say no to just one more hungry mouth. However, unlike his father who is retired and has time to sit in the sun and enjoy the company of the dogs, Matteo has the job of feeding them. And unlike Kate, who buys a large bag of dried kibble every two weeks, Matteo and his father stop at the butcher's shop every other day to pick up a trunk-load of

151

chicken carcasses, which they cook, together with pounds of pasta, for the dogs each day. Clover has taken to leaving his dry food, slipping down to join the banquet, and Niccolò threatened to do the same the other day when Kate tried to feed him sandwiches for lunch two days in a row.

Matteo's hand hovers over the plate of almond-oatmeal cookies, his eyebrows raised in question.

"Help yourself. You don't need to ask. Whatever you don't finish, I'll send home with you."

The actual amount of digging Matteo does isn't significant, but they feel better after he leaves, knowing they aren't the only ones who tire from this hard, physical work.

CHAPTER THIRTEEN

The sunrise this morning was sublime, with towering mountains of black clouds erupting over Custonaci; the predawn light eerily illuminating them from behind. The sun itself was the focal point of this morning's photographs, like the core of a volcano. Kate stood at their upstairs hallway window witnessing the gateway to their day, shivering as she clicked the shutter, as the sky lightened, until the clouds dispersed. Then, with the sun high in the sky, losing all traces of its earlier mystery, Kate crawled back under the warmth of the covers to replay the scene until it was late enough to convince Niccolò it was time for coffee.

Removing the earth to create a pool is a more strenuous job than Kate imagined, and once again she wonders if they should stop doing the work themselves to find someone to give them a hand. The deeper they dig, the harder it is to haul out the buckets of earth. Each bucket must weight thirty kilograms—almost seventy pounds. Each filled wheelbarrow is more than ninety kilograms. Each time Kate returns with another one emptied, she glances at the front gate, hoping someone will drop by to give them an excuse to relax.

When Edoardo does stop by, it is almost noon and his stay is brief. They don't even have time to climb out of their pit before he is on his way again.

When they have emptied the flowerbed to nearly six feet, they stop. "It's deep enough," Kate insists, even though they will lose some depth when the cement floor is laid.

"I'm tempted to fill it full of water straight away," Niccolò says. "I'd gratefully lie in mud right now."

On Tuesday, freed from digging their pool, Niccolò and Kate decide to relax and make cheese. Their cupboard is almost empty.

The phone rings. It is Electra. "We are heating milk for the cheese. Can I call you later?"

"Call me as soon as you finish."

"Is everything OK?"

"Yes. I spoke with Elizabeth."

"How is she? Where is she?"

"She's in Boston. She went whale watching yesterday."

"Lucky her!"

"She's having the best time! She and Stephen saw twenty whales. She said it is rare to see more than a few together."

"Amazing!"

"But she says you and Daddy are building something, and she wouldn't tell me what it is."

"It's a surprise. You have to see it yourself."

"That's not going to help me concentrate on my final exams."

"Gotta run. The milk is going to scald."

"*Ciao!*"

By now they are old dairy pros, their mistakes are limited, a little spill here, a splatter there, but the cheeses taste exactly as they would if they bought them from a dairy farm, and have the right consistency, too. However, as with the first time, Kate and Niccolò stand in awe when they lift the lid to witness the transformation from liquid to solid. It is, in their humble opinion, a miracle.

"Actually," their friend Eugenio says, "a miracle is an event that appears to be contrary to the laws of nature. This is simple chemistry."

"Thank you, Dr. Webster."

Some people don't understand when they are brought face to face with a miracle.

Actually, the more Kate thinks about it, the more she is aware that they are surrounded by miracles, all those little things they take for granted but don't really understand how

154

they work, from the sun's significance to the forming of an egg; how a radio can duplicate Handel's *Water Music* so clearly, so precisely; how the bees make honey and how the bears know to steal it. Eugenio would laugh at her, Kate knows, but it is hard not to be impressed with the workings of the world.

Just before lunch, Kate drives down the hill with two kilos of fresh *ricotta* for Angelica and the top layer of soft white cheese for Edoardo. Like a penitent to a priest, Edoardo has confessed that no matter how much *cagliata* they give him, he can't resist but to finish it all in one sitting, so Kate has divided it into three containers. She always drives to their house, going out to the road, which curves and widens before reaching their driveway, a road rutted and difficult to traverse. It is a much shorter walk through the fields, but if Kate arrives by foot Edoardo will insist on chauffering her home.

"Come in, come in," Edoardo hurries out to greet her; Angelica is right behind him, drying her hands on an apron.

"I can't stay." Kate gives Angelica the tray of cheeses, explains what they are, for whom they are intended. "I must hurry home, but we wanted you to have the cheeses while they were still warm."

"Thank you," Angelica hugs the gift to her chest. As she is always cold, even mid-summer; she is enjoying the heat from the cheeses. "Wait, I'll wrap up some eggs for you."

"Another time, Angelica. Thanks."

"Have you seen the puppies?"

Kate bends down to peer into the darkness of the undergrowth, and finds eight bright, startled eyes staring back at her. "Have you seen the mother?"

"Yes, she's one of the shepherd's dogs. I'm not sure which one. There are two with full milk sacks. She's around here, somewhere."

"I'm sorry I have to go. I left Niccolò in the kitchen with the *ricotta*."

"Poor fool. He should know better!" Edoardo walks with her through his front garden to the car. "I am going to have to pull out these daisies." He indicates a lush spread of healthy plants. "They are crowding the lillies. Look!"

Kate needs to go. Niccolò is going to be annoyed to be left with the cleaning up, the least miraculous part of the cheese-making process. Hastily, Kate shifts her eyes from the hardy daisies to the compromised lillies. In the midst of the calla leaves, still mostly scrolled shut, rises one splendid black lilly.

"Do you want to see the Agastache Liquorice Blue?"

"Next time, Edoardo, I'd love to. I really need to go home."

He holds the car door open for her, bows his head. "At least you saw the black lilly."

At first light there is a smoke signal spiraling from the other side of the valley, another farmer up early, clearing his fields, which reminds Kate that they should burn their accumulated cuttings as well. Soon, the *Forestale* will prohibit burning for the remainder of the summer.

Just after lunch, Niccolò drives down the hill with the leftover whey from the cheese, which Edoardo's dogs drink. He, too, only stays a minute.

"Did you see the puppies?" Kate asks, accepting a beautiful pear cake that Angelica has made.

"No. Apparently the mother just moved them again." He hands her the black lilly. "This is for you, from your secret admirer."

"Ah!" The lily is still furled but less than yesterday; half closed, half open.

"We must visit Edoardo and Angelica this afternoon."

"We'll wait until it cools down. We will bring them a fresh pecorino."

Kate glances at her watch when she hears Edoardo's tractor start up. It is five o'clock. She wishes he wouldn't work in this heat, but she understands the temptation to mow for a few hours before dinner. Kate carries out a basket of laundry to hang on the line behind the house. The sun is so strong she has to be careful not to let the colors fade. Even the whites turn yellow where they are folded over the line. Laundry is a problem in Erice. In the spring it doesn't dry; there is too much humidity, no matter how much wind there is. In the summer the colors fade.

An hour later, as Kate returns outdoors to check on the laundry, she sees Matteo's old Renault speed past their gate. He doesn't slow down to wave as he usually does, nor does he honk the horn. Then Kate sees an ambulance speeding behind him.

"Nicco!" Niccolò is upstairs in his study. "Nicco! Come! Quickly!"

He is down the stairs in an instant; his cellphone ringing. It is Angelica. She is desperate.

"The tractor has overturned! *O Madonna!* Edoardo is under the tractor!" Kate can hear her hysteria searing from the phone as well as through the airwaves, her voice carrying uphill, an echo, a hiccup. "Hurry! *Hurry!* Please *Please! Auito!*"

Niccolò grabs Kate's hand and they run through the fields, but after the first clumsy, tandem steps he leaves her to race ahead. He is already sliding down the decline that separates their two properties while Kate still has half a field to cross. It isn't far but the ground has been recently turned, it is full of big clods, and Kate is wearing sandals. Her slowness infuriates her but she can't go any faster. Instead, she convinces herself that Edoardo is fine. He will be fine. He is tough. He is strong. This isn't the first time he has overturned his tractor. It will make another great story.

He is strong. He is tough. He will be fine.

Finally, on level ground, Kate picks up speed.

But where are they? Kate runs past their house, through the tangle of Edoardo's garden. There is no one in sight.

"Nicco! Angelica!"

She can hear Matteo's car and the ambulance bumping down the long, potholed drive as Kate reaches the field behind their house. Where is everyone?

"Niccolò!"

At the top of a very steep field behind the house, the grass waist tall where it hasn't yet been turned under, Kate sees Niccolò.

He is kneeling down beside the overturned tractor.

She sees Angelica.

Finally, Kate sees Edoardo.

Matteo reaches his father at the same time Kate does, and together he and Niccolò pull Edoardo out from under the tractor.

Edoardo hasn't been crushed, he looks peaceful, a bit like he's had too much to drink and has lain down to doze in the rich, dark earth.

Niccolò breaks the idyllic illusion. He thumps hard on Edoardo's chest. Kate kneels down in the dirt by Edoardo's head, unties the sweatshirt from around her waist, nestles it beneath his head.

"Edoardo!"

Angelica is a distance away, watching; not watching.

They need to keep Edoardo with them.

"Edoardo!"

The ambulance drivers finally appear. What in the hell have they been doing? Admiring the view? Taking time for a smoke? They come toward them slowly, carrying heavy equipment up the steep hill. One kneels down and thumps Edoardo's heart but gently, ineffectively, without conviction.

Niccolò takes his place, resumes his thumping.

"Edoardo! *Stai con noi!* Stay with us!"

Kate holds Edoardo's hand, squeezes his fingers. Kate doesn't know if he is alive or not. He must be. How can they tell? With every last ounce of his strength, Niccolò pumps at Edoardo's heart.

Kate cradles his head, continues to call his name. "Edoardo!"

After what seems an eternity, a doctor arrives. He moves Niccolò to one side. He gives Edoardo some kind of shot. Adrenalin? The men are speaking among themselves, the doctor, the ambulance drivers, Matteo, Niccolò.

"Do something!" Kate pleads.

"Signora. É inutile. Lui non c'é piu'."

"Edoardo?"

It is pointless.

"Edoardo?"

He is not here; but far away.

There is nothing else to do.

The noise of life begins again. Angelica moves as if on automatic pilot, putting a pair of Edoardo's pajamas into a suitcase. There are issues to solve, thank heavens, something for her to think about other than Edoardo's abrupt, absolute absence.

Angelica must resolve where to transport Edoardo's body, and quickly. Should they lay him out here or bring him down to their house in Trapani?

She looks at Kate uncomprehendingly, as if Kate has spoken to her in English. She seems unable to focus on the question enough to form a decision. Angelica shakes her head, her pink scalp disturbingly visible through her thin hair.

"People will want to pay their respects," Angelica says eventually, as if recounting a dream.

Kate is sticking to her side, keeping close enough so that if she collapses Kate can catch her, but to be honest, Kate is of little help. She doesn't know what is expected on an occasion like this. There is the right thing to be done, but she doesn't have a clue what it is.

It occurs to Kate that she doesn't have to make decisions. Kate replays Angelica's questions so she can hear them anew. "People will want to pay their respects. Is it better to bring him into the house here or in town?"

"I don't know. It's so crowded here."

They don't really have a living room here, the downstairs to their house is the kitchen with a long table, lots of chairs. Where would they lay out a body? The upstairs has two bedrooms but they are both small; the staircase connecting the upstairs to the down is external.

"There is more room in town?" Kate knows the answer. Kate has been to their house many times.

"Yes. Town would be better."

But there is a problem, it turns out, bringing Edoardo into town. He has died in Erice. His residence is in Trapani. The ambulance isn't authorized to cross communities transporting a corpse. In addition, they can't do anything at all until the police arrive. It needs to be ascertained that Edoardo has died of natural causes, that no foul play has been involved. It would be too easy, it seems, for an enemy to slip in and end a life, making it seem like an accident.

This scenario seems ridiculous but apparently it is an issue.

Two issues that need to be resolved.

"Niccolò? Can you call the *Maresciallo*?"

They are friendly with Erice's Chief of Police, Antonio Croce, a friendship that started when they were returning home from the sea one day, hot and sandy, looking forward to a shower and lunch, when they found the road closed for a bicycle race. The officer in charge told them there was nothing to do but wait— two or three hours, she couldn't be more specific. Niccolò spied the authorative cap of the Chief of Police a few feet away and went to explain the situation. "Follow me!" the Marshall said, switching on his siren. They had a police escort to their house, and they have been friends ever since.

What a simple, carefree memory!

Eventually, the Marshall arrives, and fills out a report. Niccolò signs as testimony that he and Matteo found Edoardo under the overturned tractor. Matteo resolves the ambulance's problem by calling the Scaduto funeral service his family has dealt with in the past, and they agree to drive up to claim the body. They will transport Edoardo's body to the house in Trapani and prepare it for the final viewing.

It is dark and cold now as they wait for the funeral service to arrive with their hearse.

Niccolò stops Kate as she starts to climb the hill again.

"I want to go."

"It's dark, and the terrain is uneven."

He is right. It is totally dark now. Cofano is present by its absence: a blank space where stars should be. Kate leans her head against Niccolò's shoulder. "I can't stop thinking of Edoardo lying in the dirt up on the hill."

He places his lips near her ear, then whispers, "Think of him embracing the land he loved, one last time. That's the image I'm holding."

"I want to go see him."

"I will come with you."

"No. Stay with Angelica."

"Are you sure?"

"I need to see Edoardo."

Edoardo isn't there. His body lies in the same position but there is no mistaking that he might be alive.

"*Signora?*" The ambulance attendants are leaning against a tree, two sturdy, strong men, neither of them young. Kate can see the red glow of their cigarettes burning in the dark.

She was a fool to insist that Edoardo quit smoking.

"I would like to take my sweatshirt."

"Is this it?" The older attendant retrieves a wadded bunch of gray fabric lying at the base of an olive tree.

"Yes." She recognizes it even in the dark. Kate bought it for Elizabeth when her daughter was thirteen. Just the right weight for both summer or winter, it became her favorite piece of clothing. But when Elizabeth was leaving for university, Electra convinced her to give it up. 'I can't stand seeing that sweatshirt any more, you've been wearing it for five years." So Elizabeth left it behind, and Kate wears it all the time, much to Electra's annoyance.

"Do you need anything?" Kate asks the paramedics, wrapping the sweatshirt back around her waist. She is cold but it doesn't seem right to wear it. "Water? Coffee?"

"No, we have everything we need." The older attendent's voice is deep and craggy. "We will stay here until the funeral attendants arrive. We need to keep the dogs away."

The other man shines a flashlight, casting a circle of light around *Mica* and Sandy, Russ and *Orecchiella*, huddled together at Edoardo's feet. "They won't go away. I've even tried throwing stones."

"No, don't throw rocks. He was their champion. They owe him their lives."

Who is going to take care of all these dogs?

When it is time for the funeral attendants to carry Edoardo's body down the hill, Kate brings Angelica into the kitchen. Matteo stays to help the attendants. Niccolò, too.

There is pasta sauce on the stove, a plate of sliced eggplant ready to fry, dinner preparations interrupted. At the table, in Edoardo's place, there are letters open, a magazine; the saints he collected; a bottle of Coca Cola filled two-thirds with cold coffee.

"Do you want to bring this food with you to town?"

"I might as well."

"I'll start a bag. You decide what to put into it."

"See if there is anything in the refrigerator that will spoil." Angelica is eerily calm.

Kate opens the door. On a shelf next to a bowl of fruit Kate sees a container of *cagliata*. Why didn't she put it all into one big bowl and let him enjoy it to his heart's content? Why did she push him to stop smoking, when he obviously loved to smoke? She sees the futility of her insistence. He had never intended to live a long life. If only Kate had taken the time to walk through his garden with him yesterday, to admire his flowers. At least she could have given him that.

Kate has flowers in the house that Edoardo brought on Monday, two agapanthus, one white, one blue, both of which have started to wither, and the black lilly. Kate has just been out wandering through her front yard, marvelling at how many plants have come from Edoardo's garden.

Who will admire her flowers now?

It occurs to her with painful clarity that much of the work Kate has done in this garden has been to gain Edoardo's approval, knowing he'd drop by and admire her efforts. Now, who will tell her when it is time to transplant a palm, the lillies? Why didn't Kate write down all the things he told her?

It is another beautiful day. Nature's spectacle continues as if nothing has changed. But she is moving slowly, as is Niccolò. Their hearts are heavy, their feet are made of clay.

Edoardo's last words to her were, "At least you saw the black lilly."

Kate has seen it, and it has touched her deeply.

Tomorrow morning she will give it back to him.

They are late. Kate has already locked up the house but Niccolò runs back inside. He has forgotten something.

"Nicco! We are late!"

"Do you want me to die of a heart attack, too? Stop rushing me!"

They are both on edge. The funeral starts in thirty minutes, that's not the problem; the problem will be to find a parking space with all of Erice attending Edoardo's funeral.

She stands under the massive pine trees, holds open the gate while Niccolò backs out the car. Just outside the gate is a six-foot cactus; from it a single bloom. As if on time-release, it opens, all at once, a huge white flower, its pistil tingling, as if just awakened from a long rest.

"Nicco! Oh my God! Look!"

"I thought we were in a hurry."

"But look! That flower. It opened while I was standing here. It's a miracle."

"Are you coming, or am I going to the funeral alone?"

Kate climbs into the car, subdued. They speed up the hill. At the second curve in the road, Niccolò puts his hand on top of hers. "Sorry."

She feels a lump form in her throat. If she starts crying now she'll be lost. "Sorry I rushed you."

"I don't like funerals."

"I don't like death."

La Matrice, the cathedral in Erice, is packed. They move through the crowd unseeingly, a few hands reaching out to claim theirs, but Kate doesn't know or care to know to whom they belong. They find a seat at the front, on the side, where the choir usually sits. From here Kate can see Angelica in the front row, limp like a wrung out dish cloth. Yesterday, at her home, hostess to the continual flow of people who had come to pay their final respects, she was dry-eyed, composed; the only sign of weakness was the force with which she gripped their hands. Today she is crying uncontrollably. Each person who comes forward to embrace her releases a new store of tears. She seems smaller than usual, as if the tears she's shedding were part of her composition; as if her significance died with Edoardo.

She is held up on each side by her two sons, Matteo and Sergio: two pillars of strength, an illusion compromised by the tears flowing unchecked down their faces.

Edoardo's coffin is covered completely with large, elaborate, expensive flower compositions. Kate can imagine his dismissive, irreverent gesture. *"Esagerato!* Exaggerated! Overdone!" Or maybe he would like them? There is certainly a wide variety to choose from. He always had more than one reaction, as if he were playing all the parts in any given drama.

Shy of her own part in this drama, Kate waits until a family surrounds Angelica, so she can move into the nave of the church unnoticed. Kate lays the single black lilly onto Edoardo's casket, tucks it into the handle as there is no more space on the top or sides.

The lilly gives her a place to focus during the ceremony. Kate is sure she sees it quiver. She can't look at Matteo or Sergio, so sturdy and tall, young and strong; so vulnerable: pillars of salt consumed by rain. Angelica is unrecognizable, the black dress she is wearing seems sizes too large, as if she is diminishing before Kate's eyes. She listens, and doesn't listen, to the priest conducting the service. The familiar phrases and prayers that comfort and console Italians don't touch her; they remain words, void of meaning, even though many are the same psalms and prayers which move her so deeply in English.

> *He maketh me to lie down in green pastures:*
> *He leadeth me beside the still waters.*
> *He restoreth my soul*

Niccolò leads Kate out of the church as soon as the ceremony is over. They don't need to offer their condolences to the family; there will be time to speak with them later. Outside the church, as far away from the crowd as Kate can go without leaving the square, she rests her forehead against the ancient stones of the *Matrice*, walls that have witnessed every kind of human suffering for more than nine hundred years. She adds her sorrow to their collective memory.

The church bells clang, a sad, slow, empty reverberation that echoes down the narrow, cobbled streets of Erice, pouring down the hills like the perpetual fog. Eight strong men carry Edoardo's casket out of the church, among them Matteo and Sergio, keeping time to the slow, empty beat. All the flower compositions have been removed, are leaning beside the hearse awaiting the coffin, but the black lilly remains tucked into the handle.

Kate recalls the first time she saw Matteo, filled with grief as he transported the Madonna, as if that were the trial run for this greater sorrow.

164

As is the tradition, the crowd accompanies Edoardo's coffin to the city gate, a slow-moving, disorganized mull of people who were part of Edoardo's life.

Niccolò whispers into Kate's ear. "I understand now that Edoardo spent his days alone in the country because he preferred solitude, not because he lacked options for company."

They reach the gate and say goodbye, a quick hug to Matteo and Sergio.

The rest of the journey Edoardo will have to make alone.

As they are moving away, heading back to where they parked their car, Rosario elbows his way through the crowd to join them. He says, "I've fixed the appointment, *praticamente*, with the Notaio and Butterello for the 27th, at 9:30, *praticamente*, as you requested."

Kate starts to say something, but Niccolò, more composed, promises to call Rosario in a few days.

There is nothing to do but return home.

As Kate steps out of the car to open their gate, she sees the blossom on the cactus has withered. The only trace of its brief existence is a drab, brown hull.

Indoors, her vase is empty.

CHAPTER
FOURTEEN

The sunrise this morning was spectacular, if only for its total lack of color. Predawn was stark silhouettes, acute outlines; no broad strokes but all fine detail. When the sun did rise it happened as if offstage, or behind a curtain of clouds; it didn't bring color but gave the scene a sepia wash. It was beautiful, too, in a long-ago, far-away sense. Kate watched closely, but couldn't bring herself to photograph.

Into the abyss of their collective mourning, Electra arrives in Sicily, a bright light of health and happiness. At the arrival gate at Falcone Airport in Palermo, she hugs Kate with glee, not sadness, as they have been embraced repeatedly these days. In the car, they listen to the news of Electra's last days in Utrecht, a bicycle trip with friends through Hoge Veluwe National Park. Her astute observations of cultural differences between the Dutch and Italians are judicious but not cynical. Halfway to Trapani, with Segesta peeking down at them from its sacred perch high on its ancient hill, Niccolò looks at Kate, as if to say, it is time.

"Electra. I have some very sad news."

"Tell me it isn't Grandma Claire."

"No, Grandma Claire is fine." Kate hears her voice crack.

"Lizzy?"

"No. Elizabeth is fine. It's Edoardo."

"What—"

"He had an accident on his tractor on Monday. He's dead."

She is quiet for a minute. "Poor Angelica."

"Poor Angelica."

She is quiet as the news settles in. "When is the funeral?"

"The funeral was the day before yesterday."

"Is Sergio home?"

"He is. They flew him home immediately."

"Poor Sergio. Poor Matteo. Can I see them?"

"Of course."

"I'll go down as soon as we are home."

"They have gone back to town. It is easier for people to pay their respects in Trapani."

"Can we go down now?"

"Let's go home first. We can drive down this afternoon."

"Poor Edoardo."

"Yes. Poor Edoardo."

At home, Electra jumps out of the car to open the gate. "The garden is beautiful, Mama. You have been working hard." She pauses at the end of the second bank of flowers. "I especially like these colored lilies. I've never seen anything like them."

"Yes. Edoardo gave me the bulbs."

"You are going to miss him."

"Terribly." Kate doesn't tell her that she can't be bothered to water the plants in the garden since he died. What's the use, everything's going to die anyway?

"I'm going to miss him, too." Electra is dry-eyed, subdued. She gazes out at the view, but Kate can't tell if she is looking at Cofano or Edoardo's property.

"So," she says finally. "What is the big secret you haven't wanted to tell me on the phone?" A flicker of panic crosses her face, as if perhaps Edoardo's death has been their secret; then she recalls the enthusiasm with which they teased her and the pain in her eyes dissolves. "Not even Elizabeth would tell me. And I offered her several good bribes!"

Niccolò is unlocking the terrace door. "You have to find it. Look around."

"What am I looking for?"

"First clue. It's outdoors. You have ten guesses."

"You bought me a car?"

"Nine."

Electra circles the garden. "You planted the tulip bulbs I gave you for your birthday and want me to see the first shoots?"

"Eight."

"Wait! That was a joke! That doesn't count."

"Just keep looking."

Electra passes in front of the terrace and pauses, as if on an Easter egg hunt. She doesn't know the measure of what she is seeking. Instinctively, she takes the steps up onto the terrace and looks over the wall, into the structure where they have been digging.

"Surprise!"

She smiles, vaguely. "What is it?"

"We wanted to have it completed before you arrived, but it has taken us longer than we expected. Then we were interrupted."

"But what is it?"

"It's a little pool."

"Oh! Cool."

"Won't it be wonderful?"

"I'm sure it will be." She must sense her parents' disappointment. She looks again into the pit. "I am sorry I'm not more enthusiastic. I think I must be tired."

"Why don't you lie down until lunch?"

"Thanks. I might sleep for an hour."

"I'll call you when it's ready."

"Thanks." She tries to rally. "The pool will be great. Really."

Niccolò and Kate stand together looking down into the pit. "Electra is right, it doesn't look like much."

"It will. We'll start working on it again." She doesn't have the benefit of their vision: clear, sparkling water, inviting beneath the hot, summer sun. "Once it is finished, it will be hard to remove her from the water."

"We'll have to take turns in our two-person pool."

"Time to wake up, Electra." Kate rubs her foot, which is sticking out from under the pink-and-white bedspread. "Lunch is ready."

"Mama?"

"What honey?"

"Would you mind if we didn't drive down to Trapani to see Angelica today?"

"All right. Why?"

"I don't know. I think I will be better prepared tomorrow. Is that too rude?"

"I don't think they are holding a stopwatch. They know you cared for Edoardo."

"I know. I do." She shifts, straightens the cover, exposes two books on the bed beside her: *The Brothers Lionheart* and *The Poisonwood Bible*, both so consumed and dog-eared they remind Kate of Electra's baby blanket of which only a tattered corner remains. "It's strange," she continues. "I don't really feel that Edoardo's gone. But I feel terrible for Angelica and Matteo and poor Sergio." Her lip quivers. "What are they going to do without him?"

"I don't know." They are quiet for a moment. "But they have each other, which is already a lot more than some people have, and they have many friends, lots of family, who will look after them."

"But what can *we* do?"

"I've been asking myself the same question." Kate strokes her daughter's other foot, which has also appeared from under the cover. "For the moment, we can just let them know that we care. In a little bit, we can offer distraction."

"I can ask Angelica to pick blackberries with me. I can ask her to teach me to make a *crostata*."

"Exactly. In a week or two. In the meantime, we'll stop by and sit with them."

"Can we bring them cookies?"

"I think cookies would be a good idea. We'll make them after lunch."

"Mama?"

"What, honey?"

"After lunch, when it's not so hot, can you show me where Edoardo died?"

"Of course. If you are sure. It isn't a very happy place."

"I know. But it might make it more real to me."

The heat has left the air but still clings to the earth. Kate can feel it boiling up beneath her boots as Electra and she tromp through the fields.

As the crow flies, the field where Edoardo's tractor overturned is less than a hundred meters from their house. After an aborted attempt to traverse a barrier of cactus animated with pink prickly-pears, they take the long way around; their usual route. Electra calls for the dogs as they pass through Edoardo's garden, as Kate notes that the smaller leafed plants have wilted. As they trudge up the hill Electra continues to call for the dogs. Finally, Sandy appears, fat and slow-moving. "How is it possible that she's still waiting for puppies?" Electra remarks. "She was pregnant when I left at Easter."

"She had that liter. She's pregnant again."

"Mama, we have to fix her."

"That would be one thing we could do to help."

The tractor is still there, dented, overturned, the ground underneath darkened with spilled diesel fuel. The ambulance attendants have not cleaned up after themselves: there is an empty water bottle tossed under a tree, a pair of gloves removed carelessly or quickly, left discarded half inside-out. The disposable thermal sheet which they used to cover Edoardo has been wadded up and left near the rear tractor tire.

"Not exactly the memorial site I had hoped to find," Electra says gloomily.

Kate gathers up the crumpled and discarded objects, then kneels down, reaches under the tractor for a second plastic water bottle; then snatches her hand away.

"What is it?"

"Something snarled at me."

Electra is on her knees, peering under the tractor. *"Orecchiella! Vieni qui!"*

Orecchiella peers at them with unforgiving eyes and doesn't budge. They extend their hands as far as they can reach under the tractor. He sniffs their scent but keeps his distance.

After a few minutes of gentle coaxing, Electra says, "I am going back to the house to get some food."

"Clover's kibble is downstairs. There's an extra food bowl under the sink. Bring some water, too."

Kate sits under the olive tree while Electra is gone; from this angle she can see Orecchiella crouched beneath the tractor, and he can see her. His dark, worried eyes challenge her offer of concern and his unreasonably large ears swivel away from her words of comfort.

Edoardo's boots lie where they fell or were thrown. Kate knows these boots, part of his work outfit, as familiar to her as the outdated, formal suits he wore to and from town, the heirloom watch chain looping from his vest pocket. The boots are sturdy leather, thick soled; constructed to prevent accidents. Kate places them neatly side-by-side where his body fell, the first step toward constructing a memorial.

Electra is back. Her face is red and sweaty. She has obviously been running. Kate can see tear tracks in the dust on her face. She pours water from a plastic bottle into one side of the dog food bowl, kibble into the other. She splashes a little water onto the kibble, and then dumps chopped meat onto the kibble mush.

"I hope you don't mind, I took some roast beef."

"It was tonight's dinner."

"I left us some."

Electra lies on her stomach, inching as close to Orecchiella as he will permit, the food bowl extended in front of her.

Orecchiella growls.

"Orecchiella, it's me. Come on!"

"Leave the food. When he's hungry, he'll eat."

"I hope you are right." She pushes the bowl closer to the dog.

Orecchiella growls. He will not be comforted.

The last time they were at Angelica's, the house was full of people paying their respects to Edoardo. Every room was crowded with friends and relatives. Even the steps outside their house were full, Matteo and his friends crying openly.

Today the house is empty. Kate is glad they have all come. Electra embraces Angelica, which wrenches loose a sob. Electra steps back, smiles brightly through wet eyes and says, "You know we love you, don't you?"

Angelica's body heaves another sob but no tears appear: the well must be running dry. She leads Electra, Niccolò and Kate into the kitchen but forgets to ask them to sit. "You were his newest friends, his closest friends. He always said that."

Matteo tumbles into the room. "Oh, Electra!" He tries to build up enthusiasm.

"*Fratello mio.* I am so sorry about Edoardo."

Matteo shrugs, the muscle in his jaw straining. "Sit down. Please." Matteo gathers a sheaf of letters, stacks them on the sideboard next to a box of black rimmed note cards. "Would you like something to drink?"

Kate, Niccolò and Electra all decline.

"Mamma?"

"No. Nothing."

Matteo is frustrated. "She's not drinking. She is hardly eating. She is getting too weak."

"I think I will have something to drink after all," Electra says. "I hadn't realized how thirsty I am."

"A glass of juice does sound good, now that you mention it," Niccolò adds.

"Yes, I am thirsty, too," Kate says.

Matteo fills everyone's glass with juice. "Mamma?"

"Just a drop."

As if he hasn't heard her, he fills her glass almost to the rim.

Electra brings out the box of cookies, unwraps the paper and places the box in the center of the table. Matteo takes one for himself and hands one to his mother. "Yum!" He smacks his lips, the way Kate used to encourage her infants to try unfamiliar foods.

Sergio comes into the room. He has been sleeping. The tee-shirt he has thrown on is inside out. Aside from the funeral, they haven't seen him since he was called home from Lebanon.

"I am so glad you are home again." Electra says, hugging him.

"Me, too, but I wish it were for different circumstances."

"Of course."

Sergio sits for a minute, then stands again, restless. He is physically imposing, several inches taller than they are and solid muscle. In addition to his job with the military, when he is stationed in Trapani he works evenings as a bouncer. He's the guy at the gate who refuses entry to potential trouble, the one who calls a cab at the end of the evening for those who have had too much to drink. He would be an intimidating presence, except for a slight lisp, which cracks through his tough guy façade, a Sylvester the Cat without claws.

Electra has developed a relationship with both brothers. Matteo is her twin: they both love animals and are happiest exploring a hillside ruin or constructing an elaborate sand castle. Electra has also befriended Matteo's girlfriend, making sure that Tana understands that Electra isn't competition.

Sergio, on the other hand, is a player. Edoardo obviously made things clear to his son as Sergio treats Electra with the respect he would show his best friend's sister, which frees her to tease him like an elder brother. They adore each other.

Sergio leaves the room to smoke a cigarette, and Electra follows. Kate can see them talking in the little garden beyond the kitchen, shaded by lemon and mandarin trees. Matteo stays at the table with them, filling glasses with juice, passing cookies toward his mother. When he gets up to answer the phone, Angelica says, "The boys trade shifts. They don't leave me alone. I can barely go to the bathroom without company! Matteo waits until Sergio returns before going off to feed the animals. Sergio waits to go out at night until Matteo returns."

"You are fortunate to have both your sons at home. Are you sleeping?"

"Yes. I am exhausted. I can barely crawl into bed at the end of the day."

"It's good that you are sleeping."

"They have Tana sleep with me. It's so strange. I wake up in the night, look over and instead of Edoardo, who made quite a mountain under the bed sheets, there is this little lump of a girl.

"And last night I had the strangest dream!" she continues. She takes a sip of juice, recalling. "I dreamt that Edoardo was here, except it wasn't here but in the country. He was dressing up in a heavy black cloak. I didn't see his face but I could tell it was him by his voice, his posture. I called to him. 'Edoardo! Where are you going?' 'Up to Niccolò and Kate's,' he said. 'Dressed like that? You will scare them out of their wits!' He laughed. 'That's the whole idea, my dear.'"

CHAPTER FIFTEEN

In the afternoon, when Kate wakes from her nap, she finds Electra ensconced on the terrace

"What are you reading?" Kate sits at the edge of the pool. It is completely empty of earth. A *muratore*—a bricklayer, has poured the concrete floor, set the drain, built two steps, and smoothed the sides. They are waiting for the lining to be installed. It is hot

"James. *Portrait of a Lady*. What a dip!"

"Henry James or Isabel?"

"Isabel. James. Both!" Electra is not in a good mood.

Kate laughs. She remembers thinking much the same the first time she read the novel.

"If you were Isabel, would you stay married to Osmond?" Electra asks.

"I wouldn't have married him in the first place!"

Isabel is an exaggerated example of duty, more so because she is such a self-centered girl before she arrives in Europe, disguising her self-interests as a quest for independence. But when she marries, and marries wrongly to a man who is all form and no content, she moves to the other end of the spectrum. She falls into the role of dutiful wife, without an escape clause, even if the reader is rooting for her to leave her fruitless marriage.

"It was difficult for me to understand Isabel when I first met her," says Kate.

"You were my age?" Electra has moved her chair so that her legs are in the sun.

"More or less. I was in my freshman year of university, but the times were very different. Banks were being burned. All institutions were under scrutiny, including marriage. Especially marriage! The slightest imperfection was a justifiable cause for separation. I considered Isabel a dim-wit for maintaining her marriage vows."

"But if you had married a man like Osmond? Would you have stayed married to him?"

"Good question." Difficult question. Kate thinks of Niccolò's mother, who abandoned her marriage to Niccolò's father with more justification than Isabel has to leave Osmond. Then Kate thinks of Fiammetta's three-year-old son, Niccolò, the baby she threw out with the bathwater, who has scars deeper than any Kate will ever be able to heal. Did Fiammetta's pursuit of happiness justify the trauma to two small children? Would they have been less damaged if Niccolò's disappointed mother had stayed married to Niccolò's difficult father?

How can Kate hope to explain any of this to Electra, who has not yet embarked on love's many complications?

"From the other side of the marriage vows," Kate says, speaking personally, trying not to lay blame on anyone's doorstep, "I am less critical of Isabel's choices. I respect her values, even though I see that James was portraying an extreme case. This is not a portrait of a woman, Electra; it is a *Portrait of a Lady*. No matter how blessed we are in our marriages there are moments when form needs to dominate. Tempers rise; angry words are ready to flow. How easy it would be to say something mean, regrettable, something that would hang in the air long after the dispute had passed."

"But you and Daddy are respectful of each other, even when you disagree."

"It is all right to have different opinions. It's all right to argue. But it is not all right to attack one's soft spots, especially those confessed in moments of intimacy."

"If I were Isabel, I would have chosen Lord Warburton," Electra says dreamily. "He is perfect."

"Perfection doesn't make interesting novels, honey. But you have the right idea for real life."

Electra appears in the kitchen as they are putting the breakfast plates into the dishwasher. "Daddy? Could I ask you to make me a coffee, please?"

"Sure. Were you up late?"

"I was. Reading James."

"Did you finish?" Kate asks.

"Almost. Isabel is still a fool. I'll finish it this morning."

"If you'd prefer, you can come with us today."

"I don't know. I am tired." She plops down onto a chair. "Where are you going?"

"Favignana." The Egadi Island closest to them. "Ettore and Graziella have invited us sailing."

Electra sits up straight. "Do I have time for breakfast?"

"Of course." Niccolò has already prepared an espresso for her. He bought a *Pavoni* espresso machine for Kate several years ago, but the real present is the coffee he makes her every day. If Kate happens to be still in bed when she hears the hissing of milk being frothed, the sound brings her immediately to her feet. Pavlov revisited.

"Not too tired to sail?" Niccolò asks, opening the steam valve to build a head of foam.

"Never."

Ettore and Graziella pick them up at nine. The back of their station wagon, which they keep in Erice all year, traveling back and forth from their home in Milano by plane, is full of wine and water bottles clinking against each other. In other bags, plums, apricots and peaches nestle against each other as they never did on the tree. Kate sees the ends of crusty baguettes poking out of bags; the green stems of vegetables. Graziella is a fantastic cook, one of those people who can prepare an impressive three course meal in the tiny quarters of a boat's galley—in fifteen minutes!

"I hope you don't mind me tagging along," Electra says.

"We are glad to meet you, finally." Graziella is almost as tall as Electra. At nearly sixty, she moves with a model's grace, not only through an evening's festivities in her own summer designs, but from *prua to poppa*—from bow to stern, on a boat in high seas. Her body is as tan and smooth as if airbrushed, but fuller now; her décolleté is positively voluptuous. She keeps her salt-and-pepper hair as short as a sailor's so it is always neat and out of her eyes, even in wind.

At the boat yard, they quickly unload the car. Everyone grabs gear and bags of groceries. Ettore, who could fill the role of sailor from central casting, his beard scruffy, his eyebrows wild, his blue eyes bleached light from squinting into wind and sun, calls and waves across the dock to someone he knows. "Carlino! Come say hello to our friends."

They put down their bags and wait in the hot sun. Kate is glad she has already put sunscreen on Niccolò and herself. She hopes that Electra has done the same.

The two men embrace. "This is Carlino," Ettore presents. "I have known him since we were children."

They are both in their sixties, but Kate can easily imagine them as boys, escaping their mamas, their school work, to run down to watch the boats dock.

"He has been mistreating me since we were infants." Both of them are tan and age spotted. Carlo has lost his waist, Ettore has stayed trim.

"Carlino, this is Niccolò and Kate Aragona, and their daughter Electra."

"Carlo." He shakes their hands. Apart from his ill-fitting clothes, he looks like the conductor of an orchestra, his hair long, combed back from his high forehead. "Ettore is the only one left alive who still calls me Carlino." His back has a slight curve, as if from years of a raised baton. "You've got good weather. Where are you going?"

"We thought Cala Rotonda."

"There's wind from the south. You might be happier at Cala Rossa."

"Come with us?"

"I can't." He has a straight-forward, simple elegance. "I have work to do."

"The richest man in Trapani, and he can't afford to take a day off."

"That's why he's rich," Niccolò says, laughing.

"Don't believe everything he tells you," Carlo warns, as he turns to leave. "Ettore tends to exaggerate."

"We know!"

They have loaded their gear onto the boat when Carlo returns in company. "Ettore, you know my nephew, Bernardo."

"Bernardino!" Ettore says, holding out his arms. Again, introductions are made, hands are shaken. "Why don't you come with us today?"

"I would love to, but I came up to spend the day with my uncle." His voice is so soft that Kate has to lean forward to hear him. "I thought I could lend him a hand."

A counter-point to his uncle's disarray, Bernardo is tall and able-bodied; the quintessential marine cadet, at ease. His blonde hair is carefully trimmed, his clothes nicely fitted. Bernardo has all the qualities necessary to hold the group's attention, but he steps back so as not to outshine his uncle.

"Go ahead." Carlo puts his hand on his nephew's shoulder. "I can handle things here. We will catch up over dinner."

"If you are sure?"

"I'm sure."

"Get your gear, Abel Brown," Ettore teases. "You can be our boatswain."

"Are you in the boat business, like your uncle?" Kate asks.

"No. Our side of the family makes wine. We have a vineyard about an hour from here, near Sambuca."

"One of six vineyards," Ettore clarifies, "one of the biggest wine-making enterprises in Italy—certainly the most important in Sicilia. How is the newest vineyard? Where is it, near Catania?"

"Capo Milazzo." Bernardo blushes red to the tips of his ears, as if he has already spent the day in the sun without sunscreen.

Niccolò offers protection from Ettore's embarrassing exuberance. "If you go onboard, I will pass you these last bags."

Ettore's boat isn't new or fancy: its claim to fame is that it can handle the roughest seas. Kate would rather be on a safe boat than a plush one, and Ettore's boat is sleek and trim, a sailor's tool, not a toy.

Electra is eager to learn. Ettore calls out orders. Graziella shows her how to latch the *cima*, leaving the rope long and lose, ready to uncoil.

Being in a boat is a test of compatibility. As Ettore hollers a command, Kate sees a side of him she hasn't seen before: a budding tyrant. At the dinner parties they have attended

179

together Kate has always thought of him as a younger brother, accommodating to the stronger personalities in the group. However, as Captain on his boat, he is stern, no nonsense. Kate folds herself into a portside corner, out of the way. Niccolò positions himself at the stern, ready to untie the *cima*, while Graziella and Electra prepare to hoist the anchor. Ettore shouts instructions over the sound of the motor, but he can't hear what has been answered, which adds to the confusion. The atmosphere on board isn't peaceful. Ettore hollers an order to Graziella to secure a box of sliding groceries in the galley, even though she is at the other end of the boat, storing the anchor chain around the capstan.

"Ettore? Are you, per chance, an only child?" Electra asks, climbing out of the galley where she has secured supplies.

"I am! How did you know?"

They all laugh. Put a Captain's hat on an only child and there can be no doubt.

Bernardo says, in his shy, barely audible voice, "I am an only child, too."

"You and I, son, must stick together!"

"I am a younger sister," Graziella admits, before she climbs down into the galley to organize their provisions.

"Me, too," Electra says. "Younger sisters rule."

"You, Niccolò?"

"I am the elder of two," Niccolò says.

"We should start a competition: Only Children against The Interlopers," Electra says.

Bernardo smiles, then blushes.

Electra blushes at his blush.

They are forming a club of their own.

In the harbor there is more sun than wind. The sails flap, unengaged. The motor propels unpleasant fumes into the air, clouds of black smoke into the water. Kate can see that Niccolò is as unconvinced as the sails, is regretting his decision to spend the day at sea.

As Ettore steers his boat out of the harbor, into the open sea, as the wind begins to assert itself against the sails, everyone begins to relax. Ettore says to Niccolò, who is seated beside him at the helm, "I heard your neighbor died recently."

"Yes. Edoardo Oliviero."

"He was well-known and respected," he says, setting his site on automatic pilot. "Give our condolences to his wife?"

"Of course."

"Does he have children?" Graziella asks, watching her head as she lowers herself again into the galley.

"Two sons," Niccolò says, "They are consoling their mother, as well as each other."

Bernardo nods. "I know them. In fact, I think we may be distantly related. Ettore, where are we going?"

"*Cala Rossa*. Your Uncle's recommendation."

Electra says, "I heard it is called *Cala Rossa* because of the color of the coral."

"Actually, it got its name, Red Cove, during the Punic wars, when the water there ran red with blood."

"I think I prefer the coral version."

Today, the water at *Cala Rossa* looks like it has been strewn with crystals. The color of the blue is altered by the depth of the water, and again by what occupies the sea floor: smooth, white sand or jagged shoal or plant life. However, when Graziella looks down into the depths of the transparent, inviting water, she sees it is swarming with large, purple jellyfish. "*Che peccato!* What a shame!"

"We won't be able to swim?" Electra, already on the ladder, her lower legs immersed, climbs back up onto the transom.

"Sure we can." Bernardo comes to stand next to her. "I'll stand guard while you swim. We'll take turns." He sees she is not convinced. "I'll go first, if you will watch guard?"

"Starboard is clear."

From the stern, Bernardo dives. Right after him, as close as a shadow, Niccolò dives, a graceful dolphin arch.

Kate is amazed. She says to Electra, "I didn't know your father could dive!"

Niccolò surfaces, shakes water from his hair, and then floats on his back. "You are watching for jelly-fish, right?"

Kate repeats, "I didn't know you could dive." She is impressed beyond the act itself. What other surprises lie in store for her in the years to come? She is sure she showed Niccolò all her tricks in the first five minutes she knew him. Or perhaps not. Their courtship wasn't flashy. They were both tired of trying to impress. They had both settled into the philosophy if s/he wants me, s/he can take me as I am.

Something else impresses Kate about the dive. Niccolò usually edges his way into the water inch by inch, complaining about the cold, standing on tiptoe as it reaches his waist. Not today. Niccolò has turned young again, daring.

"Jellyfish on starboard, two o'clock."

Niccolò shoots out of the water, climbs back on board, just as Bernardo dives portside, far from the jellyfish. They take turns diving into the crystalline blue water, keeping watch.

"Look! The jellyfish are leaving," Graziella says, watching them propelling their way out of the cove.

They swim until they are hungry. They eat until they are full. Then everyone moves into separate corners of the boat, Kate assumes, to nap. Graziella and Kate stretch out on the bow as Kate hears a splash, then another. Electra and Bernardo are swimming toward the shore in masks and snorkels.

"Aren't you afraid she will block her digestion by swimming so soon after eating?"

Italians tend to leave several hours between eating and swimming, but Kate has another theory; that is, if you swim immediately, before digestion starts, there won't be a problem. Besides, Electra swims like a fish, and she isn't alone.

Bernardo and Electra are gone for a long time, over an hour. When they return, they are old friends. The shyness has disappeared between them. However, when Electra spreads her towel on the bow, Bernardo doesn't lie beside her. Electra keeps Graziella and her mother company. She and Kate are slathered with 30+ protection. Graziella, as dark as a Nubian, has applied another layer of cream to keep her skin moist. Niccolò, Ettore and Bernardo talk politics in the shade of the sail, pleased to learn they are of like minds, as Italians are so unwavering in their political views that to disagree is to risk a friendship.

A day on a boat is more exhausting than all the work Niccolò and Kate ever do at home, including the excavation of their little pool. To express their gratitude to Graziella and Ettore they propose taking them out for dinner, but they are secretly relieved when everyone votes for a quick ice cream instead of a meal. There will be other occasions to reciprocate.

At home, Niccolò says, "Bernardo seems like a nice young man."

"*Si. Carino.*" Electra has just dismissed him with that innocuous adjective, "nice."

"Did you give him your number?" Kate asks.

"No. Why?" Electra is stuffing her beach towel into the washing machine.

"Wouldn't you like to see him again?"

Electra thinks for a minute. "Sure. He's nice." There's that unflattering classification again. "But he didn't ask for my number."

"You could have offered it."

Electra looks at her mother as if Kate has suggested she should drop out of university.

"If he's interested, Mama, he'll find a way to get my number."

Niccolò nods. "That's right. That's my girl."

CHAPTER
SIXTEEN

Kate slept through the sunrise today. She worked too hard in the garden yesterday, far beyond her usual exertion. She was with Angelica, helping her transplant a patch of long-stemmed daisies to widen the entry path to her house. The same plants that were choking Edoardo's lilies. Usually, when Kate is in their garden, she shares this work with Niccolò. In fact, to be fair, he spades the earth ten times for her two, and each of his thrusts are deeper and more forceful than hers; should be counted double. Kate serves to initiate their work, to give him a break. He rests while Kate empties the wheelbarrow—that in itself is a tiring job—and together they use up all their energy, stopping when they have done enough.

But in working with Angelica, Kate is the stronger of the two, and if she quits spading the earth, Angelica takes over. It breaks Kate's heart to see her ineffectual attempts, probably as it pulls on Niccolò's heart strings to see Kate's limited results. Strength, as everything else, is relative.

Eventually, Angelica invited her inside for a cup of tea. Kate wanted to go home, to shower off the dirt, but neither of Angelica's sons was there yet, so Kate kept her company until one of them arrived. With some trepidation, they have moved back into the country again. It makes things more difficult for Matteo and Sergio, their lives are in town, but Angelica, surprisingly, has insisted.

"Edoardo didn't like to spend his summers in town."

There is more order in the house than when Edoardo was alive; also more silence.

Angelica made tea, found some cookies. She served Kate but kept standing, looking around for something else to bring to the table.

"Sit down, Angelica. We've been working hard."

She laughed her funny little laugh. "We actually got those plants moved!"

"We did!"

"I can't tell you how many years I have wanted to widen our walkway. I'm afraid of stumbling, especially when my arms are full, and I can't see where I'm putting my feet."

"I hate to propose another project when we have just finished this one, but I was thinking we could trim the palm tree next to where you park your car."

"The one that pokes me in the head every time I get out of my car?"

"That's the one."

"Tomorrow?"

"If you want, we could start it now. See how far we advance before the boys come home."

Kate was physically exhausted when she went to bed last night. She read less than a few pages of the book she had been looking forward to all day, the last paragraph a blur. She fumbled for her bookmark, kissed Niccolò good night and was asleep in half a breath. Drifting down on a thought-free cloud, Kate heard Niccolò's voice, distinct: "The fox is out. Do you hear her calling?" No, *Amore mio*, she hadn't heard it, hadn't heard anything at all, and suddenly all Kate could hear was the fox's call. Suddenly, Kate was wide awake, listening. She lay awake for hours while Niccolò slept peacefully beside her.

Finally, when Kate did sleep, she slept deeply. Instead of waking during the night, spot lit by the reflection of the moon through the window, or early, to photograph at sunrise, as she is apt to do, Kate woke to full daylight. No haunting shadows, no suggestive silhouettes, no gray tones transforming themselves into pastels, no passage from the dark mysteries of night to the subtle awakening of day. Rather, a jolt from dreamless darkness to full daylight, nothing sublime in the transition.

All morning Kate has moved slowly, as if she has missed the most significant moment of the day. Irrationally, she feels that the day will be inconsequential without having witnessed its awakening. This is foolishness, Kate tells herself, as Niccolò prepares coffee, as she cuts up figs, adds almonds and a spoonful of their golden plum preserves to yogurt and muesli: the day is as promising as she allows it to be. Yes, she missed a magical moment but that doesn't mean it isn't there. Does a nightingale's song fail to break the silence of the night without an audience; does it turn mute if Kate is not awake to hear it? How presumptuous to think that nature performs for her.

Hours past the unseen sunrise, it is a beautiful, clear, softly-lit morning. There is a smattering of low hanging clouds far out to sea, seemingly resting on the horizon. A broad, silver beam radiates from the clouds to the shore, the kind of light path to heaven seen in Italian Renaissance paintings. Cofano appears twice, once rising stark and majestic, every fissure, every cleft in high relief against the cloud studded sky; and once in reflection, a mirror image floating on a sea as smooth as glass. If Kate is looking for the sublime she missed from sleeping late, there it is, its details obscured and mysterious, as if the mountain had been pulled into the underworld by an impetuous sea god. And just as suddenly as Kate finds it, before she has time to uncap her camera and focus the lens, the reflection is shattered by the wake of a fleet of small fishing boats returning late to shore. Cofano's double shudders and is gone, as fleeting as a sunrise Kate can only imagine.

Kate has a heavy basket of wet laundry balanced on one hip as Electra drives into the front garden. "You look exhausted," Kate says, as her daughter unfolds herself from the car.

"I got stuck behind a really slow tour bus at the bottom of the hill," she says. Popping open the trunk, she lifts out two bags of groceries "Here, if you want to put away the food, I'll hang up the clothes. They are mostly my things anyway."

"Either way." Kate accepts the groceries in exchange for the basket. "You'll find clothespins on the line."

Kate has set down the groceries on the kitchen counter when she hears Electra laugh. Kate wonders to whom she is talking; then realizes she is probably on her cellphone. Now Kate laughs: she hasn't become accustomed to what seems like people talking to themselves.

"Mama!" Electra comes around to the patio. "You won't believe what I have found!"

Kate opens the screen door to find Electra holding two panda-bear-like puppies in negative, all black, with white markings around their eyes, on their chests.

"Where did you find them?" Kate asks, relieving her of one black puff ball, which fits snuggly into the palm of her hand. "They are adorable!"

"There are two more, just as cute."

"These must be the puppies that were in Edoardo's garden." Quivering, the little ball of fur wraps its front paws tightly around her thumb, clasps it with that same instinct all newborns grasp a proffered finger. Kate feels the veil of lethargy lift, that heavy shroud which has accompanied her since Edoardo's death.

"The mother has moved them into our woodshed."

Sure enough, from the rear corner of their woodshed peer two more sets of inquisitive eyes.

"Do you think we should be disturbing them? Won't their mother reject them if she smells a human scent?"

"I don't think that problem applies to dogs, Mama. Besides, they must be at least six weeks old. Aren't they precious! Can we keep them?"

Kate was wondering when Electra was going to ask. "I don't see any reason why they can't stay in the woodshed until we find them homes."

"Can I lay down some old blankets?"

"If we had any, we could, but I don't think it's necessary."

"I'll move some of this wood so it doesn't tumble down on them."

"They are probably safe for now." Kate positions her puppy in the huddle with its team of brothers. "Why don't you hang up the clothes while I make lunch? Then we can improve their quarters."

Reluctantly, Electra adds her puppy to the bundle. "I think I'll wash my hands before anything else. We have a brush here, don't we?"

"We do."

"And flea drops?"

"We do. But these little guys may not be old enough yet to spray. Who can we ask?"

Understandably, the conversation at lunch revolves around the newfound puppies. Niccolò wants a promise that Electra will find them homes before she leaves at the end of the summer. Kate wants promises, too: that Electra will feed the dogs and clean up the puppy poop, that puddle of pee that has appeared in the corner of the terrace; that she will try to keep the puppies out of her flower beds.

"I will, I promise." She hugs both her parents. "Although there won't be any flowers to worry about if you don't water them, Mama."

Niccolò and Electra shoo Kate out of the kitchen, agreeing to do the dishes if she will water the garden.

But Kate can't bring herself to uncoil the hose.

Instead, she changes into her bathing suit and submerges herself in the cool, fresh water of their little pool. Gazing out at the view, Kate can hear the counterpoint of voices in the kitchen, Electra asking why the air conditioner taxes the car's engine, Niccolò giving more detail about the compressor than she probably wants. Kate sinks down to the bottom of the pool, as if total immersion will clear her head and remind her why she should water the garden. She concentrates on the air bubbles escaping upward, an undeterred stream, an upside-down fountain, breaking the surface like bright crystals. As she emerges, she can feel her muscles begin to relax, as if they had installed Jacuzzi jet streams.

Is it the clouds that reflect on the sea, coloring it in shades of gray and white, or the sea itself, turbulent?

Their two regular rafts have developed leaks so Kate inflates a raft that was given to Elizabeth when she was two years old: a six-foot crocodile, surprisingly realistic, everglade-green, with pop-out eyes. It was a gift from Fiammetta's second husband, and whatever one might say about him—and Niccolò has a lot to say, if you start him on that unfortunate topic—he had a lot of kid in him. For all her closet cleaning tendencies, Kate knows better than to give away her children's childhood treasures. As Kate steadies the raft, attempts to climb on the beast's back, she is glad for the restraint.

She squints again into the distance: is it the clouds that reflect on the water, coloring it in shades of gray or the water itself, turbulent?

Unfortunately, a crocodile's shape is not ideal for a tall person to stretch out on, and Kate has a real struggle trying to throw her legs out of the water, onto that narrow, curving tail. As she is attempting to tame this beast, Kate sees Electra hiking up the hill, followed by four stumbling balls of fur. As Kate watches her daughter stretch out to sunbathe on a plastic raft, the puppies clamoring over her legs and lap, onto the book she has brought to read, Kate understands why the rafts have developed leaks: Electra has been using them to sunbathe! Annoyed, Kate throws her legs back up onto the crocodile, attempts to find balance, and capsizes into the water. She tries again, and again fails, tumbling gracelessly into the water. Each time, as Kate thinks she has finally succeeded and will be able to lie still and undisturbed, just as she is regaining her balance, the tail shifts just enough to redistribute her weight and in she falls, as if thrown, back into the water. As she slips off the raft for perhaps the tenth time, Kate hears laughter: Electra, no longer stretched out and reading, but standing on the hill with a quartet of puppies, hands on her hips, laughing with real gusto.

Kate sees herself from a distance as Electra is seeing her: a middle-aged woman wrestling a crocodile—and losing! The newest sporting trend in Sicily!

Kate can almost hear Edoardo's gravelly laugh: "Life may be futile but it is also hilarious." Kate can almost see him conspiring with Electra, stamping his feet, as he did whenever something tickled him. "Get up, *Nica*! Water your garden!" The voice is as clear as if he were seated on their terrace, awaiting a glass of wine, seeds peeking out of the cigarette pack in his shirt pocket.

Is it the clouds that reflect on the water, coloring it in shades of gray and white or the water itself, turbulent?

A moment later the clouds pass and the question is answered, although, Kate realizes, the importance wasn't in the answer but in the question.

"**M**ama? Would you mind if I didn't help you make marmalade today?"

"Not at all. What's up?" Kate is slicing open ripe figs, inspecting the bright, pink tentacles for signs of bugs. Her hands and arms are sticky up to her elbows. "Do you mind scratching the center of my back? In between my shoulder blades. There. Ahhh. Thanks."

"Bernardo has invited me out for the day."

"Where are you going?"

"*Lo Zingaro.* Bernardo has borrowed a boat from his uncle, and has invited a group of friends."

Lo Zingaro Natural Reserve is a stretch of coast between San Vito Lo Capo and Scopello, accessible only by boat or by foot; nature at its most spectacular, most unspoiled. Kate wishes she had been invited, too.

Electra reaches around her mother, slips an apron over her head and ties it around her waist. Kate is wearing work clothes. They don't really need protecting, but she appreciates her daughter's gesture.

"When is he picking you up?"

"He asked if I could meet him at San Vito." She snatches a handful of almonds that Kate has chopped for the marmalade. "Can I take the car?"

"Sure." This is the first time Electra has asked to drive a long distance alone. She's had her license for a year. She is a prudent and capable driver, but as she doesn't have occasion to drive during the school year, she feels unpracticed and unsafe on these steep, winding roads.

"Take sun screen."

"I've got it in my duffle." She grabs another handful of almonds.

"The puppies?"

"They should be OK, don't you think? Can I bring some fruit?"

"Of course." Kate scoops the almonds into a bowl. Between Niccolò and Electra's snacking, there won't be any left for the marmalade. "I have cookies made, if you want to bring some."

She rewards her with a happy smile as she pilfers two last almonds from the bowl. "I'll clean up whatever mess the puppies make when I return."

When Bernardo and Electra return that evening, he comes onto the terrace for a glass of iced tea. He is sunburnt; and too tired or relaxed to be shy.

"Did you have fun with your friends?" From the kitchen Kate hears the marmalade lids popping, that reassuring sound that marks the successful conclusion to the long, hot, splattering process of preparing preserves.

"It was just the two of us. My other friends ended up not coming."

"We had enough food to feed a fleet."

"We did."

"I ate most of it," Electra says. "He eats nothing!"

"I had two sandwiches!"

"Yea, two of the tiniest sandwiches I've ever seen. I ate at least six."

"It's a pleasure to see a woman eating more than yoghurt, although the boat did start to list dangerously on its side."

"Hey!"

There is an easy familiarity between the two of them, as if they have known each other all their lives.

"Would you like to stay for dinner? We've been invited out—"

"You have?" Electra interrupts. "By whom?"

"Renato and Diana. I think Ettore and Graziella have been invited, too. But I've made a pasta sauce for you, Electra, and Bernardo is certainly welcome to stay."

"Another time. Thank you. I promised my *Zio* Carlo I'd have dinner with him and *Zia* Anna before I return home tonight.

"Ok," Electra says, "but before you go, you have to see the puppies. Come on."

An hour later, as they watch Bernardo back out of their driveway, waving as he turns, Kate asks, "Did you have a good time?"

"Yes. It was wonderful," she says, hugging a puppy closely. "We had lunch at the *faraglioni*, just beyond the *Tonnara di Scopello*."

"On the stacks?" These are steep, vertical columns, an ideal place for seagulls to nest but hardly a perfect place for a picnic.

"No. On the boat! Between the *faraglioni*. I think it may be the most beautiful place in the world," she says dreamily, nuzzling the puppy with the white Zorro zigzag between his eyes.

"Elizabeth called last night while you were out." Electra is up and dressed, the coffee machine is on. So is the washing machine. Through the screen door, Kate can see, and hear, four puppies awaiting their breakfast. Clover is finishing his breakfast indoors. He is patient with the puppies, doesn't seem to mind that they follow him everywhere, step on his ears, try to nurse, but he isn't happy when they want to share his food.

"Oh—" Kate is sorry she missed Elizabeth. They haven't spoken with her in over a week. "Where are they?"

"They are leaving Zion National Park this morning," she says, pouring hot water over the puppy chow.

"Did she say where they were going next?"

"The Grand Canyon. They are going to stay there a couple of days." She adds a can of lamb bits and mashes it together.

"Right." For Elizabeth's birthday, Stephen bought tickets for the Glass Bridge. Every present this past year has been directed toward their holiday in the United States. Niccolò bought them luggage. Kate bought them tickets to the Aquarium in Monterey Bay and arranged through her friend Carrie's niece for two days in Disneyland. "Remember when Lizzy was a child? She couldn't decide which was her favorite, amusement parks or aquariums. I wonder if she's developed a preference."

"In Stephen's company, she's more of a kid than ever." Electra puts the food bowl down on the patio, and arranges the four puppies around it like compass points.

"That's not bad. She was too mature as a child, too serious."

"Only in your company, Mama, not with me." The dogs slobber and slurp down their food in an accelerated Charlie Chaplin mode, their tummies expanding into round, swollen balls, like time-lapsed photography. "Anyway, Elizabeth was annoyed you weren't here last night. She said she's been calling you since she left Grandma Claire's, but you are never home."

"Aren't we always home?" Kate asks, carrying their breakfast onto the terrace, careful not to trip over the dogs. They are sprawled on their sides, their eyes already shut, over-taken by the bliss of sleep-induced digestion. In the distance, disappearing into the band of bamboo, Kate catches a glimpse of their ever-present, almost-invisible mother.

"Well, *practicamente*, you and Daddy are out quite a lot these days. By the way, would you mind if I went out today?"

"Not at all. What are your plans?"

"Bernardo has invited me to go to *Levanzo* with some friends of his."

"Sure. Why not?"

"He hasn't said anything directly, but I think it's his birthday. Could you help me make a cake for him?"

"Which recipe?"

"Probably chocolate, since I don't know his taste. Everyone likes your chocolate cake."

"Will you be home for dinner?"

"I think so," she says, bending down to light the oven, "but can I let you know later?"

"We are going out," she laughs. They *are* going out a lot these days. "But I can't remember if it is dinner or just drinks. I need to check our calendar."

"Remember you are driving me to meet Emma tomorrow morning." She sets out the ingredients for the cake.

"We won't be late. You should probably be home early, as well. Are you packed?"

"Mostly." She opens a drawer to find a clean dish towel. "Mama, would you mind if I cut up this dishcloth for the rag pile. It's so faded."

"I'd rather you didn't." Kate melts olive oil with chocolate squares, and whips them together until the ribbon runs smooth as velvet.

"But it is starting to have a hole."

"Use another one if that one bothers you."

"But why do you keep it? I understand thrift, Mama, but this is going a little too far, don't you think?"

"I keep it for sentimental reasons."

"An old, faded dish cloth?" She stops whisking sugar into the batter. "With a hole?"

"Mammacita gave it to me. Do you remember her?"

"Grandma Claire's friend? The one whose long fingernails clicked on the keys when she played the piano?" Electra sprinkles flour into the mixture, a free snowfall on rich, black soil.

Kate retrieves the measuring cup from the bottom drawer. "Measure, Electra. You can improvise proportions with a sauce or a stew but not a cake." Electra accepts the cup, sets it to one side. "Mammacita was the choir director of the Methodist Church when I was a little girl. She directed the children's choir. She let me sit beside her and turn the pages while she played the piano for the older children. She directed my first solo, when I was six years old."

"But why did she give you an old towel?"

"It wasn't old when she gave it to me."

"Mama?" Electra has stopped her preparations. She waves the measuring cup, as if it is somehow related to the answer she is waiting for.

"The last time I visited her she gave me a Steuben Glass Christmas tree."

"I know it. The one you use as a centerpiece at Christmas."

"Now that I think about it, she probably gave something to all of the people who visited her. Anyway, as we were leaving, she took me into the kitchen and asked that I find a towel in which to wrap it. She was practically blind by then. This is the towel we found. Of course it was bright and new then. I think of her every time I see it, which is much more often than the Steuben Glass she gave me, which I only bring out once a year."

"Do you want me to stitch up the hole?" Electra asks, pouring the batter into a cake pan and sliding it into the oven.

"No. The hole doesn't matter. The memory won't fall through," Kate says, accepting a beater, licking off the chocolate batter as Electra does the same with the other beater.

It is late afternoon when Bernardo and his friend, Vito bring Electra home, all three of them decidedly windblown. Bernardo and Vito willingly accept the offer of cold drinks. Bernardo sits at the table on the terrace with Electra, with the calmest of the puppies, *Panda*, curled on his lap. Vito paces, a profusion of platitudes pouring forth like lava from Etna as he appraises the view, while the feistiest of the puppies, *Macchia* runs between his feet, trying to bite the leather strings of his boat shoes. Electra picks up *Macchia*, and puts him into Vito's hands. He looks at the wiggling ball of fur, appraises it critically as if trying to identify an unknown, then sits down on the top step of the terrace and ruffles its untamed fur.

"Are you sure you won't change your mind?" Vito asks Electra, his insistence somewhat calmed. Oddly enough, Macchia calms, too. He circles head to tail and falls instantly asleep.

"No. I already told you. I have to be up early."

"We can bring you back early, no problem." There is a gentle laughter trilling in his voice, mischief in his close-set eyes.

This seems to be an ongoing discussion. Electra isn't bothering to decline any more. She simply shakes her head, no.

"But why?" Vito rubs the puppy behind its ears.

Electra is going camping in the morning as part of a summer camping trip organized by her friend, Emma, who was Electra's housemate last semester in Utrecht. Emma has invited Electra to join the group of her friends.

Electra doesn't know anything about camping. She isn't even sure she likes the idea of spending five days with a group of kids she doesn't know. But she figures, if she doesn't go camping now, when will she ever?

"Where are you going camping, Sir?" Vito turns his attention to Niccolò.

Niccolò defers the question to Electra, "Where is it you are going?"

"The River Platani. Near Eraclea Minoa."

"You are not going?" Vito asks.

Niccolò laughs. "No. I haven't been camping since I was her age. I am too old to lie on hard ground in a tent. We are just driving Electra to meet her friends."

Vito turns again to Electra, "When will you be back?"

"My parents are picking me up on Friday."

"OK, we will let you go." He wags a finger at her, like an old school marm, "If you promise to save next Saturday night for us."

"Sure. I have a riding lesson on Saturday but after that I'm free."

"Actually," Bernardo begins. "Eraclea Minoa isn't far from where I live." He looks to Niccolò. "If you would like, I could save you the drive to pick her up."

Again Niccolò defers. "Electra?"

"If you are going to be driving up anyway to see your uncle, why not? Thanks."

"Are you sure you won't change your mind about tonight?" Vito insists one last time, putting down the puppy after petting it one last time. "We'll be sure to have you home in time to go camping tomorrow!"

After her friends have left, Electra joins Kate in her bedroom to help her select a dress to wear tonight. Last week, when Kate asked to borrow a blouse so she wouldn't be wearing the same outfit three evenings in a row, Electra insisted it was time she took her mother shopping. She had a point, and the sale banners in the store windows in Trapani made it easier to accept Electra's recommendation. Now, Kate holds up a sleeveless white dress with copper accents that accentuates the light tan Kate has acquired. She asks, "Why didn't you want to go out with them tonight?"

Electra has propped up the pillows on her mother's side of the bed, and is making herself comfortable. "The invitation included spending the night on Vito's boat."

"Oh." Kate takes a dark russet and cream colored sleeveless top with matching skirt from the hangers on the back of her bedroom door, and offers them for Electra's scrutiny. Even though Electra has helped her choose this casual but classic outfit, she shakes her head, nods toward the simple, streamlined Jacqueline Kennedy-style dress. "That could have been awkward."

"It would have been OK; I know how to take care of myself—"

Her confidence amuses Kate.

"—but I don't want to be tired for tomorrow." She rummages through the box of jewelry she has brought upstairs, "Besides, they started teasing me when I said I had to be home early."

"Bernardo teased you? Or Vito?"

"No. There were three girls with us today. They were totally annoying. Here—" She holds up a pair of amber earrings Elizabeth gave Electra last year for Christmas. "Try these. They'll be perfect."

Kate accepts the earrings. "Were they older than you?"

"Yea. In their thirties. And desperate. Remind me to shoot myself if I ever start acting like them."

"Vito seemed like a nice guy." Kate has slipped on the dress. Electra reaches to finish zipping it closed.

"I don't know if he's nice, but he keeps things moving." She rummages through her jewelry box again, finds a chestnut-size amber bead on a single string that matches the earrings, and the dress. "He gets a bit tiring after awhile. I would never want to go out with him alone, but I think I can convince him to adopt one of the puppies. He said he would think about it." She adjusts the dress on her mother's hips, pulls down on the hem so it falls straight from neck to knee. "There, you look great. Like a president's wife."

"Aside from the desperate girls and an agitated Vito, did you have a good time?"

"Yes. Excellent. Bernardo is really nice."

"I can't believe you guys are home! I even called Electra on her cellphone, to see if you two were all right."

"Oh, Lizzy!" Kate sets down her book and reading glasses. "I've been hoping you'd call."

"I've called every night this week!"

"Sicily is a lot more social than we anticipated."

"I guess so!" She sounds really annoyed.

"I hope I wasn't this stern a parent when you started going out?"

"I never went out! Remember?"

This is true. With a few exceptions, Elizabeth stayed at home, invited friends in. She always had one best friend instead of many; tended to invite the same few friends to spend the weekend. She's maintained almost every friendship she's ever started, reaping the benefits of these long investments. She and Stephen met when she was eighteen, at a Christmas ball at the end of her first semester at university, and they have been together ever since, mostly entertaining at home.

"Where are you?" Kate asks.

"In Big Sur," she says. Kate can hear her daughter start to relax. "I am glad we didn't follow Uncle Stuart's advice to take 101. You were right, Highway One is gorgeous."

"As long as you aren't in a hurry."

"We aren't. We stopped all along the way. We saw so many seals. They were right on the beach with us. I can't wait to show you our photos!"

Elizabeth is an excellent photographer. So is Electra. "How long are you in Big Sur?"

"We leave tomorrow for Monterey. The day after we are in San Francisco, at Carrie's."

"Oakland."

"Whatever. We decided to skip Yosemite. We will stay with Carrie the whole last week of our vacation. We've decided it's better to see less but enjoy it more."

Smart kid, Kate thinks, even if she doesn't know the difference between Oakland and San Francisco. "I suspect you will find plenty to do."

"Stephen wants to taste wine in Napa Valley, and I want to see the Redwoods. Oh, my phone card is running out! I'll say goodbye now, and we can chat until I'm cut off."

"Ok. I'll call you in a few days at Carrie's. Sorry we haven't been home to receive your calls."

"I'm just relieved I found you now. I was worried!"

"We are enjoying our new friends. I am glad you are having a wonderful time in the States."

"It couldn't be better. We are sad it is ending. This has been the best—"

The call has ended. Next time they speak Kate must remember to ask how Disneyland compares to the Aquarium.

A shiny, black Audi TT pulls into their driveway, a little too fast, and then stalls. Electra opens the door to the driver's side and steps out, laughing. "That's the first mistake I made! Admit it. I drove perfectly until now!"

Bernardo unfolds himself and emerges from the passenger side, also laughing. "My poor car!"

Kate has been digging, preparing the loamy ground for a crowd of tulip bulbs. She wipes the earth from her hands onto already muddy trousers, and comes forward to greet them.

"I promise I won't shake your hand, Bernardo. Don't worry."

"Oh Signora!" He holds out his hand anyway.

"Welcome home, Electra." Kate kisses her daughter, hoping she doesn't have dirt streaked on her face. "Did you have a good time camping?"

"Wonderful. Emma's friends were so nice. Smart. Funny. Cultured. It was a little hard getting everyone moving in the morning, but I got them up, eventually. We had a blast."

So much detail, from Electra? What has happened? Kate looks at her daughter: deeply tanned and freckled, and blonder than ever. There is something different about her.

Bernardo is smiling, confident.

"Is this a new car?" Kate asks.

"Yes, I picked it up on Wednesday."

"And you risked an accident today?"

"Mama!"

"She drove perfectly."

"You are a brave man indeed." Niccolò has joined them. Kate is not sure if she is comforted or embarrassed that his trousers are as muddy as her own. "Did you have any trouble finding the camping ground at La Riserva Naturale della Foce?"

"If I may say, Sir, your daughter has no sense of direction."

"Unfortunately, we know that," Kate interjects.

"Unfortunately, she inherited it entirely from me," Niccolò adds.

"No offense intended, Sir, surely."

"No offense taken."

"It's a good thing we have cellphones or we would still be trying to meet up. In which part of the reserve did you say the camp was, Electra?"

"OK, OK, so I got it slightly wrong!"

"*Slightly*! On the left! Or on the right!"

"The Nature reserve is divided into two parts," Electra explains guiltily.

"Each side is several hundred hectares."

"If you had waited, I would have walked out to meet you."

"You described the most beautiful beach in the world, I had to see it!"

Their teasing is ardent but neither sounds seriously annoyed. Their protesting is diminished by conspirators' smiles.

"Would you like to come in for something to drink? Eat? You must be tired after your adventure."

"Exhausted!"

"Hey! I'm the one who drove."

"My point exactly."

"Wine or tea?" Kate asks, as they walk toward the patio.

"Or whiskey?" Niccolò asks.

"A glass of water, please, and I'll be on my way home."

"Aren't you here to visit your uncle?"

"No. Unfortunately, he is out of town today. But I should be leaving. I want to see if the mechanic is still open on my way home."

"Hey, stop teasing me!"

"All right." Bernardo turns serious. "What time should I pick you up tomorrow?"

"I finish riding at six. I can be ready by seven."

"Do you want me to pick you up from riding? It's on my way."

"It's not, but thanks anyway. And I need time to wash up after riding. You don't want your new car to smell of horse."

"True. I'll be here at seven. If you will walk me to the car, Electra, I brought up a case of wine for your parents."

Electra is up early, already dressed when Niccolò and Kate come down for breakfast. Kate can see her bathing suit strap tied around her neck. "Matteo invited me to the beach. We are going scuba diving."

"Scuba diving?"

"Well, he is. I'll snorkel. There's a medieval anchor near Custonaci that he wants to show me. He says it isn't very deep." She has made sandwiches, is wrapping them in plastic. "I wish Elizabeth were here. I miss her."

"I miss her, too. What about Tana?"

"We're picking her up on the way." She rinses a grapple of grapes, wraps them into a paper towel and places them into a bag. "She's promised to be ready on time."

"You are packing a lot into one day. The beach. Riding this afternoon. A party tonight. You're not worried you'll be too tired?"

"The summer is almost finished. I need to make the most of every day."

A good philosophy, and even though Kate's summer is finishing, too, she plans to do nothing more ambitious than garden and float in the pool.

"I can't believe I have to leave Sicily. This has been the best summer of my life. Except for losing Edoardo, of course."

"It's been the best summer of my life, too," Kate says, "except for losing Edoardo."

Making the most of every remaining day, Kate accompanies Electra to her afternoon riding lesson. She is impressed by how relaxed Electra has become behind the wheel, and again impressed by how much her riding has improved this summer; how elegant and at ease she looks on a horse. All those years Kate told her to stand up straight; she should have simply given her riding lessons sooner. "She was born to ride," her instructor tells Kate. "Next summer she should start jumping."

Kate drives back up the hill as she drives faster. Electra's lesson ran long, and Bernardo will be at their house in thirty minutes.

"I should have said seven-thirty!" Electra frets.

"Don't worry. This is Sicily. He won't be on time."

She's wrong. He pulls into their driveway in another new Audi, just as Electra is stepping out of the shower.

"Have you invested in Audi stock?" Niccolò teases. Bernardo is nicely but casually dressed: linen trousers, linen shirt, both already creased at the back.

"The sedan belongs to my father. I traded him the TT for tonight."

Bernardo is driving another girl to Vito's party in Palermo, as well. Carla emerges from the Audi sedan in silk organza and tulle, as if on her way to a wedding. Her heels are so high Kate worries she'll twist an ankle as she teeters down the uneven garden path. Electra, when she appears a few minutes after seven, is decisively under-dressed. Her hair is still slightly damp, but very blonde after a summer in the sun. She is wearing a short, blue, linen skirt and a fitted blouse; a pair of sandals they bought last week together, flat and comfortable.

Electra and Carla shake hands, exchange pleasantries. Kate wonders if Carla is one of the desperate thirty-year-olds.

"Should I change?" Electra asks Bernardo, observing Carla's dress.

"No. You look fine."

"What time do you expect to be back?" Niccolò asks.

"I expect we'll be quite late, Sir."

"We trust your driving."

"And if you are tired," Electra says. "I can always drive."

"I'll call my father to suggest he increase his insurance?"

Electra appears on the terrace in her pajamas as Niccolò and Kate are finishing breakfast. Kate greets her daughter with her standard question. "How was the party last night?"

Sleepily, Electra picks up Figaro from the corner of the terrace, where he is dozing in the sun, and hugs him in her arms. "It was more interesting than entertaining."

She recounts the party: an amazing house on the water in Mondello, two or three dozen friends, everyone very dressed up. "Carla was one of the least elegant, except me."

"Was she nice?"

"Yea. Nice enough."

"Were the desperate thirty-year-olds at the party?"

"One was, but she was less annoying last night. We actually had an interesting discussion about land development in Sicily. There was an American guy. He didn't speak any Italian so he pretty much attached himself to me. I spent a lot of time trying to interest him in one of the thirty-year-olds."

"Did you have fun?"

"It was OK. It would have been more fun if Elizabeth had been there, too." She scratches Figaro under his chin. His purring becomes audible. "At a certain point Vito got a call from a friend, who had his yacht anchored off shore, and the whole party ferried out to the boat."

"What kind of boat was it?"

"I don't know. The kind of boat in that Goldie Hawn film, *Overboard!* But bigger!"

"How exciting!"

"It should have been fun, but the guy who owned the yacht was too full of himself."

Orecchiella skips onto the terrace, his expression more puzzled than ever. His tall ears pitched forward, alert to peril. "Orecchiella!" They all choral. "Vieni qui!"

Figaro squirms in Electra's arms, his fur rising along his back. He wants to jump down but isn't sure of his territory with Orecchiella so near.

"Do you know what the owner of the yacht said when he was introduced to me?"

"No. What?"

"He said, 'You're too young for me.'"

"You're kidding. What did you say?"

"I laughed." Electra's laughter dislodges Figaro. He leaps from her arms, and darts off the terrace, sprinting past Orecchiella with impressive speed for his fourteen years. "I said, 'fortunately for me!' What I should have said is 'and you are too arrogant for me'. That poor guy is never going to find a partner. He pulls up in an expensive yacht and then worries that people are interested in him for his money. If he hadn't been so arrogant I would have felt sorry for him."

"How was the rest of the party?"

"OK. Vito was a pest. He said I was the kind of girl a guy would marry, not the kind one would date! He kept trying to kiss me. He'd had quite a lot to drink. Finally, he said he'd stop if I'd kiss him on the cheek. But he turned his face as I started to kiss his cheek, so I pushed him off the sofa onto the floor."

"You didn't!"

"I did. He's such a shrimp, it was easy. That's not the way to win a kiss! At least not from me!"

"What did Bernardo do?"

"It was really funny. His mouth dropped open. Then he said, 'Remind me never to try to kiss you!'"

CHAPTER SEVENTEEN

"**Y**ou know the best thing about the party last night?" Electra is dressed in jodhpurs and boots. She is putting her cap and crop into a sports bag, along with her spurs. Her riding appointment is in an hour.

"What?" Kate has been dying to ask.

"On the drive home, Bernardo was really tired." She is putting carrots and apples into her bag, enough to feed all the horses in the stable, not just the one she rides. "So I told him, 'before you fall asleep at the wheel, I can drive. I'm wide awake.' So after another few minutes, he pulled over and let me drive."

"Where was Carla?"

"Oh, she fell asleep in the back seat as soon as we got in the car."

"So he let you drive his father's brand new car?"

"He did! I drove two Audis in two days! After the TT, I was more confident. I drove really fast!"

"Don't tell me that! I bet that woke him up!"

"It did!" She puts her riding gear by the patio door, ready to go. Kate is waiting for more details but Electra has said all she is going to say.

Kate peels an onion and then rinses it under water before chopping it to diminish eventual tears. Electra has pulled out all the vegetables from the bin, and has started chopping zucchini. They are preparing a late summer version of *pasta primavera*.

"Matteo is coming over today."

"When?"

"After I return from riding."

"How was the anchor?"

"I didn't see it, the water was too murky." She frowns, and then brightens, a momentary eclipse. "This afternoon, may I use some of Clover's shampoo?"

"Daddy and I washed him yesterday."

"Matteo and I want to wash *Mica*. She's covered in fleas."

"Sure. I have flea drops, if you want. Other than riding and washing the dog, what are your plans for today?"

"We're going to see if we can find Orecchiella. He's missing."

"Take some meat." Kate heats the frying pan, watches with satisfaction as the onions turn translucent.

"Matteo is cooking it now," Electra says, slicing and chopping the bright red and yellow peppers. "Oh, do you know what I realized today?"

"What?"

"That I am a nerd."

"That just occurred to you?"

"The book I ordered for my Economic Competitive Strategies course arrived yesterday, and I had to restrain myself from opening it until the postman left."

"It's good that you like what you are studying."

"Mama, I have already read the first three chapters! And I was seriously thinking of cancelling my plans with Matteo to continue reading."

"You are right. You are a nerd. I'll bring you the phone."

There have been too many parties this summer. They have participated in too many mundane conversations. Fortunately, along the way, scattered in, there has been real dialogue, thought-provoking conversation, with solid ideas and images. Nonetheless, Kate is looking forward to a quieter season, with more time for themselves. However, before they can relax, they must reciprocate the invitations they have received from Eugenio's friends. Niccolò and Kate set the date for September 1st. They won't tell their new friends it is the anniversary of the day they met, but Niccolò and Kate will enjoy the underlying celebration.

Preparing the menu isn't difficult. It is the guest list that causes Kate a moment's deliberation. She knows whom they must invite, that's easy, all the people who have invited them into their homes. But there are others in the group who have not had parties. Does Kate need to invite them all? Kate calls Eugenio.

"I am organizing a party," Kate says. In the background, she hears bosanova music playing.

"How nice!" There is an echo. Kate can envision Eugenio dancing through his suite of rooms, the phone on loud-speaker. "Everyone is curious to see your home."

"I hope they won't be disappointed."

"I'm sure they won't." He hums along with Jobim. "Who are you planning to invite."

Kate reads him the list, raising her voice to compensate for the Samba-like music. "What do you think?"

"You can invite the Pepolis, but they won't come. They don't go anywhere."

"But they were at your party."

"Well, they come to me, of course, we are practically family."

"I've invited Carlo Servato and his wife—"

"Anna. Another couple who never attend parties."

"Are they friends with the others I've invited?"

"They are part of the same group, but Carlo's wife is a recluse. Why did you decide to invite them?"

"Their nephew Bernardo has been very kind to Electra this summer."

"I see you haven't included Aurora and Paolo. Any particular reason?"

"No, just that our house is small, and I already have twenty-five on the list, plus us, twenty-eight."

"Hmmm."

"You think I should invite them?"

"I think it might create problems if you don't. They are part of the group. They are like little children. They will feel left out if you invite the others but not them."

"I was thinking I could invite a second group, have a smaller, second party."

"Serial B?"

"Is that how it will be interpreted?"

"I'm afraid so."

"I wouldn't want to offend anyone."

Silence.

"It would probably be easier if I just invited them."

"I'm glad you have come to the right solution."

"I don't need to invite that other couple, do I? Monica? And her husband. What is his name?"

"Beppe. No, not if you don't want to, although I have noticed Monica has been courting you, trying to win your favor at parties this summer."

"Is that what she is doing? Every time I see her she makes a rude remark about my height, as if I could do something to change it."

"You are too sensitive. You take things the wrong way."

His words ring familiar but untrue. "So do I need to invite them?" Kate is starting to feel cornered. She should have some say on whom they invite into their home.

"You don't have to invite Beppe and Monica, as long as you invite Aurora and Paolo. Do you need to borrow anything for the party? Tables? Chairs? Dishes?"

"Thanks, I think we have everything. Can we invite everyone for seven?" The days are beginning to shorten. "So they can see the view before dark?"

"You can try but I doubt anyone will arrive before eight."

He is undoubtedly right. In Florence Kate has invited people for afternoon tea at four and everyone shows up at five, the Italian hour for *merenda*. If Kate invites people for dinner at seven, they will arrive at their usual dinner hour, which is eight.

"Eight-thirty," Niccolò speculates. "South of Florence, dinner is rarely before eight-thirty. Especially in summer."

Stubbornly, Kate invites the group for seven. At least Niccolò and Kate and Electra will be ready, on the terrace, to enjoy the last light of the day.

The drinks and *antipasti* are on the patio. Platters of food have been prepared and carefully arranged indoors on the dining room table, interspersed with the few remaining summer flowers from their garden: pink and white oleander clusters, enlivened with sprigs of evergreen and miniscule pine cones. Electra has added candles, which makes the extended table more ornate, but Kate has had to take them away as she is afraid people might burn themselves as they reach over the candles to fill their plates.

The two puppies who have not yet been adopted have been collected and bedded downstairs in Electra's bedroom, with Clover as their babysitter. There will be puddles to clean up, but better puddles than puppies underfoot and the worry of a sprained ankle.

Electra and Kate have been working in the kitchen all week. They are pleased with the results. They have prepared something for everyone: meat dishes for Graziella who doesn't eat fish, fish for those who don't eat meat; vegetables, breads, savory pastries; and pasta, the only dish that requires last minute attention. Everyone should find something he or she likes on the table.

"What should I wear?" Kate asks Electra.

"Wear your new white dress, it will show off your tan."

"You don't think it is too risqué?" It is white cotton broadcloth, with navy blue trim, a large sailor's collar but otherwise backless; a full skirt flaring from a tightly fitted waist.

"No, Mama. There is nothing *osé* about it."

To make sure she's not dressing unsuitably, Kate double-checks with Niccolò. Electra has good taste but she is young. Niccolò will know.

"You look wonderful. You should dress like this all the time."

"It's not inappropriate?"

"Not at all."

At ten minutes past eight, the first guests arrive: within minutes, like a flock of migrating birds, everyone has landed. Under Eugenio's astute instructions, their friends have parked their cars side by side, precisely, like the scales of a fish, someone notes, and are on the terrace, accepting drinks.

Kate sees patterns emerging. Diana, Caterina, Graziella, Silvia and Anna ask for water or juice; they don't drink wine until dinner is served. Instead, the men, Renato, Lorenzo, Ettore, Carlo, Paolo, Bernardo, all finish their first glass of Prosecco and replenish it quickly. The six bottles Kate has chilled disappear much more quickly than anticipated. She hopes they won't run out. She has twelve chilled bottles of white wine, all from Bernardo's family's cantina, and six bottles of red open, breathing, to serve with dinner, but she can offer them with the *hors d'oeuvres*, if necessary.

Everyone, without exception, comments on the view, or its absence. By eight o'clock the view has vanished, is absolute in its darkness, except for the lights in their garden and the stars emerging. Like a chorus, the same phrase is repeated: "*Peccato! Abbiamo perso il panorama!*" What a shame! We missed the view."

Like a chorus, the women who comment on Kate's dress give compliments mixed with concern: 'How pretty you look, but aren't you afraid you'll be cold?' Caterina and Anna, Bernardo's aunt, have dressed for winter, even though the evening is warm. Silvia has worn a large, roomy, caftan-kind of dress, and many women are carrying shawls. "*Come sei bella,*" they repeat, "*ma non hai paura di sentire freddo?*"

As the hostess, Kate will be moving all evening. There is little chance of being cold.

The men are more straight-forward. Renato greets Kate, "*Principessa! Sei bellissima!*"

"*Bella come questa straordinaria notte.*" Lorenzo confirms. "The only element missing to make this a perfect night *è l'Arpa eolica.*"

"Sorry?"

"The lyre." He looks puzzled that Kate doesn't know what he is talking about. "It was one of the great symbols in the Era of Romanticism. Shelley used it in "Ode to the West Wind." Coleridge mentions it in both "Dejection, An Ode", and "The *Eolian* Harp.""

"Ah, the Aeolian Harp! Of course!"

Lorenzo has developed the habit of dropping by each week, sometimes more than once, to discuss poetry with Kate. They take turns reading Shelley and Keats and Shakespeare. Lorenzo's slightly accented English baritone eases over a caesura so that the meaning plays both at the end and the beginning of a line. Kate, despite her enthusiasm, stumbles over the lines no matter how familiar she is with a poem. She will never be comfortable reading aloud. Historically, Lorenzo is extremely knowledgeable and can put any poem or play in context. As a scholar, he has researched every line, every allusion; he has facts to support every assertion. Kate plays the devil's advocate, throwing Jungian archetype monkey-wrenches into his most elaborate arguments, as well as flashing light into the Platonic caves of objective impossibility. Despite their different points of departure, they wholeheartedly agree on the time-less beauty, the eternal significance of the lines they read.

"Up there, harp-generated wind songs emanating from the boughs of those magnificent pines," he nods toward the trees at the front gate, "which might actually have been planted during the Romantic Era."

"You are absolutely right, that would be the perfect final touch." She would like to prolong this dialogue. Lorenzo always introduces subjects which Kate would enjoy discussing at length, but as hostess she will be lucky if she participates in any conversation tonight. "I'll see what I can do about finding one for next year's party." She senses his disappointment at a conversation aborted. "Are you finding time to write, despite the summer distractions?"

"A little. Mostly I'm thinking."

"About what?"

"*Paradise Lost*. I am trying to determine who is the heroic figure, God or Satan?"

"The obvious choice would be God, no?" Kate says, setting down her tray of drinks.

"But the Archangel's description of God is certainly less than inspirational. Unless you admire bureaucratic adornments."

"Milton was a Protestant," Kate says, "if I remember correctly. He might have been objecting to the Roman Catholic version of God."

"Certainly his devil is a clever, determined figure, choosing to wage his battle against God by toying with His creation: man."

"Strategic. A timeless, never-ending battle."

"I will leave you to your duties as hostess."

"A timeless, never-ending battle." They laugh. "We will continue this conversation soon, I hope."

"*A presto.*"

"*Avete fatto una bella figura stasera*," Eugenio says, allowing Kate to refill his glass. She hopes Niccolò is filling glasses, too.

He tends to become involved in conversation and forgets his role as host, as she has just done. She glances across the crowd and sees her husband fully engaged in conversation with the Mattarellas. Fortunately, Electra is circulating, refilling glasses, offering canapés. How she wishes Elizabeth were here, too!

"Thank you." It seems they have passed inspection.

Eugenio looks pleased with himself. After all, he has introduced them to almost all these people. Kate and Niccolò could have embarrassed him; let him down if their preparations hadn't been up to par tonight.

"Do you think I can serve dinner?" Kate asks. "Everyone has had enough starters by now."

"Is everyone here? Didn't you say you invited the Pepolis?"

"I did. And they called yesterday to confirm. But it's almost nine. Don't you think people will want to eat?"

Eugenio smiles enigmatically. "It would be a ghastly error to start dinner before the Pepolis arrive."

"But they are late."

"It doesn't matter. If they confirmed they are coming, you must wait."

Kate has known the Pepolis were a respected family in Trapani, an important street is named after them, but Kate hadn't known their elevated rank among their friends. Just as Kate is wondering if she should put the duck breasts back in the oven, worrying how to keep them from drying out, a car pulls up to their front gate.

Niccolò and Kate walk together to greet the Pepolis. Kate hopes to hurry them along so that she can serve dinner, but Orlando Pepoli brings a book out of the car to show to Niccolò. It is a book that Niccolò's grandfather wrote, a children's story—one of his two ventures outside his specialty as historian—dedicated to the great-grandsons of his dear friend, Conte Pepoli. "I am the eldest grandson," Orlando is saying, opening to the front page where the dedication is printed, below which is a hand-written dedication from Niccolò's grandfather. "I could give you the book, if you'd like."

"I am deeply moved that you would offer it to me," Niccolò says, handing it back, "but I wouldn't think of accepting."

Teresa Pepoli and Kate have been standing together on the sidelines of their husbands' conversation, smiling but silent;

however, as they start to walk toward the house, she suddenly links her arm in Kate's, like an old school buddy. Kate is a little embarrassed. She has only seen this woman one time before, months ago, at Eugenio's party, where they didn't have occasion to speak. As they near the other guests, Teresa squeezes her hand before releasing her arm. "With me, it's all based on feeling."

Kate smiles. She doesn't know exactly what this woman is talking about; and doesn't know how to respond. It doesn't matter. Everyone is greeting Teresa, talking at once. The men bow over her hand, the women kiss her cheek. Orlando and Niccolò join the crowd, chatting like old friends. Orlando greets the women with the same courtly bow. He has a peculiar laugh, Kate notes, an intake of breath, almost a hiccup, but it doesn't diminish his style, or cause others to move away.

The King and Queen of the Street Name Club have arrived. Kate can serve dinner. She hopes the duck breasts won't be so dreadfully dry as to condemn her to the royal dungeon.

As their guests have finished serving themselves for what seems a final time, Kate sends Electra outside to where they are seated at tables; has her pass the platters one last time. While she is offering a last helping, Kate slips into the kitchen, bringing with her the platters that are nearly empty. Kate takes notes: no one ate much pasta but all of the stuffed porcini mushrooms are gone. The risotto with truffles is finished, too, but there are a lot of duck breasts left. Perhaps it was too dry. Or too difficult to eat. Another note: whatever meat Kate serves next year needs to be bite size.

She was right to place cards by the dishes, stating their names. Italians are suspicious of non-Italian foods, of which there were many tonight. Her winning card, Kate believes, is serving dishes that no one here can duplicate. It would be a mistake if she were to try serving *cous cous,* a local specialty.

The table is almost empty. Each time Kate re-enters the dining room to remove a plate, she brings a dessert with her.

She is back in the kitchen, arranging cookies onto a plate, when Kate hears voices on the terrace. Contrary to what Kate expected, their friends haven't divided into small groups, some on the terrace, some at the tables in front of the house. Instead, after the antipasti, everyone has gathered together in a large, lopsided circle, though it means not everyone is able to rest their plate and drink on a table. The table on the terrace, set to accommodate eight, has been empty.

Now Kate hears voices on the terrace, two. The doors from the kitchen are closed except a crack: Kate didn't want anyone looking in to see the kitchen in disorder. Picking up the plate of cookies, Kate pauses at the door in time to hear a woman say "—ma lei chi si crede di essere—who does she think she is?"

She wonders who is talking, cloistered away like this from the others.

"Marilyn Monroe, ha!"

Kate can practically see the blood dripping from fangs, the tone is so cruel.

But who are they talking about? Who are they criticizing?

"Stealing attention from all our husbands."

"Her poor husband." Kate hears Eugenio say.

"That's what he gets for marrying a foreigner."

Kate feels blood flooding into her face as it becomes clear that she is the object of their disdain.

She carries the last plate of sweets to the table; moves aside a tiramisu to make room for the plate of cookies. The table looks crowded. Unattractive. Unappetizing. The crostata Kate was so proud of this morning, made from her own fruit preserves and elaborately latticed looks pretentious now. Kate selects a few flowers from her desk and tries to position them attractively, but nothing makes the table pretty. Kate swallows hard.

A sadness settles on her like dust, at first lightly so that Kate doesn't even notice it has worked its way into her nose, her eyes, her ears, covers her skin so that even her pores have difficulty breathing; as though her heart has been dusted, too. Now Kate knows why she keeps to herself, why Kate prefers individuals to groups. She reaches into the downstairs cupboard and retrieves a dark, plum-colored shawl; wraps it over her bare shoulders.

Electra bustles into the house carrying two empty trays. "I don't think I can convince anyone to eat anything more," Her voice is bright and cheerful. "Except dessert. They are all waiting for your desserts. Especially Bernardo."

"Can you set those trays in the kitchen?"

"Sure. Are you cold?"

"No." Kate shivers.

Electra rests the trays on the dining room table. "Are you ready to invite your friends in for dessert?"

"In a minute." Kate knows it isn't logical to feel this way, all she has to do is look into Electra's happy face, and her world will come back into focus. But her heart won't listen to reason; it remains heavy and dull; clotted.

"Mama, what's happened?"

"Nothing." Such a silly thing, emotions, intangible, insubstantial, but with the strength of a near tidal wave to knock Kate off her feet, pull her under, keep her spinning until her reserve of strength is completely exhausted, and she must give in to the turbulence.

"Mama?"

"Just give me a minute, Electra." The pain Kate feels is intensely physical. She would have more success ordering a migraine out of the room.

"But what happened? Did somebody call? Have you had bad news?"

"No." Kate swallows. She has to tell Electra, so she will stop imaging someone dead. "I just overheard two *friends*—" she laughs at the irony "—criticizing me."

"Who?" She is incredulous.

"I don't know. Eugenio and someone whose voice I didn't recognize."

"Oh," Electra says dismissively. "They are probably just jealous."

Jealousy! All her life Kate has worked to avoid it.

"I knew I shouldn't have worn this dress! I was a fool to be flattered by you and your Daddy."

"Mama, you look fantastic. All evening I've been proud that you're my mother. I've received a dozen compliments about you. Are you going to let two gossips spoil this lovely evening? Mama?"

"I don't know, Electra. I feel pretty miserable right now." Whoever the *friends* are, they have stuck their swords deeply into her Achilles' heel.

"Mama!" Electra moves into her line of vision, forces her mother to look at her. "Just because two old gossips haven't outgrown their middle school malice, doesn't mean that you have to return to your teenage insecurities. Listen to me! You haven't done anything to deserve their criticism so stop acting as though you have."

Kate can feel her face burning. She feels a flush of heat rush through her body. Kate throws off her shawl. Kate needs fresh air.

"I am glad to see you have come to your senses, finally."

"No," Kate laughs, fanning herself. "I just had a really intense hot flash!"

The sadness crests and then passes. Kate is left shored and sandy, skin prickling, as if from the sting of salt water; but safe, no longer in danger of drowning.

"At least it has brought the color back to your face. Come on!" Electra insists. "Get moving! Everyone is waiting for dessert."

Electra is preparing two suitcases, one filled with the things she will need in Utrecht, which is largely empty, as she wants to leave room for her riding gear; and one is full of the things she wants her parents to bring back to Florence for her. All her lightweight clothes are being folded and placed neatly in her drawers, so they will be in order when she returns next summer. Kate is impressed. She has never seen Electra so well organized.

"Bernardo asked if he could pick me up from riding today."

"That was nice."

"He said he wanted to watch me ride."

"It sounds serious."

"It isn't."

"Are you sure?"

"Mama, he hasn't even tried to kiss me. How unserious can you get? He's just a nice guy, that's all."

"You've enjoyed his company this summer."

"I have." She is chewing her lower lip, masticating an idea. "You've always told me to have faith, to trust that things will happen as they are supposed to happen."

"I have."

"That if something is meant to be, it will happen, if we are open and receptive to receive it."

"That's right."

"So, if it is meant to be, it will be. If not, I have made a good friend." She picks up a photograph of herself and the puppies, drops it into her suitcase. "It's a win-win situation. How can I have any regrets?"

Kate nods. How can she argue with perfect logic? She looks at a row of books standing side by side on top of her daughter's dresser; two speakers from her stereo serving as bookends. "You've done a lot of reading this summer."

"It's been a great summer." She runs her finger across the spines of the books, scanning the labels. "There are a couple of books I want to bring with me," she says, selecting two. "Not that I will have a lot of time to read, with Econometrics and Competitive Strategies this semester."

"There's always time to read, even if only ten or twenty minutes in a day."

"I'm going to miss you, Mama."

"I'm going to miss you, too."

"Christmas vacation seems awfully far away."

"Maybe we will fly up to see you before the harvest."

"That would help. Or maybe I can come home to Florence mid-term."

"That's even better. Whichever you prefer."

"By the way," she says, snapping shut the suitcase for Florence. "Bernardo says he's going to come up to Utrecht one weekend in September. Can you give me the name of the bed and breakfast you liked?"

Matteo and Angelica are returning to the city. When Edoardo was alive, the Oliviero family never returned to the city before the end of the olive harvest, mid-December, but this has all changed now that Edoardo is gone. Matteo needs to study for an exam in October. He is working toward his master's degree in Marine Archeology. His study group meets every afternoon from three until dinnertime; sometimes continuing after dinner. He finds it too demanding to drive up to the country at the end of the day. Sergio has returned to duty in Lebanon. He will finish his assignment at the end of October; then he hopes to be stationed in Trapani. The Italian Armed Services will be sensitive to his request to stay near his recently widowed mother.

Angelica has told Kate that they will be leaving the day after tomorrow. Her voice is matter of fact, resigned. She is going along with what she is told to do, even though she would have other preferences. Kate invites her in for tea. Her hesitation is habitual. In fact, Angelica does have time these days for tea, if not an appetite.

She wraps her black, cable-knit sweater around her shoulders as she looks at the dish of meat marinating at the end of the counter.

"What are you making?"

"Carpaccio. I am trying to build up Electra's strength for a cold winter up north."

"What's your marinade?"

"Olive oil and lemon, salt and pepper, thyme, oregano."

She laughs. "When I was a little girl, my father and his brother inherited a farm from their father. They divided up the land, that was easy, but my grandfather had two animals, a *vacca* and a *vitellino*—a cow and a calf. 'What will I do with a *vitellino*?' my father asked. 'I'll take the calf,' my uncle said, 'and you take the cow.'

"So my father took the *vacca*, he called the *macellaio*, and made an appointment for the butcher to come to pick up the *vacca* the following day. My father didn't have a barn; he wasn't that kind of farmer, so he put the *vacca* into a storage shed for the night. The next morning, when he went to open the shed for the butcher, they found the cow lying on its side. Against the wall was a 100 kilo barrel of olive oil that the beast has broken open with its horns. It had consumed almost half the oil. The butcher didn't want to take the *vacca* but my father gave him a discount and said 'You can sell it as marinated beef.'" She laughs. "I can't remember why I told you this story."

It doesn't matter. It is good to see Angelica laughing again.

In theory, Angelica and Matteo will come up from town daily, Matteo to feed the animals, Angelica to do the many things left undone: the last vegetables in the garden, large, misshapen pumpkins and the last fruit on the trees, hard-as-rock *mele cotogne*—quince apples. Some days Kate and Niccolò see them driving by in a hurry, Matteo having slept late, or worried that it will start to rain before they light the fire to cook the food to feed the dogs. Some days all they hear of them is the double beep of their car's horn as they pass. Other days, they stop for a minute to chat. It isn't the same. They feel Edoardo's absence anew. Kate wanders in her garden alone.

The dogs are in their garden every morning when Kate wakes, except Orecchiella, who has disappeared. Matteo and Angelica still hope he will return, but Kate knows he won't. Too much time has passed. He has gone to find Edoardo.

Niccolò tries to engage the dogs' interests, tries to throw a pine cone for *Mica* or Sandy or Russ, but after a few minutes they lose interest. They are waiting for Edoardo. When he doesn't appear, they wander off. Kate can see them at the edge of their property, positioned strategically to see Edoardo's car if it comes into view.

As Matteo and Angelica have left, the shepherd and his flock have returned. The shepherd himself could be from any epoch, his beard long, his hair clipped haphazardly—perhaps by the same sheers used to crop the sheep? But his *modo di fare*—his way of being—has turned modern. In the springtime he herded his animals up the hill, out of the valley, on a *motorino*—a motor scooter. In the autumn Niccolò and Kate find him comfortably ensconced in a car, an old Renault, the windows open, his arm extended to keep his flock moving.

The bellwether—the leader to this drove of sheep—is a handsome, bearded, tawny fellow who knows the way to the pasture where they will spend the day, but either the hill outside Kate and Niccolò's house is steep and tiring and requires rest, or he and his friends are tempted by the *frassino*—ash—tree growing along the upper edge of their garden. Whatever the reason, the herd stops halfway up the hill, creating an impasse so that the road in front of their gate is thick with shaggy, mulling sheep. They nibble on the lower branches of the *frassino*; the goats rise up onto their hind legs, resting their front hooves on the guardrail to enjoy the more tender leaves.

If the front gate is open, they wander in to see what looks appetizing: the daisy bush, Kate's pride and joy, gets trimmed radically if she or Niccolò is not right there to shoo them away. Eventually, the shepherd's car catches up, he bangs his hand against the side of the car door, and they start moving again, bells clanging; a cacophony of metallic chimes coming together like an oddly instrumented Gregorian chant. Sometimes the shepherd smiles and waves, sometimes he calls out a word of greeting, but today, as he herds his flock back toward their nightly shelter, he has his cellphone to his ear: between steering his sheep, steering his car and his conversation, his attention is fully engaged.

Kate continues dividing the agapanthuses, preparing to transplant the new growth onto the ridge above their house. It is delicate work: she has to be careful not to break the bulbs. At the end of the operation, when Kate finally looks up, she sees that Cofano is gone! So is the meadow below their house! Abruptly, Kate is wrapped in a coat of white fog, the likes of which they haven't seen since Easter.

She gathers up her spade and shovel as she hears Niccolò move through the fog to join her. "The seasons are changing."

"Dramatically. Here, take my sweater. I'll take your tools."

Before Kate can slip his sweater over her head, the fog lifts, is heading up the hill toward Erice. Cofano is back, bathed in brilliant sunlight.

At night, after dinner, sitting on their terrace, enjoying a glass of *Ben Ryè*, the lack of human presence is absolute.

"The summer has passed too quickly," Niccolò says. "It should be the start of July just about now."

"Don't worry," Kate reassures him. "The day after tomorrow it will be July again."

She can see him nodding in agreement, but is this a reassurance, time slipping by so quickly that the autumn and winter and spring slip by in an instant; like the sun warmed sand they let fall through their fingers the day before yesterday at Cornino? His glass sits empty. He lifts it tentatively, then puts it down, then lifts it again, as if unaware of what he is doing. Kate pours another inch of *Passito di Pantelleria* into his glass but he lets it sit; lets the tiny flakes of sediment settle.

They are not surrounded by silence. A distant sheep's bell clangs as one animal shifts against another in their crowded stall, like distant church chimes. There are owls and foxes calling but not to one another, presumably. Occasionally there is wind, which adds a dimension of sound, as the darkness beyond the terrace adds another dimension to the light encircling them, until Kate switches it off and they are engulfed, made one with the night. There are no voices. No human movement. They sit in their relative silence feeling no need to talk.

Even the distant lights at the shore have stopped moving. No car lights progress down roads. Not even roads are visible, just pinpricks of coastal lights, a necklace of pale color, as if moonlight were reflecting off water-weathered amber glass strung along the edge of the sea. This solitude is an illusion, of course. They know that restaurants are full of people up the hill in Erice, and down the hill in Trapani; in Bonagia, on the coast, there is movement and conversation.

The stars are as close, as far away, as the lights on the coast. Tonight they are plentiful, playful, twinkling. Niccolò stretches his legs, slouches down in his chair, leans his head back so that his neck is supported, and gazes.

Kate is given the flash of a fallen star and though she waits for another, the first is all she receives.

Everyone agrees that *Calvino's* has the best pizza in Trapani, but everyone has his own opinion where they should go for a real meal tonight.

"I vote for *Tentazioni di Gusto*," says Renato, leaning back in the corner of his sofa, legs crossed, nonchalant. Kate is struck again how much he reminds her of Cole Porter, not just in looks but in style: cool, calm, collected, composed. The only component missing is a long, ivory cigarette holder.

"The waiters treat him like royalty," his wife, Diana interrupts. She, too, could be from the Cole Porter era, not from her dress, which is last minute fashion, but from the way she carries herself: precise, studied, contained, a style that hasn't made its way into the twenty-first century. Graciously, she passes a tray of attractive, color-coordinated *hors d'oeuvres*.

This is the first time Kate has seen *The Street Name Club*, as she has started to call this group, since her party. After the conversation she overheard, she hasn't felt like seeing them.

Even now, though Kate can't really believe that any of these women would speak spitefully about her, Kate tries to recognize the voice on the terrace. It isn't Diana, whose vowels are roundly articulated, her consonants crisp and clear; her enunciation as perfect as her dress and manners.

"*Tentazioni di Gusto* is good," Niccolò says. "You are right, but the food can be a little too original, at times. Salami and figs as a starter may be old hat but they work together in a way that figs with salmon never will."

The day after their party, Kate told Niccolò about the conversation she overheard. He was angry but incredulous, unable to believe that any of their new friends would betray them, especially in their own home. But Niccolò is Latin in temperament: quick to lose his temper, quick to forget a transgression. Kate is more like an Anglo-Saxon elephant, never forgetting, never forgiving. She has questioned the wisdom of their continued involvement with this group, but Niccolò wants to give them another chance. They have compromised. They have declined invitations to two larger parties, but they have accepted an invitation from Renato and Diana, to spend an evening with three of the couples they especially like.

"My favorite trattoria is *Al Solito Posto*," Caterina offers. The Same Old Place.

"The Same Old Place is my favorite, too," Lorenzo agrees. "The food is traditional but there are enough choices on the menu to keep from getting bored."

"The service is quick, efficient, and the prices are reasonable," Caterina adds, like a bridge player, reinforcing her partner's hand. She smiles at Kate, and winks.

No. It can't be Caterina.

"Ettore and I like *Cantina Siciliana*," Graziella lays down her card shyly, her voice soft, breathless, immediately recognizable.

"It is excellent, isn't it," Diana says, "but it's tiny, five tables—no more than thirty people can be served in an evening. I doubt they can seat us without a reservation."

"I'm willing to call," Niccolò offers, casting his vote. "The food is exciting and the wines are excellent."

"It's a little more expensive than *Al Solito Posto*, but it's worth it," says Graziella.

Kate has grown bored with this exchange. She glances at Lorenzo, who shrugs an eyebrow and smiles resignedly. "Are you sure you don't miss the limitations of academia?" He says quietly in his gentlemanly English.

She takes his question literally rather than a comment on the lightness of their present conversation. "I miss being among readers, I miss the easy exchange of books being recommended. I am always hungry for a good read."

"The best book I have read this year is *The Winter Vault*. Not a fast read but every line is poetic."

"I will order it tomorrow. I can recommend—"

"I know a restaurant that is excellent!" Ettore interrupts, as if having awakened from Sleepy Hollow. "An *enoteca* near *Torre di Ligny*. And it costs nothing!"

Ettore's statement revitalizes Kate's attention. She is always keen to find an excellent, reasonably priced restaurant.

"For ten euro, you are given a glass of wine, sardines on bread, all the olives you want, and a hard-boiled egg!"

"Ettore!" Graziella slaps his hand. "They aren't interested in that old sailor's dive."

"And if that isn't enough," he continues, undeterred. "They will serve you a second hard-boiled egg for free!" He is earnest, but it takes a minute to realize he's speaking from heartfelt enthusiasm, not making fun of them.

The best deal in town!

Renato and Diana are choking with laughter. Caterina and Graziella, too; no one is able to reply, as if they've all swallowed that second hard-boiled egg, have it stuck in their throats and desperately need yet another glass of wine to wash it down.

In the end, Renato drives them to a new little place he has wanted to try: *Le Tre Salette*. It is even smaller than *Cantina Siciliana*, three tiny rooms, one of which is the kitchen. In the smaller of the two rooms there is one long table, set for eight. Ettore, who has a knack for positioning people at the table and isn't slowed by the difficulty of eight, seats Kate between Renato and Lorenzo. Kate glances at Graziella and Caterina to see if the seating arrangement has evoked any resentment, but they are both chatting with Niccolò, who is seated between them. Ettore rises to wash his hands. Diana slips into the kitchen to appraise the fish. She returns enthusiastic.

"*Principessa mia*," Renato places a hand over Kate's. "What will you have to eat this evening?" He has been calling Kate his princess all summer, after Kate confessed that she wore a Grace Kelly-style *Escada* ball gown in a charity fashion show in Florence a few years ago, and it made her feel like a princess.

Is this flirting? With his wife and her husband across the table? Renato's hand rested briefly on hers, true, but it was in plain sight, not on her knee, not under the table, a gesture of affection, certainly nothing more.

The waitress hands Niccolò the wine list. He, in turn, passes it to Kate. She looks at it briefly, and then passes it to Ettore. Kate knows something about Tuscan wines but she is the least qualified to chose a Sicilian wine.

Ettore doesn't open the list but says to the waitress, "Do you have *Planeta's La Segreta? Bianco*, naturally?"

"No."

"*Donnafugata?*"

"Of course."

"Then bring us *Vigna di Gabri*. Well chilled."

Caterina says, "We were sorry you didn't come to Aurora and Paolo's party last night" She looks directly at Kate, then Niccolò.

"We had other plans." In truth, they stayed at home and read.

"And we missed you at the Ricci's party last week," Graziella says.

Kate decides to confide. "We are going to limit our social activities a bit."

Niccolò supports her. "We've been going out too much."

Diana sits up straighter. "Well, some of our group can be a little—what can I call it?"

"—provincial." Caterina finishes.

"But do you find some of them vicious?" Kate asks, before she can censor herself.

Caterina and Diana exchange looks, puzzled. "Everyone has their limitations, but—"

"—vicious is a little strong," Graziella adds.

"The only way to maintain long-term relationships in a small town like this, generation after generation," Diana counsels, "is to ignore friends' little weaknesses."

"They don't really amount to much," Graziella adds, "just a bit of irritating gossip."

"But how do you deal with it?" Kate asks, looking from one to the other, addressing everyone at the table.

"Keep in touch."

"Don't take it personally."

"Act as if nothing has happened."

"*Stealing their husbands' attentions.*' Those aren't words easily ignored."

Renato looks at Diana, Lorenzo looks at Caterina, they all look at Ettore, then Graziella. Everyone is stunned.

"Who said that?" Diana inquires.

"I don't know," Kate admits. "But it sounded pretty vicious."

"I don't understand," Ettore says. "Who said what when?"

"At our party. On our terrace. I overheard Eugenio talking with a woman who was slandering me."

"Someone in our group?" Caterina asks. "Impossible."

"You and Niccolò are like a breath of fresh air—"

"Someone who hasn't already heard our stories a hundred times—"

"You love Sicilia as much as we do, but you aren't embarrassed to admit it."

"No, my dear, you are surely mistaken."

Her face red, Kate repeats again what she heard at their party, finishing with 'That's what he gets for marrying a foreigner!'

Caterina has twisted the corner of her napkin until it has begun to fray. She clears her voice. "You are right. What you heard is unkind."

"Unkind but not unjustified," Diana says sharply.

"But they weren't speaking about you, dear," Caterina clarifies.

"My cousin, Giuseppe, married a young French woman some years ago," Lorenzo explains, "and she has brought much unhappiness to their marriage."

"Ha! She's committed more indiscretions in the last three years than a stray dog in heat!" Ettore says.

Renato laughs. "It isn't fair of us to speak badly of Céline, but she has earned herself a few distinct criticisms."

Diana reaches across the table, squeezes Kate's hand. "We are all glad to have you and Niccolò as friends."

Out of the ashes rises the Phoenix.

"Even if you do have too vivid an imagination," Lorenzo adds, his bright, sky-colored eyes alight with Puck-like conspiracy.

Everyone at the table laughs, a sound that washes over Kate like the tide over ragged rocks on the shore, smoothing them until they are soft and even, no longer a danger to bare, tender feet; least of all her Achilles' heel.

"We will miss you when you return to Florence."

"*Principessa mia.*"

Yesterday Niccolò and Kate worked in the garden all morning. There was a pine growing on the hill near the front gate which Niccolò had looked at dubiously ever since they moved in. A fire catcher, Kate called it: just the right height and dimension to pull a forest fire into their garden. Their twin, hundred-year-old pines would be safer from the threat of fire without a smaller pine as kindling at the base.

However, as often happens when they start to work, the job designated for their morning labors is only the starting point of many lateral projects. In order to cut the tree at its base line, they had to hoe away a mountain of earth, in which they found the bases of cactus, which had to be hacked out with a pick ax. The earth they pulled away was unusually fertile, so as they dug and raked, Kate created a bed for the geranium cuttings she intends to prune before they leave mid-October.

Two gargantuan geraniums grow on either side of their terrace. They need to be pruned so that the wind doesn't break them and so that they don't cover the view from the terrace. With the pine about to be displaced, a bed of rich, velvet-leaved geraniums will be a picturesque backdrop against exposed granite.

Niccolò pulls on the cord that ignites the chain saw and down comes the tree. That is the easy part. Now they strip the branches from the trunk, and heave them, javelin style, down the hill onto their driveway where they will retrieve and drag them—most of them taller than Kate, all of them nearly as weighty—to the other side of the house where they will be burned. That accomplished, the two of them together hoist up the heavy trunk and carry it down the hill where tomorrow Matteo will come with his tractor trailer to haul the trunk away. He can burn pine in the outdoor fireplace he uses for cooking the dog food, while they can't risk the resin buildup in their chimney flue. They have learned to clean up after themselves at every stage; otherwise, they find themselves with too many branches to tow to the bonfire at the end of the morning and not enough strength. Then, inevitably, something interrupts their afternoon's program to finish the work started in the morning—an unexpected visitor or weather—so they clean up as they go.

In front of the mounting pile of branches to burn, Kate stops to twist off a particularly beautiful pine cone, then another, equally striking but completely different from the first, even though they grow on the same branch. Kate starts to think what they could have for lunch. They can't have sandwiches as they don't have anything to put into them and even if they did, the little bit of bread that remains is needed for breakfast tomorrow. They are out of everything, Kate realizes. Once again she must shop for groceries.

But that doesn't solve the problem of lunch. Kate should go inside, now, put water on for pasta so it can start boiling while they finish transporting the limbs. As Kate dumps her load of branches onto the building pyre and returns for another load, Niccolò passes her with his bundle, twice the size of hers.

"You are moving as slowly as if you had mud stuck to your boots!"

"I think I must."

"Do we have any leftovers from last night's dinner?"

"Ahhh, we do!"

Lorenzo came over yesterday afternoon to discuss Shelley's long poetic dialogue, "Julian and Maddalo", and at the last minute they convinced him to stay for dinner as Caterina was helping to prepare for a charity banquet. Lorenzo has unlocked the heart of the Romantics for Kate, a gift that reasserts itself as each new day unfolds, in every sublime sunrise she photographs, in every sunset she pauses to witness. Before this summer she could have said that she had read "The Rhyme of the Ancient Mariner," but did she *know* Coleridge? No. Keats? Kate has read "Ode to a Nightingale." She probably wrote a paper on it, but did she ever understand how beautiful it was or how much it addresses the issues that have become her life? A willingness to live with uncertainty, recognition of awe in nature: the presence of the sublime beneath beauty.

Kate made her variation of an Italian classic: *aglio, olio, and peperoncino*—garlic, olive oil, crushed peppers. To these three basic ingredients, she added a fistful of chopped parsley, chopped capers, and half the ripe tomatoes she had in the basket on the counter. It was delicious last night and will be even better now, with all the flavors amalgamated and steeped into the pasta.

There's not a lot left over but perhaps it is enough. Kate quickens her step, eager to finish with the branches, pausing only to twist off another couple of really special pine cones before she heaves her last load of branches.

Her family teases her because she collects pine cones. An avid advocate of un-clutter, everywhere they go, wherever pine cones grow, Kate collects. If they are travelling by air, she settles for one perfect exemplar to pack into her suitcase, but if they are travelling by car and have room, Kate is likely to fill the trunk. Most of these pine cones are consumed each winter; they make easy work of lighting the stove in Florence in the late afternoon. Yet, even when Kate is cold and in a hurry, impatient to start the fire, she appreciates these perfect cones. Some, Kate doesn't burn. She has a little ceramic bowl near the fireplace filled with tiny, starfish-like pine cones collected from a friend's garden along a fiord in Norway, and she keeps one on her desk that Electra brought her from Holland, no larger than a miniature marigold bloom.

Lunch is on the table in the time it takes Niccolò to dump his last load of branches and wash his hands. The meal has grown to include tomatoes, fresh basil and a braid of mozzarella, and figs picked yesterday from Angelica's property. And almonds, which Niccolò shelled last week and Kate toasted yesterday. Kate contemplates bringing out the bottle of white wine they opened last night at dinner but decides against it: they are too tired to drink even one glass of *Inzolia*.

At the far end of the table, together with the pruning shears and gloves that Kate was too tired to put away, is a tiny sprig of pine that she has saved from the burning pile. Niccolò moves the shears and gloves onto the seat of an empty chair, and slides the little branch into the center of the table. A drop of resin forms a translucent bead where the branch has been separated from its base. Its scent acts as a smelling salt to their lagging energies, a centerpiece for their meal.

The wind picks up as they eat. They won't be able to burn their clippings this afternoon. Even though it has rained occasionally in the past several weeks, the wind can carry sparks and the result can be devastating. In a way they are relieved. They are tired, and burning is another demanding job. Usually the wind blows over the castle ruin from the west, but today it blows from the southeast. In Florence Kate knows where the winds come from and what they mean. If big, heavy storm clouds blow across the Arno Valley from the west, from Prato, downtown Florence might flood but on their southwesterly hill it won't rain. If the wind blows from the east, which it rarely does, they are in for a Siberian cold spell. Most of the time the wind arrives from behind them, from the southwest, and if it brings clouds, it will rain.

It took Kate years to understand the wind and rain tendencies in Florence, but now they seem easy, wholly predictable, especially when compared to the eight possibilities of wind that haunt this corner of Sicily. So far the only one Kate recognizes in Sicily is the *Scirocco*. It is the easiest one, although not necessarily the most pleasant, coming as it does from the desert of North Africa. It is hot and dry and it reminds her of California's Santa Ana wind. Here, too, it carries the threat of fire. Reportedly, it lasts for three days. But the others, *Libeccio, Ponente, Greco*, they are all still names to her. To make it more confusing, oftentimes two or three winds blow simultaneously.

She stops trying to make sense of it all and leans back into her chair, the muscles in her arms and calves pleasantly sore but no longer exhausted. Niccolò has picked a cluster of grapes from the vines that grow near where the bonfire will be. They are a pretty, deep purple, almost black, small and crowded tightly on their stem. Kate and Niccolò eat a few, the flavor is sharp, the sweetness secondary. Each tiny fruit is full of seeds, which are deposited on the edge of their plates together with the thick, dark skins. A lot of effort for a little inner juice, but they keep nibbling.

"We are a long way from the seedless perfection of California grapes, aren't we?"

"We are. And we can't even argue that the flavor of these little guys is better."

Yet still they snack.

The breeze from the sea is soft, warm, and at once discernible from the fog shrouded wind that has started gusting down from Erice. Kate can't name either wind but she feels them come together, distinctly. Niccolò plucks off the last grape on the grapple and offers it to her. In the twenty four years of their marriage, Kate can't remember him ever reaching for the last portion of any food without first offering it to her. She loves him for this simple, quotidian consideration. It is better than any jewelry store gift. Kate accepts the grape; polishes it between her thumb and forefinger until it shines brightly, then pops it into his mouth. He smiles at her as sweetly as if it were the tastiest grape in the world. Her centerpiece.

CHAPTER
EIGHTEEN

Up the hill from the castle ruin, there is another road, steep like theirs but narrower, a path that descends towards the cliffs above the sea, but which, like theirs, doesn't reach the sea. Along this road there are several small ruins. Thick walled, one-or-two room houses are now occupied by trees growing from dirt floor interiors. Weeds and brambles climb up buckled chimneys, and floors are paved with bits of broken roof tiles. The more Kate and Niccolò descend toward the sea, the more the road diminishes in width, crowded on both sides with sticker bushes lush with berries, the tartly sweet cluster of juice suspended between glistening black seeds.

The painters have been at work this morning, a fluff of clouds in anti-colors. Shades of gray and ginger are contrasted with a dozen shades of white.

Kate has always thought of white as the simplest color, the absence of color, a space holder providing rest to the eye between other colors. But as the summer ends, as her collection of cloud photographs expands, she has come to perceive white in a multitude of shades—and textures—which seem to alter white's color, as well.

Kate doesn't know where they are going. They don't have a destination. They woke up wanting to take a walk, and decided to explore their neighborhood, if you can call it that, as it lacks neighbors. Judging from the number of abandoned houses they are passing, this area was once a neighborhood.

A car couldn't traverse this road, this path, so narrow now, so overgrown with shrubbery. Niccolò and Kate proceed single file.

231

It is a warm day and Kate has worn a sleeveless blouse. She can feel thorns scratching at her arms, like newly clipped fingernails. One step ahead of her, Kate sees that stickers attach themselves to the sleeves of Niccolò's polo shirt, testing their strength against his stride. He moves forward, disengages; they win by pulling a thread.

Closer to the cliffs, the road widens, as nothing can grow on the sheer rock cascading on the right. The steep cliff is intimidating: they hug the side of the road with the sticker bushes, preferring the thorns to the abrupt drop.

As they round the last curve, they are greeted by a breeze. It removes the moisture from Kate's face deliciously, as if with a cool cloth; finds its way between the buttons of her blouse, under the edges of her shirt tails. It flutters at the hem of her three-quarter-length trousers to dry the sheen on the back of her knees.

In front of them rise five ancient, wind-blown Mediterranean pines, the only growth on this otherwise desolate stretch of land. They appear unexpectedly, like ancient Baobab trees on an empty African plain.

It is easier to walk now, and fresher. The wind has picked up, has lifted the hair off her neck, has caressed it with a cool, refreshing stroke. The road has ended but the land is relatively flat now. They walk through a field, far from the cliff.

Ahead of them, partially hidden by a knoll, there is another ruin, but as they pass the hummock they see it is not a peasant's house but a mansion, perched at the very edge of the cliffs, as if ready to dive.

"Amazing!"

It, too, has lost its roof. The center structure, perhaps a tower, has crumbled on three sides, leaving part of it at its original height, three stories above where they stand. Its remaining walls show fine stone work, classic columns, chiseled stone windowsills; evidence of a majestic edifice.

To one side of this palace, there is another building, a single room that has resisted the elements, has remained intact. It looks like a sentries' post, its westerly wall open with a large stone framed window, with a view of Trapani, the coast, the salt beds, Marsala, the islands and beyond.

The view is 360°, so extraordinary, so vast, that it takes time to comprehend all its elements. Beyond the steep cliff, which demands its own appreciation, Trapani covers the basin. Its pale limestone and gray stone spreads out like water to fill its perimeter. The coast borders the city gracefully. It curves and stretches against protruding rocks, sandy beaches, ports and harbors, salt beds and windmills, from Pizzolungo directly below where they stand, to Marsala some thirty kilometers in the distance, *in linea retta*, as the crow flies, before the coast bends and disappears inland, leaving only the sea until it blurs into infinity.

"I bet you can see Pantelleria on a clear day."

This is an aspiration for all of Trapani: to the north, on a clear day, to see Ustica; to the south, some 150 kilometers away, to see Pantelleria.

Today, easily, Kate can see the Egadi Islands, Favignana, the closest, so clear the *tufo*—limestone—caves are visible rising out of the light turquoise blue water. *Cala Rossa*—Red Cove—is full of boats, whitened by taut sails.

Niccolò has wandered off to explore. He calls to Kate. "There is another little building on the other side of this ruin."

It is hard to pull herself away from this unbounded view.

"Come look at it."

There are pillars to climb over, and Kate has to watch where she places her feet. The structure Niccolò is exploring has one of its two stories fairly intact. The roof has partially collapsed but as the tiled pavement is solid, undamaged, no trees or plants have grown through.

"Actually, this *little* building isn't so small."

"It just seems undersized in comparison to that massive structure."

"Relativity revisited."

The wind has increased and Kate is suddenly chilly. It is a good feeling on a warm day.

"I wonder who it belongs to." Niccolò voices the first of two questions that have been gnawing at Kate.

"And I wonder who could have let it deteriorate like this."

They stand in wonder, equally moved by its beauty and neglect.

By the time they reach home, they have devised a wild plan. They will investigate the ownership to see if it is possible to buy, and if it is, they will restore this sad ruin to its former glory.

The research to discover the ruin's owner is easier than they expected. It belongs to the State. It is *Il Faro*, well known in Trapani, a historical landmark. Its dilapidated condition is a statement of Trapani's decline after the devastating bombings in the Second World War.

Much of Trapani has been restored. The entire downtown historical center shines with clean, refurbished facades. Granted, there are parts of Trapani that still need work. The upper stretches, built without guidelines in the 1960s are not attractive. They have been built in a hurry to accommodate rather than inspire the masses. Nonetheless, the main thoroughfare which runs from the top of the city to the old historic center has been planted with oleander and hibiscus. The old trees are well established, and have been carefully pruned and nurtured. The newer buildings have a certain charm. On the whole, Trapani is moving toward being a beautiful city, the Santa Monica of Sicily. True, there are still bombed out lots, abandoned fields in the midst of tall communist-bloc style constructions, but even these are starting to disappear. The old warehouses near the Tower of *Ligny,* full of disintegrating fishing nets and termite infested bait boats, which couldn't have been given away ten years ago, are being bought by people who know that the good deals won't last long.

Now that they know its name, *Il Faro*—the Lighthouse—they learn it was built at the beginning of the 1800s as a military station. They also learn that construction workers from all over Trapani come here to pick up antique stone work to enhance new construction. The more Niccolò and Kate learn, the more they are drawn to saving this abused building.

Trying to buy it is harder.

One can imagine the bureaucracy involved in trying to buy a property from the State of Italy, but the reality is much more complicated.

To clear themselves of the spider web of bureaucracy, they spend a lot of time at the Lighthouse, sitting on the fallen pillars, considering the merits of its purchase. The eight winds, they soon learn, are all present, almost all the time. Performing at full force, one blasts like a geyser from below *Il Faro's* cliffs while another gusts around the skirts of its foundation. Yet another whips through the glassless windows like wind in the sails. Another tunnels through the wreckage like a ghost in a nightmare. There are often times they do not risk sitting on the parapet wall.

"Are we crazy to want to buy this property?"

"Probably."

But still they talk about it as a real possibility. They come back to visit as if they already owned it.

"We will need sturdy, double-glazed glass."

"Even so, we won't be able to sit outdoors some months of the year."

"We can create open, inner spaces, protected from the wind."

"The road is going to be a problem."

"It's going to be very expensive to construct and maintain."

"Is there water? Does it have a well?"

"Electricity?" Kate knows Niccolò is envisioning a modern windmill, but Kate is afraid there is too much wind here, from too many directions.

"We *are* crazy."

But the lure holds.

There is something in the still standing cornerstones that asks to be restored to its former splendor; something in the perfect classical proportions that calls to be reinstated; something in the building's *anima* that begs to be saved.

In addition, there is the view that will never exhaust the eye, a view so complex, so diverse, and so complete it will require examination for generations to comprehend its entirety.

"But we aren't young," Kate reminds Niccolò.

"We would be building a home for our children's children."

The possibility of restoring *Il Faro,* it occurs to Kate, is Niccolò's answer to letting go of L'Antica. For better or worse, he was born into a family who lived in palaces in town and villas in the country. For Niccolò, it makes a certain kind of sense to want to buy The Lighthouse.

But for Kate? A sensible American?

"Already we have two houses, one in Florence—"

"Which isn't ours," Niccolò reminds her.

"And one in Sicily."

"Two in Sicilia," Niccolò corrects her, as they have just acquired the little house up the hill from theirs.

They are crazy to consider buying The Lighthouse!

Niccolò agrees, at least part of the time. In his rational moments he says to her, "Do you know how much it is going to cost us to reconstruct that property!" as if it were she urging him to buy and restore it, not some inner part of himself.

"I do." Actually, she doesn't. Her wildest guess is probably not even close.

"Do you know what it will be like to live with workers for at least a year?" Niccolò demands, as if she were forcing him to act against his better judgment.

Kate wonders how much their friendship with the Street Name Club is driving Niccolò toward this decision. When their friends come to their house for dinner, they applaud their choice of simple living; however, when Kate and Niccolò go to *their* parties, the large, heavy, cast-iron gates are stemmed in nobility. They creak open onto long driveways winding past statues and fountains, drives that eventually open up to frame a colossal villa or castle. Idle chatter gains another dimension when seated on seventeenth century velvet sofas, under the three tiered, graceful arms of a Murano chandelier, overseen by family portraits and debutante photographs of their heirs as they were presented to society in sepia-toned pinafores. Even an American can become used to these excursions into past glamour: like stepping onto a James Ivory set in bright day light, it makes sense to unfurl a parasol.

When, at Niccolò's request, the Lighthouse is finally designated for public auction, he introduces the possibility to their daughters. He has been tempted to discuss it with them before now, but in the past Niccolò and Kate have shared enthusiasms with them too early, and Elizabeth and Electra's disappointment has exceeded that of their parents' when a dream didn't materialize, for whatever reason, like the pool at L'Antica.

Niccolò calls to discuss the possibility of bidding on The Lighthouse. The response he receives from Elizabeth and Electra does not contain surprise, as if they have been consulting for months on what to say when this question arose.

Niccolò presents all the details, finishing with the price at which it has been put up for auction.

"Daddy, that is nothing!" Electra says. "I know the property. I hiked there with Matteo."

"How many bicycles would that be?" Elizabeth asks, her inimitable way of making sense of large sums of money.

At this price, it is an once-in-a-lifetime occasion. It will cost another hefty sum to put it in order, but a property like this, at a price like this, is unlikely to come along again in their lifetime.

The Lighthouse restored is a one-of-a-kind masterpiece. Priceless. One of those properties only realized through inheritance.

Elizabeth says, "If you want to buy it and restore it to live in yourselves, I think that's great. But to be honest, I would rather you stopped investing and started to enjoy some of your money. You've worked hard. Travel more. Hire more help in the fields at L'Antica. Electra and I have everything we need, and soon we will be working."

Electra says, "The lighthouse would be amazing. We could have the best parties! But are you sure you want the headache of another big, expensive project? For me, I'd love to live in the Lighthouse, but I don't even know if I'll settle in Sicily or Rome, or some other country. Don't you think it's time you stopped investing and started spending some of your money?"

The ball has been thrown back into their court.

Everyday Niccolò and Kate walk the two kilometers road that separates their house from the Lighthouse. When they are there, no matter how the wind blows their hair, no matter how it manages to work its way under their clothes, they are convinced that they should take the leap, bid enough to guarantee that they own this property. The siren holds them captive in her song all the way back to their house. The view remains bright in their vision. The possibilities excite them, taunt them, convince them that the only choice they have is to restore *Il Faro*.

But lying in bed at night, in windless darkness, Kate has her doubts. Beside her, she can almost hear Niccolò thinking, the tick tock of his thoughts penduluming back and forth. But unlike a pendulum, Niccolò's thoughts aren't swinging free between options. He has become obsessed. He needs to own the Lighthouse.

"Just bid on it," Kate says the next morning at breakfast. "At worst, we can let it sit as it is, put up a fence to protect it from further vandalism. We don't have to restore it at once."

"At the very least, it would be a good investment."

"So bid on it," she says. "Or don't. But please stop fretting."

"What do you want to do?"

"I would like to own it. As you say, it is a once in a lifetime opportunity."

"It is!"

"At the same time, I am also happy to simplify our lives. I like having time to sit on the terrace to talk. I enjoy being able to pick up a book after lunch to read for an hour. I didn't enjoy having the construction men here to finish our pool."

"Except Pino."

"Pino was wonderful. But those other two men who installed the pool lining were uncivilized. You and I would both have been happier not having them in our lives. And they were just here for two days."

"They were arrogant."

"They were horrible. We might be lucky to find a crew of pleasant workers to rebuild the Lighthouse, but we might be unlucky, too. For sure, something will come up that isn't agreeable. The question is do you want to spend a year of your life supervising a construction crew?"

"No."

"Wouldn't you rather, as our children suggest, spend some of the money you have worked for, travelling, visiting them, discovering parts of the world you've always wanted to see?"

"I've always wanted to visit New Zealand," he yields. Kate can see the pendulum swing free. "You've wanted to visit Bali."

"In another ten years, we may not feel like travelling far. In another ten years, we will probably have grandchildren. Sooner or later we are going to start feeling our age."

"You make us sound old. We are still young."

"We are. And we are healthy. But will the lighthouse add to our well-being or diminish it? Do we really need it, Niccolò?"

"Can you look *Il Faro* in the eye and say it is a bad idea?"

She pauses. Kate remembers when Niccolò and she married, the days of ceremonies, parties, house guests, *confusion*, when all Kate wanted was to slip away with her husband to be quiet, to look in his deep brown eyes and repeat their vows. Her mother, Claire, and her sister, Leslie, had come for the wedding, and since this was her sister's first time in Italy, Kate promised to take her to see Venice the day after the ceremony, before Niccolò and Kate left for their honeymoon. On the train, in a cozy, steam-windowed cabin for six, the man seated opposite Kate, smartly dressed and distinctly handsome, with a casual, successful attitude, openly flirted with her, despite—or because of—the new shine of her wedding ring. When they descended from the train at Santa Lucia in Venice, as he lifted her bag from the overhead rack, his hand lingered on hers a moment too long. Instead of looking up to confirm what this gesture implied, Kate kept her eyes lowered as she said goodbye.

At times it is better not to look temptation directly in the eye.

Temptation is real and ever present: another cookie, another coffee, another purchase they don't really need; a deep, meaningful look shared by two strangers.

In the years they've been married, Kate has come face to face with other temptations. She keeps her eyes lowered. She already has what the stranger on the train was looking for. Besides, it would be unrealistic, unfair, to ask Niccolò to remain faithful to a wife who is keeping her options open.

She'd be a fool to risk spoiling the trust between them. She'd be a fool to look for more when she already has everything she has always wanted.

There will always be larger houses, more expansive views.

Her pendulum stops swinging.

"We have two houses in this amazing valley. I am happy, Niccolò, really happy with what we have, regardless of what happens with Villa L'Antica."

In the end, Niccolò decided not to bid on the Lighthouse.

In the end, it wouldn't have mattered if he did. He had planned to offer 30% above the asking price. It sold for 60% more.

Whoever bought it got a great deal.

Whoever bought it, Kate hopes they will restore the Lighthouse to its former dignity.

She looks forward to walking over together with Niccolò, to watch *Il Faro's* transformation. Kate will walk over to admire its beauty, and return home faithfully to Cofano, a most fortunate woman.

CHAPTER NINETEEN

The air is warm enough for Niccolò and Kate to work outdoors without a jacket but cool enough to wear long sleeves. They are removing earth from the bank beneath the upper garden, uncovering the outcropping that runs half the length of their garden: inch by inch, wheelbarrow by wheelbarrow. It isn't the excavating that is hard but the collecting of the soil and carting it away that takes time and tests their muscles. But every day they whittle away another batch and thus far they have revealed almost 25 inches, approximately 60 cm more of rock face.

"Whose idea was this anyway?" Niccolò asks, fatigued.

"I hope it wasn't mine," Kate says, as she unravels the hose. Playing with water is the satisfying end of the day's activities: spraying the hill to remove the last traces of dirt, to make the black rock glisten.

As they take turns with the hose, Kate notices, not for the first time, the distinct, black-peppery fragrance emanating from the large, sprawling Dichondrifolium geranium, its scent awakened with water. It is dark and mysterious, like *Guerlain* cologne for men—*Pour Homme*.

The phone rings, and Kate runs for it, slowed by her muddy boots. Fortunately, she has remembered to bring it out of the house or they'd have an additional chore of floors to clean after answering it!

"Mama!"

"Lizzy! Welcome home."

"It's really nice to be home, but there is a ton to do. Loads of laundry. Classes start tomorrow, but we've mostly unpacked. I was gardening until it started to rain. I got soaked."

"Poor you."

"We need the rain. A lot of our flowers died this summer. Seems there was a drought of sorts."

"I thought it always rains in England."

"Apparently not."

"Your Daddy and I are still in the garden. He's watering. I'm supervising."

"Is there still light?"

"Not really," Kate notices for the first time. On the coast the lights have come on. Cofano is covering herself in a dark, velvety veil.

"Why don't you go in, then?"

"We will. Soon. But it is lovely out, still warm. The scents are amazing."

"Funnily enough, I was thinking the same thing. The rain brought a burst of fragrance, here, too."

They laugh. The first year Stephen came to Florence, he used the phrase *funnily enough*, and Kate challenged the word's existence. The next morning when Kate came down for breakfast, she found the English-Italian dictionary that Elizabeth had given him for Christmas, opened to the letter F, the pole of a miniature unfurled British flag underlining *funnily*.

A sweet yet musky perfume emanates from the Angel Trumpet tree. "Have you looked at your calendar to see when you can fly down to Sicily?"

"That's why I'm calling. What about next weekend?"

"Excellent."

"We fly into Trapani Thursday afternoon late and leave from Palermo Sunday afternoon."

"You can miss classes on Friday?"

"Once, yes, at the start of the semester. Don't worry; we'll study on the plane."

"I'm not worried." If there is one thing Kate doesn't worry about, it's their studying. Stephen inevitably has a book open on his lap on those occasions when they watch a film together, reviewing anatomy during the slow scenes. When they are at dinner together, in the middle of a discussion about a BBC wildlife series, for example, Elizabeth might ask Stephen confirmation about a nerve ending. If Elizabeth finds an unusual shell, it will remind Stephen of a concha, a shell shaped, small bone located along the outer side of the nasal cavity. Medicine isn't merely course work. It is their lives. They are not only a couple, they are a dedicated team.

Niccolò has switched on the lights in the garden. Dozens of soft lights hidden amongst the plants illuminate the flowers and the glistening rock. "I'll let you tell Daddy your plans."

"What plans?" Niccolò accepts the phone.

Kate starts to recoil the hose but it is too heavy, still full of water. She opens the nozzle and lets the residue drain into a Princeanum geranium, its white flowers marked with dark purple, vaguely imitating a pansy. Kate is rewarded with a whiff of orange aroma emitting from either its flower or its leaves. Kate doesn't know. It doesn't matter. Whatever is making the scent, it is heavenly.

"Elizabeth has good news to share with us," Niccolò says a minute later, coming to help her coil the last of the hose.

"Hmmm." Kate keeps her foot on the loop so it won't unravel. "It's bound to happen sooner or later."

"Hmmm." Niccolò sets the wheelbarrow on end; even if it doesn't rain, the mist alone can deposit several inches of water; initiate the rusting process. "I hope the weather holds for their visit."

"I hope the Angel Trumpet blossoms open. There are millions of pods."

"At least fifty."

They both inhale deeply and then laugh. Electra says her parents are the same person, in two different bodies. In some ways she's right. Their sensibilities are compatible: their hands meet as they reach to raise the heat in the car, lower the volume of the radio, open a window, reach for the second blanket at the foot of the bed. But in other ways they are distinctly different. While Kate reads, Niccolò thinks, and his thoughts are far different than hers. He will more likely be inventing some financially viable energy-conserving device whereas Kate will be studying the effect of light or unraveling some kind of metaphor.

"Do you think these scents are present during the day but we don't notice them because our sense of sight is stronger?"

"*La Bella di Notte* don't have a scent during the day, I've tried."

She bends to ruffle the tops of the Four O'Clocks, whose flowers have been opening as the evening progresses; they release more of their perfume at her touch. They are called Night Beauties in Italian, appropriate for a flower that reveals its splendor, visual and aromatic, as night arrives. Their English name is Four O'Clocks. "I wonder in which part of the world these flowers open mid-afternoon?"

"I wonder if there is any chance of dinner tonight."

"What are you hungry for?" Kate asks, as they scrape thick cakes of mud off their boots. "I have the ingredients for mud pies."

"I'd prefer pasta and pomodoro?"

Kate could ask Niccolò every day of the year and his response would be the same. He is easy to cook for, undemanding, but Kate can't eat tomato sauce more than a couple times a week. "Let's see what we have in the kitchen."

He stands in front of her, grabs hold of her boot to pry it loose. He carries her boots and puts them into the basin next to his, which are already soaking. There is a lot of clay in their soil. He washes his hands again, which have been dirtied from her boots, and shakes them dry.

"Do you want to shower first?" Kate asks. "I'll put the water to boil."

"You don't have to ask twice."

All the ingredients for *pesto alla Genovese* are on the counter: a beautiful bunch of pungent basil, pine nuts, parmesan, garlic, olive oil. Kate blends them together quickly, and then adds a dollop of yogurt to unite the flavors. As the water heats, Kate sets the table, then cuts up a *Casaba* melon for dessert, its rich, ivory interior tinged with pink.

She doesn't mind preparing dinner. She enjoys transforming ingredients into meals. To be honest, Kate doesn't really mind washing the dishes after dinner—although she wouldn't say this loud enough for Niccolò to hear. But if Kate is left alone to clean up the kitchen, she can be sure it is because Niccolò is doing something else for them. Kate is free of any suspicions that he is not carrying his load. True, he never does the laundry, but then Kate rarely washes the cars. What matters is that they are rowing in the same direction.

"Nicco?"

"Dressing! One minute!"

She won't throw in the pasta until he arrives—sometimes his one minute can turn into ten. Spaghetti cooks quickly and needs to be eaten immediately; otherwise, it turns gluey.

Kate waits for him outdoors, stares into the darkness. On the horizon, a cruise ship makes its way south, its bright lights fairy faint and alluring in the distance. From here, the ship looks magical, a myth in the making, far different from the reality of crowds and loud laughter, too bountiful buffets and staged entertainments. From where Kate stands, the night air is so light and sweet, it seems impossible that their summer will ever end.

Off shore, on a far horizon, Kate sees a fleet of tall ships, their sails raised, masts billowing broadly with the wind. The sea beneath them is frothing white, pulsating, rising to great heights before plunging. Sails bulge fantastically, until Kate realizes, through the lens of her camera, they aren't tall ships at all but phantoms: a galleon of capricious clouds crossing the horizon.

"Nicco! Come look at these clouds. They look like tall ships!"

Niccolò studies the horizon. "Ships, no," he says. "Horses."

When Kate looks again she wonders how she could ever have imagined they were a fleet of ships. They have transformed themselves into a herd of stampeding stallions.

Another depository of clouds forms as they return midmorning from gathering the last figs of the season. The lower clouds are black as slate, upon which a foam of pure white effervesces, whiter than the frothy milk of Kate's morning's *cappuccino*. The two colors are so distinctly separate it is like witnessing the extreme ends of a rainbow's spectrum, void of the colors in between.

Perhaps it is the weight of the rain contained in the darker clouds that keep them low lying, perhaps the tumble of white knows no restraint due to some inner buoyancy, but it is

245

impressive how they pass each other without blending, without taking on each other's absolute absence of color.

And then the drama starts! An electrical storm sets off its fireworks right behind the upper pile of white clouds, flashing them with back lighting, then inner lighting, making the clouds seem as if they are about to explode with light. The lightning bolt itself remains unseen.

Kate tucks her camera into her blouse as they scurry for cover as huge drops plummet from the clouds. They should go inside, change out of their wet clothing, lay out the figs, but this theatre is too dramatic to miss, a final chapter for her series of clouds. They huddle side by side on the terrace, shivering, to witness the heavens performing their mysteries. When Niccolò starts sneezing, Kate stops photographing and moves them indoors. The last thing they need is a cold or a fever, with Elizabeth and Stephen arriving at the weekend.

After a night of intense rain, the sun has returned, as shamelessly as if it had never been eclipsed. The fields have soaked up the excess water, and grass has sprouted green, overnight. If a dove flew overhead with a soggy olive branch clamped in its beak, it wouldn't be inappropriate or unexpected.

That same fleet of tall ships flanked the horizon again this morning, their sails raised to catch the wind gusting from the west, but Kate was only fooled for a minute before she recognized them as clouds. They held her attention as they sallied forth, a whole armada breezing along, until they transformed themselves back into a distant bank of clouds and sailed out of sight.

Kate walks down to the Oliviero's house to make sure it hadn't suffered from the rains, and finds Angelica and Matteo standing at the edge of their tractor shed, talking with a distant relative who is willing to take two of the dogs. Matteo has dedicated his summer to taking care of all the dogs, but since he and Angelica have moved back into town, he is finding it inconvenient to come up every day. In the heart of the winter, the chore will weigh more heavily. All of these dogs are in need of a real home.

Mica is so friendly, so adorable; cousin Guido doesn't hesitate to take her.

With some effort Matteo catches skittish Campanellino, a high-strung young bloodhound, and puts him into the Guido's car, from where they can hear him yelping tragically.

"And if you were to take Sandy, too?" Kate tries.

"I had thought to, but I tried to pat her when I first arrived, and she snarled at me."

"Sandy is a sweet-tempered dog," Matteo tries to explain. "But she has had two litters—"

"—one right after the other."

"All the pups in both litters perished."

"Why?"

"We don't know why," Matteo adds, sadly.

"She might not be a good mother," Guido speculates.

Kate hates to admit it but she has had the same suspicion. Sandy is too young to breed, she's hardly more than a puppy herself, but the shepherd's dogs scented her first heat and have been relentless. Kate has seen them lure her away from her newborns. Larger dogs aren't prey for the foxes but puppies are defenseless.

"None of this would have happened if Edoardo were here." Angelica speaks what they are all thinking.

"I am happy to help out," Guido says, "but I don't want trouble. I'll take these two dogs for now. I'll ask around if anyone wants her."

"We can arrange to have her fixed, if that would make a difference."

"I'll let you know, but first impressions are telling."

Matteo picks up *Mica* and hugs her tightly. Kate remembers when *Mica* first arrived, tiny as a bunny, and how she protested that Edoardo had given the dog her nickname. *Mica* was a good substitute, it rang well enough at the time, even though *Mica* means *an absence, a negation; the lack of something more than a presence.*

And now she, too, is gone.

And Matteo's face is streaked yet again with tears.

Last night there were three storms brewing off-shore. Kate watched lightning illuminate vast stretches of sea that had been lost to darkness a few hours earlier with the setting of the sun. Usually the lightning off-shore is as elusive as a hummingbird's hiatus: Kate sees it out of the corner of her eye but by the time she takes a real look, it has passed. Her attention span is precisely a tenth of a second shorter than the next flash. Normally, her only hope of catching a lightning flash is through the speed of her lens. But last night the flashes were frequent and lengthy. Mt Cofano was thrown into full light, as was San Vito lo Capo and all the clouds beyond. Niccolò and Kate were closing up the house to drive down to Trapani to meet the Pepolis for dinner, and they risked being late to watch this unusual, delayed-reaction electrical storm.

On the ride into town, down their steep, mountainous road, they passed several, significant mud slides. Some trees—dead from forest fires—had slid into the road. As they drove down the mountain toward Trapani, the storm beyond Cofano and San Vito lo Capo continued to roll, but their attention was drawn to another storm off the coast. It was a little less dramatic than the first one but nonetheless remarkable. The stretch of sea off *Pizzolungo* flows unencumbered for some 300 kilometers, toward *Sardegna*; the closest interruption is *Isola dei Cavoli* off *Sardegna's* southeastern coast. These islands are never visible; they are beyond the eye's most ardent reach. However, during the storm, with the lightning flashing far out to sea, the dark, ominous clouds were pulled close to the water, weighted down by an incomprehensible amount of water. They appeared as islands in the near distance, engaged Kate's eye and imagination. A third storm was raging rampant farther south, originating somewhere beyond Marettimo, lighting up all three of the Egadi Islands and the sickle-curved coast of Trapani.

Whole parts of the city were flooded. All along Via Fardella the water was ankle-deep. At Via Marsala, the road was closed. People were wading through knee-high water, barefoot, with trousers rolled, or in fishing boots. Improvised barriers, lumpy sandbags, blocked the entrance to the shops to keep the water out. All the city street lights were off, but the houses and shops and restaurants had electricity.

Oddly enough, perhaps due to the storm and the flooding, there was little traffic driving down via Fardella, and they arrived at their meeting place early. Niccolò parked the car at the statue of *il Re galantuomo*, Vittorio Emanuele II, whose sculpted, fleece-lined cloak weighs too heavily for Trapani's usually moderate climate, and they walked to the sea where all three storms were performing. It was warm, there was wind, but it wasn't raining.

Standing at the railing, watching the storms, trying to photograph the spectacle, Kate had the same slightly stressed sensation she had as a child trying to follow the activities in a three-ring circus. Impossible to concentrate on three points of interest at one time, Kate focused on one storm for a few minutes, then another, then a third. When she put down her camera, she saw Niccolò—his face attentive, wholly absorbed—light up in the flash. His hair, recently washed and not a hundred percent dry, was standing straight up on top of his head, a thousand silver, silky antennae receiving electrical beams from above. It was an absurdly comical sight, especially on this otherwise serious, dignified man, but instead of making her laugh, Kate felt the pang of an inescapable inevitability. She took his hand, large and sturdy and slightly calloused, in an attempt to anchor them forever to this moment, even though she knew the futility of her grasp. Kate is as essentially powerless to protect him from the thunderbolts of fate as he is to protect her.

CHAPTER TWENTY

In the half hour Elizabeth and Stephen have been home, they have paid homage to the garden and approved of the little pool—even if there is no chance of them using it this late in the season. Niccolò has opened a bottle of *spumante*, and they sit together in the garden, under the canopy of the giant pines, to admire the view. Elizabeth's ash-auburn hair shimmers twenty shades of autumn. She looks relaxed, healthy and happy to be reunited in Sicily.

The clouds turn grapefruit pink and sherbet orange, at first modestly, a blush, then vividly, boldly, a flock of flamingos in flight, flamboyant, until the whole sky is ablaze with disharmonious colors.

"In any other setting but the wide-open sky, a display like this would seem unsightly," Stephen says.

"The color volume is set too high."

"It looks as if the sun is setting behind Mt. Cofano," Stephen says.

"It does look like the sunset," Elizabeth agrees. "But isn't this east? Isn't this where the sun rises?"

Not everyone in their family is an early riser.

"It is indeed east," Kate blinks, than blinks again, and the tones have softened two shades. The scarlet red has run back to peppermint pink, the violet subdued to lavender. She is photographing as quickly as the shutter will allow, but is certain she isn't capturing every shift of light. "It's impossible, of course, but the illusion is so strong it makes me doubt my senses," Kate shares her thoughts, "as if the sunrise is occurring

251

at the wrong hour of the day. Or the sun has decided to retreat to its birthplace, instead of setting in the west."

"Right then," Stephen says.

"I think we might be ready for dinner," Niccolò speculates, taking his wife's glass and setting it on the tray.

"I've hardly had half a glass!" Kate protests and then notices that Elizabeth is shivering, that Stephen is rubbing his hands rigorously along her arms. "Maybe we should go in now."

Still, they stay where they are, standing under the pines, watching the sky until all the colors descend into blacks and grays, until the city lights pop on; string themselves along the coast like bright beads against cocktail black velvet.

"Would you like us to show you the photographs of our trip before or after dinner?" Elizabeth asks.

"After, if it's the same to you. If you want to wash up, dinner will be on the table in five minutes."

Twice during dinner, Stephen has cleared his throat, as if he wishes to speak. Twice they have paused to listen but he has retreated, has let the silence fill with chatter. They have heard all about their trip to the States, the reunions with family, their visits with old friends. They have listened carefully to the descriptions of the whales in Boston Bay, the giant redwoods in Napa Valley and San Francisco's Amazon Forest museum.

"What was your favorite moment of the trip?" Niccolò asks.

"Eating Cracker Jacks while watching the sunset in Arches National Park, from the highest rock formation we could climb."

"Stephen?"

"Definitely drinking lemonade post-hike to Angel's Landing in Zion National Park. It was a much more ambitious hike than we had expected!"

"What else?" Kate asks.

"Watching the sun set at the Grand Canyon, eating ice cream."

"I hear a theme emerging."

Dinner has been over for almost an hour, but they are still at the table, nibbling on the chocolate covered almonds Kate made this morning. "Here's the big question—"

Nervously, Stephen and Elizabeth look at each other. "Yes?"

"Which did you prefer, the Monterey Aquarium or Disneyland?"

"Disneyland."

"Although the Aquarium was spectacular," Elizabeth is quick to add, as it had also been a gift from Kate. "Unfortunately, it was really crowded when we were there, full of noisy kids."

"But Disneyland was fantastic. And as we were there for two days, we didn't have to rush. We could repeat our favorite rides."

"Stephen said that Disneyland is even better as an adult than as a kid."

Stephen laughs, "Because we didn't have to ask our parents for money whenever we wanted to buy something."

"I'm glad you had such a good time."

"It was a perfect trip," Elizabeth says dreamily. "If you think about it, with all the things that could have happened, nothing went wrong. We never even got lost."

"It was brilliant."

"Perfect."

"It's going to have to hold us for a long time."

This time next year Stephen will be working full time: extended holidays will be a thing of the past. Elizabeth, one year behind him, has another summer to relax, but then, she, too, will have limited holidays. Niccolò and Kate can't expect to see them at Christmas for the next several years, at least until they achieve seniority.

"And how are your parents, Stephen? I'll bet they were glad to have you home for a visit."

"They were. Although they were disappointed we stayed so briefly."

"Didn't you stay a week with them?"

"Actually, no."

Elizabeth and Stephen look at each other. "Actually, Stephen had a job interview."

"We didn't want to say anything, in case it didn't turn out."

"The competition was terribly stiff. Med students from Imperial College in London and Cambridge, even full-fledged doctors. There were more than six hundred applications for ten posts."

"I understand why you were reluctant to raise your hopes," Niccolò says.

"I figured it was good experience, even if I wasn't given the job. An additional interview is always good practice."

"That's the right attitude, though I am sorry you weren't hired."

"But he was!" Elizabeth exclaims.

"You were?"

"Not only did he get a position, he got his first choice of location."

"Stephen, this is excellent news!"

He beams.

"He'll be positioned in Norfolk for the next two years."

"Except the first three months, when I have to commute forty minutes to the Paget Hospital in Great Yarmouth, all my assignments are at the N&N."

"Ten minutes from home!" Elizabeth is even more excited than Stephen. "We'll be together while I finish my last year of studies!"

This is excellent news, indeed, to have Stephen's intelligence so concretely confirmed, his hard work rewarded; and to know that Elizabeth's last year of medical school won't be compromised or lonely.

"Knock 'em dead!" Kate toasts, lifting her glass to Stephen.

"Actually," Stephen says, "That's not the best expression for a doctor—or a taxi driver."

"Mama, how did you know that Daddy was the right person for you to marry?"

Kate glances up, clutching the fistful of weeds she was about to pull. Elizabeth, who is helping her weed, has looked away, as if to lessen the magnitude of her question, studying the sky as if following the flight of a bird Kate can't see. From the way Elizabeth has lifted her chin, just a degree higher than usual, Kate sees the importance of her question. But what can Kate tell her? She doesn't have a ready answer.

"It was a lot of things, Lizzy—" Kate adds a fistful of yellow-headed dandelions to the wheelbarrow at her side.

"Specifically?" She seems so grown up, and, at the same time so young, eager for a concrete answer to a question that depended more on feelings and intuition than anything as real as a relatable fact.

"Well, actually there were two things that convinced me."

Elizabeth looks hopeful. Kate feels unequal to the question. She wonders if her daughter will understand the significance of what she is about to share with her.

"Several months after your father and I started living together, Daddy was in Florence for the morning, and I was at home editing photographs. I made the mistake of consuming an entire *panforte*—"

"That really sweet, dense cake from Siena?"

"Exactly. We had been given one for Christmas and I nibbled on it all day long, one tiny sliver after another, until it was gone. And then I went into sugar shock."

"Oh no!"

"I had a blood sugar problem before you were born."

"Pregnancies can do that sometimes, reset imbalances."

"Anyway, I knew better than to eat something that sweet without balancing it with real food, but I was engrossed in my work. I was alone. It was delicious. I kept nibbling."

"What happened?"

"I couldn't stop shaking. It felt like my jaw was locked. I got into bed and pulled the covers up over my head. It was horrible."

"Poor you!"

"When Daddy came home, he wanted to take me to the hospital straight away, but I said no, just to bring me a large bottle of water so I could start to flush the sugar out of my system. I also asked him to bring me my night guard. I couldn't unclench my teeth, and I was worried I might break the porcelain crown I'd had fitted for a molar before I came to Italy.

"I had some trouble explaining to your father what my night guard was—his English and my Italian—plus it was difficult to speak clearly through a clenched jaw. But finally he found it and I put it on."

"And you were so grateful that's when you decided you to marry him?"

Kate laughs, carefully dropping a spiky-stemmed thistle into the wheelbarrow. "We would probably be divorced by now if that had been my motivation."

"Then why?"

"Well, a few days later, when the sugar shock had passed completely, and I put away my night guard, your Daddy confided that he had seen the night guard container in my bathroom the first week we knew each other, and had assumed I had false teeth."

"You're kidding!"

"No. All those months he had been watching me brush my teeth, trying to figure it out. He told me he had assumed dentures were more sophisticated in the USA, a kind that didn't need to soak overnight in a glass on the bedside table. He said that he admired everything else about me, my honesty, my intelligence—your father has always known the right thing to say—that he would be a fool to throw it all away for an imperfection as superficial as false teeth.

"You know, the Italians place a lot of importance on aesthetics, which is fine, as long as aesthetics don't become the only criterion. Your Daddy's willingness to accept me, despite false teeth, showed me that his priorities were right, that he wouldn't stop loving me when my looks faded, when my body lost its shape, as bodies inevitably do. Not even when my teeth fall out."

"I bet Stephen wouldn't care if I had false teeth."

"He might care. He's entitled to his reaction. But would it interfere with his overall feelings for you? That is the question." Kate struggles to stand.

"Let me give you a hand, Mama. We'll empty the wheelbarrow."

"Ok, but let's take out the thistles first, we don't want them taking root in the compost."

"God forbid." Gingerly, they remove the thorny plants, laying them on the pavement to dry in the sun.

"It's too bad about all the thorns. The flowers themselves are quite pretty."

"They are. But Mama, you said there were two things. What was the other?

"It has a long story attached to it, as well."

"There are a lot of weeds left to pull."

"Well, before I came to Italy, there was another man, an American, who wanted to marry me."

"The guy with the beautiful voice?"

"No. Brian was my boyfriend at university, and even though we were together for four years, I don't think either of us seriously considered marriage."

"He seemed to me like a really great guy. Lots of fun."

"He is. He was. But we were kids. Playing house. You haven't met the man I'm talking about. His name is Gerald."

"Did you want to marry him?"

"Let's say I was flattered that he wanted to marry me. I liked it when we discussed having children—"

"Stephen and I talk about children. We even have names chosen—"

"—but I wasn't convinced that I should marry Gerald. Then, one night I had a dream. And in the dream I was sobbing because I knew that Gerald wasn't the right man for me to marry. I remember that dream as clearly as if I had it last night. When I woke, I knew I would never marry him. It was a matter of months before we separated, and another couple of months before we stopped tormenting each other and ourselves."

"So you weren't really in love with him?"

"It wasn't that simple. I did love him. I could see his soul by looking into his eyes. But on a practical level we weren't good together. He was a photographer, too, and his work was extraordinary. He loved it when I told him how much I respected his work, but he didn't like it when I looked into my lens instead of his eyes, or disappeared into my studio to work. He became terribly competitive. He was a wonderful person, deeply sensitive, an artist in the truest sense of the word, but not the right person for me to spend my life."

"So what does this have to do with knowing that Daddy was right for you?"

"From that dream about Gerald I understood that my dreams could reveal the path that is right for me, if I listen to them. I have also learned that I can pose a question before sleep, and sometimes, oftentimes, I will receive an answer during the night. A coded answer but an answer nonetheless.

"So when Daddy and I were discussing marriage, I posed the question: would it be right to marry him? And the dream I was given was of an old couple walking along a winding, rock strewn path, hand in hand."

"Which means?"

"It isn't obvious? That we would traverse the difficulties together, hand and hand. From the condition of the path, I suspected our lives wouldn't necessarily be easy—few lives are—but that we would grow old together, travelling along the same road."

"That's a great dream."

"I thought so. Soon after, we set the date to be married, and a day or two after that, you were conceived."

"You could tell you were pregnant straight away?"

"It was the strangest sensation. I could practically feel the cells dividing. So we rescheduled the date, married at the end of the summer, and you were born a couple of days after the date we had originally scheduled for our marriage."

"And you have been living happily ever after since."

"Despite a few rocks in the road."

"I can't wait to sleep tonight. I have so many questions to ask."

It rained all night, a hard hammering on the roof. All morning the sky continues to unload its tons of water. Stephen and Elizabeth take turns getting up to stand at the front door, looking for a hiatus that doesn't appear. This is not the holiday in Sicily they had planned.

After a late lunch, the rain stops abruptly. The sudden silence brings them all to their feet.

"Let's run up to see the new little house!" Niccolò suggests.

Kate checks the sky, studies the high-flying wisps of clouds to the east, then notices the dark clouds gathering to the west. "Let's go quickly, before it starts to rain again."

"Let's drive up," Elizabeth proposes.

"Not a bad idea."

They could walk, it is certainly close enough, but they don't know how long this window without rain will last. Elizabeth,

Stephen and Kate stand at the front gate, appraising the clouds for the next rain, while Niccolò brings the car.

This is the first time Elizabeth and Stephen have seen the new house that Rosario has helped them acquire. They are full of compliments, but the truth is there is a lot to do before this little house will be presentable. However, as Niccolò un-shutters the windows, the small, dingy rooms are transformed by light. The view here is even better than from their house a hundred meters below. Here, in addition to the sea, the whole valley is visible, the neighboring hills and the heights of Erice.

"It's going to be magnificent."

"Will it be ready for next summer?" Elizabeth asks.

"Probably not." There are many considerations. There is another ruin on the property and they don't know if they should combine its footage to construct a larger house or build two smaller, separate houses. The solution will present itself, if they are patient. In the meantime, with the transformation of the garage, they can all fit into their present house.

They are walking back to the car, which Niccolò has parked at the entrance to the driveway, when they hear, and feel, a tremendous shudder. Kate is sure the mountain behind and above them has avalanched, but she can't see any sign of rocks sliding.

"Oh, no!" Niccolò is the first to detect the noise's origin. "Our pine! No!" Niccolò runs down the hill, ignoring the danger of the wet, slick road.

"No!" Kate is right behind him, side-stepping the mud and scattered gravel.

The lower pine, the more inclined of the two, has crashed down across the entrance to their driveway, crushing one of the stone pillars and the wrought-iron gate they've left open. No longer regal, it now resembles a slain, prehistoric beast, as large as any dinosaur. It's last act, on its way down, has been to catch and annihilate the electrical lines.

"We could have been killed."

Thirty minutes earlier Elizabeth, Stephen and Kate were standing in this exact spot, opening the gates, waiting for Niccolò to bring the car. Two minutes later, they would have been driving through the gates again. The pine has crushed where they always sit on the low stone wall.

Niccolò is the first to break their reverie. "It's going to be a long, dark, cold weekend without electricity."

Kate glances at her watch. It is four o'clock. Friday. "We had better call ENEL, fast."

Elizabeth hurries indoors to collect candles. Stephen returns up the hill to fetch the car. He brings it down, and parks it outside the gate.

Niccolò calls ENEL. They register the problem but can't say when someone will be up to repair it. With all this rain, they are swamped.

"Do you want to call *Maresciallo*?"

"Good idea."

While Niccolò is on his cellphone, Kate returns indoors to help Elizabeth, but she has everything under control. She has located candles and has distributed them throughout the house. She has even prepared individual candles for bedtime.

In the kitchen, Kate organizes what they will need for dinner while there is still daylight. Elizabeth sets the table, aligning eight tea candles down the center. Kate locates a box of matches. Once night falls, every simple task will be complicated. Fortunately, they cook with gas.

"Did you speak with the Marshall?" she asks Niccolò.

"I did. He's out of town until tomorrow, but he said he will call his officers to have them report our electricity outage as a public hazard. Now all we can do is wait."

"In the meantime, let's call Orlando."

"Do you think Orlando knows someone at ENEL?"

"Probably not. But Orlando will know what to do with this fallen pine. He had one fall in his garden in August, remember?"

"Right. I hope my phone battery lasts."

Forty-five minutes later ENEL arrives, hauling their long, extendable ladders down from the top of their van, rigging their safety devices around their waists before climbing up the tall pole. They work long past dark to repair the wires. When they finish, Niccolò invites them in, but they are in a hurry. "With so much rain, we are working around the clock. How did you move to the top of our list?"

"I don't know, but I'm thankful you came in a hurry." Niccolò slips ten euro into the senior worker's vest pocket. "For a coffee," he says. A coffee they can accept.

"Let's leave the candles," Elizabeth bids. "I was looking forward to a romantic, candlelit evening."

"You've watched too many old films. It's not really fun living without electricity."

The next morning at seven-thirty, two men ring the bell at their gate, even though the gate itself is crushed open and they could have approached the house to knock on the front door. These are Orlando's workers, come to lend a hand. The younger man, Enzo, is the manager of Orlando's property—several hundred hectares in Paceco—young and bright, energetic and organized. Accompanying him is an older man, more brawn than brain, who welds a long bladed chainsaw to Enzo's instructions.

"*Bravo, Zio* Ciccio," Enzo addresses his senior worker with respect, even though Enzo is the higher paid employee.

They cut a ten foot section of the pine tree that Niccolò and Kate felled recently and carry it on their shoulders to prop up the enormous fallen pine just short of where they will cut it, so it doesn't further damage the pillar on which it balances, or the other, undamaged gate.

Slice by magnificent slice, they are fashioning what looks like a set of stools for large forest dwellers. Everyone who stops by to view the fallen pine, Angelica, Matteo, Gaetano, the shepherd, Rosario, the Marshall, all comment on the emerging set of rustic furniture.

"You are welcome to it," Kate says. "Help yourselves."

In Florence, at the end of their terrace, just outside their gate, in the closest part of Fiammetta's garden, there is a similar style table and chairs, large and rustically fashioned. Before Elizabeth and Electra were born, Fiammetta and her friends used this table for their summer bucolic dinners. But as the years have passed, the humidity in the garden has begun to annoy Fiammetta and her friends, so they dine indoors, after cocktails on the terrace in front of her house. The bulky, hand-crafted furniture, which was covered in black plastic at the end of a season many years ago to protect it against the winter

261

elements, remains covered. For a spring birthday party, when the children were little, Niccolò asked permission to use it, but Fiammetta hadn't felt inclined to have her gardener uncover it. Nor had she felt inclined to let them do so, either. She was probably afraid they wouldn't re-cover it correctly, if her thoughts extended that far. In any event, year after year, the table remains covered in black plastic, its chairs tilted forward and protected by the same plastic, as if permanently inhabited by spooks. It is all of it held together with odd bits of mis-matched twine. At best it's an eye sore; at worst, a reproach.

Kate would not like a replicate of the furniture on their property in Sicily.

Matteo promises to come up with his tractor trailer in the early afternoon to haul it all away.

By noon, Enzo and Zio Ciccio have freed the gate. Niccolò tries to pay them for their time, but Enzo refuses, absolutely: "I am on salary from Conte Pepoli; my time has already been paid for. Please, you are putting me in difficulty by insisting."

"Ok, I won't insist." Niccolò tucks the money into Enzo's pocket, saying, "Just something for a coffee." Enzo will be back in Paceco before he discovers how many coffees Niccolò has given him.

In the early afternoon, the iron monger arrives to remove their bent gate for repairs. A few minutes later, Matteo and his friend, the cute, shy one who was studying in Bologna, come up with the tractor and trailer to haul away the huge sections of pine. Stephen is impressed. When Sicily functions, it surpasses every other place in efficiency.

Elizabeth and Stephen mull around the garden. It is a shame to lose all this time as they are all together such a short time, but Niccolò won't leave things as they are. They must be cleaned up and put into order. Elizabeth snaps photos to send to Electra. Kate photographs Elizabeth photographing.

Everything is back to normal again in time for dinner on Saturday night, and they all relax with a second glass of wine. The conversation has turned to Cardio-Vascular disorders, and Stephen is in his element. He is explaining, very simply and clearly, what happens when Niccolò's heart goes into fibrillation. Kate is impressed. For the first time in the twelve years that Niccolò has engaged medical help for his heart problem, Kate fully understands what is happening.

"You might want to consider teaching, Stephen, not as an alternative to practicing medicine but as a parallel track."

"I have thought of it as an option."

"You have a talent for taking a complex matter and making it crystal clear."

"Without being condescending."

"The heart is fairly simple to understand—" Stephen starts.

"Easy for you to say," Elizabeth contradicts.

"It seems complicated because a lot of the parts overlap and interact, but the heart is elementary plumbing, with a little electrical wiring thrown in."

"*Contrariamente a quello che il mio dottore vorrebbe che io credessi*—Contrary to what my doctors would like me to believe." Niccolò has lapsed back into Italian. Whenever Stephen is with them, Niccolò speaks in English, but it's a tiring mental effort, and at the end of an evening he inevitably slips back into Italian. Kate is glad. She loves the sound of Niccolò's voice in Italian: the intricate construction of his phrases reveals the elaborate workings of his mind. In English, while he makes himself understood well enough, his word choices are limited, and his mistakes make him seem uneducated; uncultured. In English he walks with a limp, in Italian he soars.

Automatically, Elizabeth slips into Italian, too. "*I medici tendono a mantenere i misteri della loro professione.*" She turns to Stephen to translate. "Doctors tend to maintain the mysteries of their profession."

Kate sees by the affectionate expression on Stephen's face that he, too, likes to hear Elizabeth speak Italian. "I forget she's bilingual. There are few occasions to hear her speak Italian in England."

"My Italian gets rusty," Elizabeth admits. "I never speak Italian, except when Daddy calls."

"It's lovely. You should call more often," Stephen says to Niccolò.

"Stephen laughs at me because I don't know the correct words to English nursery rhymes, but what he doesn't realize is that I don't know all the right words to the Italian nursery rhymes, either."

"The other day," Stephen says, "Lizzy was in London with two friends from the States, and she sent me a text message." He pulls out his phone, quickly locates the message he has saved, which reads: 'Dinner tonight at a Mission and Star. So excited! Wish you were here.'"

Kate and Niccolò look puzzled until Stephen explains. "You know the Michelin Star ratings, for extraordinary restaurants?"

Elizabeth tries to defend herself. "I've always thought it was Mission and Star."

"Unfortunately, you'll never be perfect in either language," Kate says, laughing. "Bilinguals can have a total fluency of 180 percent but that's only 90 percent in each language. Mistakes are inevitable."

"But it is impressive how effortlessly Liz switches between English and Italian. How did you manage?"

"I have always spoken to her in English," Kate explains. "When she started to talk, if she answered me with an Italian word, I would repeat it back to her in English. Niccolò did the same in Italian. It took extra effort but we wanted her—and later Electra—to feel at ease in both languages."

"What do you and Niccolò speak to each other?"

"Now that the kids are away from home, we speak mostly in Italian."

"Unless she gets mad, then she speaks in English."

"Always best to disagree in your native tongue." Kate sets a bowl of walnuts in the center of the table. She cracks open a nut for Niccolò, then hands Stephen the nutcracker. "The unexpected benefit of having two languages is that the world opened up for Elizabeth and Electra."

"How do you mean?" He holds a walnut in his left palm, and splits it in two perfect halves. He passes the nutcracker to Niccolò and one of the halves to Elizabeth.

"If everything has two names, there is no way to think of things singularly."

"No chance of being close-minded or provincial."

"And we could tell secrets in English when we were surrounded by Italians," Elizabeth adds, attentively removing the nutmeat from the shell. "And in Italian when we were in the States."

"Were there negative aspects?"

They all laugh, all start to speak at the same time. "Outside the family," Elizabeth says, "our conversations are hard to understand by those who aren't bilingual." She passes the nutmeat back to Stephen but keeps the shell. She has a slight intolerance to nuts. They make her ears tingle.

"Difficult because you switch between Italian and English?"

"That, too, although we try to stick to one language when we have guests. It's just that some words sound better in one language, so we substitute an Italian word into an English sentence, and vice-versa."

"Lizzy, put your *bambole* and bears into their *carrozzino* so I can vacuum your room."

"Niccolò, *potresti portare fuori la* trash?"

"She's always asking me to take out the trash!"

"Electra had some problems learning to read and write two languages at the same time."

"What did you do?" Stephen looks at Kate, then at Niccolò, but it is Elizabeth who answers.

"They took us out of the International School and sent us to an Italian school," she laments. She has acquisitioned the unbroken walnut shells from everyone's plate, is picking clean the membranes; an art project materializing. "That was the end of Halloween celebrations!"

"*É risolto il problema?*" Stephen has asked this in perfectly correct Italian. Did that solve the problem?

"*Non completamente*—not completely."

"Electra's problem was aggravated by two languages but the problem itself remained."

Niccolò and Stephen pass the nutcracker back and forth, each trying to open the walnut without breaking the shell. Each time Stephen is successful, Niccolò is successful, too; each time he fails, breaks the shell in bits, Niccolò fails, too, almost as if he is following Stephen's lead.

"Dyslexia?"

"Not exactly."

"Dysgraphia?"

"It would have made things easier to resolve, perhaps, if we had been able to put a name on the problem, but we could never identify it beyond something spatial. In the long run, Electra

265

has learned techniques to compensate. Her intelligence was never in question, but her self-esteem suffered along the way."

Kate takes the nutcracker from Niccolò. They are cracking open all the walnuts but are leaving them uneaten on their cream colored, gold-borderless plates. Two boys playing games.

"Especially in the Italian school system, where memorization is rewarded."

"You might have done better to keep us in the International School," Elizabeth adds.

"Hindsight has twenty-twenty vision."

"Electra provided us with some pretty humorous misunderstandings."

"Do you remember when our first swimming instructor told her to hold her breath before dunking her head under water?" Elizabeth asks.

"How can I forget?" Kate was at the side lines. She could see them but couldn't hear. All Kate saw was four-year-old Electra clapping her hands over her chest, then sputtering under water.

"Why?"

"She thought he said, 'hold your breasts.'"

"Fortunately, Electra's difficulties disappeared as she matured."

"She is certainly doing well in university!"

"Who would have ever thought she'd get better grades than me?"

"Medical school can't be easy, Lizzy, even if Stephen likens it to plumbing."

"Besides, we don't have grades," Stephen says. Their medical school uses a pass-fail system to curtail competition between future colleagues. "*É un casino!*"

"Actually, that's not a word to use, Stephen."

"Mama, everyone says *casino* to mean confusion."

"I know how it is used. I just don't think you want Stephen using it."

Niccolò kicks Kate under the table. Stephen has turned sullen, has retreated into himself. Kate doesn't know whether to further explain the reasons not to use the word *casino* or to try to move on to another subject. Finally, after an awkward moment, Kate stands up. "Would anyone like anything more from the kitchen?"

"It's late. I think we'll go to bed now, Mama. Unless you want help with the dishes?"

"We'll clean up the kitchen," Niccolò says. "Good night, 'Lisabetta. Good night, Stephen."

"Good night."

"Good night."

Kate is scraping pear peelings and broken bits of walnut shells into the compost bin as Niccolò brings in the plates from the table. Silently, they load the dishwasher. Kate covers and puts away the leftovers; wipes the crumbs from the counter. She hangs the dish towels to dry.

"I wish he wouldn't sulk," Kate says finally.

Niccolò takes her hands in his, gently. "You must stop correcting him."

"But if he is going to speak Italian, he should—"

"*Amore.*" He kisses her hands. "Even if his Italian is flawed, it doesn't reflect on you."

"But—" Kate tries to remove her hands but Niccolò keeps a steady grip.

"Let him be. He isn't perfect, none of us are, but he loves our daughter and she loves him."

Niccolò always has been a wonderful, steady father. Clearly, he will be an excellent father-in-law. But above all, in this awkward moment, Kate appreciates what a good husband he is: how he supports her, is on her side, even when he believes she has erred. Honestly, Kate loves Stephen. She is dismayed that she could have led anyone to think otherwise. She appreciates how smart he is and admires his unfailing persistence; but more importantly, she loves his honesty, his loyalty, his fundamental goodness. He is everything she could have wished for Elizabeth.

"I never meant to be critical of Stephen," she says shamefully.

"I know." He kisses her hands again, and then rubs her wedding band gently, as if it needs polishing. "I know."

"Do I need to apologize?" Embarrassed, she looks away, focuses on a point in the distance. She prays for a word of assurance.

"Not in so many words, no. Just let him be. Give him time. What does it matter if his Italian isn't perfect when in every other way he is an ideal partner for our daughter?"

Kate mourns the absence of their pine.

She understands now that its demise was her fault.

Last May, a furious wind twisted one limb back behind the pine's trunk, like a wrestler's hold, where it hung dislocated, perilously low, over their gate. Kate asked Edoardo if Matteo would help them remove it. Despite his obvious fear, Matteo climbed into the pine with his chain saw and severed the twisted limb. But as soon as it was cut, he hurried down, his shirt drenched in sweat. "*Io io io*—" he stuttered, "It's a lot higher than it seems from here. And there's no place to hold onto."

We should coat that cut with *catrame*,' Edoardo had said. 'I have some tar in the shed.' But Matteo was obviously relieved to be down on the ground, and Kate didn't feel like sending him back up. She couldn't be bothered to call someone else to correct the problem. Rain infiltrated the massive tree, and it snapped, like a matchstick, just below the cut.

Hindsight. What she'd pay to have a dose of it ahead of time.

Fortunately, one regal pine remains, perhaps more impressive now that it stands alone. Its branches are already filling with birds that had nests in the other fallen tree.

Niccolò has called a team which is coming up tomorrow to remove the base of the fallen pine. He is afraid water will seep into it, as well, and weaken the roots of the remaining pine. While they are up there, after they have painted the scars with tar, Kate will ask them to hang an Aeolian harp.

CHAPTER
TWENTY-ONE

They had clams for *antipasti* last night, a big steaming platter brought out and placed into the center of the table at their favorite restaurant, from which they and their friends, the Pepolis, served themselves. They invited Orlando and Teresa to join them as a thank you for having sent up his workers to resolve the fallen pine. It was a lovely, thought-provoking evening, and they arrived home late. Niccolò and Kate shared observations about the evening as they prepared for bed.

"Are you nearly finished?" Niccolò has hung up his clothes on the back of the door in his study, and is waiting to use the bathroom.

"Almost." Kate puts away her toothbrush. "I seem to have a piece of clam caught between two molars."

"Floss."

"I can't. We've run out." Kate hands him his toothbrush, dries her hands and leaves to give him privacy.

In the morning at breakfast Kate can feel her gum is swollen. It is too tender for her toothbrush. She buys dental floss, but cannot dislodge anything. The next day her gum has progressed from swollen to atrophied, as if the tissue holding her tooth in place has lost all its tone. The right side of her face is tingling, sensitive to the touch, especially around her eye. Kate tries to ignore it as there is work to do. They are closing up house, preparing to return to Florence.

The weather has changed. There will be no more dinners on the terrace. Breakfast outdoors these last few days has been a test of endurance. Even gardening has lost some of its appeal. They decide to make cheese one last time before they leave.

Wood is burning in their fireplace, the scent of pine and a whiff of smoke makes the room fragrant. Niccolò and Kate can't go to bed yet because the cheeses are absorbing their second layer of salt and will need to be rinsed at midnight, before they can put them, and themselves, to bed. Kate snuggles next to Niccolò for warmth. They are both having a second glass of red wine, an antidote against the cold; nevertheless, they can see their breath.

"What a shame they built this house without heat."

"A lack of foresight," Kate says, unfolding a throw from the back of the sofa to cover their legs.

"What can we do, short of drilling the walls full of holes for radiators?"

"The fireplace is lovely," Kate says, watching a flame embrace a log. "But it isn't very efficient."

"We could buy an insert for the fireplace," Niccolò proposes. "We'd use a lot less wood, and it would warm the house more adequately."

"It would make a difference, I think, if we could come down to Sicily whenever we felt like it, instead of just in the summer and autumn."

"Are you planning to move here full time, and this is your way of letting me know?"

"No. I love our home in Florence, and I know we need to be there. But having the possibility to come here whenever we want would be comforting."

"I'll call Pino tomorrow. Let's see what he thinks."

Pino, bless his heart, thinks an insert is an excellent idea. He takes the measurements of the fireplace and sends Niccolò and Kate to a shop in town, where after careful deliberation they buy a handsome *Jøtul*.

Before they return home, they stop to see Angelica, to fill a shelf in her refrigerator with yesterday's production of cheese.

"*Grazie! Grazie mille*! I'm sorry to rush but I'm having lunch with my sister and her husband." Angelica is happy to see them, and they are relieved to find her busy, engaged. Her clothes are starting to fit again, and Kate is pleased to see Angelica is quick on her feet. "I will come up to see you tomorrow," she says, shooing them out of the house, "before you leave."

Pino stops by on his lunch break and helps them carry the *Jøtul* into the living room. He measures the fireplace, measures the insert, and frowns. "This is going to be a tight fit."

Niccolò has also taken measurements, just to be sure, but both he and Pino have forgotten to leave room to attach the flue to the insert, which needs to be jimmied up into the chimney. "Is it possible?"

"We won't know until we try. I'll be back when I finish work this afternoon, around four."

Pino is one of those workers who takes pride in finding solutions rather than succumbing to difficulties. When he returns that afternoon, he puts his shiny bald head far up into the chimney flue. His short, squat body follows with surprising agility: a balloon rising weightlessly into the clouds. Complications slow him but don't stop him; rather, they speed up his determination. Despite his delicate efforts, soot dislodges from the flue and blackens his head and fills the cups of his ears. Even his long lashes are darkened by soot. Work boot footprints appear on the floor like Arthur Murray's diagramed ballroom dance steps.

Too late, Kate runs for newspapers to protect the floor. As she opens the drawer where the newspaper is stored, she finds a fleet of tiny boats made from walnut shells and toothpicks, their sails a snipped triangle of Italian green, white and red. Onto a sea of newspaper are drawn two parallel lanes of waves, and in between the waves, in Elizabeth's steady, elegant calligraphy, are printed the words: "We, too, will traverse all difficulties together. We, too, are on the same path. Keep dreaming and we will see you soon. E&S."

Afternoon turns into evening. Another worker would have left hours ago. But Pino doesn't quit until the insert is installed, and he waits while they light the first log, to make sure the connection doesn't leak smoke.

Niccolò invites him to stay for dinner, but Pino laughs. "My wife would assume I had a girlfriend if I skipped one of her meals."

Niccolò has made a list of what they need to do to close the house as it would be easy to forget an important detail in their hurry to leave. Angelica has stopped to say goodbye, so has Matteo and lastly, *praticamente*, Rosario. This evening, as an alternative to the long drive, Niccolò and Kate will embark in Palermo on an overnight ferry to *Civitavecchia*, a coastal town not far from Rome. From there, it is a three hour drive to Florence. They should be home by noon tomorrow.

Water turned off? Check!

External light sockets turned off? Check!

Keys for Florence? Check!

Gas?

It feels like only yesterday they were turning it on.

One last glance at the Angel Trumpet Tree with its hundreds of perfumed pods starting to open; a farewell to the succulents which any day now will raise their bell-like clusters of bright orange flowers.

And Kate won't be here to see them.

She buttons her cardigan; turns its collar up high. She feels as if she is saying goodbye to a lover.

"What is that on the horizon?" Niccolò asks, as Kate places the food hamper into the car in the last available space between their two seats, close enough to be able to reach it easily, far enough away from the dog and cat.

"Could that be Ustica? Where have I put my camera?"

Most days of the summer, with the sun bright, the shore line clear, the island of Ustica hasn't been visible. During their first months living in Sicily it had become a joke between them. Everyone, especially Edoardo, acted as if Ustica was just off the coast, usually visible; it was only Niccolò and Kate who couldn't see it. All summer long they've been trying to catch a glimpse. Kate has begun to doubt its very existence.

Actually, that's putting it too strongly. She knows Ustica exists. It is documented on all the maps. A dot along the northern coast of Sicily, it is presumably eighty kilometers away. Therefore, it isn't the existence of the island they began to doubt but its visibility, its presence from their house. If they can't see it, for their purposes it is as good as nonexistent.

But now, as they are leaving, their eyes adjust to the light and look! There it is! So close! So large, just five inches off the end of San Vito Lo Capo!

How could they have doubted Ustica's existence?

There it is, perched on the horizon, solid and tangible, not at all the stuff of myths.

Cat? Dog? Tranquilizer drops? Check!

Kate helps Clover into the car, onto a floor mat where he will sleep by her feet. Indoors, Figaro is hiding behind her desk, his eyes white and glassy; unable to walk a straight line. Kate zips him into his box, the top of which she'll open once they are on their way, when he is used to the car's movement. She will box him again to board the ship, transporting Figaro and Clover to the cabin.

Niccolò bolts shut the front door, switches on the alarm.

"Look! Ustica is gone."

Just as quickly as it appeared.

But having seen it, they can't doubt its existence. It is always present, even when they can't see it.

"Say goodbye to Cofano!" Niccolò says.

"Our constant."

They arrive home mid-day on the 15th of October. They free the animals, who stumble into their environment as if they never left. Figaro heads straight for a tree trunk to sharpen his nails while Clover finds a soccer ball that has spent the summer under a rosemary hedge. He drops it at Kate's feet, barks at her, ready to play. Niccolò unloads the suitcases while Kate fixes a quick bite for lunch. They change out of their travel clothes and walk across the garden to tell Niccolò's mother they are home.

They find Niccolò's sister, Federica, in the garden. She is puzzled to see them, then happy, then irritated, all in a matter of seconds. The agitation wins: *"Aspetta!* Wait." She moves toward the front gate. "Mamma just left, not ten seconds ago. She might not be gone yet."

But her car is gone.

Federica uses her cellphone to call. "Mamma! Wait. Niccolò's here! He's just arrived."

Niccolò takes the phone. "Mamma!" A boyish enthusiasm resounds in his voice. "We've just returned."

"You've just returned. I've just left."

Silence.

Federica fills in. "She's going to her friend's, Gaia, for the weekend," she tells her older brother. "She's back on Sunday night for Alessia's birthday dinner. Ask if you can come, too."

Niccolò speaks into the silence. "Federica says you are having Alessia's birthday dinner on Sunday night. If we can come, too, it would be good to see the family."

"*Sarà difficile*. It will be difficult. *Sabina ha già fatto la spesa*. Sabina has already done the shopping." *Silenzio*. Silence.

Clover has followed them into the garden. He has found a dried Magnolia cone, and has laid it at Niccolò's feet. Ignored, he starts to bark.

"*Va bene*." Niccolò's voice is still dignified but it has lost its sparkle. "If it is possible, it would be nice. If not, another time. Enjoy your weekend."

"*Grazie*. And please remove your dog from my garden before he makes a mess."

Immediately, Kate is sorry to be back in Florence. For all her resolve, for all her determination, Kate feels the wind knocked out of her sails yet again. How can this woman yield such power over her sense of well-being? Niccolò seems more at peace with the situation, and she is his mother. Maybe he expects less? But Kate has lowered her expectations to zero and still she feels wounded. Suddenly, she misses Sicily, as if they have been away for years.

A good night's sleep helps. Their bodies turn collectively in the night, a familiar dance, her arm thrown over Niccolò's chest; his arms wrapped around her as they close their twenty-second year of marriage. They wake, still entangled, to begin their twenty-third year.

It is their wedding anniversary today, but that doesn't preclude a long list of errands to run, chores to do which include resolving a leaky toilet, a dead battery on Niccolò's tractor, a flat tire on hers. They need to order fuel for the furnace. There are prescriptions to fill. They need to shop for groceries. They scribble a list and drive into town. On their way home, they stop at the butcher to buy a Florentine steak which will be the main course of their anniversary dinner tonight.

The butcher, Maurizio, completely white haired despite being several years younger than Kate, looks at her warily, as if she's betrayed him; then his expression lightens as memory returns. "Have you just returned to Florence?" After Sicily, the Tuscan accent seems more pronounced to Kate's ear: his **c** hardened into an **h,** his **t** slurred into a **th** cause her to smile.

"Yesterday."

"You can find good meats in Sicilia, but not *la bistecca alla Fiorentina.*"

"Certainly not." In Sicily, the meat is less tender as the animals are allowed to graze openly; their muscles are toughened by their liberty. Instead, the Sicilian fish is so fresh it practically swims onto their plates. Kate looks at the huge slab of aged beef on the butcher block. "Do you have a cut with filet?"

Maurizio disappears into the back room and returns with the best looking flank of Chianina beef Kate has ever seen. The fillet is as large as the contre filet. He cuts it extra-thick, as he knows they like it. It weighs one and a half kilograms—three pounds of dark, aged beef. She asks for a bone for Clover.

They stop to buy vegetables and fruit, too, returning to their favorite little shops. It is easier to shop in Tuscany, where all the markets are in one valley. In Sicily, half the stores they frequent are in Trapani, half in Valderice; both valleys twenty minutes away from their home.

Their last stop today is at their favorite ice cream store where Kate buys pistachio for herself, *Bacio* for Niccolò, chocolate fondente for them to share.

And while Niccolò is otherwise engaged, Kate sneaks into an *enoteca* to buy a tiny bottle of twenty-three-year-old balsamic vinegar. At home she wraps it carefully before putting it in an aquamarine Tiffany's shopping bag. Kate puts it on Niccolò's plate as he is setting the table.

"But I didn't buy you a gift."

"I know." He never buys her a gift for birthdays or anniversaries, unless the kids are home to take him shopping. It doesn't bother her. He is generous spontaneously. At Christmas, as the kids nag them that they don't have any gifts for themselves under the tree, they have learnt to wrap up the gloves they need to work in the fields, a case of the coffee they prefer, objects they would buy anyway, simply so they will have something under the tree. One year Niccolò wrapped up a twenty-five-liter can of grease and the pump to inject it into the joints of the tractor. Wrapping and unwrapping the gifts transforms them into the Christmas spirit, although everyone agreed that the grease was pushing the limit of what could be considered a Christmas present.

"I bought this for the two of us."

"Then you open it."

"No. I wrapped it. You open it."

He is embarrassed, made awkward by the Tiffany's bag, but suspicious when Kate says that she has wrapped it. He takes forever to open the package, snipping the tape, the ribbon. Kate can see he plans to save this tiny square of paper to use again. He unfolds it carefully, then sees the writing on the box: *APOTEOSI*—Apotheosis. "Perfume?"

"Open it."

He breaks the seal on the perfume bottle and sniffs cautiously. "*Balsamico?*"

"Exactly!" Kate hands him a teaspoon. He pours a few drops of the thick black nectar, lifts it to his mouth, and inhales as he sips.

"Stunning!"

He pours more into the spoon for her: it is tart and sweet, thick and smooth.

"Perfect." He reads the bottle, an elegantly scripted label with the years, 23, added by the owner's indelible ink.

"Is this Stravecchio?"

"Almost. I could have more easily bought a bottle of Vintage balsamic, twenty-five-years-old, but with a little persuasion—"

"We Italians are suckers for a good story."

Kate laughs. Niccolò can envision the scene. "I convinced the owner to decant a twenty-three-year-old balsamic vinegar instead of selling an already packaged bottle twenty five years old. As he lovingly funneled his precious nectar into the tiny sculpted bottle, the creator of the vinegar said 'Nearly a quarter of a century in the making. The slow osmosis of liquid, precious woods and time resulting in a perfect balance.'"

"Like us."

"Like us. Happy Anniversary."

This little bottle won't last long, even if they are prudent, but Kate can buy another bottle at Christmas, which will give them something to open under the tree.

Having lived for nearly six months without objects to dust, it is a pleasure to pass a soft cloth over old ceramics, pieces of silver, glass; to polish old wood. They see their paintings anew as they wipe away a spider's web from the corner of the frame; notice details that have been lost or forgotten. They give as much pleasure as a new acquisition, as an old friend re-found.

It is less of a pleasure to wash the floors and vacuum, but it all has to be done, and quickly. November is harvest time for them, and once it starts there won't be time for putting the house in order. They beat the carpets of the dust that has accumulated in their absence; position them snugly beneath the dining room table, under the chairs and sofas, as two birds supply the finishing touches to their winter nest. When they light the wood burning stove for the first time, the house takes on a warm, cozy feeling. Figaro has reclaimed his place by the fireplace; Clover positions himself beneath their feet, wherever they are. They are home and settled for the winter.

Cofano remains in the forefront of Kate's memory: crystal clear, reflected in still, blue waters, as if in a mirror; a halo of clouds hovers over her head, twice.

Sunday evening arrives without a phone call from Niccolò's mother.

"What would you like for dinner?" Kate asks cheerfully, as it becomes clear they are not being invited. Clover perks up, as if he has been invited to dinner.

"*Pasta and pomodoro?*"

"How about *pancetta e pomodoro?*"

"Perfect."

"We have some grilled vegetables leftover from lunch. I can mix them into a salad."

"With a drop of the balsamico, please."

"You can toss."

As Kate puts on water to boil, Niccolò's cellphone rings. It is Federica. "Mamma says she has tried to call you but couldn't reach you."

"Doesn't she have my cellphone number? Couldn't she walk across the garden to knock on our door?"

Federica ignores the questions. "You are invited to dinner tonight."

"At the last possible minute."

"Are you coming?"

"Are we going?" he asks Kate.

"Your mother, your call."

"We'll be there in fifteen minutes. Time to dress."

"Don't be late."

Dinner at Niccolò's mother's home is a study in form. The table is set beautifully; the indigo borders of the *Ginori* porcelain are recalled in the sapphire crystal under plates—chargers—and a fine, embroidered blue line in the otherwise unadorned white linen napkins. The centerpiece of flowers is white velvet gardenias, their perfume wafting through the room as Fiammetta's servant, Sabina, passes with a large steaming platter of pasta. The flower arrangement finishes with three small clusters of azure hyacinth, to carry on the color theme.

The food is good and abundant: a first course of tagliatelle with fresh porcini mushrooms, followed by tender meat surrounded by new potatoes and creamed spinach. Everyone busies themselves with eating and compliments about the food. The tension in the air is palatable: there is an indignant edge to Fiammetta's voice as she criticizes Bulgari's new collection of handbags. "What on earth could their designer have been thinking? Who on earth would buy such a large, vulgar purse? Doesn't anyone have any taste anymore?" No one contradicts her, everyone chatters on about nothing—clothes, holidays, mutual acquaintances—keeping the tone light and cheerful, as it should be to celebrate Alessia's twentieth birthday.

Alessia is a lovely girl. She has a bright, open smile that lights up her entire face. She is seven months younger than Electra and they are fast friends. Their reunions at Christmas and Easter, sometimes for birthdays, reassure them that the future is promising for these cousins.

"We have a peculiar birthday present for you," Kate tells her niece.

"Even more peculiar than usual," Niccolò adds.

"We are buying you a ticket—plane or train, whichever you prefer—to visit Electra in Holland."

Alessia attends university in Italy. She is studying to be a lawyer, but she is spending an Erasmus semester in Brussels, a few hours away from Utrecht, where Electra is currently studying.

They have a present for Vittoria, too, Alessia's younger sister, as they were away on her birthday: another promised ticket to visit Electra in Holland, or Elizabeth in England, if she can't arrange a visit before Electra returns to Rome in February. "You'll have to coordinate your schedules, and then find out when Electra is free from exams."

"Maybe we can include Elisabetta." Alessia and Vittoria look at one another excitedly.

Vittoria, usually reticent, adds conspiringly. "Could she fly over from England for the weekend?"

"It will take more planning, you all have busy schedules, but we will pay for the reunion whenever you can make it happen."

Niccolò's mother has put up with this conversation long enough. Kate knows she equates Holland with drugs and its red light district, and interprets their gift to her nieces as license to corruption. From the way Federica is frowning, Kate is afraid she shares her mother's sentiments. "Explain again why Electra is in Holland when she should be in Rome?"

Niccolò starts to explain, even though both he and Kate have already told her many times. But Alessia interrupts, "It's like my program, *Nonna*. My university is in Milan; and, as part of my course, I am spending six months in Brussels."

Kate can see that Alessia's explanation has further confused her grandmother rather than clarifying.

Annoyed, Fiammetta changes the subject. "When do you intend to start the harvest?" It is the first question she has asked them all evening. No questions about Sicily, no questions about their daughters, nothing about themselves. Kate touches her fingertips to the side of her face and winces.

"On the 21st."

"Not on a Tuesday or a Friday, I assume." There is a superstition against starting anything on those days, a journey, a marriage, a harvest, and even though they don't believe it, there is no reason to tempt fate.

"The 21st is a Thursday. In four days."

"Is it going to be a good year?"

"The trees are full of olives," Niccolò says. "A light rain would be welcome now, as long as it's without wind."

"Dial a weather prayer," Alessia says.

"You'll take what you get." Fiammetta doesn't mean this cruelly, Kate believes, but it comes out sounding like another reprimand.

"I'll bring you a bottle of oil on the 22nd."

For the last ten years Niccolò and Kate have been taking care of his mother's olive groves. Before they took over, Fiammetta had other people work the fields in exchange for half the product, but as she didn't supervise the work, the fruit was harvested but the trees were neglected. Trees—and workers— unattended, always yielded less, until finally only a trickle of oil flowed back from her 3,000 trees.

Eleven years ago Niccolò and Kate stood in their garden watching three workers loading gunny sacks of olives into a car that headed down hill, then four sacks into the car that drove up to deliver the daily yield into their cantina. 'Another bad year,' the worker lamented, removing his cap to scratch his head. Niccolò's mother didn't really care, as long as she had enough olive oil for her table.

What bothered Niccolò most was the audacity with which the workers stole, not even bothering to hide. He asked his mother if they could take charge of the harvest. She said no. She didn't want to upset the apple cart, which meant she didn't want to confront the workers. However, a few months later, when one of the workers died and his widow said she wasn't up to harvesting the olives herself, Niccolò's mother found it convenient to let her son take over that parcel of land. As Niccolò and Kate climbed ladders to pick the olives, they could hear the other workers in the distance laughing at their ignorance, but when they brought in more olives from those 400 trees than from all the other 2,600 trees combined, Niccolò's mother agreed to rent them the property, if they could convince the workers to leave.

In ten years they have transformed the groves, if not to golf course standards, at least so the trees are producing to their full potential. Trees that had been difficult to harvest in the past had been left to be overgrown by forests. Borders were brambles of sticker bushes towering over their heads. In several abandoned fields, they could see the top branches of olive trees poking out from an otherwise impassable forest, bearing fruit, poor things. Niccolò bought a tractor and they rolled up their sleeves, clearing fields, pruning trees to manageable heights so their workers wouldn't be tempted to truncate the upper boughs; could reach the product from the ladders. In putting the groves in order, Niccolò and Kate built up a ten year store of firewood from the pruned trees. In putting the groves in order, they have tripled the amount of olive oil they produce.

It is hard to imagine unless one has experienced it oneself, but land can empty bank reserves if one isn't careful. Once Niccolò understood the danger, they made an agreement that they wouldn't spend more to take care of his mother's property than they could earn from selling the olive oil.

Kate set to work on a marketing plan. On a rainy day they shopped for bottles, driving down the small roads around Vinci, marshes where Niccolò's father had hunted for ducks when Niccolò was a boy. At a house with a yard full of geese, with a warehouse full of sterilized bottles shrunk-wrapped in the back, they found a tall, elegant dark beauty normally used for Grappa—and came home with two Swan Geese, in the bargain. They designed their label using an etching of Villa L'Antica from the 1800s. Finally, they chose to enhance the product with a little booklet describing the oil and the villa, in English and Italian, together with a stainless steel pourer which they hung from the neck of the bottle. In the evening, muscles aching but otherwise enthusiastic, Kate went on-line to search for retail sellers. Eventually, their olive oil found room on the shelves of specialty shops in Europe, Asia and America. They bought themselves a second tractor, another mower; a second trailer so

Kate could retrieve the crates of olives from the fields while Niccolò drove his trailer full of olives to the press. They were making the groves pay for themselves!

And then terrorism hit the Twin Towers and the world economy began its downward spiral.

They have limped along ever since. Whatever they earn, they spend on the property. When they earn nothing, they do all the work themselves, except for the harvest, when they hire help, almost always Sri Lankans.

The maintenance of the property requires more strength and hours than they are able to give it, especially now that they are spending half their year in Sicily. For the six months they are in Tuscany, they work in the groves every day, weather permitting, doing what they can and trying to be content with the resulting imperfection. It is a little like raising children: no matter how much one gives them, they always need more. As with kids, if one gives one's time consistently, the results are usually positive.

Before Niccolò and Kate left for Sicily last spring they mowed for weeks, knowing that if it rained during the summer, they would find the grass tall and would need to mow again before the harvest. The summer has been dry in Tuscany, so they don't need to mow. However, the olives have suffered and a small part of their product has fallen to the ground. Past generations recuperated the fallen olives, but Niccolò and Kate don't. If the skin has been bruised or broken, fermentation has already started and the olives need to be pressed immediately. One never knows how long the olives might have been on the ground.

Alessia has forgotten to turn off her cellphone during dinner and when it rings, right before dessert, she brings it out of her pocket to silence it. It is a new model iPhone, and Niccolò comments, "Bello!"

Vittoria, who has been silent throughout the meal says, "It's from Papà and me."

Federica grumbles. She and her husband have been divorced for more than five years, and she blames her ex for everything, especially a disrespect she perceives radiating from her daughters, like a phone ringing during a meal. Federica leaves her chair and walks out of the room, supposedly to help assist with the decision of the champagne, which frees Alessia to roll her eyes toward heaven.

"Twenty years old today?" Kate says to Alessia, "the end of adolescence?"

"For me, definitely. But what about Mamma?"

Federica returns to the table with the champagne, feeling the injustice of her divorce as if it were new. Fiammetta suddenly turns cheerful. Niccolò pops open the champagne as Fiammetta holds up her glass, amused as the bubbles threaten to overflow.

"A toast!" she proposes grandly. "To my beautiful niece."

"To Alessia, happy birthday!"

Sabina brings in the cake, two fat candles instead of twenty, and everyone sings *Tanti Auguri,* except Federica, who has returned to her unhappy past and sees no reason to sing.

Fiammetta sings with uncharacteristic good cheer. She smiles seductively at Niccolò, lifts her champagne glass and winks at Kate. As the cake is cut and served, she conspires with her nieces to give her instruction on how to use the new cellphone, beguilingly admitting her ineptness in the face of modern technology. The woman is absolutely charming, and Kate recalls, many years ago, that this is the woman she used to know as Niccolò's enchanting mother.

What has become of her over the past twenty years? Why has she soured, not just with Kate and Niccolò, but with Elizabeth, who was for years her favorite granddaughter? As Federica spirals deeper into her unlimited resources of misery, Fiammetta compensates, becomes brighter, wittier, more expansive. Finally, Federica has had enough. She excuses herself from the table, says good night, and leaves the party.

"She's just like her father," Fiammetta stage-whispers, pretending Federica's daughters aren't present or can't hear, or won't disagree. In case her comment is overlooked, she shakes her head and repeats, "Just like her father."

Unfortunately, Fiammetta is right. Federica is very much like her father. Fiammetta says it's the DNA, there is nothing that can be done; it's all in the genes. But having lived with Niccolò, having seen his father's gestures surface in moments of what Kate calls *automatic pilot,* when habit rushes in before rational thought, Kate disagrees with her mother-in-law's verdict. Having watched Niccolò free himself of these gestures,

283

just as he has freed himself of some old, redundant, politically incorrect attitudes, Kate believes Federica's similarity to her father has more to do with Federica's fear of not having an identity of her own.

Both siblings suffered when Fiammetta left her difficult husband. Insults were hurled at her back, in front of the children, in front of the neighbors, eventually in front of the judge who granted Niccolò's father custody of the two children. How they survived, Kate doesn't know. In some fundamental way, Federica didn't survive. What grew up in place of her trusting youth is a sad, wounded replica of her father.

It is a miracle that Niccolò is the man he is: positive, optimistic, full of love and caring, determined to do the right thing for himself and those around him.

What strikes her now, as Kate watches her mother-in-law reinventing herself as cheerful and carefree, is that Fiammetta acts in response to the people around her. If her ex-husband was incensed and self-righteous, Fiammetta would compensate by playing out the role of the happy-go-lucky, irresponsible divorceè (although divorce wasn't legal in Italy until twenty-two years after they separated). When Niccolò's father was alive—a self-appointed victim of life's injustices—Fiammetta balanced his act with gaiety and generosity—a good time for all!

That is the woman to whom Niccolò introduced Kate, the woman she enjoyed without reservation. When Elizabeth was born, Fiammetta showered her granddaughter with the affection Niccolò never knew as a child, healing hard feelings; reconstructing bridges. When Niccolò's father died, the balance shifted again. There was no longer any need to compensate, to prove her ex-husband the bad guy. A few years later Fiammetta's second husband died, and she turned cold, self-centered and unsympathetic. While maintaining appearances, she pushed them all away; blamed them for her unhappiness.

The more Kate knows of other flawed parents, the more she accepts her own. Kate needed her father to love her, which he was unable to do. She needed him to make her feel safe, which he didn't understand. However, now that she has had the privilege of knowing Niccolò's family well, she has less complaint with her own.

CHAPTER TWENTY-TWO

In the days before the harvest, Kate disappears into the kitchen to make a big pot of minestrone and a quantity of *ragu* sauce for hearty, last minute meals. She makes batches of *pesto*, using the basil in the pots on their terrace before the leaves blacken from frost, and stores it in little jars under last year's olive oil.

The day before they start the harvest, Niccolò drives her into town to see their dentist, Donatello. The gum around her tooth has regained sensation, but the skin on the right side of her face is very sore, and her eye is slightly puffy.

The drive to town at eight in the morning is sluggish. The roads are crowded with people travelling to work. Mothers and fathers have left their cars double-parked to accompany their children into school, to chat with teachers and other parents. There is nothing to do but shift from first gear to second, second to first, apply the brakes, shift again, and aim for patience.

The drivers in Florence are more skillful than the drivers in Trapani but they are also less forgiving. Horns are honked at a stalled engine or a second's delay in responding to a green light. Slow reactions are rewarded with insulting gestures. The drivers in the other cars are not allies, they are enemies. The assumption seems to be that one is intentionally thwarting their progress. As the diverse roads to town merge into one lane, and cars have no choice but to yield, it is interesting to watch these drivers who face this bottleneck five if not six days a week, refusing to let their fellow commuters enter, without the benefit of a rude gesture and an insulting remark.

In Trapani the driving is more chaotic but less aggressive. The streets are reduced to a single lane as cars are double and sometimes triple parked on both sides, which demands negotiating with on-coming traffic for the right to progress. The difference is that most cars do let you pass. They also slow to let the side street traffic scoot across an intersection. There are few horns, no rude remarks, not even those mean, accusing stares which unnerve Kate most in Florence.

Kate is a confident driver. She grew up in California where they say the residents learn to drive before they walk. Kate has lived in New York City with a car, although she wouldn't recommend it to anyone she loves. Electra learned to drive in Florence but perfected her skills in Trapani. While she was next to her daughter, Kate often held her breath to help them ease through the trafficked streets, as she did on the curvy, switchbacks between town and home. Electra has driven in both Florence and Trapani and she, too, agrees that Trapani is better. Other drivers, for the most part, are accommodating. If you are in a hurry, they will let you pass. If they are in a hurry, you let them pass. It doesn't alter one's sense of importance.

Driving in Florence is like travelling through the centuries, Kate thinks. They proceed along the broad boulevard constructed mid-1800s when Florence was briefly the capital of Italy, at the pace of a horse-drawn carriage. They pass the grand palaces from the sixteen hundreds, the Renaissance Fortress, *Fortezza da Basso*, built by the Medici in the fifteen hundreds to defend itself in an uprising against Pisa; past *Piazza della Libertà*, its neo-classic *Arc de Triomphe* mostly hidden by tall, broad-limbed trees; down narrow, medieval streets to Donatello's office, with its high ceilinged, echoing entry hall, its broad, marble stairs, all the ingredients for grandeur but without the proportions to render it attractive.

Donatello doesn't keep them waiting, but they lose several minutes hearing about his summer at *Forte dei Marmi*, the Bridgehampton or Malibu Colony of Tuscany. After examining Kate's mouth, he listens to her story of the piece of clam caught between her teeth, the tingling of her face, and the swelling of her eye. He positions the x-ray machine, places a piece of hard cardboard into her mouth and tells her to clamp down.

Between one x-ray and the next, he admits that her story confuses him. "If it were an upper tooth that could perhaps trigger a reaction in the eye," he says, as he positions another hard square of cardboard in her mouth, its wings biting into the soft skin under her tongue, "but the nerves from the lower jaw aren't connected to the eye or the cheek. It is impossible."

He may be right; he undoubtedly is. He is the expert. Kate is just relating the course of events that have brought her into town today. Whatever the logic, something is creating a problem in her eye.

Donatello returns with the exposed x-rays, props them onto the light box for them to see, and explains that the work that he has done eight months ago on her lower molar is perfect. "Everything is fine."

His concern, Kate realizes as she leaves his office, is that his work is not at fault.

Time is wasted on the first day of the harvest as Niccolò and Niroshan, their harvest coordinator, explain the process to the workers. More time is wasted making sure the workers' documents are in order, in registering them for this temporary work. Kate begins the process of connecting impossibly long names with unfamiliar faces, a process that is complicated by the use of various nicknames. Kate is told to call Peiris Malalage Sucilintha Amarasinghe by the name of Sucil, while his colleagues address him as Peiris and his friends call him Amarasi.

It is late morning before the workers are in the fields, but an abbreviated first day is not a mistake. Muscles are used in harvesting that are not otherwise called into use, and a reduced day will be appreciated at bedtime. As Niroshan divides the workers into teams, Kate notices a cluster of the bright yellow enameled flowers, the same ones Concetta transplanted into the garden in Erice. Once her eye recognizes that they are not merely dandelions, Kate sees another cluster and another, their olive groves dotted intermittently with these shiny, tiny works of perfection.

On the second day of the harvest they fall into a rhythm they will maintain daily, until the last of the olives are picked, unless they are interrupted by rain. Kate arrives at the bus stop at seven a.m. to pick up the first group of six workers. At seven-thirty she is there again for the second group. At eight she returns for the third and last time to pick up the stragglers. As Kate is taxiing them up the hill, Niccolò and the first group are putting nets and ladders and crates into Kate's tractor's trailer.

Once they have driven all the teams to the fields, Niccolò and Kate start loading his tractor's trailer with yesterday's olives, and once the larger trailer is full—twenty tons—Niccolò drives up to the press, a half hour away. While he is having the olives pressed into oil, Kate takes the smaller trailer and returns to the fields to pick up the morning's first produce. In exchange for every crate that weighs twenty kilos, Kate gives each squad a ticket with the number of boxes they have produced. At the end of the week, they trade in their tickets for cash.

Niroshan stops Kate as she climbs back on her tractor. "Madam?" His ebony skin is smooth over the planes of his face.

"Yes?" Kate is expecting him to ask her to buy bread. One of the teams always shows up without bread—especially in the first days—which makes their lunch of thick, spicy, curry sauce incomplete, insubstantial. Kate is trying to figure out when she will have time to drive into town to buy bread, an errand that might overturn her carefully organized day into chaos. Maybe Kate has an extra loaf in the freezer?

"Are you well?" Niroshan asks instead.

"Yes. I'm fine, thank you. Why do you ask?"

"Your eye."

"Oh." Kate touches her fingers to her temple and tries not to wince. Niccolò has asked her the same thing this morning. "No, it is nothing. I am just a little tired, that's all."

"But not as tired as you will be when the harvest ends!"

"That is the truth." Kate starts the engine to her tractor.

"Madam?"

"Yes." Kate grinds into first gear but keep her foot on the brake. A bank of clouds is settling low over the Arno Valley. The dome of the Cathedral is hidden within, like Cofano, Kate thinks nostalgically. She hasn't had her camera out since they returned to Tuscany.

"Can you bring a loaf of bread when you return?" He reaches into his pocket to offer her a euro coin. "One of the groups has forgotten to bring bread."

She refuses the coin. "I'll see what I have in the freezer. Tell them to remember their bread tomorrow."

When Kate returns home, she unloads the boxes of olives. She runs her hand through the crate, enjoying the heft and the color of the unripened green and mature black fruit. Niccolò and Kate easily move box after box together, and Kate can do it alone, if she must, but it is asking for back problems so she has devised a ramp to ease the crates off the tractor. A certain amount of lifting and shoving is still involved but at least she is not moving forty or fifty twenty-kilo boxes alone.

By the time Niccolò returns with the olive oil, Kate has prepared lunch. These meals would never be classified as gourmet. They are quick and light, nourishing enough to give them strength for the second half of the day but not heavy enough to make them want to nap. It is a moment to sit, to relax, to regroup their energy.

After lunch Niccolò and Kate transfer the olive oil he has brought home into the first of the eighteen 500-liter stainless steel containers standing against the east wall of the cantina. Once the 50-liter plastic containers are empty of oil, they need to be washed and dried for tomorrow's transport. While Niccolò prepares the equipment for the next day's pressing, Kate fills the trailer with empty crates for the crews, and returns to the fields to pick up what the workers have boxed, leaving them with however many boxes they think they will need between now and closing.

"I'll return at 4:30," Kate tells each group as she climbs back onto her tractor.

"Signora, if you can please come at 5:00."

Three or four workers join together to form a crew. The fastest ones make reasonably good money. Other teams are slow and they make just enough money to scrape by. Niroshan organizes the workers, settles disputes and translates their instructions—some of the workers speak English, some Italian, some only Sri Lankan. She doesn't know what they would do without him.

Niroshan started as a worker ten years ago but quickly made himself indispensible. He shows the workers how to pick more efficiently and admonishes them when they skip over the less plentiful trees in favor of the full ones, telling them all trees are to be picked in a row. No exceptions! He won't listen to excuses, calls some of the workers lazy, but Niccolò and Kate have picked olives, and know how hard it is. If they had to earn their dinner by picking olives, they would undoubtedly starve. Niccolò has been tempted to give a minimum wage for a day's work but Niroshan assures him he is courting disaster if he does so. The slower workers will move even more slowly since they know their earning is guaranteed. And the faster workers will resent the slower ones being rewarded instead of themselves. So Niccolò gives them exactly what they earn, no more, no less, and at the end of the harvest he and Kate reward reliability: they give a bonus to the ones who have stayed throughout the entire season.

Everyone wants to be the last team picked up so they can bring in another few kilos, earn a little more money, which means that they return home long after dark every day. Their trailer is weighed down with the last two dozen boxes of olives, all the nets, the ladders and all the workers who are too tired to walk home. It is quite a scene. The Sri Lankans are indisputably exhausted on the ride home but there is laughter and good humor emanating from the trailer as they drive through the dark.

It is a magical moment of the day. Niccolò invariably drives. Kate perches beside him on the fender of the little tractor, her arm around the back of his seat, holding on as they bump along. She enjoys the movement of his back against the inside of her arm. It is a moment of suspended happiness. There is more work to do when they reach the cantina. Kate still has to drive the workers back to the bus, and they, poor souls, have long bus rides home, often several transfers. All of them have dinner to think about. The lucky ones will enjoy hot showers and clean clothes. All of them will feel the burn of sore muscles. But for the moment, proceeding through the dark at a slow, leisurely pace, too heavy to hurry, too tired to care, the stars pin-pricking their way into the night's black fabric: the world is a magical place.

By the time the tractor is unloaded and the equipment stored, the first workers have changed back into their street clothes, and are ready to be taxied down to the bus. The second ones are ready when Kate returns. Niroshan is always the last to leave. He makes sure that someone—and not the same someone—sweeps up the olives that fall from the cuffs of the workers' trousers and boots, as squished olives on the cantina pavement will be messy. And slippery.

By the time Kate returns from the bus for the last time, eight-thirty or nine, Niccolò has already showered. He puts pasta water on while Kate showers, defrosts a package of the ragu. If they have the energy, they make a salad. If not, they find other ways to enjoy their newly pressed olive oil: *bruschetta*, toasted bread scraped with garlic, dribbled with oil. Or thickly sliced tomatoes, dribbled with oil, or a dish of white cannoli beans; cooked *cavolo nero*, black cabbage. It doesn't matter how commonplace the vegetable or bean is, a dribble of new olive oil transforms it into a celebration of flavors. It is sinfully delicious. It reminds them why they do this back-breaking work.

Kate must remember to take a bottle to Niccolò's mother.

When Elizabeth and Electra lived at home, it was their job to start the pasta, but when the girls were home Niccolò and Kate had to help with homework after dinner, so the trade-off is even. Now, with the kids away, they finish their dinner, put the kitchen in order, and spend a few minutes on the phone with their girls, hearing their news, giving them theirs.

They are almost always in bed by eleven, asleep by eleven-o-one. Their sleep is deep and their dreams are of olives: raking, shifting them in their nets, removing the leaves. And the oil, of course, its pungent scent, its vivid color, pours its way like a fluid ribbon into their dreams.

The next day, right before lunch, before Niccolò returns from the press, Kate fills a bottle of bright, pungent new oil for Fiammetta. She changes out of her work clothes to cross the garden. She times her visit carefully so as to arrive fifteen minutes before Fiammetta will be served lunch. Kate doesn't have the time for a longer visit, and it isn't up to her to decide when a visit is over.

Fiammetta has imprisoned herself in proud isolation. When Niccolò calls his mother, no matter what time of the day, she is busy and doesn't want to talk; then she complains to Niccolò's sister that they never call. If Kate invites her to join them for dinner, she finds a reason to decline, then complains again to Federica that she never sees them. Like the genie inside the lamp, each day she worsens her threat of what she will do to the person who frees her.

Unfortunately, no one can free her.

For the two months a year that Fiammetta is in residence at L'Antica, Kate tries to visit with some kind of regularity. Truthfully, she does it as much for herself as for her mother-in-law. Kate doesn't want to be a person who neglects an old, lonely woman, related to her by marriage or not, even if Kate is given every reason to justify her distance. She tries to peer through Fiammetta's murky glass of antagonism and superiority, to see the needy person inside, as Kate did when her children were obnoxious and whining, inviting them to sit on her lap instead of sending them to their rooms.

Like the uninvited guest she is made to feel, Kate always brings something to buffer her intrusion, something that will give them an opening and closing conversation: a jar of marmalade, a round of cheese, a recent photo of Elizabeth or Electra, a slice of a dessert she has made for their dinner. Today's gift is easy. Fiammetta is as proud of the new oil as if she made it herself.

It breaks Kate's heart to find Fiammetta sitting in front of a soap opera. From her worried expression and the nervous way she is picking at the cuticles along her red, varnished nails, Kate sees she is thoroughly involved in the drama. In fact, after she magnanimously accepts the bottle of oil, and they are perched opposite each other on two uncomfortable sofas, the television program continues to add its voice to their conversation. Kate has to repeat her comments several times, and then Kate can't really hear Fiammetta's answers over the volume. Eventually, Fiammetta manipulates the remote control so that the volume is off, but Kate sees her peering over her shoulder, surreptitiously trying to follow the mute drama. It is obviously a relief when she is called to lunch. Before Kate is out the door, the volume is back on, the drama continued.

CHAPTER TWENTY-THREE

"How long does the harvest last?" Mark asks.

Normally they discourage friends from visiting during the harvest, but Mark, an American, is traveling through Italy with his eleven-year-old son, Joshua, after the recent death of his wife, Julie. Kate doesn't feel they can deny them their font of distraction.

"It varies from year to year," Kate explains, wiping up a drop of oil from the table. Mark and Joshua have spent an hour in their fields picking olives before lunch. In a few minutes Kate and Niccolò will need to leave to resume their afternoon chores. "In a spare year, we can finish in less than a month. In a good year, it takes about two months. Last year we started on the twentieth of October and finished two days before Christmas."

"Five days a week?" Mark asks.

"Normally we work every day, weekends included, and break when it rains. But that year it didn't rain at all."

"How many hours a day do you harvest?"

"The workers start around eight and finish around six. Our work starts at seven and we finish, if we are lucky, by nine." Kate stifles a yawn.

"Fifty-eight, fourteen-hour days," Joshua announces, shaking his head to remove the fine, sandy hair from his eyes. "For a grand total of 812 hours!"

This kid is going to be fine. Kate looks at the father with the same fine hair just beginning to gray. His attention is wholly engaged by the olive oil on his plate. As he dips his bread into the oil, careful not to spill a drop, a glimmer of enthusiasm makes its way through the pallor of inherent sorrow. They are both going to be fine.

As Kate stands to clear the table, she finds Joshua at her elbow, bringing his father's plate to the sink as well as his own. She stops herself before she can compliment him on a skill his mother probably taught him. Instead, Kate rewards him with a quick "thanks" as she would acknowledge Niccolò's help or her daughters'.

But Joshua lingers at her side, obviously wanting something more from her.

"What is it, sweetie?"

"I was wondering?" Joshua is suddenly shy.

"What?"

"Could I maybe drive your tractor?"

Kate hesitates. She has already given them more of her time than she should today. Niccolò and she will finish hours later than usual tonight to make up for the luxury of a leisurely lunch. Kate is beginning to regret having said yes to their visit in the first place. This kid has asked to drive her tractor as casually as if he were asking to borrow a pencil.

"Do you know how to drive?"

"No. But I was watching you, and it doesn't seem that difficult. You could teach me?"

It is the question mark at the end of the phrase that is the decider, the tremor of doubt behind the presumptuous request. Kate is annoyed with herself that compassion is her second reaction. She almost missed an opportunity to give this child something to smile about, to do what? The dishes?

"Sure. I'd be happy to teach you. I bet you're a natural."

Mark, who has been silent until now, pushes his chair back from the table. "I'd be happy to finish up those dishes for you."

"No, let's leave them to soak. You should come with us." Suddenly Kate is enthusiastic. "Bring my camera."

"And your stop-watch, Dad!"

As Mark rides down the hill with Niccolò on the John Deere, Joshua climbs onto the fender of Kate's Carraro. Kate explains the process. "First, I am not going to do anything dangerous, so you don't need to be afraid."

"I'm not afraid."

"Good. Hang on. We aren't going to go fast but the terrain isn't even, so you need to hold securely to the back of my chair. Keep your feet here—" Kate points to the mud shield "when we go downhill, and here—" Kate indicate a small space, "when we go up hill, but don't step on this pedal. Better to uncross your legs. If there is an emergency and you need to jump clear of the tractor, you don't want to lose time uncrossing your legs. Duck down," Kate warns, as they pass beneath a low hanging olive branch.

"This is great! Tell me when I should jump. *Dai!*"

Kate laughs at his Italian imperative. Joshua and Mark accompanied Kate to the supermarket earlier today. She had needed to pick up bread for two workers who had forgotten theirs, and a few staples. The elevator door was closing when three teenage Italian boys pushed their way in, and in loud, argumentative voices, debated whether to go up to the top floor, meat and poultry, or down to the produce. "Su!!!" said the one with the scruffy, day-old beard, jabbing the elevator buttons. "Dai! Giu!! Dai! Giu!" argued the other two, jabbing the other buttons.

Mark leaned close to whisper. "Do we need to be afraid?"

"No, why?" She looked at the kids, typical *ragazzacci*—boys with attitude, but nothing to worry about. She looked again, to see if she had missed some important sign.

"Are they anti-Semitic?"

"No, I wouldn't think so. Why?"

Whispering, he says, "They keep repeating 'Die Jew, Die Jew.'"

"Ahhh—" She explains through controlled laughter. "*Giu* means *down*—even if it is pronounced like *Jew*. And *Dai*, which is pronounced like *Die*, means, in this case, *agree with me,* or *give in*. No, you don't have anything to worry about."

Kate brakes the tractor as they cross a narrow juncture. "I doubt you'll need to jump, Joshua, but the secret to driving a tractor is to keep your eyes and ears open all the time, even if the movement is routine, even if you think you know the terrain by heart." They are headed down a steep, narrow decline; the front left tire rises as it passes over the remains of a once ingenious water channel system.

"Wow, what was that?"

"In the old days, when dozens of workers tended this land—instead of just the two of us—the property was beautifully terraced with double stone walls, one wall to hold the earth, the other to let pass the water."

"I can see the walls. There!"

"Josh! Hold on. Yes, the walls are still there but trees have grown between them, blocking the water, sending it off course, which in turn causes the walls to collapse."

"Why don't you put the walls back the way they were? It would be pretty."

"We would if we had the time and energy. It's on our list of things to do, just not at the top. Duck!"

He bends at the waist as they pass beneath another olive tree. Kate has learned to resist the temptation to lift the branches as she passes, as she has damaged both her shoulders, first her left, then her right, from lifting and holding branches as she passes under trees. Once too often, her hands have become entangled and unable to release the branch as the tractor moves forward, tearing ligament. It takes longer to repair than rip, so now Kate passes farther from the trunks of the trees, even though it annoys her to leave a patch of tall grass unmowed. Kate sighs. There is only so much they can do. She tries to look at what they have achieved rather than what is left undone.

"Is re-opening the tunnel at the top of your list?"

"Not exactly in pole position." There is a tunnel that starts under the floor in their cantina, which runs the two kilometer distance to the nearest town, Mosciano, designed nearly a thousand years ago to facilitate escape between L'Antica's tower and the church's promise of sanctuary. Niccolò's maternal grandfather had its entrance closed with bricks at the beginning of the Second World War, as he did the cantina itself, which they have reopened. Earlier, as Kate was preparing lunch, she heard Niccolò confess to Mark his desire to reopen the tunnel. It's all a question of priorities. It would be lovely to have the money to hire someone to repair the dry walls, to open the tunnel, to make it safe enough so that they could allow their friends' children to traverse it. "In the old days," Kate tells Joshua, "which spans back to the Renaissance and forward until the Second World War, numerous families maintained this

296

property. Able-bodied fathers with strong sons, everyone pitching in, wives and daughters-in-law, grandmothers, everyone worked to make this land efficient and profitable."

"And beautiful."

"Well, I think nature is largely responsible for the beauty."

"But the walls."

"Yes, the walls are beautiful, even if they are in disrepair." Kate doesn't tell him how sad the neglect makes her feel. Instead, she pulls the tractor into a large, relatively flat field, a field that doesn't receive much sun in the winter and is therefore sparsely populated with olive trees. "Ready for your first tractor driving lesson?"

She climbs out of the seat so he can take her place.

"You'll stay with me, right?"

"Of course." Kate perches herself on the fender and begins to explain the transmission. She keeps it brief: all he really needs to know is that the figure of the rabbit means fast and the tortoise means slow. Kate positions his hands on the wheel and his foot on the brake while she operates the clutch. She adjusts the accelerator lever to a slow crawl. If they were walking, they would be going faster, but Joshua is as focused as if they were speeding in a sports car along the *Targa Florio*. Kate sees his father in the distance, photographing. "You are doing fine."

"Am I?"

"I think you are ready to drive it alone."

"You do?"

Kate jumps down from the slow-moving tractor. "I'm right here, if you need me." She feels like a pony-master but is glad for his self-esteem that her tether is invisible. "Just remember to steer," Kate calls after him. "And stay away from the trees."

Mark keeps his distance, continues to photograph. Kate can see a team of Sri Lankans pause to watch, the longing on their faces apparent even at a distance.

Please don't ask, Kate whispers to herself, or we'll never finish the harvest. And if we don't profit, we will never begin to rebuild these beautiful stone walls.

The harvest is demanding but it is beautiful, too, as long as Kate remembers to pause from time to time, to raise her gaze to the distant hills, to photograph mentally the images as they present themselves. The Arno valley is swept clean of summer's heavy air, the clouds are high; the sun is bright but not hot. Unless it rains, it is a pleasure to be outdoors. Surely, they would have lost the experience of autumn if they hadn't been harvesting, if they had been sitting warm and cozy indoors in front of the fireplace.

Having been in Sicily for nearly six months, Kate is struck anew by the beauty of Tuscany. To be honest, it's not that she ever forgot its appeal, but its beauty has been compromised by the smog of frustration. Today, a fog has flooded the entire valley, has covered everything man has worked so strenuously to create; nevertheless, the tops of hills emerge like islands in a sea of white, as if Kate has re-opened a page to a beautifully illustrated fairy-tale.

At the end of the second week of harvest, Kate wakes with her eye swollen shut. She tries to ignore it as she dresses for work, tries to disregard the inquisitive looks from the Sri Lankans. When Kate returns from bringing up the last carload of workers, she finds that the first workers have already loaded the trailer with olives, and Niccolò has changed out of his work clothes, is wearing a jacket and tie.

"Where are you taking me?" Kate hopes he will hear flirtation in her voice, not fear.

"To the optometrist at I.O.T."

"I know the way. I can go alone. You can stay to follow the harvest."

He looks at her sternly. "Do you really think I would send you off by yourself?"

As they travel along the southern edge of the Arno Valley, Simona Collura sings *Caruso*; the passion in her voice belies her youth. For a moment it feels as if they are out on a pleasure drive rather than driving to see a doctor, with all the time in the world instead of stealing minutes from the harvest.

Normally, Kate brings a book to read in a doctor's waiting room, but with one eye puffy she can't read comfortably. Niccolò paces. They have different methods to pass the time. Today, Kate looks out the large, not very clean window to a spacious, unattended inner courtyard. She can imagine how pretty it looked in the architectural rendering of this clinic, but the reality is sad, a motif of abject abandonment and neglect. Even the tree branches are empty. Their leaves lie in wet piles on squares of pebble-studded concrete. A sad statement at the center of a hospital.

When she is admitted to the optometrist's office, he agrees that her eye is puffy but can't find a cause. Finally, he suggests that she might have a case of shingles behind her eye, which is causing the swelling. He prescribes eye drops, suggests Kate has a TAC—a CT Scan—and sends her on her way.

"When I have the results of the TAC, to whom should I show them?"

"If the eye is still swollen after a week with these eye drops, I'd suggest you visit an *Otorinolaringoiatra*—an Ear, Nose and Throat doctor." He scribbles down a name. "There is nothing wrong with your eye. Everything is fine."

During the day Kate's eye improves with the drops so that by mid-afternoon, when she picks up the crates, it is almost normal, barely puffy. She doesn't dare touch her cheek with her fingertips as it is painfully sensitive, so she solves the problem by resisting the temptation. She has a headache, a relentless thudding, like a prisoner's muffled chisel and hammer escape.

They have fallen behind schedule. *Il frantoio*—the press—is annoyed that Niccolò forgot to call to say he would be late. Grabbing a sandwich and a grapple of grapes, he has set off in high gear to haul the heavy, overflowing trailer up the hill to the press. Kate sits on the old stone bench in front of their cantina. She pulls on her boots to start her rounds. She has a sandwich in her hand but she is not hungry. Piece by piece she feeds it to their dog. Clover eats it all, even the thick slices of tomato, and then lies at her feet, his chin resting on the toe of her boot. Kate stares out at the distant view of Florence. The whole Arno valley, from Vallombrosa to Abetone, is clean and clear today. This is a view celebrated by artists since the beginning of time, not the least Leonardo da Vinci. But however hard Kate tries, however hard she scans the horizon, she is blind to its beauty, as if the problem with her eye has shrouded her internal vision.

Niroshan sends two workers back to the cantina with her to unload the crates from the trailer, and these two strong, healthy men—Sucil and Tangi—have the crates unloaded in minutes. They return to the fields to pick up more filled crates, as Kate is late in her rounds and they have been working hard. Sucil and Tangi return with her again, even though it means that their daily harvest will be reduced because they have lost time helping her unload the trailer.

For the rest of the week, each time Kate drives out to pick up the filled crates of olives, Niroshan sends back two workers with her. After the first day, they are rotated. Not one of them expresses impatience, even when Kate makes an error backing up the trailer and positions it far from storage, which adds many steps to their heavy work. They are always cheerful and polite. No one ever asks her what is wrong with her eye, but Kate can hear them speculating among themselves. She can't understand their words but their gestures leave no doubt that her eye is the subject of their conversation.

Every day Kate wakes up to her eye swollen shut. Is it getting better? Worse? Are the drops making a difference? It is hard to say. Certainly, it takes more time for it to diminish its puffiness during the day. At first it stays swollen through breakfast but is gone by lunch; then it stays puffy through lunch but is fairly normal by dinner. By the end of the week it is swollen all the time.

Driving to pick up the workers each morning with one eye swollen shut isn't particularly difficult. Even the persistent headache doesn't deter her. The road from their house to the bus stop is mostly a single country lane. Kate knows the places to pull over when faced with an approaching car. The swollen eye, her right, keeps her from seeing the worried expressions on the faces of their workers. The ride up the hill is unusually silent, absent of the usual cheerful banter. The workers leave the car with heads bowed, as if in mourning.

Each morning, when Kate returns with the last carload of workers, she finds the trailer already full. This new routine saves Niccolò and her an hour a day of exhaustive labor.

Too often, Kate returns to find her husband changed into city clothes, another doctor's appointment to announce.

Kate's friend Carrie has told her what to expect from a *TAC*—a CT Scan. She has told her about the noises and the duration; also the claustrophobia. Kate's mother has commented on the claustrophobia, as well; has said that she had to take a Valium before entering the tunnel.

Forewarning has prepared her for everything except an exceptionally rude attendant. He is fat and unshaven; his white lab coat is noticeably dingy at the cuffs. Someone has burnt his toast this morning, and he is taking it out on Kate. He has her lie on her stomach and turns her head tightly to one side, straps her into a position she won't be able to maintain if the CT Scan takes fifteen or twenty minutes, as she has been told. When she tries to explain the difficulty she is having with the position, she sees hatred in the technician's eyes. His words are not reassuring, either, and he tells Kate if she can't cooperate, she can just go home.

"All right," Kate says. "I'll be happy to leave, if you will un-strap me."

A second attendant comes forward, unties the restraints; helps her up.

The sadist relents, "We will film your head from the front, if you are capable of lying on your back."

What is his problem?

Twenty minutes later Kate is released. She leaves the chamber without voicing a single one of the scalding phrases she has crafted while in the tunnel.

"How was it?" Niccolò asks, his face a portrait of concern.

"It was OK—not too bad," Kate lies. Why burden him with the details when he can't do anything about them.

On the way home they listen to Federico Berto singing *Io Canto!* I Sing! Kate lets his enthusiasm wash over her, cleansing her of the anger and resentment that built in the *CT scan* tunnel. By the time they reach home, Kate is happy to be dressing in her work clothes again. She is looking forward to seeing how many olives have been picked this morning. She can't wait to be on her tractor.

As Kate is backing out of the cantina, Niccolò stops her. "Keiji just called." Kate can see he has good news to share.

Keiji Tanaka is their principle olive oil customer; in fact, their only significant client these days. About the same time that they took over the care of the fields, he opened an elegant Italian restaurant in Athens, Georgia. Every year he orders ten pallets of oil from them, some thirteen thousand half-liter bottles, which he puts on the tables of his fine restaurant, for the pleasure of his clients. He is the only one of their clients who has not decreased or cancelled his order after 9/11.

"Keiji called to say that he is opening a new restaurant."

"That's marvelous."

"He called because he hopes to increase his order from ten to fifteen pallets this year, and wanted to know if we would be able to accommodate the larger order."

Niccolò knows they can. All the work they've done over the years means that their trees are producing more olives. They definitely have the oil. It is good news indeed to learn they have a place to sell it.

Most evenings Niccolò or Kate calls one of their daughters to report on the harvest. They want to hear news of their studies, the details of their lives: Electra has found a stable just outside of Utrecht in which to ride twice a week. Elizabeth has spent the weekend planting borders of cyclamen and pansies. Niccolò has mentioned Kate's eye, but at her bidding he has down-played it: there is no reason to alarm them. They are far away, there is nothing they can do, and worry will keep them from focusing on their rapidly approaching exams. They are both happy to hear that Keiji is hoping to increase his order, and promise to lend a hand bottling the oil when they return home on holiday.

In the third week of the harvest, Kate wakes up to find her eye not only swollen but discolored; a sickening black and green and yellow. Kate hands Niccolò a digital camera, and asks him to take a close up to e-mail to Elizabeth. What's the point of having an almost doctor in the family if they can't consult freely?

Elizabeth phones them almost immediately. "It is probably nothing serious, but as there are several possibilities that are not pretty, don't lose any time in getting it looked at, please."

Her tone is professional, her words are calm, but it is the please at the end of her phrase, extended with the extra Italian syllable that tells Kate she is alarmed.

"Don't you worry. We are taking care of it."

"Good. Here is Stephen. He wants to say something, too."

"Hello, Kate. Stephen here. I just wanted to mention that my uncle in London is a specialist in maxillofacial surgery. He might have an idea what's wrong with you eye, or at least be able to point you in the right direction."

"Thank you, Stephen. I appreciate your concern. Let's see if I can resolve this in Italy. If not, there's time to contact your uncle."

"I also would like to reiterate what Elizabeth has said: it's best to take care of this problem straight away. I am here if you need me for anything. Here's Lizzy again. Goodnight."

"Goodnight."

"Goodnight, Mama. We will phone you tomorrow to hear what the doctor has said."

Perhaps the medical system is miraculously efficient in England, or perhaps it is Elizabeth and Stephen's wish for her well-being, but seeing a doctor today is unlikely in Italy. Or is it? True, it can take time to be given an appointment if the case isn't urgent, but when it is urgent, the doors fly open. Maybe Kate should be treating her eye with more urgency instead of assuming it's going to be all right.

"Shall we try to see an Ear, Nose and Throat man?"

"I'll fetch our coats." Niccolò has been stimulated by Elizabeth's words as well. "We'll go to the emergency room of the hospital where Electra had her tonsils removed. Maybe Dr. Spezi will be on duty.

Dr. Spezi is on duty, and after a relatively short wait in uncomfortable, anatomically-incorrect chairs in a dreary corridor, they are admitted. The doctor hears Kate's story about the infected gum around her molar, the tingling in her face. She doesn't need to say anything about her eye; it is as puffy at three o'clock as it was when Kate woke in the morning. Dr. Spezi repeats the same thing their dentist said: that it is impossible that the lower jaw could enflame a nerve in the upper part of the face.

Before Kate can quite register what he is doing, the doctor has inserted a very long tube attached to a tiny camera down her nose, into her throat. She wants to scream. The burning is intolerable. It is as unpleasant an examination as Kate has ever had, and just when she is sure she is going to faint, he pulls it out. As Kate was suspended in suffering, Dr. Spezi was viewing the inside of her passages with a micro-camera. "It's all clear. Nothing here to worry about." He looks again at her CT scan. "You need to have an optometrist look at this."

"I have had an optometrist look at it."

"What did he say?"

"He sent us to an Ear, Nose and Throat man. To you."

The doctor looks irritated, as if someone is playing a trick on him. He looks at the CT scan again. "No, you definitely need to go back to the optometrist."

The next morning they don't even bother to dress in their work clothes. Kate drives down to the bus to pick up the workers dressed for a visit to the optometrist, and Niccolò supervises the loading of the trailer in his city clothes, as well. Niroshan directs the workers to a field close to their house, so that Kate will be spared driving them and their equipment a distance in her tractor. Usually, the fields that are close to the house are reserved for days threatening rain, but today Niroshan has foreseen the need to send Kate and Niccolò on their way quickly.

The optometrist isn't surprised to see them. He doesn't remember having seen them before. Looking into one person's eyes at this close distance must be very much the same as looking into another's. He dilates Kate's eye, then examines it again. Again he finds nothing. He looks at her CT scan. He suggests that Kate makes another appointment with the Ear, Throat and Nose doctor.

Do they laugh or cry? Do they nod in agreement or scream in protest? All four possibilities push themselves forward for consideration, until they decide to go home, take care of their responsibilities in the fields, and consider their options.

The question of what to do next is waiting for them at home. Niccolò is bewildered. Kate can see it in the lowering of his eyebrows, as Kate tugs on gloves to load the last remaining crates of olives onto the trailer. "Why the frown?" Kate asks.

"Among other things, I am trying to decide if I should re-schedule my trips to the press. There just isn't time to drive up there every day."

"You could schedule for every other day instead of daily?"

"Exactly."

Many people take their olives to the press just once a week. In the olden days—before Kate and Niccolò took over the farm—the olives were collected and stored on the floor of the cantina, thousands of kilos forming fermenting mountains, only transported to the press at the end of the harvest. Kate would not like to know the acidity count in that olive oil.

Niccolò and Kate err on the other side. Their friends who also have olive groves say that Niccolò is fanatical. However, the result is the finest quality of olive oil.

"Next time I go to the press," Niccolò says, folding Kate into his arms and pressing the side of his face against the un-inflamed side of hers, "I want you to come with me. It's the best part of the harvest, and you haven't been once this year."

They used to go together. It was the culminating point of their day, giving purpose to the effort. However, in the last several years, in the name of efficiency, they have started dividing chores. "I would love to come with you next time," Kate agrees, returning the pressure of his arms wrapped around her. Without being present to witness the final phase of the transformation of olive to oil, the harvesting of the olives remains a labor-intense chore rather than a process of creation. "Maybe I'll bring my camera." Maybe she can focus with her left eye.

"If we press every other day, we will have more time for everything else that needs to be done."

"We could ask the men to store the boxes half full—ten kilograms each—to keep them from fermenting under their own weight."

"And we can set up fans to keep the air circulating."

"The press is going to be annoyed at another change." Already, Niccolò has shifted his appointment to mid-day, right after lunch instead of the morning. It means he will return home late in the day, just before Kate brings the workers in from the fields. It means putting the oil away after dinner. They won't be in bed before midnight.

Niccolò says, "Go upstairs to rest. I can take care of these crates."

But rest isn't the solution to her problem, and Niccolò will drop from exhaustion if she doesn't give him a hand. "I'm OK."

"That's what you always say." There is an undertone of anger in his words. "I'd like to know how you are really feeling."

"I'd rather work than fret." She is surprised by the presence of anger in her own voice. "OK?"

"OK."

"And since you are asking, I would like to consider our options before we schedule another appointment with another doctor. Can we pause for a few days?" Anger shifts into exasperation. "Really, Nicco, I need a moment to catch my breath."

Kate has had health issues in the past, nothing serious but issues nonetheless. Sometimes they need to be dealt with immediately but sometimes, more often than one would suspect, they take care of themselves, if allowed to follow their natural course. Waiting is good, sometimes. The question is when is it the right time to wait, when it is right to rush ahead?

Kate can see Niccolò considering her request to pause. There is a real urgency to resolve this problem before it worsens, but in chasing after a solution, they risk running around in circles. He understands this as well as Kate does. Kate watches as his eyebrows lower, settling into a decision. "OK then. If you stand on the ladder, I'll pass you the crates."

"Good." She kisses him lightly between his brows, hoping to erase the furrow. "Then we both will rest."

As if someone has heard their need to pause, as they are preparing for bed that night, the sound of rain on the roof brings both of them to a standstill. At first it is a quiet patter; neither of them is sure they are hearing rain or wind. Then, to remove all doubts, the drops increase in size and splatter down insistently on their roof. In an instant it is pouring.

"Do you think it is too late to call Niroshan?" Kate looks at her wrist watch. It is eleven-thirty.

The phone rings before they can formulate an answer. It is Niroshan. "Madam." He pauses. "You are sleeping?"

"No, I was just about to call you. It's raining here."

"Yes, here, too." He lives in the center of town, only eight kilometers away but sometimes—oftentimes—they don't share the same weather conditions.

"We will suspend the harvest. Will you call the workers?"

"I will. They will be happy for the rest."

"Good. We can use the break, too." It hasn't rained yet this season, and they have been harvesting for nearly four weeks. Everyone is tired. "Good night. I will call again tomorrow afternoon."

"Thank you, Madam. Good health."

Happily, Niccolò turns off the alarm clock, pulls the curtains shut so they can sleep past first light. Kate lifts a book from her bedside table. It has been weeks since she's read anything. Kate removes the bookmark as she tries to remember what has happened in the first third of the book, and then notices Niccolò looking at her, shaking his head.

"Not tonight, *amore mio*," he says gently, closing her book, switching off the light.

It is almost nine when they awake the following morning, rested and renewed.

Kate is a weather dependent cook. If it is hot and sunny, their meals are light, mostly fresh, uncooked ingredients tossed together with pasta or salad; more time is spent chopping than cooking. But when it turns cold or rainy, Kate becomes inspired. The kitchen windows steam up. The air fills with aromas of cinnamon and nutmeg; of yeast breads rising; of meat stewing with onions. Kate grabs a spatula from the counter and scoops around the edge of a cake batter, decidedly happier than she has been for weeks, then notices that she has already used the same spatula when preparing the spinach for a quiche. "Oops!" Kate retrieves a second spatula and eases the batter out of the bowl, into its pan.

The table in the center of their kitchen becomes crowded with crusty breads and flaky rolls, with trays of cookies and loaf pans of rising dough waiting their turn in the oven. Kate can hear the rain pounding on the roof. She doesn't even remember her eye until Niccolò reaches out to wipe away a smear of flour from her cheek.

Every now and then he slips into the kitchen to empty the sink of dirty dishes.

"May I?" He reaches toward a butter horn crescent roll, a recipe from her maternal grandmother. It tastes the way bread should taste, light and airy; it dissolves before it can be chewed.

"You may."

"Why don't you call Costanza, invite her to tea this afternoon? We haven't seen her for a long time."

Costanza is an old friend of the family. She was Niccolò's friend before Kate met him. She was married in her early twenties to a boy she met when she was in middle-school, and they had two daughters. Then, tragically, her husband died. Niccolò met her a year after the accident, and Kate met her a couple of years later. Neither of them has ever seen or heard anything but wisdom and strength in Costanza, miraculously balanced with a bristling sense of humor and good will. She has a store of anecdotes that keep them laughing—and thinking. She has suffered more tragedy in her first thirty years than most people know in a lifetime, but there isn't anything tragic or bitter about her. She is just a person doing what she can to make the best of the life she has been given. She is Electra's godmother, a role she takes seriously. In addition, she has adopted the role for Elizabeth, as well, whose godmother is neglectful.

"I'll let you decide what you would like for tea."

Costanza's eyes pop open with wonder when she enters their kitchen. She is like a kid in a candy shop, filling her plate with pumpkin bread, a slice of persimmon cake, an oatmeal-raisin cookie, a cluster of chocolate orange peel. Niccolò, too, fills his plate, concentrating on the nuts: chocolate coated almonds, brown-sugar dusted walnuts and chocolate, caramel-covered pecans. Kate takes only pear cake to start, as she doesn't like to mix her flavors.

They settle into the dining room, gathered at one end of the long table. They talk about their daughters, her summer, theirs. Figaro jumps into Kate's lap, and as they have finished eating, Niccolò doesn't protest.

Costanza asks, rather pointedly, Kate thinks, for Costanza is always diplomatic: "And how are *you*?"

Before Kate can answer, Niccolò says, "Are you going to give her your usual answer or the truth?"

His words jar Kate. She is used to being stoic. She doesn't see how complaining about her aches and pains will make them better or their guests happier, but Kate hasn't thought of herself as untruthful.

"How much do you want to hear?"

"I want to hear it all."

So Kate tells her, figuring, if she can't trust Costanza to listen to her saga, who can she trust?

She tries to keep it short, but Niccolò keeps jumping in, to fill in the details Kate has meant to skim over. When Kate finally finishes, she asks, "If you were in my situation, what would you do?"

Without a pause Costanza says, "I would go to the Emergency Room at *Careggi* and see someone in Maxifacciale. Immediately. But before you go," she says gravely, "I have one question."

"What?"

"What is the significance of the spinach leaf in the persimmon cake?"

They invite Costanza to stay for a quick dinner. After these snacks, no one is very hungry, but a bowl of beef stew that has been simmering on the back burner appeals to them all, and somehow they find room for a few biscuits, too. Costanza helps Niccolò put their plates in the dishwasher while Kate runs upstairs to shower and put on clean clothes, just in case. They make the long drive across town to *Careggi* Hospital, waving goodbye to Costanza just past the *Ponte alla Vittoria*, the Victory Bridge.

In traffic, this drive can take more than an hour but because it is dinner time, they arrive quickly, in less than half an hour. And because it is dinner time, when every patient at the hospital is being visited and fed by a family member, it takes them another hour to find a parking space.

They wait in the corridor of Maxifacciale for another hour, watching as severely disfigured patients are wheeled in, victims of car accidents, falls, fights, all of whom are hoping to have their faces restored by these highly specialized doctors.

Finally, they are invited into the examination room. They are seen by a middle-aged, balding doctor who says that, according to her CT scan, there is nothing wrong with her eye. This is both good news and bad. Obviously, Kate doesn't want to find something wrong with her eye, but she would like to have explained the puffiness and the tingling. The doctor tells her to sit on a bench while he writes up a prescription for two other exams.

While he is writing up his prescription, another doctor, scare-crow thin and young enough to be a medical school classmate of Elizabeth's, approaches her to ask, "May I take a look?"

Kate hands him the CT scan. His youth is counter-balanced by confidence as he pins the scan up to the light box. He confers with another young doctor with wild, straw-like hair, both of them pointing and talking softly. After a minute or two, they approach the middle-aged doctor, who is writing up her prescription.

In a low voice, the scare-crow says, "I don't like the looks of this shadow area."

The second doctor, the one needing hair gel, also young enough to be in class with Elizabeth, leans in to add, "It looks like the bone has deteriorated." He points to an area in the scan. The original doctor looks more closely, but Kate can tell that he can't see anything. The other two doctors continue poking their fingers at the shadows of her CT scan.

"No, this isn't good," the older doctor concedes, either because he has finally seen the danger the younger doctors report or because he wants them to think he has. "You need to have an MRI, immediately."

The young doctor says, "The administrative office is closed at this hour, but you must contact them first thing in the morning to schedule an appointment."

"Will it be a long wait?" Kate dares to ask.

"On second thought, perhaps it is better if I contact them myself. Expect a call as soon as they can fit you into the schedule."

They return home just after midnight. The rain has stopped but the fields are wet. The trees are dangerously slippery. Grateful for any small blessing, they are granted another day's reprieve.

They lie side by side in the dark, Kate's hand folded into Niccolò's, each of them far away with their respective thoughts, until sleep overtakes them.

At seven o'clock the next morning, the phone rings. It is Niroshan. He is at the bus, with the first group of workers.

"Are you coming, Madam?"

Kate looks out the window; the sun has risen into a sky without clouds. The fields will be wet but it is possible to pick olives, if the workers stay out of the trees.

"I'll be down in ten minutes."

"Slippers!" Niccolò reminds her, as she is reaching for her keys.

"Right." Kate runs back upstairs to exchange slippers for shoes.

Niccolò makes breakfast while Kate drives down the hill. *La brina*, the frost, lies softly, like a blanket, between the vineyards. Farther down the hill it covers entire fields with silver. At the bottom of the hill the car skids over a puddle of ice. By the time she drives back up the hill with the first workers, the fields have lost their ghostly sheen.

Kate eats her toast and marmalade and savors her coffee while Niccolò drives down to pick up the second group. There are no stragglers. The attrition rate in field labor is high, especially after a rain.

"The hospital called," Kate says when Niccolò returns. "I have my MRI appointment tomorrow."

"Who says the health service isn't efficient in Italy? At what hour?"

"Eight-thirty."

"Eight-thirty," Niccolò repeats.

"How will we manage to be across town at eight-thirty and pick up the workers?" Kate asks what he is thinking.

"We will figure it out. We always do."

Since it rained yesterday, there are no olives to load into the trailer; no olives to deliver to the press, so once they drive the workers out into the fields, their morning's chores are complete.

They have several hours before they need to pick up the first crates.

"Why don't we lie down for an hour?"

"Yes. A rest sounds good."

They lie together like two old tarnished spoons. And then they sleep.

A week later—a week without rain, a week in which they have brought in 2,100 kilos of olive oil, despite many interruptions—they are back at *Careggi* Maxifacciale to present the results of her MRI. They arrive Friday afternoon, as Niroshan has positioned the workers near a woodshed where the olive crates, nets, and equipment can be stored overnight. It is close enough to the house for the workers to walk back at the end of the day. Niroshan has the automatic gate remote control and the keys to the cantina, and they have hired a friend of his to ferry the workers down to the bus at the end of the day. All is set into motion so they can resolve the problem of Kate's eye.

Unfortunately, the hospital shifts have changed, and they don't find any doctors they recognize. Furthermore, all the doctors present are busy with victims from an accident on the motorway. Everyone present is far too busy with real, immediate drama to read her MRI. Kate sits patiently and waits while Niccolò paces.

The afternoon passes into evening. They watch the doctors change shifts and still no one will speak to them. Finally, tired and hungry—it is well past the dinner hour—Kate accosts a doctor in the corridor who has made the mistake of making eye contact with her.

"We were told to come back once we had my MRI results, but we can't find anyone to read it. Can you please take a look?"

He is dressed in surgical scrubs. He checks his watch. "My patient is being annestisized now, but I'll look quickly—"

He doesn't have the MRI out of the envelope before his cellphone rings. "Sorry. My patient's on the table. I must go."

"May I wait?"

"Feel free." He is halfway down the corridor. "But it will be a couple of hours."

So they wait a couple of hours. Niccolò walks to the café on the other side of the hospital and returns with two stale croissants and two small bottles of pear juice. "They were closing. This was all they had left."

They wait.

Kate has been feeling sorry for herself and Niccolò, sitting on these uncomfortable plastic chairs in a bare-walled corridor, nothing to read, nothing to say; but when she sees how tired the doctor looks when he exits from surgery, her sympathy shifts. If he is surprised to see them, he covers his shock, calls upon a new source of energy and graciously unlocks the examining station for them.

He is silent and pensive as he studies the MRI. He is still wearing his surgical garb; his mask hangs around his neck instead of the customary stethoscope. Tiredly, he pulls off his surgical cap to reveal thick, recently barbered salt-and-pepper hair. After what seems like a long time, he comes over and looks into her face. Just looks. Kate watches his eyes flickering from right eye to left, although there is less to see at this late hour; the swelling nearly gone. He touches the side of her face, near her temple, with his forefinger and thumb, applying pressure. "Does this hurt?"

"No, not much. Just a little sensitive."

"Here?"

"A little."

"Here?"

"A little. Not much."

"Here?"

"Ouch!"

He swivels his chair back to the MRI and studies it again, compares it to the CT scan. He checks the dates of each exam printed on the outside envelop. Then he swivels his chair back to face them directly. He is still wearing the once-sterile paper booties over his shoes.

"Your MRI is not encouraging. It appears you have something growing behind your eye. And judging from the size of it, from the time you had the CT SCAN to when you had the MRI, it is growing rapidly."

"What is it? Can you tell? Do you know?"

"I can't say for certain, but what causes me concern is that whatever it is, it is chewing on the bone, consuming the structure of the eye socket."

"What should we do?" It is Niccolò who has the presence of mind to form the question.

"You will need to have a biopsy to determine what it is. But because the tum—growth—is in a delicate position, you need to have the needle biopsy done while you are in the midst of an MRI. I am going to make an appointment for you in Padova."

"Padova? Padova is three and a half hours away. Isn't there anyone in Florence, at *Careggi*, who can do it?"

"There are lots of doctors in Tuscany who could do it, but the only one I would trust for a growth in this delicate position is in Padova. His name is Dr. Borgo. Hold on. I'll call. Otherwise, it could be months before you are given an appointment."

He leaves the room to call.

Kate can see that Niccolò is scared. He starts pacing in the small, confined office space. He reminds her of Senesh's last poem:

One - two - three... eight feet long
Two strides across, the rest is dark
Life is a fleeting question mark

Instead, Kate is feeling unexpectedly hopeful. Finally they are getting somewhere! Finally they are going to resolve this problem. The dice aren't yet cast. Kate may win! "At least he's not sending me back to the optometrist!"

The doctor is back before Kate can make Niccolò stop frowning.

"Thursday, nine a.m."

"Tell us what you think it might be."

He purses his lips together tightly, and when he speaks Kate can hear the accumulated fatigue of his day. "In my opinion there are three possibilities. It could be Giant Cell Arteritis, which is an inflammation of the lining of your arteries. It causes headaches, jaw pain, and blurred or double vision, all of which you have."

Niccolò has taken a pen out of his glasses case. He is writing on the back of a receipt he has found in his wallet. "What kind of consequences are we talking about?"

"Blindness—sometimes stroke." He doesn't linger. "Or it might be an orbital tumor. You have proptosis, a bulging to your eye. The most common causes of proptosis are thyroid eye disease and lymphoid tumors. But it might be hemangiomas, which is a blood vessel tumor, or lachrymal, a tear gland tumor."

Niccolò's hand trembles as he writes. His script is barely legible.

"The third possibility is Idiopathic Orbital Inflammatory Disease, also known as an orbital pseudo-tumor. This is perhaps the rarest of the three possibilities, but the easiest to resolve, if the tumor can be reached."

"Worst case scenario?"

"Let's not ask that question yet." He places his hand on Niccolò's shoulder. "Let me know the results," he adds, taking Kate's hand firmly in his. "Good luck. I will be thinking of you."

There are five days between their visit to the hospital and their appointment in Padova: too much time, not enough time.

"What are we going to do about the harvest?" Kate asks Niccolò, on the way home.

"I think it is time we called it off. What's left on the trees can stay on the trees."

Niccolò doesn't waste anything. The water doesn't run when he brushes his teeth. He turns off the shower when he lathers up. Lights are to be switched off when the last person leaves a room. The dishwasher doesn't run until it is full. Kate finds him scanning the web in search of high tech energy sources, one of his favorite pastimes. He is conservative in the most fundamental sense of the word. So when he suggests they interrupt the harvest, leave fruit un-picked, Kate knows he is worried.

"Let's work until we leave," Kate counters. "We can do a lot in four more days. We can ask Niroshan to find more workers. It will give us something to think about instead of my eye."

"Fair enough, but let's not add any more workers to the crew. It's stressing enough having so many people around every day. The ones we have are already familiar with the routine."

"We can ask Niroshan's friend if he will drive the workers down to the bus on Wednesday."

"Or they can work half day on Wednesday."

"We can let the workers decide."

"No, let's just give them two days off. We'll resume work on Friday. That will give us time to return home without pressure."

Neither of them is willing to discuss any other possibility although Kate will pack a suitcase before they leave.

"I've never been to Padova. Let's look on line to see what the city has to offer."

CHAPTER
TWENTY-FOUR

Between Florence and Padova the autostrada rides high on the back of the Apennine Mountains. The stretch between Florence and Bologna is one of Italy's most treacherous. With trucks on the road, the two-lane highway is reduced to one, and when trucks decide to pass each other on the steep, uphill grade, the single lane is slowed and dangerous. An accident, no matter how minor, can bring traffic to a dead standstill for hours. Niccolò decides to book a hotel for Wednesday night rather than travelling on Thursday morning. They will make this a little holiday.

Traffic flows easily on Wednesday. The autostrada has been improved, a new lane has been built along stretches of this difficult road, and they arrive in Padova before dark. The hotel they have reserved is across the street from the hospital. From the somber atmosphere in the lobby, everyone who is staying there has an early morning appointment. They leave their bags in the modern, impersonal room, to take a tour of the city.

Padova is a charming little city. The streets are full of young people, students from the university. Niccolò and Kate set out to explore, prepared to lose their way. They always lose their way. It doesn't matter. Their appointment isn't until the next day, and they aren't in a hurry.

It is cold out, and humid, but people are on the streets, riding bikes, chatting on street corners, coat collars pulled up and scarves tightly wrapped but otherwise nonchalant about the cold. Niccolò and Kate continue to walk, arm in arm, but they quicken their pace.

They stop at the Basilica of St. Anthony. Kate has heard the Sri Lankans speaking of St. Anthony. This is one of the places they choose to visit before Michelangelo's *David* or Botticelli's *Nascita di Venere*—Birth of Venus. Unaccountably, these non-Catholic immigrants will skip a day of work, a day of pay, to visit this venerated saint.

Apparently, it's not only the Sri Lankans who revere him. A plaque acclaims that more than five million pilgrims visit St. Anthony each year. The altar is crowded, at the front, the sides and especially at the back. People are kneeling, fervent in prayer. A young woman sobs, silently. Niccolò disappears around a corner of the Saint, busy with prayers of his own. Gaining faith from the faith that surrounds her, Kate touches her fingers to the altar and prays for the strength necessary to deal with whatever is coming to her.

At a quarter to nine the next morning they are in Dr. Borgo's waiting room, but there are a dozen other people already waiting as well. Appointments in Italy are not given by the quarter hour. Everyone is given the same appointment, and is seen in the order in which they arrive. This makes sense when you allow that Italians are notoriously late, and rigid programming would hold up later appointments. Still, it takes getting used to. Years ago, Kate received an appointment for 9:13. She was impressed by the precision; applauded Italy for taking steps forward in their organizational skills. However, when Kate arrived at the designated time and found a room full of people, Kate asked the receptionist, who laughed. "You are expecting too much from us, Signora. Appointments are between nine and one o'clock, 9 –13.

When her appointment with Dr. Borgo comes, Kate's first question is about the needle biopsy.

Startled, he looks up from reading the medical history she's given his assistant, adjusts his reading glasses lower on his long nose. He peers at her myopically. "Not today." He is an elderly man, his hair as white as his carefully ironed doctor's coat. Kate knows of his reputation: they have looked him up on internet. He is the expert they say he is, but Kate looks to see if his hands are steady. "We don't work that way," he says, scribbling something in the column of her file. "I need to see you, study your case. Then we schedule an appointment. My secretary will call you, as soon as we have an opening."

"But when?" Niccolò asks. "Should we book our hotel for another night?"

"No. It will be some time."

"But my wife has this thing growing behind her eye," Niccolò protests.

"Yes, I understand. But I have many patients and only one MRI machine. I will do everything I can to make the appointment sooner rather than later. In the meantime," he turns to Kate. "I want you to take this medicine. It is a steroid."

The Prednisone makes her very anxious, as if there is a wire pulled too tight under her scalp. Every time she speaks, every time anyone speaks to her, the vibration feels exaggerated, like a violin cord ready to snap. In short, Kate feels like jumping out of her skin. If she could bite someone's head off, she would, but as the Prednisone has altered her taste buds so that everything tastes like soggy cardboard, Kate is reluctant to take a bite of anything. Despite the side effects, Prednisone works wonders, and after a few days, her eye is less puffy.

"Nicco, would you please call Angelica?"

"Can't you call her?" He is at the computer, updating the spreadsheet for the harvest's expenses, surrounded by a mountain of receipts.

"I don't really feel like talking with anyone, but I don't want her to think we've forgotten her."

He sighs, takes off his reading glasses. "Of course I'll call her."

Angelica and Niccolò speak at length. The sheep have been in their fields again. They don't mind if they nibble the grass in their pasture, but the shepherd isn't attentive and his animals come up into the garden and devour everything they can find.

"Matteo has passed his last exam," Angelica tells Niccolò. "I'm relieved that he can help with the harvest now."

"We are nearly finished. How is yours progressing?"

"It would help if the rain would stop. The fields are so muddy, it is impossible to harvest," Angelica says.

Niccolò signals to Kate, mutely asking if she wants to speak. She shakes her head no. Kate doesn't have the patience even for dear Angelica.

"What on earth have you done to your eye?" Fiammetta greets Kate one afternoon when she brings her mother-in-law another bottle of newly pressed olive oil. Kate has avoided visiting Fiammetta while her eye has been puffy, and she has been too agitated to visit her mother-in-law while taking Prednisone. Today, puffy eye or not, Kate can't avoid a visit. Niccolò comes too, although he has been putting in overtime. Today he accompanies her to help balance the comments they know they will hear.

"I have an irritation," Kate says, kissing one cheek, then the other, trying to make light of the situation.

"I hope it's not contagious!" Fiammetta steps back.

"No, I doubt it is."

"Probably from an olive leaf," Fiammetta decides. She writes all their scripts and probably wishes she could supply more appropriate actors for her carefully elaborated roles.

"It might well be." Kate is happy for an innocuous explanation and she can see that it soothes her mother-in-law, too. Perhaps Kate has underestimated Fiammetta's ability to empathize.

"Well, I hope you won't go out in public with your eye looking like that, the way that other woman did, wearing that wooly ski hat to dinner parties."

She is referring to their good friend, Gioia, who died last year after four years of fighting cancer; the most courageous person Kate knows.

"Are you referring to Gioia Strozzi?" Niccolò asks.

"Just make sure you don't make the same mistake." She looks at Kate's eye and shivers in repulsion. "People are still talking about that ridiculous hat."

"Don't worry. We don't feel much like going to parties these days. With the harvest and all," Niccolò adds.

"There is nothing stopping *you* from accepting invitations," she says to her son. "It would do you good to get out a little, socialize."

"Do you think I would go out without Kate?"

"People do, you know." She is looking annoyed. "All the time."

Kate knows what her mother-in-law is thinking: How did a modern woman like herself raise a son to be so close-minded?

'People abandon their kids, too—' Kate can hear her husband thinking, but fortunately he stays silent. It is pointless to worry that old bone.

"All I am saying is that she could have at least bought a proper hat—"

"Mamma!"

"Or better yet, a wig. They have wonderful shops in Florence, exactly for this reason. No one needs to know when one is unwell. Right, Kate?"

After a few weeks of Prednisone the puffiness is hardly discernible, even in the morning. When the three week's treatment is finished, Kate regains her appetite. She starts to feel less irritable.

However, just as Kate is starting to feel well, is starting to remember what health feels like, her eye becomes inflamed again. It does not diminish during the course of the day. Niccolò thinks she should start taking Prednisone again, but Kate doesn't want to do anything without consulting a doctor. Her eye gets puffier and stays puffier longer. The headache returns, with a vengeance. They are back to square one.

CHAPTER
TWENTY-FIVE

They finish the harvest with a loud, anti-climactical clap.

Niroshan has predicted another week; then, mid-week he announces, "Sir, we finish tomorrow."

"Tomorrow?"

"Yes. There are nineteen trees more. Each with at least one hundred kilos of olives." He smiles boyishly, his large, square teeth just a shade lighter than the tea he drinks. "I have been saving them for the men who work to the end."

They always start the harvest with twenty workers. They lose three or four after the first days—the work is too hard or pays too little, the bus ride too long—whatever the reason, the following days are always slow; even the workers who do return have aching muscles. By the end of the first week Niccolò can predict pretty well who will stay; who will not return after the first pay check. Niroshan keeps a reserve list of workers so that at the beginning of the second week they are back to twenty.

Inevitably, by the end of the harvest they are reduced to working with three teams of four men. Kate still makes three trips to the bus every morning because someone always arrives late; but she only drives down the hill twice in the evening.

On the last day, the work finishes mid-afternoon. Kate pays the workers, Niccolò thanks them, and they pass out their bonuses. Each man requests a bottle of olive oil, which Kate has already prepared for them. They do not use the oil for cooking but for cosmetics: the bottle is sent back home to their wives, their mothers, their sisters, who use it in their hair, on their skin. It is considered precious and these men are proud of their part in producing it.

"Madam?"

"Yes Niroshan?" They have just paid him, have tipped him generously. Niccolò has said goodbye, has returned to the house to close the harvest data in his spreadsheet, but Niroshan is lingering.

"I can ask you a question?" He seems nervous and Kate knows what is coming. She should have expected it. It happens every year.

"My brother-in-law, Sucil. You can give him a contract, Madam?"

"I can speak with my husband."

"Yes, please speak with Sir. And Madam?"

"Yes?"

"He will need help getting his documents in order."

"But I saw Sucil's work visa when he signed up for the harvest."

"You didn't look closely at the photograph, Madam."

Kate remembers the photograph: blurry, unclear; it could have been any dark skinned person. "We are not inclined to give a contract to someone who has lied to us," Kate says.

"He had no choice, Madam. He had to work or he would have starved."

"You couldn't help him?"

"I can. I do. He sleeps on my floor. He eats what we eat. But I also feed my wife, my sons, my wife's brother and my two cousins."

The generous bonus they have given him suddenly feels inadequate. But what are they to do? They are not making much of a profit selling olive oil.

"Please, Madam, if you give Sucil a contract, you will not be sorry. He is a good worker."

Sucil has been extremely helpful during the harvest. He is always among the first to arrive in the morning; is always the last to leave in the evening. They don't speak: he doesn't know any English or Italian, and the two words of Sri Lankan that Kate knows—*loku aliya, podi aliya pateya*, big elephant, little elephant, allusions to their two tractors—don't take her far into conversation. But Kate can tell by having watched Sucil that he has been making up for his lack of linguistic skills. His group always brought in the most olives, even though he was the first to volunteer to help her unload the trailer, thereby losing precious picking time. If Kate had taken the time to think about it, she should have suspected that he was hoping for a contract. Poor guy. He deserves a better job. In a fairer world, he wouldn't be working so hard for so little, hoping to prolong field labor beyond the season.

Niccolò and Kate dread Niroshan's request to give a contract to one of his relatives. Niroshan always assures them that his brother-in-law or cousin—they are all related in some way—will pay their own taxes, but that promise disappears the moment they receive their first paycheck. So Niccolò ends up paying his side of the taxes for a worker they don't really want, and the worker's taxes, as well. In addition, Niccolò loses a lot of time standing in lines in offices where otherwise he would not set foot.

Despite their reluctance, they have given contracts to many workers over the years, always at Niroshan's insistence. Some of the workers have repaid them with consistently good labor. Unfortunately, just as many have taken advantage of their year's contract and appear sporadically, if at all. These workers are always the most surprised when Niccolò chooses not to renew their contract at year's end. Niccolò has become cynical over the years and although Kate has been impressed with Sucil in the last weeks, she wonders how he will perform once hired.

Upstairs, Niccolò delivers her a bad piece of news before Kate can relay Niroshan's request. "We have an email from Keiji." He doesn't soften the blow. "He says that with the recession, he won't be taking any oil for the new restaurant this year—"

"That is bad news."

"—to make things worse," he pauses, to make sure Kate is listening carefully. "He is reducing his order from ten pallets to three."

"This is terrible news."

Three pallets won't even begin to cover the costs of the harvest.

"What are we going to do with all our oil?" Niccolò worries.

Just this morning they had stood in their cantina giving thanks for this year's abundance.

"I'll search for new clients. The oil is excellent, someone will buy it."

Niccolò sighs, not convinced but too tired to voice his pessimism. "What did Niroshan want?"

She should wait, this isn't the right moment, but Niroshan is downstairs, expecting an answer. Kate is tired and discouraged, as well.

Niccolò's temper flairs. "Every year is the same! How many contracts have I given over the years? Haven't I done enough already?"

She can see the vein in his temple throbbing dangerously. Kate knows not to push the issue. "OK. Relax. No one is forcing you to do something against your will. You have the right to say no."

"So tell him no, then. *No.* Tell him to stop asking. Can't he see I have too much on my mind already?"

Kate leaves Niccolò in his study, descends the two flights of stairs and crosses through their entry hall, through the bottling room, through the cantina and out into the front yard. Niroshan is seated on the cold stone bench, his hands folded, his head bowed, his lips moving slightly.

All of the Sri Lankan's stories are heart-rending; they all have wives, babies, unwell mothers. Niroshan's own story is so sad that Kate wonders it hasn't made him bitter for life: his family's property mortgaged to pay the agents who transported him, illegally, to Italy; being dropped instead in Kosovo, in the middle of a war; being made to panhandle for food when the agents disappeared. It took him two years by foot to reach Italy from ex-Yugoslavia. Twice, he was caught and turned back at the border. When he finally did enter Italy, it was to learn that his family's property was being sold, as he hadn't paid the mortgage payments. When Niccolò and Kate first met him, he was sickly-thin and fiercely proud; nonetheless, he begged to be allowed to pick olives for the season.

For ten years they have helped Niroshan as he has helped them.

But after ten years of cultural incongruities, the arteries to their collective hearts have started to harden. Niccolò is angered every time he catches Niroshan—or one of the other workers— in a lie. "Why can't they simply tell the truth?"

Truth is rarely simple.

"They can't afford to. If *your* wife and kids were hungry, you'd lie, too, if that's what it took to feed them."

They are taking opposing sides of a non-existent argument. Kate agrees with Niccolò. He agrees with her. The difference is that Kate was raised on Dr. Seuss, whose message behind the silly rhymes was distinct: Yertle the Turtle mustn't be allowed to build his kingdom on the back of poor Mack. Niccolò, on the other hand, grew up in postwar Italy, where capitalism struggled for equal footing with communism, creating a welfare generation that were granted advantages long after it had become a thriving middle class.

However, Kate can't compare the Sri Lankans' situation with the Italians. It's a whole other ball game which Kate is not qualified to referee. All Kate sees is need and need is always real, despite the misconstrued attempt to cover it up with face-saving lies.

Niroshan smiles hopefully when he sees her. She doesn't have the courage to say no. "Give us a little time," she tells him. "Let us think about it."

They have three days before her appointment in Padova, and they use it to put the cantina in order. They mend the nets, which are full of gaping holes where the ladders without their rubber bases have pressed through the webbing. They repair the bases of the ladders, too, and hoist them high overhead where they will lie in storage until next autumn. The boots are inspected for holes; the broken ones discarded, the sturdy ones scrubbed clean of caked-mud and olive leaves. For some unexplainable reason they always end up with many more left boots than right, just as they end up with more right gloves than left. Despite the condition, they request that all gloves be returned at the end of the harvest, even though they all have holes and need to be thrown away; otherwise the gloves discarded in the fields clog Kate's tractor—*podi aliya pateya*— when Kate mows the tall grass in spring. A glove caught in the cogs of the mower can interrupt work significantly, but not nearly as much as when Kate mows over a forgotten gunnysack the workers have left under a pile of leaves. Once the grass

327

starts growing, everything is hidden. Her clever little elephant finds it all.

Niccolò appears with a big black garbage bag into which they toss all the clothes left behind by the workers. This is waste Kate can't understand. None of these workers is rich—they wouldn't be working for them if they could afford not to—but all of them waste as if they were. The clothes they leave behind are in good condition. They might not be the latest style—she is not to judge—but a tee-shirt worn under a shirt for warmth, does it need to be a brand name? They present the bag to Niroshan, out of principle, even though they know he will dispose of it. He shakes his head. "They are shameful." Kate can see his question about Sucil poised and waiting, but to his credit he doesn't ask. He accepts the trash bag full of clothes and squeezes it between his feet and knees onto the floorboard of his battered *motorino*. He will throw it into the first trash he passes.

Niccolò and Kate bring out the *idropulitrice*—the pressure washer—and hose down all the crates until they are free of the residual bits of olives. They are then stacked and stored at the end of a long tunnel that passes under the garden of the villa, in the old servant's quarters and vast kitchens and laundry rooms of a previous era. The tunnel that connects these storage rooms to their cantina is more than a five hundred years old. The atmosphere Kate imagines helps shorten the steps they need to make until the two hundred and twenty-odd crates have been carried, six at a time, and stored. Next, they pressure-wash the twenty plastic chairs that the workers have been using as their changing station, until they shine like new; after which they, too, are dried and stacked and carried down the tunnel to await next year's harvest.

Once all the clutter has been removed, they sweep the two cantinas: the one where they have been unloading and storing the olives, which results in satisfying mounds of dirt and leaves and crushed olives; the other cantina, which runs perpendicular, is where the workers have changed. It is also where they store the oil in eighteen large, stainless steel tanks stationed side by side on their stands. Along the opposite wall of this second cantina are old wooden casks where Niccolò's predecessors stored wine. They are enormous, much too large to fit through the doors, which leads them to believe they were constructed on site in the 19ᵗʰ Century. Kate can envision the quarter sawn staves being bent into shape over an open fire, as evidenced by the charred ceiling—from white oak growing on the property. Both rooms are longer than Olympic swimming pools. It takes Kate and Niccolò several hours of sweeping and washing, employing the pressure washer in both rooms. The final result is satisfying: the worn, stone pavement is as clean and shiny as if it has been polished with oil.

They have made it through the harvest!

As Kate puts away their laundered work clothes, she wonders where she'll be for next year's harvest. Up to her knees in mud, she hopes, out in the fields with the rest of the workers, seeing, feeling, freed of this infernal problem.

Finally their appointment arrives.

Again they find traffic flowing unobstructed to Padova. Again they visit San Antonio. At night, in the same impersonal hotel room, they lie side by side in the dark, their feet, and their hands touching but otherwise separate. In the morning Kate wonders if she has slept at all, but she must have, as she remembers awakening abruptly to the sound of the alarm clock. She studies Niccolò's reflection in the bathroom mirror as he shaves, the pouches under his eyes dark, especially in contrast to the white foam on his face. He looks like he hasn't slept at all.

At eight, Kate is given a room on the day-hospital ward. She has brought a book for herself, a book for Niccolò, and they sit together, reading separately or not reading at all. At ten o'clock a very short, chubby, cheerful nurse—Rosanna, her name tag announces—comes to fetch Kate. She collects the woman in the next room, as well, and together they follow her down a series of corridors, like two naughty students on their way to the principal's office, to another room where they are asked to wait again.

This other woman also has a puffy eye. Without the preliminaries of exchanging names, they compare notes tentatively, in the way that people exchange stories in waiting rooms all over the world. They are both frightened but their fears are different. Kate is afraid of the upcoming process, of a needle being inserted into a hard-to-reach area behind her eye. The other woman is afraid of what the biopsy will reveal. As Kate listens to the woman's fears, she realizes that she herself is at peace with her fate. Her prayer to have the strength to deal with whatever she receives has been delivered. She is prepared to address whatever diagnosis she receives, with dignity and grace; philosophically.

With bitter-sweet recognition, Kate understands that she has accomplished everything she has hoped to in this life—and more. If it must end, let it end, but spare her the suffering, please.

The longer they wait, the quieter they become. They retreat into themselves and look up only when someone in a white coat passes through the room.

Finally, Kate is called. She is led into a large, white room, and strapped onto a table; her head is put into a brace. It is important that Kate not move, not even a little, she is reminded, especially while they are doing the biopsy. The table glides into a tunnel and the sloshing noise begins. It sounds like she's in a washing machine. Kate lies there as the minutes pass, tries to find an image she can hold peacefully in her mind. Surprisingly, she finds herself trying to reconstruct a poem her friend Lorenzo has sent to her, *Ithaka*.

> *As you set out for Ithaka*
> *hope your road is a long one,*
> *full of adventure, full of discovery.*
> *Laistrygonians, Cyclops,*
> *angry Poseidon—don't be afraid of them:*
> *you'll never find things like that on your way*
> *as long as you keep your thoughts raised high,*
> *as long as a rare excitement*
> *stirs your spirit and your body.*
> *Laistrygonians, Cyclops,*
> *wild Poseidon—you won't encounter them*
> *unless you bring them along inside your soul,*
> *unless your soul sets them up in front of you.*

Perhaps Kate has misunderstood. Perhaps they will do the MRI first, then the biopsy. She forces her mind to try to reconstruct the rest of the poem.

> *Keep Ithaka always in your mind.*
> *Arriving there is what you're destined for.*
> *But don't hurry the journey at all.*
> *Better if it lasts for years,*
> *so you're old by the time you reach the island,*
> *wealthy with all you've gained on the way,*
> *not expecting Ithaka to make you rich.*

She can't tell how much time has passed, but she would guess nearly half an hour, maybe more. Kate is starting to feel cold, and as often happens when her body temperature drops abruptly, her hormones react with a hot flash. In any other situation, a hot flash isn't a big deal. She strips off any extra clothes she is wearing for the minute or two it takes to pass. She has learned to dress lightly, with an easy to unbutton cardigan, for fast action. She has noticed that flashes are most likely to occur whenever she is slightly embarrassed, like when she is confronted or if she has said something inappropriate. It happens sometimes if she mistakenly finishes an Italian word as masculine instead of feminine, *il bottiglio, il merendo*. It is like an exaggerated blush and she uses it to investigate whatever it is that has made her uncomfortable. But lying on a table, strapped down, Kate has no option but to wait it out. She feels like she is lying beneath a very hot sun. She knows she is perspiring. At least there aren't mosquitoes!

It passes as quickly as it came, the perspiration dries, and Kate is back to wondering why they aren't proceeding with the biopsy? She repeats the poem again, unsure if she has remembered the lines correctly. She can't remember the poems' ending. Nonetheless, it has served its purpose as a distraction.

The sloshing noise ceases. The table moves out of its circle, and Dr. Borgo is at her side, unfastening the straps around her head, under her chin.

"Signora, we have decided that a biopsy is unnecessary."

"What?"

"The growth has diminished so that it is insignificantly present. My colleague and I believe it would be dangerous to try to biopsy such a small mass. If it is diminishing of its own accord, we feel we should not disturb it."

"It has disappeared?"

"Yes. Almost completely."

"I am free to go?"

"Of course."

Kate leaps off the table. "This is the best news I could have hoped for!"

"We are also very pleased. Believe me, *Signora*, we do not like to see growths like this in such a difficult position."

"May I leave?"

"Yes. Return to your room. I will pass by in a short while to speak with you and your husband."

Kate doesn't wait for the wheelchair that is offered, she pauses only long enough to tell the woman in the waiting room what has happened; to wish her luck.

She runs—prances—the distance back to her room. Niccolò is standing by the window, his book discarded on the table. "We have a miracle!" Kate tells him. "They didn't even do the biopsy. The growth has almost completely disappeared."

Now his eyes turn red and puffy, and it occurs to Kate that her earlier acceptance—resignation—has been unwittingly selfish. She has been thinking about herself, coming to terms with *her* fate, but she had neglected to consider her family. Her absence would destroy Niccolò's security and truncate their daughters' easy progression into adulthood. Any decision Kate makes, now and in the future, must reflect her family's wishes as well as her own. Suddenly, Kate recalls the closing lines of the poem that eluded her before.

Ithaka gave you the marvellous journey.
And if you find her poor, Ithaka won't have fooled you.
Wise as you will have become, so full of experience,
you'll have understood by then what these Ithakas mean.

The nurse of this morning, Rosanna, comes to the door, ready to help. They share the good news, which she receives with tears of her own. It doesn't matter that they have known her for less than three hours. She cries as if Kate were her daughter. They are in the midst of a miracle and a shower of tears is the least they can do to acknowledge it.

As Kate uses her phone to send a message to Elizabeth and Electra, then Costanza, Niccolò picks up his cellphone and calls Niroshan. Without preamble, he says "Tell Sucil I will give him the contract."

No doubt about it, Kate has chosen Lord Warburton.

There is some traffic on the drive home, but they don't care. Nothing could interfere with their sense of well being.

Niccolò's cellphone rings but as he is driving, Kate answers.

"Why didn't you tell me?" Fiammetta doesn't bother with pleasantries or preliminaries.

"Why didn't I tell you what?" There are so many possibilities. Kate puts the call onto the loud speaker so Niccolò can hear his mother's conversation.

"That you were—that your eye was—" She can't bring herself to say the words. "Did you assume I wouldn't care?"

Again, there are many possible answers but there is a tremor of emotion in her mother-in-law's voice that keeps Kate focused. "I thought you wouldn't want to hear about my health problems."

"Of course I don't. Who would? I can't stand old people who sit around talking about their intestinal disturbances. But you are family. How could you not tell me you were—?"

"You are right." Kate feels the justice of the reprimand. "I should have told you, but at least now I can give you good news. The problem is resolved. By the way, who did tell you?"

"Federica. She heard it from Costanza. She didn't know anything either."

Actually, Niccolò had mentioned it to her sister—to explain why Niccolò couldn't attend a condominium meeting yesterday, but obviously it hadn't registered. Kate hadn't counted on Costanza speaking with Federica. Florence is a smaller town than Kate is willing to admit.

"Anyway, everything is fine. I have had an examination, and there isn't any problem."

"Thank goodness. I have been out of my mind with worry."

"Nothing at all to worry about." Kate hears herself sounding like the many doctors they have consulted in this long, unpleasant ordeal. "We will be home in another few hours. We will stop by as soon as we unpack."

She puts Niccolò's phone on the car's console. Neither of them speaks. Finally, Kate says, "I guess we've been wrong."

"A complicated woman, my mother."

"Who would ever have thought she'd be concerned?" Kate is bewildered.

"Strange way of showing it."

"True. But I am touched, nonetheless."

"Just don't expect consistency."

"Maybe that's our error." Kate covers his hand with hers. "Instead of appreciating her good points, we cancel them because she isn't consistent."

"That and other things." He speeds up to pass a slow moving truck, then returns to the slow lane; she keeps her hand rested on his as he shifts gears. "At least Claire is dependable."

"Don't let me forget to call my mother when we are home." They are silent for a minute. Kate folds her hands into her lap, as she was taught to do as a child, left grasping right, as if in agreement; a strategy to confound fiddling. "We must let that be enough—" she offers "—consistency from one mother instead of two. Anyway, I am glad your mother called."

"I am, too." He keeps his eyes on the road, both hands on the wheel. Traffic has grown heavy. The right lane is slowed by an uninterrupted progression of trucks grinding their weight uphill in second gear; a single left lane must suffice for all cars, fast and slow, patient and impatient. Niccolò compensates for the tailgater behind him by leaving extra space in front of him. "My father was consistent, if nothing else."

Uncharitably, Kate thinks: *constant in the darkness, where's that at.* "At least you had that. My father was anything but consistent.

"But your father was a genius. Full of brilliant, unusual ideas."

"Instead of letting their poor qualities impoverish us," Kate says, unfolding her hands and gesturing like an Italian. "How rich we would be if we could cash in on their good qualities."

CHAPTER TWENTY-SIX

"Nicco?"

"Tell me." He looks up from his computer, sees the expression on his wife's face; clicks *save* on the spreadsheet he's been working.

"I know we had planned to stay in Florence all winter, and I know I need to busy myself to find someone to buy our olive oil, but could we go back to Sicily for a week or two?"

He takes off his reading glass, folds them and places them in their case. "It will be cold."

"I know." Kate removes a stack of papers from the chair beside his desk. "But we can dress warmly." She sits beside him. "I would like to see Cofano again."

"You wouldn't rather fly up to England?" He takes the papers from his wife, lays them on his desk in between the other piles of papers awaiting his attention. "We could have Electra fly over from Holland." He takes her hand, surprised for the millionth time by the fragility of the bones in her fingers. "We could spend a long weekend with our girls."

"Not yet." She removes her hand, as if he has squeezed it too tightly. "I want to put another experience between me and my eye before I see them." They have told them that her eye problem is resolved, but haven't shared all the details. There will be time, the right occasion. "They are coming home for Christmas. By then it will all be a faint memory."

"You really want to see Cofano?"

Gently, as if exhaling an expectation, she lays her hand on the back of his; a gesture of healing, an offer of protection, despite the discrepancy in strength, in size.

"Fair enough," he says, accepting the gesture of comfort he hadn't known he needed. "Book our flight."

Two days later Rosario picks them up at *Birgi* airport. They have left a little car at the house so they can fly back and forth from Pisa to Trapani, but they need a ride from the airport. On the empty road between Birgi and Trapani, Rosario drives in third gear, keeping his engine reved high.

"If you shift into fourth gear," Niccolò coaches, "you'll save wear and tear on your engine, and also petrol."

Rosario follows Niccolò's advice for a few kilometers, then downshifts again. Without the engine reved, he doesn't feel engaged.

It begins to rain as they stop at a market to pick up a few groceries. By the time Kate returns with eggs and cheese, milk and pasta, it is pouring.

As they drive towards Valderice, the rain stops as abruptly as it has started. "Rosario, would it be all right to stop quickly for vegetables?"

Rosario, ever obliging, drives them to a farmer's house, a little side room off a garage full of vegetables from their garden. Today it is full of people. Kate selects more than they need simply because the vegetables are so beautiful: long stalks of Swiss chard, lime-green spiky cauliflower; baby tomatoes tied into a garland, drying for the winter months; several varieties of artichokes, their stems still long, their buds tightly closed. Kate buys a pumpkin, too, not because they will have time to eat it, but because its pale, jade green form, dusted with gray, is as beautiful, as subtle, as an oriental still life.

Patiently, Kate stands in line, waiting her turn. The man in front of her has finished collecting his fruits and vegetables, shuffles forward, but when it becomes his turn to pay, he seems paralyzed; frozen with his wallet half open. The owner of the little shop, the farmer who has grown all these vegetables, is brown from years in the sun. His fingernails are broken and black. He doesn't hurry the man along. "Are you ready for me to ring up your sale?" There is another woman, not in line but in a rush. The farmer nods at Kate, includes her in his decision to let this other woman pass first. His politeness is inherent, even if his voice is gruff and his undershirt isn't very clean.

How good it is to be back in Sicily!

The rain has stopped, the clouds have passed. The sun is trying to shine. Kate closes her eyes against the view of Cofano as they drive up the mountain.

"Are you car sick?" Niccolò asks. Rosario's driving is fast and these roads seem to have more curves than ever.

"I'm fine." She wants to be alone when she sees Cofano for the first time.

They say goodbye to Rosario in the driveway, promise to take him and Franca out to dinner one night before they leave. Niccolò unlocks their front gate, which has been repaired and treated with an anti-rust component, but still needs to be varnished black. They pick up their bags of groceries and their little suitcase. They are in their garden again.

Kate turns to see what Cofano has to say.

The sea itself is dark, a somber, blue-black, seemingly darker juxtaposed to an undercurrent of near white. It looks as though there is a stream under the sea, as distinct as if the painter creating this scene hadn't yet blended the two separate colors.

The white near the coast is untainted, as if the water has risen up to cover pure, white sand, lightening its own blue body to a pale, transparent turquoise.

Each time Kate looks up, the brush stroke has broadened, lengthened.

In the middle of this dramatic backdrop, Cofano rises proudly, majestically, a single wisp of cloud forming a crown over its head in an otherwise serene, monotone blue sky.

"Look, there is a rainbow!" Kate says.

Niccolò steps close behind his wife and wraps his arms around her, whispers in her ear. "There are two."

He is right. One bright and clear, as if drawn by a child's crayons; the other incomplete, half finished, but undisputedly a rainbow. "Don't expect anyone to believe two rainbows. It's too much of a cliché to be credible."

"There is nothing cliché about a miracle."

337

Side by side on the sofa after dinner, Niccolò and Kate are warmed by the glow from the fire. The flames, contained in their airtight box, take on a life, a dimension of their own. Snuggling against each other as if it were still cold, they let themselves be hypnotized by the flames. They have winter-proofed their house. They have made a home for all seasons.

Lynn Rodolico divides her time between Tuscany and Sicily. She is married and has two grown daughters.

For questions and comments,
visit Lynn Rodolico
@
www.lynnrodolico.com